# "Stop it, Caro," Jeremiah said, more softly this time, but with the same commanding tone.

"Do you want that whole pack of knaves topside to believe you've lost your wits?"

"I don't care a fig what they believe!" With a cry of wounded frustration, she struggled to pull free and tried to strike him again, but he was so much larger, so much stronger! "And you don't care, either, not about what they think! All that matters to you is that I obey, like some well-trained little dog, so that you can feel free to go off alone and get yourself killed with a clear conscience. That's it, isn't it? *Isn't it?*"

"How can you say that after all we've done together?" he demanded, his eyes glittering like green fire. She'd never guess how deeply her words cut into him, as surely as any knife…!

Dear Reader,

This month, award-winning Harlequin Historical author Miranda Jarrett continues her dramatic saga of the Sparhawk family in *Sparhawk's Lady*, a sweeping tale of danger and romance with a dashing hero who is torn between duty and desire. Don't miss this stirring adventure that was given a 5★ rating by *Affaire de Coeur* and a 4+ rating from *Romantic Times*.

And from author Suzanne Barclay comes *Lion of the North*, the second in her new medieval series featuring two clans of Scottish Highlanders, the Sutherlands and the Carmichaels, who have been fighting for generations.

Our other titles for June include our warmhearted WOMEN OF THE WEST title, *Saddle the Wind*, by author Pat Tracy, and the first Western from author Kit Gardner, *Twilight*, a story of love and redemption.

We hope you'll keep an eye out for all four selections, wherever Harlequin Historicals are sold.

Sincerely,

Tracy Farrell
Senior Editor

---

Please address questions and book requests to:
Harlequin Reader Service
U.S.: 3010 Walden Ave., P.O. Box 1325, Buffalo, NY 14269
Canadian: P.O. Box 609, Fort Erie, Ont. L2A 5X3

# MIRANDA JARRETT

# Sparhawk's Lady

## Harlequin Books

TORONTO • NEW YORK • LONDON
AMSTERDAM • PARIS • SYDNEY • HAMBURG
STOCKHOLM • ATHENS • TOKYO • MILAN
MADRID • WARSAW • BUDAPEST • AUCKLAND

ISBN 0-373-28871-9

SPARHAWK'S LADY

This edition published by arrangement with Harlequin Enterprises B.V.

Printed in U.S.A.

---

## MIRANDA JARRETT

was an award-winning designer and art director before turning to writing full-time, and considers herself sublimely fortunate to have a career that combines history and happy endings, even if it's one that's also made her family regular patrons of the local pizzeria. A descendant of early settlers in New England, she feels a special kinship with her popular fictional family, the Sparhawks of Rhode Island.

Miranda and her husband—a musician and songwriter—live near Philadelphia with their two young children and two old cats. During what passes for spare time, she paints watercolor landscapes, bakes French chocolate cakes and whips up the occasional last-minute Halloween costume.

For the Unholy Trinity—
Teri, Raine, and Theresa

You make me laugh,
you let me cry,
you give me the joy of
your friendship
(and don't forget the kitten handouts!)

# Prologue

*Portsmouth, England*
*May 1787*

With growing panic, Caroline Harris stared at her reflection in the mirror as her mother's maid tied the sash at her waist. Soon it would be time to leave the ladies' retiring room and join the gentlemen in the salon, and then it would be too late.

Why, why was there never enough money?

"I can't do this, Mama," she whispered hoarsely. "I know you say we've no choice, but I can't. *I can't.*"

"You can, and you will," snapped her mother with the angry irritation that Caroline had come to know too well these past two weeks. "You're all I have left to me, girl, and I won't die a pauper."

Caroline nodded, not trusting her voice to speak. If she cried, she would be cuffed. She'd learned that lesson quickly enough. Tears would make her eyes red and puffy, and then no gentleman would want her.

But what *gentleman* would want her anyway, dressed like this? Her flowered silk gown had been re-made from an old one of her mother's, cut down so far that her nearly all of her high, small breasts showed above the neckline, the darker rose of her nipples peeking shamelessly through the gauzy neckerchief. Her stays were laced so tightly she could scarcely breathe, and her feet were squeezed painfully into pointed, high-heeled shoes meant to give her a dainty, swaying walk.

Her hair, usually as straight and fine as corn silk, had been crimped and set with sugar water into high, stiff, fashionable curls she'd been forbidden to touch. The jewels that glittered against her pale skin were paste as false as the rest of her, and when she looked at the masklike way they'd painted her face—black kohl around her eyes and rouged circles on her cheeks—she wanted to weep all over again. She looked like a cheap wax doll that no one would ever value, let alone love or cherish.

And not even her mother had remembered that to-day was her fourteenth birthday....

Miriam Harris clutched possessively at her daughter's arm as she, too, stared at the reflection, the resemblance between them obvious in the high cheekbones and the wide-set blue eyes. But that was all; the consumption that would soon claim Caroline's mother had left her face tight and gaunt beneath the dyed black hair, her body bent and wasted, and the life she'd led, a Cypriot always dependent on the favors of gentlemen, had long ago destroyed the innocent charm that lit her daughter's face.

"You're too weedy by half, Caroline," she declared with a broken gasp, and coughed into the lace-trimmed handkerchief she was never without. Swiftly she wadded it into her reticule, but not before Caroline had seen the bright red blood on the white linen. "Look at you, half a head taller than me! I shouldn't have wasted my money for all those years to see you raised in the country if this is how you turned out."

With a sharp pang of homesickness, Caroline thought of the thatch-roofed house in Hampshire where she'd lived until last month, of ruddy-faced Mrs. Thompson who'd treated her like one of her own children, of sunlight and fresh milk and apples and fields to run through and kittens in the barn to play with. She remembered, too, the careful dreams she'd nursed of her parents: her father a handsome officer in a fashionable regiment tragically killed defending his king and country before he could wed her mother, the kind, beautiful lady in London who sent money each month for her care and would, as soon as her circumstances permitted, come herself to fetch Caroline away.

A lovely dream it was, a fantasy Caroline had played over each night before she fell asleep, and years and miles away from the reality of the ravaged, dying woman clinging to her arm. True enough, Miriam had finally come for her daughter, but not for the genteel family life that Caroline had always imagined. No, nothing like that, not in the mean lodgings that were her mother's home now, with nearly everything of value stripped away and sold for food and medicine, and once again Caroline felt the tears smarting behind her eyes.

"No weeping now, daughter," warned her mother, lowering her voice so the other women around them, most dressed in the same expensive, revealing fashions, wouldn't overhear. "Sir Harry will look to you to ease his troubles, not to be burdened with your own."

Caroline shook her head with a final, desperate show of defiance. "We don't have to live like this, Mama. I could sew, or seek a position with a milliner. There must be other ways than this!"

"What, and squander the one true gift that God gave us both?" Her mother's laugh was short and bitter. "Your face is your fortune, girl, and with it you'll earn more in a week than any squalid little seamstress in a garret could in twenty years."

"But Mama—"

"Don't gainsay me, you foolish girl!" hissed her mother, her thin fingers tightening on Caroline's arm as she led her from the room. "You're all I have, and this is all I know. I mean to see you launched while it's still in my power. If you please Sir Harry Wrightsman tonight, he'll treat you finer than you can ever imagine, far better than you deserve."

At the arched doorway Caroline shrank back. To her, the room before them was unbelievably grand, with gilded walls and mirrors and hundreds of candles. The beautiful women and the men who clustered around them terrified her, their gestures too free, their conversation and laughter too loud, nearly drowning out the musicians in the alcove. No matter what her mother said, she knew she didn't belong here.

"Oh, Mama," she whispered, her face pale beneath the rouge. "I beg you, please, can't we go, please, *please?*"

"Hush, don't shame me!" said her mother sharply, tugging Caroline along. Already smiling for the benefit of the others, she looked past her daughter to scan the crowd of people. "It's too late for begging. The thing is done. You must prosper on your beauty and youth alone, Caroline, and you'd best pray that's enough for Sir Harry."

With her own eyes downcast, Caroline sensed the stares of the others, felt their curiosity closing in on her like a heavy cloak. If her mother's fingers had not dug so deeply into her arm she would have turned and fled. But there'd be no escape now. Though she was young, she wasn't a fool. The moment she'd come into this room, her innocence and her good name were irrevocably gone. As her mother said, the thing was done, and Caroline's fear settled into an icy dread. This night would be the worst of her life, and she prayed for the strength to survive it.

Beside her, Miriam called greetings to her friends in a voice far sweeter than any she'd ever used with her daughter, a voice laced with gaiety and the promise of love.

*Oh, Mama, if only you'd shown that love to me...*

"So this is your prize chit, eh?" said the man eagerly, and Caroline's heart froze. "By God, Miriam, but she's a pretty piece, even finer than you claimed!

Come now, missy, don't be shy. Let's have a proper look at you."

Roughly he seized her chin to turn her face up toward his and forced Caroline to meet his gaze. He was old, far older than she'd expected, his face florid and lined, his eyes nearly buried in the fleshiness of his cheeks, and when he smiled, his remaining teeth stained yellow from tobacco, the stench from his breath nearly made her faint. Powder from his old-fashioned wig sifted down onto his sloping, velvet-covered shoulders, and though his clothing was costly, no tailor in London could disguise the corpulence that swelled his waistcoat. This was the man she'd been sold to; this was the man whose bed she was to share, the man to whom she must willingly give her body.

Dear Lord help her, she couldn't do it, not with him. *She couldn't do it.* With a little sob she jerked free and backed away, her hand over her mouth.

Sir Harry was displeased, and so was her mother. "Maidenly fears, my lord, that's all," said Miriam quickly as she put her hands around her daughter's shoulders, a show of maternal concern that also kept Caroline from retreating further. "I told you she's only a fortnight from the country."

"Only a fortnight, eh?" The greedy lust in his eyes sickened Caroline. "Then you swear she's still a virgin?"

"Never touched by any man, my lord," said her mother, fighting back a cough. "Not even kissed."

"Then come with me, little maid," he said with a satisfied leer, "and I'll teach you all you need to know." His arm snaked around Caroline's waist and pulled her close. Twisting frantically against his arm, she caught one final look of her mother, standing alone with the blood-soaked handkerchief pressed over her mouth, the tall plume in her hair nodding gently over her carefully expressionless face.

*Oh, Mama...*

The music continued, the conversations around them never paused, as Sir Harry pulled Caroline, stumbling across the floor toward the doors that opened to the garden. Dear Lord, the garden: he meant to be alone with her already. He wouldn't even wait until they'd returned to his house. She balked, catching the heel of her shoe in her skirts, and with a little cry pitched forward.

Swearing, he jerked her back to her feet. "Come along, you little hussy. Spirit in a woman's one thing, but outright defiance is quite another. Unless that's your game, eh? You play the wicked lass, and I'll correct you?"

Shaking her head, Caroline stared at him with desperate bewilderment. "No, sir, forgive me, I never meant to play any games on you!"

His small eyes narrowed as he suddenly twisted her wrist so sharply that she yelped with pain. "On me or under me, we'll try them all in time, won't we, my little cat?"

"Release the lady, Wrightsman," said a mild voice behind them, and, her heart still pounding with fear, Caroline turned to see her defender. He didn't look like a hero—thin and ungainly as a crane in a plain brown silk coat, his gray-streaked hair cropped short in monastic severity—but in Caroline's eyes he was already worthy of a white horse. "I don't believe she wishes to keep your company any longer."

"What she wishes doesn't matter, Byfield," growled Sir Harry. "She's Merry Miriam's daughter, and I've bought her services from Miriam herself."

The gray-haired man frowned. "Her own mother sold her to you?"

"Aye, and drove a harder bargain than any moneylender," said Sir Harry sourly. "I'll have you know I've paid a king's ransom for this little whore's maidenhead."

"If she still has a maidenhead, then she's hardly a whore," reasoned Byfield. "For that matter, to my eye she looks too young for any sort of venal activity. Since when have your preferences turned to children, Wrightsman?"

Sir Harry snorted. "Since Christmas week in Bath with that infernal actress. Left me with the French pox, damn her eyes! Even an old puritan like you must know the only real cure comes from lying with a virgin, and that means the girl's bound to be young. How else can a man be certain the chit's what she claims?"

Incredulous, Byfield stared down his nose at the other man. "You would knowingly ruin the poor girl that way? Pox her in the empty hope of curing yourself?"

"She'll be paid well enough for her trouble, you can be sure."

"I don't care what you gave that sorry excuse for a mother, Wrightsman. I won't stand by and let you do this. Come round to my banker in the morning and you shall have double what you paid."

"Damn your interference, Byfield, it's the girl I want, not the money!"

"Triple it, then, and find yourself a new physician instead. Who can put a price on an innocent's soul?" His smile grave, the sixth Earl of Byfield held out his hand to Caroline. "Here, child. You're coming home with me, and I swear no one shall ever touch you against your will again."

And at last Caroline wept.

# Chapter One

*April 1803*

He would not be afraid.

Jeremiah took a deep breath and rested his hand over the open top of the lantern's globe, sealing the candle and its flame within beneath his palm. As the air was exhausted, the flame slowly began to flicker and dim, and the shadows in the bedchamber grew darker, deeper, closing in on Jeremiah as the small light faded. He could feel his heart pounding in his breast, his blood racing, every muscle tensing to run and escape the blind, irrational panic that was swallowing him as completely as the night itself. The little flame twisted one final time and guttered out, leaving only the smoking spark on the wick and the endless, silent, eternal blackness.

With a choking sound deep in his throat, Jeremiah lifted his hand, his eyes desperately intent on the tiny glowing spark. His breath tight in his chest, he willed it back to life, struggling to concentrate on this last dot

of light as the only way to fight the blind terror that
would smother his life if he let it.

*Come back. Damnation, come back! Don't die and
leave me alone in the night!*

God, why had he let it go so far?

Slowly, as if it heard him, the spark glowed brighter,
stronger, until at last it became a flame again, dancing double in the curved globe. Still Jeremiah stared at
it, unable to look away. For now the shadows were
gone, the demons vanquished. But how long would
they stay away, how long before he found any lasting
peace? With a groan of despair he dropped back onto
the bed, his arms thrown across the pillows beneath his
head.

What the devil had happened to him? It hadn't always been this way. He was a Yankee, a Rhode Is-
lander by birth, nobody's fool, a deep-water captain
raised on the Narragansett. The first time he'd fought
for his life he'd been only eleven, beside his privateering father in the War for Independence, and through
two more wars he'd never turned his back on a fight,
whether with swords or pistols or his own bare fists.

He'd battle hurricanes at sea or thieves and rogues
on land. Who or what made little difference to him, as
long as he won. His temper was notorious, his courage undoubted. He stood over six feet tall with shoulders to match, and years of hard living had made his
body equally hard, scarred, lean and muscular.

No one who knew him would ever call him a coward. No one would dare. But he himself knew the
truth.

He, Captain Jeremiah Sparhawk, was afraid of the dark.

He stared up at the pleated damask canopy overhead, still struggling with the terror. He was safe here, safe in his sister Desire's great house on the hill outside of Portsmouth. She was a fine lady now, his sister, married to an English nobleman, Rear Admiral Lord John Herendon. If Jeremiah listened he could just make out the sound of their guests in the music room below, the laughter and merriment that he'd wanted no part of this evening, or any other since he'd been brought here four months ago. Yet Desire had welcomed him when he'd needed a haven, sat by his bedside when the pain and fever had threatened his sanity, and not once had she questioned him when he'd begged to leave the lantern lit at night.

*That other night there'd been no moon, no stars, nothing to mark where the midnight sky met the sea. The hot wind that carried the* Chanticleer *eastward across the Mediterranean had strangely died at sunset, and with the ship becalmed, the men on watch had grown drowsy, lulled to complacency by the warm air and the gentle slapping of the water against the hull.*

*But he was their captain. If they erred, the fault and the blame was his alone. He should have sensed the danger before it was too late, before the devil was there on his chest with the cold, curved blade pressed tight into his throat....*

He woke with a ragged cry, soaked with his own sweat, and instinctively lunged for the pistol he kept beneath his pillow. Clutching the gun in both hands, he rolled over onto his back, ready to challenge the demon that dared follow him here into the light.

"Forgive me if I startled you, Captain Sparhawk," said the woman standing beside the bed, "but you can lay that pistol down. At least you won't need it on my account."

Still not sure if he was dreaming, Jeremiah stared at her with the gun gripped tightly in his hands.

"Please," she said gently. "I promise I'm no threat."

She didn't look like any nightmare he recognized. Far from it. She was so beautiful it almost hurt him to look at her, dressed all in white, from the egret's plumes in her blond hair to the toes of her white satin slippers. If no devil, then an angel?

But heaven's angels were neither male nor female, and the way the white silk of her gown spilled over the full curves of this one's body left little doubt that she was decidedly female, decidedly of this earth. Her mouth was full and very red, her eyes very blue, widely set and tipped up at the corners. She watched him evenly, not at all embarrassed that he wore trousers and nothing else, waiting for him without any sign of fear.

*Fear.* Dear God, had she been here long enough to hear him cry out against the dark like a terrified child?

He uncocked the pistol and lowered it slowly, that gentleness in her voice making him wary. He didn't want sympathy or pity, especially not from a woman he didn't know. "How did you get in here?"

"The customary way." Now that he'd put the gun down, she stepped closer to him, the diamonds on her bracelets glittering in the light of the single candle. "Through the door."

He cursed himself mentally for forgetting to lock it. Was he getting so old that he'd already turned careless? "Then you can damned well leave the same way you came. Clear off, and leave me alone."

She shook her head solemnly, the white feather in her hair brushing against the curtains of the bed. She was near enough now that he could smell her scent, jasmine and musk, and in spite of his wish to be left alone, he felt his gaze drawn inexorably to the soft, full curves of her breasts above the white satin. It didn't make any sense. Why was she here, so beautifully available? He hadn't had a woman since they'd brought him back to England, and his body was reminding him, a bit too obviously, that he'd recuperated long enough.

"Ma'am." Consciously he forced his eyes back up to hers. Beautiful or not, he didn't need the kind of entanglement she'd bring, not now when his life was in such a shambles. "Look here. Where I come from, ma'am, a lady doesn't visit a man's bedchamber unless she's blessed sure of her invitation. If she comes prowling around on her own, then she's generally something less than a lady. Now will you take yourself back downstairs with the others, or am I going to have to haul you down myself, for all the world to remark?"

Suddenly imperious, she lifted her chin a fraction higher, and he saw now that she was older than he'd first thought, no young girl dabbling at flirtation.

"You shouldn't address me so familiarly. I am the Countess of Byfield."

"Well, hell." He scowled at her, unable and unwilling to recall his sister's careful coaching on English titles and forms of address. "I'm Captain Sparhawk of Providence, and by my lights that's considerably more impressive. At least I earned my title."

"So did I." She smiled with an open charm he hadn't expected, her lips curving upward like her tip-tilted eyes. "Forgive me. I forgot that you're an American, and that a countess would be an anathema to you. Perhaps we'll do better if you simply call me Caro."

"I'm not going to call you anything." He grunted, wishing she didn't use hundred-guinea words like *anathema*. "I'm tired, and I want to go to sleep. I'll just say good-night and then you go on back down to my sister and the rest of your friends."

"But they're not my friends." Impulsively she sat on the edge of his bed and leaned toward his hand, her blue eyes searching his face. "I don't go out much, you see, and I've never met your sister. It's you that's drawn me here, Captain Sparhawk, you alone, and now that I've found you I've no intention of leaving quite yet."

"I've drawn you here?" he repeated softly, staring at her parted lips so near to his own. Her gloved hand brushed against his hand, just enough to make the hair on his arm tingle with anticipation. "A craggy old Yankee shipmaster with white in his hair?"

She smiled again with the same openness. "You're not so very old, Captain, and I'm not so very young. Together, I think, we could find some common ground to share."

Her fragrance was like a drug to his senses, filling them so completely he could almost taste her already. He knew she expected him to kiss her. When he'd been younger, it had happened to him all the time. Barmaids or countesses, women generally made their wishes felt the same way. It would be so easy to draw her into his arms and beneath the sheets, to lose himself in the soft, willing pleasure she was offering.

So easy, and so wrong. Just because he'd been careless enough to let her into his room through that unlocked door didn't mean she deserved a place in his life, however fleeting, or even one in his bed.

Purposefully he shifted away from her, focusing instead on sliding the pistol back beneath his pillow. "It's late, ma'am. Good night."

He heard her sigh, and felt the mattress lighten as she rose to her feet. "Jack warned me you'd be like this," she said sadly. "But I thought at least you'd be willing—"

"Willing for what?" demanded Jeremiah. With humiliating clarity the answer came to him. His brother-in-law was so hopelessly besotted with Desire that he believed love alone could cure every other man's ills, as well. How many times before this had Jack urged him to find a ladylove of his own? "So help me, if Herendon put you up to this—"

She turned sharply. "Whatever are you saying?"

"You know damned well what I'm saying! What did Jack tell you of poor old ailing Jeremiah? Did he tell you I was so lonely that I'd welcome the attentions of a woman, any woman, who showed a breath of interest in me?"

By the light of the single candle her eyes flashed bright as her diamonds. "What he told me was that you were proud and hot tempered, but oh my, I never dreamed he meant this!"

"But you came anyway, didn't you?" Shoving himself from the bed to stand, Jeremiah saw how her eyes widened at his size as he loomed over her, how she stared at the jagged new scar that sliced across his torso. "Was I that much of a curiosity, a foreigner, an American, that I seemed worth the effort of seduction?"

"*Seduction!*" She tipped back her head and her laughter rippled merrily from her lips. "You think I came here to seduce you?"

He was in no mood for teasing, and he never liked being laughed at, especially not by a woman this pretty. "Aye, what other reason could there be for you creeping in here while I slept, every bit as bold as any barkeep's daughter?"

"You left me no choice." With her head cocked, she looked at him shrewdly. "You never leave this house. How else was I to find you?"

"You found me well enough in my bed, didn't you?"

"You really do believe I came to seduce you," she said incredulously, lifting her gaze to meet his. "Lord, I wouldn't know how to begin."

"Like this." He rocked her back off her feet and into the crook of his arm before she could protest. He swallowed her startled little cry into his mouth, his lips moving deftly over hers. He would show her that he wasn't some laughable American savage. He'd prove to her that he didn't need her pity, or her curiosity, or whatever other contemptuous impulse had brought her here tonight. She tasted every bit as sweet as he'd hoped she'd be, soft and warm in his embrace, and with a low groan he slid his hands along the satin, down her back to settle on the curve between her waist and hip.

Yet for a woman brazen enough to chase him to his bed, she seemed oddly uncertain. She lay stiffly in his arms, her hands curled defensively against his chest, and though her lips had parted for his, she waited for him to lead her. Were English gentlemen so self-centered that they left their women as unschooled as this one so obviously was?

With a new gentleness he deepened the kiss, exploring the most sensitive corners of her mouth until she began to answer him, tentatively at first and then with growing ardor. Her hands crept up his chest and around his neck to draw him closer, and, charmed by the ingenuity of her response, he felt his anger melting away, replaced by an intense bolt of desire. Lord, it *had* been too long! Countess or not, perhaps it wouldn't be such a bad thing to take what she offered. He lifted her against him and she moaned deep in her throat, and he knew then she wanted him as much as he did her.

And then she jerked free and slapped him as hard as she could.

He stared at her, his cheek stinging where she'd struck him. "What the devil was that for?"

"You—we shouldn't have kissed like that," she said breathlessly. Her face was flushed, her lips still wet from their kiss, her hair disheveled and her plume cocked to one side. "It wasn't right."

"It seemed right as rain to me." Strange how he wasn't really angry with her. Disappointed, yes, but not angry.

"No, you don't understand." She lowered her gaze, her clasped hands twisting together. "You don't understand at all."

"You've called it well enough there." He sat heavily on the edge of the bed, still rubbing his face. She'd caught him on the jaw with the edge of one of her bracelets, and he knew he'd have a bruise in the morning. "You're not making much sense, sweetheart."

"I don't, not when I'm distraught." She fidgeted with the clasp on one bracelet as she struggled to regain control of her emotions. "Frederick says it's one of my greatest failings, and he has worked quite hard to rid me of it."

Though Jeremiah waited for her to explain who Frederick was, she didn't. Her husband, most likely. If she was a countess, then somewhere there had to be a count—no, an earl. But whoever Frederick was, Jeremiah would be damned before he'd ask.

"Don't tell me," he said instead. "You have a list of failings as long as my arm."

"No, Captain, I don't, no matter how much you wish to believe the contrary." She closed her eyes briefly and sighed. "Good night, then, and forgive me for disturbing you."

"Just like that?"

"Just like that, yes." She gave her shoulders an odd little shrug, almost a shudder. "I've caused us both enough trouble tonight, haven't I?"

He caught her arm as she turned toward the door. Beneath the silk, her skin was warm and he felt the quickening of her heartbeat at his touch. "You can't go now."

She looked pointedly at his hand before she raised her gaze to meet his. "Why not? You've been telling me to leave ever since you woke."

"Use your ears, ma'am, and you'll know. All's quiet below. It must be well past midnight."

"Then I can let myself out. I'm hardly helpless, you know. My coachman will be waiting with the carriage where I left him, at the bottom of the hill."

"Well, you're not going alone." He released her arm, reaching for his shirt and tugging it over his head. Helpless or not, she wasn't going to traipse off into the darkness by herself as long as he had anything to say about it.

"I assure you such sudden chivalry isn't necessary," she said indignantly. "I'm quite capable."

"Oh, aye, I'm sure you are." He shrugged on his coat, not bothering with a waistcoat or hat, and smoothed back his hair. "And don't mistake it for chivalry. If you're found in the shrubbery tomorrow with your throat slit and your diamonds gone, I don't want to be the last one who saw you alive."

She made a disgruntled, undignified sound in the back of her throat that made him smile. He liked her better this way, when she wasn't so busy being a great lady. Given the chance, perhaps in the moonlight beside her coach, he'd kiss her again.

No, he wasn't being chivalrous at all.

He took the lantern from the table beside the bed. "Along with you then, ma'am."

"If you can't bring yourself to call me 'Caro,' then you must use Lady Byfield," she said irritably as she followed him. "'Ma'am' is common."

"Common or not, it's what we call ladies in my country," he said drily. "I fought a war with your people over such things."

She didn't answer, or maybe she was ignoring him, but he didn't care so long as she was quiet and didn't wake the rest of the house. He'd no wish to explain any of this to his sister, or worse, to his brother-in-law. Oh, he meant to have a few words with Jack in the morning, all right, but not with the subject of their discussion present the way she was now.

The long hallway to the front stairs was dark, and the single candle lit their way only a few shadowy feet before them. Fiercely Jeremiah lifted the lantern higher, determined to control the wariness that could turn so easily into fear. He'd walked this hall a hundred times, no, a thousand, in daylight without coming to harm. What difference, then, could there be in the dark?

He felt the woman beside him tentatively take his arm, and he patted her hand self-consciously to reassure her. If it had been a long time since he'd lain with a woman, it had been longer still since one had turned to him for comfort. He smiled wryly to himself, wondering what she'd do if she'd learned the truth about the sorry champion she'd chosen.

But once outside, she scurried away from him, skipping down the stone steps with her white gown fluttering out behind her in the moonlight. He followed more slowly, for the wound still pained him if he moved too fast, and he'd no wish to begin wincing and gasping like an old man before her.

The moon was almost full, the sweeping lawns around the house lit nearly as bright as by day, and Jeremiah relaxed. No demons here; here his only company was this sprite of a countess. The gravel of the drive crunched beneath their feet and with an exasperated mutter she stepped onto the grass instead.

"You'll ruin your slippers," warned Jeremiah as he joined her. "The dew's already fallen."

"I don't care. It won't be the first time, and I doubt it will be the last." She paused, waiting for him to catch up. "I refuse to stay off the grass simply because ladies' slippers are so insubstantial. It vexes Frederick, of course, but I lived in the country as a child, and if I could I'd go without shoes and stockings and garters altogether."

"Then shuck them off now. Where's the harm?" The night was warm for April, and Jeremiah liked the idea of her vexing this infernal Frederick.

She grinned at him. "I could, couldn't I?"

"Of course you can," he said easily. "I won't tell."

"Then I shall do it." Modestly she turned away from him as she lifted her skirt, but as she bent to untie her garters, the white silk gown draped over her round, upturned bottom in a charming, if unintentional, invitation that Jeremiah found far more provocative than any mere show of her ankles ever could be. When he'd been younger, women had bundled themselves away in layers of petticoats and buckram, but the scanty fashions now were worse—or better—than if they'd come out walking naked. And this woman before him would tempt a saint to sin.

Purposefully he looked up at the stars overhead and away from her. "I was raised in the country, too, and we didn't wear shoes from May till September, excepting when Granmam made us dress for church on Sundays."

"On a farm?" she asked eagerly. She was upright again, safe for him to look at as they once again began walking down the hill toward the gates and the road. In the swinging circle of the lantern's light her bare toes peeked out from beneath the hem of her gown. She held her slippers in one hand and her stockings in the other, the fine-gauge silk of the stockings still keeping the shape of her calves as they drifted out from her hand. "I've always liked farms."

"It was a plantation, really, though all that means is a bigger farm that the owner doesn't work himself."

"A plantation? That sounds very grand."

"For Rhode Island, it was," he agreed, remembering the last real home he'd had before he'd gone to sea.

"My grandfather made a king's ransom from privateering, and he must have spent half of it on that house alone. But I expect it would pale beside what a countess would call home, even in the country."

"Indeed," she said softly. "A proper countess most likely would."

"You'd know better than I." There was no mistaking the wistfulness in her voice, and he didn't understand it. He brushed the back of his fingers lightly across her arm, just enough to make her look back at him. "Exactly why did you wish to see me, Caro? You must have come with some reason in mind."

She frowned as she realized he'd finally used her given name, and rubbed the place on her arm that he'd touched.

"It doesn't matter now," she said swiftly, her words tumbling over one another. "I thought that we might help each other, but now I see how foolish an idea that was. I hadn't expected—oh, but I'll never see you again, so none of it matters anyway, does it? Look, there's my coach, just beyond the gate. There's no reason for you to come any farther."

"Don't, lass." He reached for her, but she scurried across the grass beyond his reach. "Damnation, I said I'd see you to your carriage!"

"And I say it's not necessary. Good night, Captain Sparhawk, and goodbye."

She turned and ran, holding her skirts up above her bare feet. He called her name, but she didn't look back, and he let her go. She was right: most likely they would never see each other again. She was an English countess and he was an American shipmaster, and in another week, a fortnight at the most, he meant to be gone, back to Rhode Island to pick up the shattered pieces of his life as best he could.

He watched her disappear through the door beside the gate, and he smiled to himself as he thought of her bare pink toes. He hoped she didn't catch hell from Frederick when she got home. The man should take better care of his wife.

But still Jeremiah wished she'd stayed a little longer.

# Chapter Two

Caro's feet skidded on the slippery grass, and the oath was already halfway from her lips before she swallowed it back. She hadn't sworn like that in years; swearing had been one of the first bad habits that Frederick had convinced her to abandon. Ladies didn't swear, and she *was* a lady, a countess, wife to a peer of the realm.

But ladies didn't let strange men kiss them, either, and for the first time the magnitude of what she'd done swept over her. She'd crept into the bedchamber of a man she didn't know, a foreigner, with a question that she'd finally been too fainthearted to ask, and instead she'd smiled and laughed and behaved as commonly as the barkeep's daughter he'd accused her of being.

It didn't matter that she'd gone there with the best intentions in the world. The truth remained that Frederick deserved better from her. He'd cherished her and loved her and educated her far beyond her station, and then, finally, had raised her up to his own by giving her his name and his title. There could be nothing finer for her than to be the wife of a man so endlessly kind and generous, and in return she loved him more than she'd ever loved anyone else. Because he'd told her so, she'd always believed that that love alone would be enough to redeem her.

And dear Lord, it wasn't, not now that she'd finally been tested. It wasn't even close.

The carriage loomed before her in the shadows, the Byfield crest barely visible on the side. The horses had been loosened to graze, but there was no sign of her coachman or the footman, either.

"Ralston?" she called uneasily. She touched one of her bracelets, recalling what Captain Sparhawk had said. She didn't believe that the grounds of an admiral's house would harbor footpads and cutthroats, but here on the Portsmouth Road she wasn't as sure. "Ralston, where are you?"

"And where have you been, my dear aunt?" drawled the young man who stepped from behind the coach. "I don't want to tell you how long I've been waiting."

"What a pity you've waited in vain, George," said Caro sharply, inching around him to reach the coach's door. "I've no more to say to you here than I do anywhere else. If you insist on your rude and impertinent questions, then I must refer you to Lord Byfield's solicitor."

"A solicitor, Auntie?" said the young man as he lounged back against the coach and stretched his legs before him to block her way. He wore a tall-brimmed hat cocked forward that hid his eyes, but for Caro his insolent smile was more than enough. "That's deuced uncharitable, even for you."

"Then perhaps I should call on Mr. Perkins myself, and arrange for charges to be brought against you," she answered, her irritation growing. "Surely there must be laws against your kind of vile harassment."

"So unkind, Auntie, so cruel!" He clucked his tongue in mock dismay. "And what of the laws against adultery, eh? Laws to protect husbands from a set of cuckold's horns from their slatternly wives?"

She gasped. "How dare you defame Frederick and me that way!"

"Dare I? Dare *you,* more's the point." His smile widened as he crossed his hands over his chest, the moonlight reflecting off the twin rows of polished buttons on his coat. "Oh, I'll vow you've been most discreet. These past months there's never been a hint of scandal about you. Until tonight, of course. Your slippers in your hand, your legs bare, your headpiece askew—what gossip I'll have to whisper over cards at Lady Carstairs's tomorrow night, eh? I didn't think you'd be enough to tempt gallant Admiral Lord Jack, but then his wife's breeding again, and to my own joy, you've never shown much inclination that way."

With an incoherent shriek, Caro dropped her slippers and flew at George's smirking face, determined to hurt him as much as he'd hurt her. It was bad enough for him to believe she was Jack Herendon's mistress, but to be taunted about her childlessness cut her to her heart.

But George's reflexes were unclouded by anger, and he deftly caught her wrists before her fingers reached his eyes. In the next instant he twisted and shoved her back against the side of the carriage, pinning her hands over her head and trapping her with his body.

"A widow's portion's not such a bad thing, Caro," he said, breathing hard as she struggled against him. "Once you're the dowager Lady Byfield the world will expect you to take lovers. Say the word, and it's done. So simple for you to have your freedom, and be rid of the old bastard for good."

"You're the bastard, George, not Frederick!" Furiously she fought against him. "Ralston!"

"Save your breath, Caro. I sent them off with a bottle of rum so we could talk in private."

She glared at him. "You've no right to do that! They're *my* men, not yours!"

"But for how long, eh?" He pressed closer, near enough that she could smell the same rum on his breath. "Dowager or not, Auntie, you're not so old I couldn't oblige you myself, and keep it all in the family. It's time you had a taste of a man young enough to remember what a woman desires most."

Caro stared at him, too stunned by what he was suggesting to answer.

He smiled, taking her silence as acquiescence, and leaned his mouth closer to her lips. "Simply say the word, my dear, and please us both. You'll find I'm generous with both my gold and my company."

"You're despicable." She practically spat out the words, forcing him to draw back. "Let me go at once!"

"Not yet, Caro, not before—"

"You heard the lady," said Jeremiah, his voice unmistakable to Caro. "Let her go. And do it now."

George twisted around, searching the shadows for the man who'd spoken. "What the devil—"

Jeremiah stepped forward. In the moonlight he looked to Caro like some wild forest giant, his size accentuated by the shadows around him, his face sharply planed and his thick black hair loose to his shoulders. He stood with his legs widespread and his whole body so tensed and ready to fight that the primed pistol in his hand seemed almost superfluous. In her small, sheltered world she'd never known a man like this one, and she flushed at the memory of how she'd let him kiss her, how much she'd enjoyed it before the shame had stopped her. And oh, what sorrowful mischief George would make for her if he ever learned what she'd done!

"Look here now," blustered George. "This is a private matter between Caro and me, and it don't concern you, whoever you are."

"I told you to let the lady go," said Jeremiah again, his voice rumbling deep. "I'm not a patient man, and I'm accustomed to having my way."

"Mind him, George," whispered Caro loud enough for Jeremiah to hear. "He has a gun, and I've no wish to be shot to death by some highwayman on account of your stubbornness. Lord knows we're probably already surrounded by his confederates in the trees."

*A highwayman?* thought Jeremiah, frowning. Confederates in the trees? What the devil was she up to now?

"A highwayman!" George's voice squeaked upward as he let Caro go, his eyes still turned toward Jeremiah. "Damn it all, Caro, you would be wearing those diamond cuffs, too! They must be worth a thousand guineas if they're worth a penny."

"They're worth ten times that if they'll save my life." She turned bravely toward Jeremiah as she slid the bracelets from her wrists. "Here, sir, they're yours, and my earrings, too, if you wish them. I know you'd take them by force anyway, but I pray because I've been so accommodating you'll spare me and my—my companion."

"Hear, hear," echoed George faintly, staring at the pistol.

Jeremiah's frown deepened. Here he'd thought he'd saved her from some ruffian's attack, yet instead the man had some sort of claim to her, enough that she'd protect him like this. Not that he was worth it, in Jeremiah's estimation: a fancy-dressed little Englishman so cowardly he'd let a woman defend him. But what was all this nonsense about highwaymen and bracelets?

"I'm sorry, ma'am," he began, "but I don't —"

"Oh, please, sir, please!" she begged, clutching her hands piteously before her. "Don't be so hasty in your judgment!"

Jeremiah shook his head in bewilderment. Whatever he'd blundered into belonged on a London stage, not here on the high road to Portsmouth. He glanced toward a rustling in the bushes and saw two wide-eyed men in livery cowering in the shadows, and curtly he waved at them to join the others. No matter what the woman intended, she hadn't really left him any choice but to go along with her game, at least for now.

George sniffed derisively at the two servants. "Is this how you display your loyalty to Lady Byfield, leaving her alone to be accosted like this?"

"But sir," protested Ralston, "that be what you wanted o' us!"

"None of your bickering, you silly fools," snapped Caro, her glance darting from George to Ralston and back again as exasperation temporarily overcame her show of terror, "else I'll leave you all as hostages."

George sniffed again. "You shouldn't bargain with ruffians like this, Caro. It ain't decent."

"I'll do what I must." With her jewelry cupped in her hands, she walked slowly to Jeremiah, her bare feet silent on the grass.

"Here you are," she said softly, her eyes so beseeching Jeremiah knew now he wouldn't give her away before the others. "I pray it's enough to ensure our safety."

He scooped the jewelry from her hand and stuffed it into his pocket with what he hoped was a proper highwayman's nonchalance. He'd been a great many things in his life, but this was the first time he'd been a thief, and he wasn't quite certain how it was done. "The gentleman has a purse, doesn't he?" he asked gruffly. "And that cut-stone ring there, on his little finger."

George opened his mouth to argue but Caro glared at him, her open hand outstretched. "Give it up, George, and consider it cheaply done. If you hadn't followed me here and interfered, none of this would have happened."

Glumly he handed his purse and ring to Caro, who brought them back to Jeremiah. "I fear that's everything, sir," she said sadly. "Oh, please, please, say it's sufficient to let us go!"

Though her words were meant to sway the hardest heart, there was still an impish gleam in her upturned eyes, meant for Jeremiah alone. She'd protected this man George, true, but she'd also enjoyed taking his purse. Jeremiah was glad, for the man was both a fool and a bully.

"If there's anything else you want," she continued when he didn't answer, "anything else that could sway your decision, so that we might be on our way."

Jeremiah looked down at her, struggling to appear as if he were weighing her plea instead of wondering if she'd intended a double meaning to her words. What else did he want? He wanted to send the three men on their way, and keep her here with him so she could explain. And kiss her again. Oh, aye, he wanted that very much, even if the reasons against it seemed even stronger after this silly masquerade. Her upswept hair had slipped further to one side, the egret's feather now bent at a jaunty angle over one eye as she looked up at him through her lashes. She was a charming, bewildering creature, no mistake, but with a start he realized she'd made him forget his own miseries, however briefly, for the first time since he'd been brought to England.

Her diamonds sat heavily in his pocket, a lump against his thigh. At least now he had a decent reason to see her again, if only long enough to return her jewelry, and knowing that made it easier to let her go.

Over her head he motioned to the coachman. "You heard the countess. She's ready to clear for home. And you, Master Georgie, you leave the lady alone, or you'll answer to me."

Even in the moonlight, Jeremiah could have sworn the other man paled. "See here now," he said weakly. "You can't threaten me like that. I'll see you hung, see if I don't."

"If you catch me first," said Jeremiah, and though he smiled, not even George could miss the threat in his voice. "But if I hear you've mistreated this lady again, I'll hunt you down. And God help your cowardly hide, when I find you you'll wish I hadn't."

He bowed his head briefly to Caro, still watching the other man. "Good night, ma'am. Sleep well."

She grinned swiftly at Jeremiah from beneath the feather, more than enough thanks to please him, before she turned and ran to her coach. He didn't wait to see her leave, not knowing whether or not the coachman might carry a gun beneath his box, but as he retreated back up toward the gate he could hear her adamantly refusing George a place in the carriage, with Ralston agreeing.

He uncocked his pistol and slipped it into his coat pocket on top of the diamonds as he retrieved the lantern from the lawn where he'd left it earlier. He still didn't know why she'd come to his bedchamber to see him, let alone why she'd let him rob her. He thought of her neat pink toes beneath the dew-marked white silk, and the way she grinned at him like a fellow conspirator. Behind him he heard her voice raised again, this time over the noise of her carriage, as she called George a name more usually found in the vocabularies of seamen.

No, Caroline, Lady Byfield, wasn't like anyone's idea of a countess.

And for the first time since he'd lost the *Chanticleer*, Jeremiah laughed out loud.

"Go on, lad, it's yours if you like raspberries." Jeremiah held the jam cake out in the palm of his hand, coaxing his nephew, Johnny, to take it. "Myself, I'd choose the apple, but your mama does them both blessed well."

The little boy stared seriously at the cake, his lips pursed with a four-year-old's intensity and his hands clasped behind his waist in imitation of his father, the admiral. But that was the sum of his father that showed, for with his green eyes and dark hair, Johnny was all Sparhawk. If he'd ever stayed in one place long enough to father a son himself, thought Jeremiah with a little pang of regret, his boy would look like this one.

"Take it, lad. I swear it's not poisoned." Still the boy hesitated, looking back over his shoulder to his nursemaid for reassurance. Not that Jeremiah blamed him. He hadn't much experience as an uncle, and this was the first time, quite by accident, that he'd been alone with the boy without Desire to ease the awkwardness. "Be bold now, Johnny. If you see a prize you want, why, you must seize it and make it your own."

Johnny frowned, considering, and grabbed the cake and stuffed it into his mouth in one messy bite. Then he smiled at his uncle, displaying teeth so covered with crumbs and bits of raspberry jam that Jeremiah, appalled, found it very hard to smile back.

"Oh, Johnny, you know you're not supposed to bother your uncle!" cried Desire as she hurried into the breakfast room as quickly as she could with her second child, Charlotte, clutching onto her skirts.

"No bother, Des, I swear," said Jeremiah with more relief than he'd intended. "I thought he still seemed hungry, that's all."

"He's always hungry for sweets." She plucked a napkin from the table and bent down to scrub at the boy's face while he squirmed and Charlotte gloated. "But that doesn't mean the little rogue has to come begging to you."

"He didn't beg. I offered."

"Truly, Jere?" She was slow to straighten, one hand on her back to balance the weight of the third child she carried within her, due in June. But still a beauty, thought Jeremiah proudly, the kind of tall, comely American woman that put all the little whey-faced English ladies to shame. "I've told him you've been ill, but children don't always understand."

"Stop fussing, Des. I'm as well now as I'll ever be, and the boy did no harm." He slipped his hand around his sister's shoulder and guided her to her chair at the head of the table as the nursemaid herded the two children from the room. "You're doing well enough by him, that's clear. One look at him and you know he's a sight more Sparhawk than Herendon."

"Don't forget whose roof you're under," Desire scolded, reaching out to smack his hand with her teaspoon. "No matter if it's true, Jack will have your head if he hears you say it."

"Hear you say what?" asked her husband as he came to stand behind her chair. His blond hair glinting in the morning sun, Admiral Lord John Herendon was the model of an English gentleman and officer, tall and handsome in the white and navy uniform he seemed born to wear. Desire smiled as she turned her face up toward him, her cheeks coloring with pleasure, and he rested his hand gently on the swell of her belly as he bent to kiss her.

The warm intimacy of the gesture made Jeremiah look down at his plate. If any two people in this world loved each other, it was Desire and Jack, and despite Jeremiah's own misgivings about his sister's choice of a husband, he had to admit that the marriage had brought her happiness and contentment.

He raised his gaze long enough to see them still wrapped in one another, his sister's eyes blissfully closed. Though married for nearly five years, they behaved as shamelessly as newlyweds, perhaps because so much of that time they'd spent apart. For the first year, Desire had sailed with Jack on his flagship while the British Admiralty had benignly looked the other way, and Johnny had been born at sea in the admiral's cabin and Charlotte begotten there. But then the war with France had worsened, and Desire had been forced to make a safer home alone on land for their children until the Treaty of Amiens last spring had brought Jack back to Portsmouth and the Channel Fleet.

Self-consciously buttering toast he had no real interest in eating, Jeremiah considered the dangers of loving as completely as Jack and Desire did, of placing all hope for joy and happiness in a single other person. He'd never known that kind of love himself, or particularly wanted it. Why should he? For him life seemed too uncertain for such unconditional devotion, and he'd been hurt enough by all he'd lost too soon—his mother, his father, his brother, friends and comrades—to willingly risk more.

Besides, he'd be thirty-seven his next birthday, far past the age for sentimental follies. He enjoyed women well enough—he thought again, pleasantly, of Lady Byfield—but he'd never found one worth giving up his freedom for, or would any of them, he thought wryly, consider him much of a bargain as a husband.

He looked up from the toast to his sister and brother-in-law in time to see them exchange one final kiss before Jack went to his own chair at the opposite end of the table, one more moment of such wordless tenderness that Jeremiah again looked hastily away with the same unfamiliar pang of regret he'd felt with little Johnny. What must it be like to love, and be loved, that much?

"You're looking well this morning, Jeremiah," declared Jack heartily, unaware of Jeremiah's thoughts. "Though Desire was ready to give you up, I knew it would take more than that single sword swipe to finish a man like you."

"I never gave him up!" said Desire indignantly. "I knew he wouldn't die. Jere's too ornery, even if that 'single sword swipe' was a gash as long as your arm, and then there was the infection on top of that, and floating in the sea for days on end."

"It wasn't quite that bad, Des," said Jeremiah uncomfortably, wishing they'd find something else to bicker over. He was feeling better this morning, well enough that for the first time he'd dressed in the new clothes his sister had ordered for him when his own were lost. A fop's rags, he grumbled as he'd looked in the mirror, but still he'd admitted to himself that the dark green coat looked handsome enough, and he'd taken extra care with how he'd tied his neckcloth and brushed his hair. The world seemed a more promising place this morning, and he didn't want to be reminded about how close he'd come to dying. "Though I suppose I should be grateful for your confidence in my orneriness."

"Orneriness be damned," said Jack as he cut into the ham and poached eggs that the servant had placed before him. "If Jeremiah's looking well this morning, I'm more willing to credit it to his own constitution and a good night's sleep."

"I wasn't much for sleep last night. No time." Jeremiah pulled Caro's bracelets and earrings from his coat pocket where he'd left it for safekeeping and shoved them across the polished mahogany toward Jack.

Desire gasped, and Jack frowned and lay down his knife and fork.

"I had a visitor," continued Jeremiah. "A lady who first found her way to my bedchamber and then tricked me into cozening some old sweetheart of hers into believing I was a highwayman. Gave me her jewels to prove it, too, as well as the man's purse."

Jack groaned. "Caro Moncrief."

"Caro Moncrief?" repeated Desire incredulously. "In my house? In my brother's bedchamber?"

"Aye, in my bedchamber." Jeremiah was enjoying the sight of his usually unruffled brother-in-law squirming a bit, though for Desire's sake he hoped the woman wasn't yet another of the admiral's former sweethearts. "Now, Jack, maybe you can explain how she came to be there. She said she'd told you all about it, which is a sight more than she ever bothered telling me."

Jack sighed as he toyed with the fork on the plate before him. "She didn't tell me everything. Caro never does."

"Oh, honestly, Jack, if you're not going to tell my brother about her, then I will," said Desire. "The Countess of Byfield is even more lowborn than we poor Americans are, Jere. Her mother was an expensive woman of the town who actually *sold* her daughter to Byfield when she was scarcely more than a child. You can imagine the talk when the old earl married her."

"Is he that much older?" Jeremiah remembered the stiff, startled way Caro had responded when he'd first kissed her. No wonder, with that kind of experience.

"Oh, Byfield's vastly older!" said Desire with relish. "You'd take him to be her father at the very least,

maybe even her grandfather. They almost never go out
in society, but when they do it's clear enough that
they're both, well, a bit peculiar. Goodness only
knows what they do together in private. He makes her
dress all in white, sometimes in classical dress all the
way down to sandals on her bare feet and leaves in her
hair, and he encourages her to do and say whatever she
pleases as if she were some child brought down from
the schoolroom to act clever for company. And then,
of course, there is the dragon-of-a-dowager countess."

"Desire, love," said Jack mildly. "You're gossiping."

Desire rolled her eyes with mock dismay. "I'm not
gossiping, Jack, I'm merely warning my brother before he becomes too enchanted with the creature."

"To protect my virtue from a fallen woman?" asked
Jeremiah with amusement.

"No, you great idiot, to keep you out of the courts!
She's never given the earl any children, so the heir is
his nephew, and when the poor old man was lost at sea
two years ago—"

"You mean she's a widow?" That surprised Jeremiah; from the way Caro had spoken of her husband
he'd assumed the man was snoring safely in his bed at
home.

Desire shrugged. "Well, that's what the world as-
sumes. But Lady Byfield refuses to believe it and have
her husband declared dead, and you can imagine what
the nephew says about her to anyone who'll listen.
He'll seize on any chance he gets to discredit her—
what he'd make of her meeting a lover in our

woods!—and I'd rather you didn't get yourself tangled in the middle of it."

"And I think your warning comes too late, sister mine," said Jeremiah smugly as he swept the jewelry from the table and into his hand. A widow, and a baseborn one at that. His spirits rose a little higher. Maybe Caro Byfield tumbling into his path was a sign that at last his luck was changing. Lord knows it couldn't get much worse, but she'd be a first-rate way to improve it. "Her being a widow changes everything, doesn't it? You know I've always had a special fondness for consoling widows."

Desire's brow puckered with concern. "Oh, Jere, please don't! This isn't some whalerman's merry lady that you can dally with for a week and then leave behind."

"Two weeks, Des, two weeks." His smile widened as he rose from the table. "Then I swear I'll put the whole Atlantic Ocean between me and the pretty little countess. Now if you'll excuse me—"

"Jeremiah, wait." Jack's expression was troubled as he, too, rose to his feet, the heavy damask napkin in his fist. "She didn't ask you, did she?"

"To come to call? Nay, she didn't, not in so many words, but I'd think her tossing her diamonds at me was invitation enough."

"Not that, Jeremiah. She means to ask you about Hamil Al-Ameer."

Jeremiah stopped, frozen with his hands gripping the back of his chair. She meant to ask him about *Hamil*. Hamil Al-Ameer: the man who'd robbed him of his ship, his crew, his friends. The heathen bastard

who'd destroyed his peace, made him a shaking coward, kicked him bleeding from his own deck to die in
the black waters of the night.

Blindly he stared past Jack and his sister, struggling to find something, anything, to make himself
forget. Outside the window, Johnny and Charlotte
were playing with a small, fat dog with pointed ears
that jumped into the air for the ball they tossed. Desperately Jeremiah tried to focus on them: the two
laughing children dressed in white, the green lawn still
glittering with dew, the fat little dog jumping and
twisting again and again for the red ball, innocence
and sunshine and laughter.

But not for him. God help him, never again for him.

## Chapter Three

Blackstone House, home to the last six earls of Byfield, was much as Jeremiah expected. Larger than his sister's house, surrounded by far more land, Blackstone House was an elegant jumble of architectural fashions, from the oldest, sprawling wing of Elizabethan brick to the front facade of pale green limestone, a model of Palladian order, and arches with Doric pilasters that rose the full three stories high to the roof.

But nary a black stone in sight, thought Jeremiah wryly as he walked his horse down the long gravel drive. He didn't like these ancient, overgrown English houses, reeking of endless capital and family histories so much older than his own country. As Desire explained it, Lord Byfield was only a middling sort of nobleman, yet his home was more grand than any to be found in New England, and Jeremiah thought of what a fool he'd been to babble on to Caro about his grandfather's plantation house on Aquidneck Island. Crescent Hill would fit into the stables of Blackstone House and not be missed, but at least Caro Byfield would never have to know that. No, once he returned her jewelry, she wouldn't learn another word about him.

As he climbed from his horse, a groom came running to take the reins, and slowly Jeremiah began up the long flight of steps to the door. He took his time, telling himself he wouldn't wish to be winded before the countess, but reluctance slowed his steps far more than any exertion. If the diamonds hadn't been so valuable, he could have sent them back with a messenger and been done with it, and with her.

His jaw tightened as he remembered what Jack had told him. Why would any lady want to speak of Hamil? Damn her, he wouldn't talk of what he'd been through for her cheap amusement! Jack and Desire had pieced together the barest details from what the men who'd rescued him had said and from his own delirious ravings, but he'd refused to tell them anything more. Even if he could, what was the use of it? Better to forget. It was done, finished, and all the yammering in the world wouldn't bring back the men who'd been slaughtered. Men who would still be alive if he hadn't been so—

"Good day, sir." The eight-paneled door swung open and a butler nearly as tall as Jeremiah himself gravely met his eye. "Your name, sir?"

"Captain Sparhawk, but it doesn't signify since I'm not staying." Still on the step, he held out the small flannel bag—Desire's contribution—that held Caro's jewelry. "Give this to your mistress, and be quick about it. Go on, man, take it, don't keep her waiting!"

"Why Captain Sparhawk, how splendid to see you again so soon!" Caro poked her head around the butler's arm, crowding him in the doorway. "Do show him in, Weldon. He's quite an agreeable man, for all he's glowering fit to burst at present."

Stiffly Weldon stepped aside, bowing his powdered head as slightly as he could.

But Jeremiah chose not to enter. "Thank you, ma'am, but no," he said as he handed her the little bag. "I've only come to return your property, and that done, I'll wish you good day."

"Oh, fah, don't be so pompous!" Impulsively Caro seized him by the sleeve and tugged. "Why else did you dress yourself so handsomely if you didn't mean to call on me?"

"I cannot, ma'am." Jeremiah tried to disentangle his arm while she laughed and clung to him and Weldon's disapproval grew more and more apparent. The devil take the woman for making him feel like such a fool! "My sister expects me to return shortly."

"I'll vow a man like you has never answered to a woman in his life, let alone his *sister*," said Caro, her tone shrewd as she released his arm. She smiled gleefully. "But then I should remember that myself, shouldn't I?"

"Aye, ma'am, perhaps you should." Jeremiah tried to look stern. Here in the morning sun he could see she wore no paint nor powder on her face, and little gold freckles that matched her lashes were scattered beguilingly across the bridge of her nose. Her cropped hair was simply dressed with a white ribbon across the brow, and only a narrow band of white work decorated the hem of her muslin dress.

She drew herself straight, folding her hands neatly before her as she carefully composed her expression. To Jeremiah's surprise, she succeeded, for though nothing else had changed she suddenly looked every inch an imperious, aristocratic countess. Frederick, wherever he was, would be proud.

"If you would be so kind as to favor me with your company, Captain," she said, her smile now no more than the merest genteel curve, "I would be quite honored. For a moment, that is all I beg of you. Only long enough so that I might thank you properly for your— your services last night."

The butler sniffed, and inwardly Jeremiah groaned, guessing too well what services the man was imagining. At least if they went indoors they'd be free from Weldon. "Very well, then. But mind, not long."

Jeremiah followed her down a long hall with a marble floor like a checkerboard. Lining the hallway on either side were life-size statues raised up on half-column pedestals. Some of the statues were men, some women, and all were mostly naked, and worldly though he considered himself, Jeremiah's pace slowed as he passed beneath the line of sightless marble eyes. He'd been in his twenties before he'd seen a statue like these, in an expensive Jamaican fancy house, and he and his mates had marveled over the ancient goddess's marble breasts and bottom for days afterward. What must it be like, especially for a lady, to live with such things every day?

As if she read his thoughts, Caro turned to face him, running her fingers lightly along the knee of young man with a kind of shawl draped over one shoulder and not a stitch more.

"He looks rather bashful, don't you think? Almost shy," she said. "Not very good for a warrior, which is what Frederick says he's supposed to be. I never remember his true name, something ancient and foreign, so I call him Bartholomew instead. Bart's one of my favorites."

Jeremiah made a noncommittal sound between a grunt and a cough. "He doesn't look like any Bart I've ever known."

"Ah well, he'll always be Bart to me." She patted the statue's muscular thigh with a fond familiarity that unsettled Jeremiah. She glanced up at him archly. "But then, of course, you'd prefer the ladies. Gentlemen do."

She laughed merrily as she walked away from him. At the end of the hallway was a tall arched window, and the sunlight filtered through the sheer muslin of her gown, silhouetting the curves of her body as plainly as the statues that flanked her. Jeremiah swallowed, unable to draw his eyes away though he knew he must. For her to be ignorant of how much the sunlight revealed was bad enough, but what if she knew the effect, what if she'd planned it to entice him?

"Ma'am." He looked down, away from her and away from the statues, and was surprised to see his hands clenched in tight fists at his sides. "Ma'am, I told you before I didn't have much time."

"Then it's just as well we're here," she said as she reached the end of the hallway and threw open the double doors to the right. "This is the Yellow Room. *My* sitting room. Not even Frederick can enter without knocking. He calls it my—oh, what was it?—my 'sanctuary.'"

He would have known this place was hers even if she'd said nothing. Unlike the chilly formality of the rest of the house, this room was warm with color and cheerfully cluttered. The paneled walls were white with gilded trim, each centered with a painting of overblown roses spilling from baskets. More flowers formed the design of the soft wool carpet underfoot, and real ones—daffodils, hyacinths, Dutch tulips that filled the air with their scent—in Chinese porcelain vases clustered along the mantelpiece and tabletops among figurines of commedia dell'arte characters and sly-faced cats. The hangings and upholstery were all of yellow silk damask, and piled in the chairs and sofa were plump down-filled cushions with gold tassels.

Caro dropped into one of these, propped her feet up on a gilded stool as she carelessly tossed the bag with her bracelets and earrings onto the table beside her. She waved her hand airily for him to sit in the chair opposite hers. As if, thought Jeremiah, they were the oldest of friends; as if he hadn't come here intending never to see her again.

"I really must thank you for saving me last night, Captain Sparhawk. Not that George would have done me any genuine harm, but your arrival was quite fortuitous. And, oh my, to see how he squirmed before you as a highwayman!" She clapped her hands with the fingers spread so only the palms touched. "I trust you won't return his purse and ring to him, too. He'd only squander it on gaming, and besides, if he learned to do without then he might stop badgering me for more."

Still standing, Jeremiah frowned, not liking the sound of a man who badgered a woman for money. "I dropped them both in the poor box at the seamen's chapel in Portsmouth."

"How perfect! Most likely it's the first time he's ever given a farthing to anyone other than his tailor." She tugged on one of the ringlets held back by the ribbon, twisting the hair around her finger, and though she smiled, it seemed to Jeremiah that some of her merriment had slipped away. "You were very good to come to my rescue, especially since you'd just sent me on my way for trespassing. You were quite right, of course. I'd no business being there in your room that way without any reason, good or bad."

He didn't answer at first, and beneath the weight of his silence her cheeks slowly flushed. "You had a reason," he said, wishing she'd told him the truth. "At least that's what Jack told me."

"I thought he might." She pulled a daffodil from the vase beside her, pretending to study it to avoid meeting Jeremiah's gaze. "He's been so good to me through this, you know, always telling me whatever he could from the admiralty, but even he can't perform miracles."

She looked at him wistfully, her eyes bright with tears. "I thought you might be like that, too, for no other reason than that I wished it so. More likely you judge me as great a fool as the rest of the world, but I won't believe that Frederick's truly gone. I *can't* believe it. That's why I couldn't let you kiss me, you see. You're a very nice man, and a handsome one, too, but I love Frederick, and he's my husband. If I'd kissed you, that would be as much as admitting that he wasn't coming back. And God help me, I can't do that.''

Jeremiah watched her unconsciously tear apart the flower in her hands, her thoughts turned inward to the husband she'd lost. Once again he was faced by the power of love, a locked room that he'd never enter. Widow or not, Caro was one woman who wouldn't need the kind of consolation he could offer.

With a sigh he headed toward the door, pausing by her chair to lay his hand briefly on her shoulder. "I'm sorry, Caro," he said gently. "Sorry for everything."

She bowed her head, staring down at the torn yellow petals scattered across her lap, and he walked past her to the door.

"Your friend David Kerr is still alive," she said softly, so softly he almost didn't hear her as his hand turned the latch.

But he'd heard enough to disbelieve it. "What did you say?"

"I said that David Kerr is still alive."

"How the hell would you know about Davy?" In two steps he was back before her chair. Roughly he seized her by the shoulders, his fingers crumpling the fragile muslin as he dragged her unwillingly to her feet. "David Kerr is dead, along with all the others. I saw their bodies with my own eyes, their blood black on the deck at my feet. Can you do better than that, Countess? Can you? Because by God, if you're trifling with me—"

"I wouldn't trifle with you. Not about this or anything else. Believe what I say. Your friend Mr. Kerr is alive, and I know where he is."

Jeremiah's fingers tightened into her shoulders as he clung to her as desperately as he was clinging to this last, insane hope she was offering him. "Then tell me where. Tell me *now.*"

Caro lifted her chin defiantly, trying to hide her fear. It wasn't him that she was afraid of, despite his size and strength and the anger and pain she saw in his eyes. No: what she feared was that she'd once again lose the courage to say what she must, or worse yet, to speak but choose the wrong words. This American was her last hope of saving Frederick's life. There wouldn't be another.

She swallowed hard, searching for the right plea, the perfect bargain, that would make him help her. And dear Lord, all she'd done so far was make him so angry he probably wouldn't hear a word she said.

"I'm waiting, ma'am," he said, and she heard in his voice the same velvety threat he'd used last night with George. "And I don't like waiting for anyone."

"You won't force it from me," she whispered hoarsely. She was too aware of how close he stood to her, of the warmth of his hands as they covered her shoulders, of how his mouth had felt on hers last night. Jack Herendon had told her of his brother-in-law's temper, but why hadn't he warned her of the raw power of his physical presence, the animal power that made her pulse quicken and her limbs turn to butter when he touched her? "If that's your intention, it won't work."

Instantly he released her, swearing to himself in frustration. "I'm sorry, all right? I didn't mean to hurt you. Now *tell* me."

She shook her head and backed away, rubbing one shoulder where he'd held her before she self-consciously began to smooth the crease from her sleeve instead. "I won't tell you a word about your friend until you tell me everything you can about Hamil Al-Ameer."

There, she'd done it, and there'd be no taking back the words now. She'd expected him to rail more at her before he answered, even call her names, the way Jack had warned her. But she wasn't prepared for what she saw now.

"Hamil," he said, his voice as hollow as his eyes. He seemed to age before her, his broad shoulders bowing down beneath the weight of his grief and pain. "What would a fine lady like you want to know about a thieving bastard like him?"

She remembered how he'd been last night when he'd jerked awake from the nightmare, the wild, haunted look that had followed the anguished cry of pain and terror. What could have happened to reduce a man like Jeremiah Sparhawk to that?

"Pray forgive me, Captain," she began, "for I didn't mean to upset—"

He drew himself up sharply. "No pity, ma'am. I'd rather be scorned than pitied."

"I don't intend to do either. I wouldn't ask you of this man Hamil if my reasons weren't most urgent."

"Then you'll understand if I prefer to keep my past to myself," he said wearily. He wasn't angry anymore, just tired. "David Kerr is dead, and so is every other man who served with me on the *Chanticleer*. I don't know what Herendon told you, but I won't dishonor the memories of Davy and the rest by speaking their names in the same breath as that heathen bastard Hamil."

"You would rather retain your stubborn sense of honor and propriety than hear in return what I have to say of Mr. Kerr?"

He sighed. "Honor or no, ma'am, I'm not in the habit of making bargains with ladies. Good day, Lady Byfield."

"No, wait, I beg you!" she cried, rushing after him. "This isn't a bargain that I ask of you, only an exchange of information, a way we might help each other!"

Though her desperation was unmistakable, he refused to be swayed. "If you're like every other woman on this earth, you'd merely tell me what you believed I wished to hear, whether it was true or not."

"No!" Frantically she rushed back to the little table beside her chair, yanking the drawer in it out so forcefully that the vase of yellow flowers toppled over. She pawed through the papers until she found the one she sought, then held it up to read, her fingers trembling and her voice shaking.

"'Kerr, David, mariner, first mate, surviving of the brig *Chanticleer*, of the city of Providence of Rhode

Island in the United American States. Of medium height, not above five and one-half feet, in age thirty-seven years, fair complected with brown hair, both ears pierced for the wearing of rings. Marked by a crooked left arm, broke long ago and ill-set, a star-shaped powder burn on the upper right back shoulder—"

"Let me see that!" Jeremiah lunged to tear the paper from her hands but she darted clear.

"You didn't believe me, did you?" she said breathlessly, dancing just beyond his reach. "You wouldn't trust me because I'm only a silly, ignorant woman, because I couldn't possibly feel the same loyalty as a man for those I love!"

His green eyes were as wild as a madman's as he shoved a chair aside to try to reach her. "What the devil is it, anyway? God help you if you lie!"

"The messengers of the Pasha of Tripoli do not lie, Captain Sparhawk, not when there is ransom to be earned from prisoners!" she cried, bunching her skirts in her fist as she ran from him. "From Naples this comes, from King Ferdinand's own secretary, but I won't read another word unless—"

She hadn't heard the knock at the door, and turned with a hiss when Weldon entered the room himself. She froze beneath the butler's scrutiny, as did Jeremiah, both panting and flushed amid the overturned furniture. The only other sound was the slow drip of water from the upset vase onto the carpet.

Weldon's expression remained unperturbed. "My lady needs assistance?"

Caro pressed her palm to her forehead. "No, Weldon, I do not, nor do I appreciate your entering this room unannounced!"

"My apologies, my lady, but I did knock. I did not realize you were engaged." He looked pointedly at Jeremiah. "But Mr. Stanhope has arrived, and demands a word with you at once."

"Damn Mr. Stanhope! Tell him I've no wish to see him, that I'm not at home, or better yet, tell him to go—to go straight to Hades!"

Weldon nodded. "Very well, my lady."

"Oh, Weldon, stop being so provokingly literal! Of course I'll come and speak with him, but only as far as the door. I won't have the wretched man in my house, acting like it's already his."

"Nay, ma'am, you'll do no such thing," ordered Jeremiah. "I won't have you running off like a frightened chicken until we've settled this between us!"

"I'm not running, Captain, you can be sure of that, not until you reconsider your own position." Her face still flushed, she glared at him, folded into quarters the paper she'd read from and shoved it down the front of her gown. "You wait here. I shall return directly."

As the door shut behind her and the butler, Jeremiah struggled to control his frustration, and failed. Over went another chair, followed by the needle-point-covered footstool he heaved across the room. Damn the woman! Either she did have news, real news, of Davy, or else she was the most convincing liar he'd ever met. He thought of how she'd toyed with him, teasing him along with stolen kisses and contrived robberies and statues of naked women, when here she'd been keeping a secret he'd kill to have. Davy alive, Davy a prisoner. Sweet Jesus, could it really be true?

With an oath he jerked the drawer from the table where she'd taken the first paper and dumped the contents onto the sofa. Receipts from dressmakers, half-finished letters dated months ago, a sheet of music to a love ballad. He scanned them all and found nothing more from Naples.

*Double damn the woman!* Jeremiah sank heavily into an armchair, his head in his hands. He'd known David Kerr since they'd been boys, one of only a handful of men he'd call friend. They'd sailed together, sought whores together, fought together. He'd stood up with Davy when his friend had wed Sarah Wright, and he was godfather to their oldest boy. Of course he intended to call on all the widows and orphans left by his crew as soon as he returned to Providence, a grim, heartbreaking responsibility for a captain, but telling Sarah would have been the hardest of all. And now, perhaps, he wouldn't have to do it. But what did Caro Moncrief expect from him in return, and what did it have to do with Hamil?

The ormolu clock on the mantel chimed three times. Jeremiah sighed impatiently. The countess had been gone nearly an hour, far longer than she'd indicated. He rose and walked to the window, pushing back the heavy curtains with two fingers as he looked toward the driveway.

Before a hired carriage parked at the base of the steps stood Caro and a man. Though Jeremiah was too far away to hear them, it was obvious they were arguing, Caro waving her hands in short, angry motions to emphasize her words. Abruptly the man turned to speak to the driver on the box, and Jeremiah recognized him as George from the night before, the man he'd guessed was the countess' lover. So much, thought Jeremiah cynically, for all her careful pledges of devotion to her husband.

As Jeremiah watched, Caro twitched her skirts away from George and, with her head high and the last word, began up the stairs. But before she'd taken three steps, George had thrown his arm around her neck, and pressed a handkerchief over her mouth. She fought against him, tearing at his hands as he dragged her down the steps to the carriage, until her struggles became weaker and by the time George lifted her into the carriage she was limp and still in his arms.

Though he knew he'd be too late, Jeremiah raced from the room and down the hall, reaching the front door in time to see the carriage disappear behind the first stand of beeches on the way to the road.

"Lady Byfield regrets that she will no longer be able to continue your interview," said Weldon behind him. "She has been unexpectedly called away."

Jeremiah swung round to face the butler. "Damn your impudence! Where are your eyes? She wasn't called away, she was kidnapped! That man drugged her and hauled her off without so much as a by-your-leave!"

"Mr. Stanhope is his lordship's nephew and heir," said Weldon with infuriating calm. "I do not believe he would wish her ladyship any harm."

"That bastard's the old earl's heir?" How neatly the pieces now fell together! No wonder George Stanhope wanted her money, and no wonder, too, that she didn't want to give it to him. Besides, he was relieved she had better taste in men than to choose such a sorry specimen, and mentally he apologized for doubting her loyalty to her husband.

"Yes, sir. That is, he is not a bastard, but the son of my lord's sister Lady Stanhope." Weldon let a gleam of smug contempt flicker briefly in his eyes, and Jeremiah remembered how the illegitimate daughter of a prostitute had become a countess. Trust a servant—an *English* servant—never to forget the scandalous details. "Mr. Stanhope is a fine gentleman. It will be an honor to serve him in time."

"No time soon, if I have anything to say about it." Jeremiah stared out into the direction the carriage had gone, already making plans. They wouldn't get far before he found them, for though Stanhope was impulsive, he wasn't particularly clever. He'd find them and rescue her, for Davy's sake, as well as her own.

"And Weldon."

"Yes, sir?"

"As the lady said, Weldon, you go to Hades, too."

# *Chapter Four*

Jeremiah found Desire in her garden, sitting alone with a book turned open on her knee, in the shadow of a tall boxwood hedge. It was late in the day, too close to dusk for reading any longer, and she had pulled her cashmere shawl over her shoulders and around her arms against the chill. Preoccupied with his own thoughts, he failed to notice how she was here alone at this hour and not inside with Jack or the children, or speaking with the servants concerning supper, and in his eagerness he began speaking as soon as he'd spotted her.

"That woman, Des, that woman's told me the most amazing thing! She swears that Davy Kerr is still alive, and I'm almost halfway to believing her."

Desire looked at him sharply. "Whatever are you talking about, Jere? You're making no sense at all. What woman?"

"Caro Moncrief. Lady Byfield. You know, that pretty little countess who tossed me her diamonds." He sat on the bench beside his sister, resting his hands on his thighs as he stretched his legs out across the grass. "Though I haven't learned how just yet, she's come by some sort of paper to the King of Naples that lists prisoners in Tripoli up for ransom, and Davy's name's on the list."

"And you *believed* her?" asked Desire with dismay. "Oh, Jere, I thought you'd promised not to go near her again!"

"I never promised you anything of the kind, and a good thing, too." Her lack of excitement disappointed him. Of anyone here in England, he'd expected Desire to be the one who'd understand. "Just as she was explaining it all to me, that same whining little bastard from last night—George Stanhope's his name—appears on her doorstep, quarrels with her, and when she doesn't say what he wants, he slaps some sort of smelling spirits over her face and hauls her off in his carriage, just like that! And the worst of it, Des, is that her own people, her butler, who saw the whole thing, are pretending none of it happened."

"So of course you've appointed yourself her savior?"

"I can't let him get away with kidnapping her, not when she knows about Davy!"

"Or says she does." She took his hand in hers. "Listen to me, Jeremiah. You can't let yourself get tangled in Lady Byfield's affairs. She could have trumped up this whole business about David simply to draw you into her quarrel with George Stanhope. The whole county follows it like a sparring match. It's been going on for years, all the way back to Frederick's mother."

"But Des—"

"No, you listen to me! Most likely Caro learned enough of your past from Jack to appeal to you, and because she can be quite—quite charming, you believe her. Even Jack's willing to forgive her all manner of impositions, and he's known her for years."

"That's Jack's folly, not mine. I'm no greenhorn, Desire." Indignantly he pulled his hand away, folding his arms across his chest. "The woman knew too much about Davy to be cozening me."

She sighed with exasperation. "Listen to me, you great fool! Even *if* you manage to separate her from Stanhope, and *if* she has proof enough that David lives, what then? Go to Tripoli to rescue him, too? Or have you forgotten that America's at war with the Turks, and that if you're captured again, this time they'll make sure they kill you?"

"Oh, aye, and what do I say to Davy's wife? I'm sorry, Sarah, but I couldn't go after him from fear of soiling my trouser hems?"

"And what do you say to *me,* Jeremiah?" demanded Desire. "We're all that's left of our family, you and I, and I don't want you risking your neck because some pretty little chit winks and simpers your way. When I think of how close to death you were when they brought you here—"

Suddenly her voice broke, more emotion than he'd expected spilling over into her words. "I can't lose you, too, Jere. I can't. I want you to forget Caro Moncrief and all her foolishness, and I want you to sail for home the way you've planned, so I can picture you there in our old house, safe at last."

She closed her eyes and pressed one hand over her mouth to try to stop the sob that broke through anyway. With her other hand she cradled her belly, striving to calm the child within her, who'd sensed her agitation and grown restless.

"Oh, sweetheart, forgive me," said Jeremiah, remorse sweeping over him. Awkwardly he slipped his arms around Desire's shaking shoulders and she buried her face against his chest. She wept from the heart and he let her, patting her back to comfort her as best he could. She was right, they were the last of their family, and he alone understood the depth of the sorrows they'd shared together: the early deaths of both their mother and father, and then, again too soon, that of their younger brother.

The candles and lamps had been lit within the house before she finally grew quiet, and he held her still a little longer to be sure.

"We'd best be off now, Desire," he said gently. "Jack will be sending out the guard if we don't go in soon."

"He's gone, Jere." She pushed herself away from him with a final fragmented sob, and took the handkerchief he offered. "He left this afternoon, while you were out."

"What do you mean he's gone?"

"What other meaning can there be?" She sniffed loudly, fumbling with the handkerchief as she struggled for her composure. "His orders came for him to rejoin his ship, and by now I expect they've cleared Portsmouth to chase after Frenchmen again. He says the Peace of Amiens is nearly done, that this horrid

General Bonaparte will break it any day now. Jack's known for days, but he said he didn't want to spoil our time together by telling me before he had to.''

Her voice wavered precariously. "He said...he said...oh damn, Jere, I don't want to cry anymore!''

"Hush now, sweetheart,'' he said gently, wishing for something, anything to say to ease her pain, "it will be all right.''

"No, it won't,'' she said bitterly, "not as long as men insist on making war, killing each other for their precious honor, or their king, or some forsaken scrap of land like this wretched Malta. God in heaven, Jere, I don't even know where Malta *is,* and for its sake I may lose my husband!''

"Do you know exactly where he's bound, how long he'll be gone?''

She stared down at the handkerchief, rolling it tighter and tighter into a soggy ball in her hand. "You know he can't tell me any of that, Jere. He can't tell me anything beyond that he's leaving. Jack's like that with his orders: the word of the admiralty lords is his almighty God.''

"Then perhaps it's time he bowed down to something a bit more exalted than his blasted navy.'' Although Jeremiah had come to grudgingly respect his brother-in-law as a man, he could never accept Jack for what he represented, the pomp and authority of King George's Royal Navy, the same navy that had killed Jeremiah and Desire's father when they'd been little more than children. "How he can abandon you like this, so close to your time—''

"No, Jere, I won't hear it from you again!" Awkward though she was, Desire rose swiftly to stand before her brother, her hands where her waist used to be. "Jack loves me, Jere. I've never once doubted him since we wed, and I never will. He's a loyal, honorable man, loyal to me and our children and to his country, and I would no more question his right to do what he believes he must than I'd ask you to, oh, quit the sea and become a tinker instead."

Jeremiah scowled, unable to follow her reasoning. She could preach all she wanted about loyalty, but the fact remained that her husband had left her when she needed him, and as her older brother, the one who'd always protected her, he hated to see her hurt like this. "I'm trying to be serious, and all you can do is make jests about tinkers!"

"And here I thought I was being serious, too." She rested her hand with the sapphire wedding ring on his arm. "What I'm trying to say, Jeremiah, is that as difficult as it may be, I love Jack enough to let him go. Can't you understand that?"

"No, sister mine, I cannot. After all the trouble the man went through to win you, he should damned well want to keep by your side!"

"You'll never change, will you?" she said sorrowfully. She swallowed hard, her fingers tightening on his sleeve. "But maybe you'll understand this. As much as I wish I could keep you here, I want you to sail for home now, tomorrow, before the French try to blockade the channel again."

"Desire—"

"Hush, hear me out! If you're healed enough to chase after Caro Moncrief, you're more than well enough to travel. You've no real reason to stay here. I've had Jack book passage for you on an English ship bound for Jamaica, and from there you'll have no problem finding a sugar sloop for the voyage up the coast to Rhode Island."

"I can't do it, Desire," he said softly. "I'd be a coward if I did."

"At least you'd be a live coward!"

"Since when has that been an issue for our family, eh?" He touched her cheek with the back of his hand, her face pale and anxious in the twilight. "If you'd taken the safest course, you'd still be a spinster knitting stockings in our grandmother's parlor on Benefit Street. We Sparhawks don't always do the wisest thing, but we're never cowards."

"Oh, Jeremiah." She sighed with resignation and leaned against his shoulder. "I thought at least I could try to convince you."

"You might as well try to coax the moon from the sky. Likely you're right about Lady Byfield. Likely she doesn't know any more about David Kerr than she's already told me. But if she does, and if there's even a breath of a chance that I can save Davy or any of the others..."

"Of course you must." She sighed again, and with her handkerchief in her fist, she struck his arm. "It's the very devil being a Sparhawk, isn't it? Think if our great-grandfather *had* been a tinker instead!"

"Us Sparhawks tinkers?" Jeremiah snorted. "We'd all have died out from boredom long ago."

"Well, we're never bored now." She searched his face, her eyes still too bright. "You will be careful, won't you? If there's another war with France, then the whole continent will be turned upside down."

"Ah, but Des, I'm an American, and none of it will bother me." With his own handkerchief he wiped away the last of her tears. "If this Napoleon's fool enough to go after England again, then he'll get the whipping he deserves and right soon, too. You'll see, this war, if there is one, will be done in no time, and your Jack will be home in time to see this baby christened."

"Dear God, I pray you're right." Her smile was shaky, but at least, thought Jeremiah, it was a smile. "But Jere, please, *please,* tell me you're doing this for Davy's sake alone and not for that silly Byfield woman."

Jeremiah saw the concern in his sister's face, and thought of Caro Moncrief. Yes, Lady Byfield was silly. She was beautiful, too, and charmingly unpredictable, and she'd made him laugh for the first time in months. She was also married, and no matter what the rest of the county gossiped about her, she was clearly in love with her husband. But all that mattered to Jeremiah was that she needed him, and for that he wouldn't abandon her.

Yet the deeper truth was something he couldn't admit to Desire. She'd always looked up to him as her big brother, counting on him to be strong. How could he tell her how uncertain he'd become inside? How could he admit that because Caro needed him, he needed her, too?

"Oh, aye, of course I'm doing this for Davy," he said softly, wishing he didn't have to lie to Desire. "Come, sister mine, let's go in the house."

Slowly, painfully, Caro struggled to force her eyes open. There was a sticky sweet taste in her mouth and her head ached so badly she felt sick to her stomach. What *had* she eaten for supper? If only she could reach the chamber pot beneath her bed and not retch all over the carpet!

The shadowy figure of a man leaned over her. "Come now, Auntie, don't play the sleepyhead with me. The servants said you were stirring and I haven't all day to wait on your pleasure."

*"George?"* Her voice was scarcely more than an ineffectual croak as she tried to focus on his face. "Leave my bedchamber before I have you tossed out!"

"How charming, Caro. Your eyes aren't even open and already you're giving orders as if you were born to it. Pity you weren't, isn't it?"

Her head still spinning, she weakly pushed herself up against the pillows. "You've no right to be here, especially to insult me. Where's Weldon? Why did he let you in?"

George laughed, enjoying her confusion. "Weldon didn't let me in. Rather he let you *out.*"

To Caro's dismay, she realized he was right. Now she remembered how she'd argued with George on the steps of Blackstone House, how he'd grabbed her when she'd turned to leave him, and the same sickly sweet smell of the cloth he'd pressed over her face as he'd pulled her into the carriage.

"You're my guest now, Caro," he continued, "and I mean to be a most excellent host to you during your stay here."

Caro's dismay deepened as she looked around her. The slanting, water-stained ceiling overhead didn't belong to any room she recognized, and the single casement beneath the eaves framed no more than a sliver of sky through the narrow, dirty pane. Watching from beside the window, the grim-faced woman with her arms crossed over her breasts bore no resemblance to her own laughing, lighthearted lady's maid. The linens Caro lay upon were patched and dank, the bedstead hard and narrow, a servant's bed without curtains or bolster, and beneath the coarse coverlet, she wore not her cambric night rail but only her shift. With an indignant gasp, she clutched the coverlet over her breasts and glared at George, seated beside the bed on the room's only chair.

"I'd hardly describe myself as your guest, George," she said tartly, striving for as much dignity as she could muster under the circumstances. "As despicable as you are, I didn't think you'd lower yourself to kidnapping."

He cocked his head, striving to look contrite. "Kidnapping seems a bit harsh. Think of it instead as an opportunity for you to reconsider certain of your...misconceptions."

"Don't try and put a pretty face on it, George," she snapped. "It's kidnapping, nothing less, and I'm certain the magistrates will agree with me. And my only 'misconception' was to trust you as much as I did.''

In her mind she was already framing the words she'd use to swear out a writ against him. Even with Frederick's title to protect her, she'd have to be careful: to a magistrate, George would seem more a model English gentleman than a villain. He was a small man, the same height as Caro herself, and because his features were fine boned, almost too pretty, he favored expensive boots and coats cut to make him look like some bluff country squire. In a group of men George Stanhope was always the one who laughed the loudest, and among ladies he was known as a witty, agreeable partner, free with compliments and trinkets.

Yet from the first time George had bowed over her hand, Caro had not been fooled. She, too, was a sparrow made bright in false plumage, and she was quick to recognize the wish for the same in George. But where she would have loved a penniless Frederick for his kindness alone, all of George's fawning attention had been dependent on her husband's wealth and generosity. It was his expectations of Frederick's death that paid George's tailor and bought the gewgaws for his mistresses, and those same expectations that had made him bring her here.

He smiled now, still trying to charm her into compliance. ''I didn't ask for your trust, Auntie, only your common sense where poor old Frederick is concerned.''

''Frederick will have your head when he learns of this, and then you'll find there's nothing poor about him.'' She tugged the coverlet higher. ''Now that you've had your little amusement, would you please bring me my clothing so I might dress and go home?''

"I told you, Caro, you're my guest, and I won't part with your company just yet. But such a wifely, if belated, show of modesty!'' Insolently his gaze flicked over her bare shoulders. "These last hours while you've been unconscious I've had time enough to acquaint myself with your most intimate charms.''

"But that woman...'' She glanced at the grim serving woman across the room. Wherever her clothing had gone, she'd assumed that the woman had undressed her, not George.

George shrugged. "Oh, Mrs. Warren is paid well enough to watch—whether it's you, me, or both of us.'' He leaned closer over her, and she forced herself not to draw back. "Your husband is a far more fortunate man than I'd suspected.''

"You didn't,'' she said slowly. "Not even you would dare do that.''

He shrugged again, his very carelessness suggesting a one-sided intimacy.

Fighting against her own uncertainty, she refused to believe all that smirk suggested. Could she really have been that vulnerable? Surely she would know if he'd— he'd used her the way he implied. Unconscious or not, her body couldn't have been so insensitive, so unknowing, that she'd feel no different now. She closed her eyes, unable to meet the implication in his, and instead she saw another man's hands reaching for her, grabbing her, his gnarled fingers digging into her trembling, terrified flesh....

George trailed his forefinger along her cheek, the nail grating just enough across her skin to jerk her back to the present. She was a woman now, not a child. She knew how to fight back. Furiously she struck his hand away from her face.

"Don't you ever touch me again, George!" Anger and hatred made her voice icy cold. "Can you understand that? Never!"

George's lips pressed together into a tight, narrow line, as all vestiges of his customary charm vanished. "Save your protests for when they're justified, Caro. I haven't laid a finger on your dubious virtue. You are, after all, merely a bit of garnish beside a much richer meal, and as delicious as you likely are, you're not worth risking the whole."

"You are vile!" She nearly spat the words.

"No, Auntie, I'm simply weary of waiting." He pushed the chair back from the bed and walked over to the window, the morning sun making a bright halo of his golden hair. "Your room here has a most excellent prospect of the harbor. You'll also note that you're four stories above the ground. The door will be locked—to protect you from harm, of course—and Mrs. Warren will see to your meals and other needs. I'll keep your gown and slippers myself, so they won't become soiled."

"You can't keep me here, locked away as your prisoner!" cried Caro, fighting her panic. She must not show any weakness before George. "Weldon must have seen what you did to me. He'll send for the authorities, and they'll—"

Smiling to himself, George tapped lightly on the window. "Weldon's no fool, Caro. He knows how his bread will soon be buttered. He saw nothing unusual in your departure, and he'll tell the other servants that you've gone."

"You bribed *my* servants!" Unable to lie still any longer, she flung the coverlet around her shoulders and slid unsteadily from the bed. "First you kidnap me, and then you poison my people against me with your own worthless promises! This time I *will* go to Mr. Perkins and swear against you! When he realizes I've disappeared—"

"But he won't, you see. Perkins believes you have gone to visit a friend to the north."

"Not Perkins, too!" she cried. "God in heaven, George, when I tell this to Frederick—"

"But you won't, Caro, because Frederick is dead." He turned away from the window and headed toward the door, nodding curtly at Mrs. Warren to follow. "The sooner you accept his death and agree to begin the proper proceedings, the sooner you can leave."

"No, George, I won't do it! Frederick's not dead. I would know it in my heart if he were! Somewhere he lives, somewhere he's waiting for me, I know, and nothing you can say or do will change that!" She lunged for George's arm to stop him before he locked her away, but her feet tangled in the trailing coverlet and she stumbled forward, her knees and arms hitting hard on the bare floorboards. "Wait, George, damn you, wait!"

"How charming," said George, pausing with the door half shut. "The curse of an illegitimate child prostitute, seducer of a man old enough to be her father. You let Mrs. Warren know when you've come to your senses, Caro, and then we'll speak again.''

She looked up as the key turned in the lock, and with a muffled cry of despair she sank back down to the floor, burying her face in the coverlet.

She tried to think of Frederick, to remember how his smile lit his blue eyes with pleasure when she played the pianoforte for him, no matter how many wrong notes she struck, to recall the faint fragrance of his tobacco on his coat and the contented sigh he made when he sat in the bargello armchair at the end of the day. She tried to imagine what he'd say to her now, if she could once again kneel on the floor beside him with her head resting on his knees, how gently he would stroke the back of her head and tell her not to fuss and worry, that life was too dear to waste it on ill feelings.

Why, then, was such hatred and greed destroying everything that Frederick had valued most? Why, why had he left her when she needed him so?

With a little sob of loneliness she curled deeper into herself, striving for the elusive comfort that her husband's memory might bring. And then, strangely, the memory shifted. It wasn't Frederick's voice she heard in her head, but a deeper one, rumbling thick with an American accent.

*"I'll set it all to rights, sweetheart,"* Jeremiah Sparhawk *was saying as he held her against the hard muscles of his chest. His large hands along her body were warm and sure, a caress that fired her blood and*

*made her heart race. "I won't let that thieving bas-
tard hurt you."*

She gasped and sat bolt upright. What had come
over her? It must have been whatever drug George had
used to rob her of her senses, returning again to steal
her wits. Only once had she let the man kiss her, and
here she was daydreaming of him like some moon-
struck serving girl! She certainly had no business
looking to Captain Sparhawk to rescue her, any more
than she had the right to turn to him for comfort. He'd
been furious when she'd left him at Blackstone House.
What must his temper have been when she didn't return as she'd promised?

She sighed deeply, rubbing her fingertips across her
forehead. The American had been her last hope for
finding Frederick, and even then Jack had told her
she'd only have two weeks to convince Captain Sparhawk before he sailed for home. Now most likely he
wouldn't even speak to her, let alone risk his life to
help find her husband.

Slowly she pushed herself up from the floor, drawing the coverlet around her shoulders like a shawl as
she went to the window. From the houses across the
street, she realized George had brought her to the attic of his own lodgings. She was surprised that he'd be
so obvious, but then why should he bother to take her
to a more secretive spot? No one would suspect him
because no one was looking for her.

She stared down at the paving stones in the courtyard four stories below and groaned with frustration.

She'd never be able to help Frederick as long as she was locked away up here. Somehow, she must find a way to escape.

Somehow she must, and soon.

## Chapter Five

"Oh, aye, sir, that be Mr. Stanhope's house," said the scullery maid, swinging the market basket before her as she smiled winningly up at Jeremiah. "Or leastways it be where he lives for now. Grand prospects, sir, that be what Mr. Stanhope has, on account o' him bein' heir to a great title. The Earl o' Byfield, that's what he'll be."

"Too grand he'll be for the likes of us, eh, lass?" said Jeremiah as he returned the girl's smile. He'd waited all morning for someone to come from the house, and finally luck had sent him this guileless little red-haired girl, fresh from the country. "But tell me: does he have a lady staying with him now?"

"Eh, sir, when don't Mr. Stanhope have a lady there, that be the more proper question!" The girl giggled and glanced nervously over her shoulder, hoping that neither the cook nor the butler would catch her talking to the stranger. Of course she'd been warned against dawdling with men on the street, but this one wasn't some randy, pigtailed jack-tar from the fleet. No, this one was a gentleman, and handsome, too, with his green eyes and shoulders as wide as a house. Where could be the harm? "As Mrs. Warren's always sayin', sir, Mr. Stanhope likes his ladies, an' the ladies like him."

"Then you'd best look after yourself, sweetheart, once he finds what a little beauty he's harboring under his own roof." The girl blushed and giggled more just the way Jeremiah knew she would, the same way women always did. Or almost always: it certainly hadn't been as easy with Lady Byfield. "But I've a reason for asking about this particular lady. I'm asking for a friend whose sister's run off with a gentleman, and I'm afraid it may be your Mr. Stanhope."

"Oh, lud!" The girl's eyes widened, delighted as she was to be party to a possible scandal. "Now Mrs. Warren did say there was a new lady come yesterday, an' grumblin' she was because Mr. Stanhope ordered her t' take the trays up t' her special herself. Mrs. Warren don't gossip overmuch, an' course she wouldn't tell me the lady's name, but she did say this one be prettier than most, with silver hair an' blue eyes turned up like a fairy's, even if she do be vexin' the master with her chatterin'."

The girl leaned closer, lowering her voice to a conspiratorial whisper. "Mrs. Warren says the master had t' take away her clothes t' keep her quiet an' lock her up in the room under the eaves! Can you fancy that, sir? Takin' away a lady's clothes on account o' her speakin' out!"

Indeed, he could fancy it, and a good deal more graphically than this little country girl would ever guess. Of course the woman was Caro. With upturned blue eyes and too much chatter, it couldn't be anyone else.

For a moment doubt flickered through his conscience. Desire had said the battles between Lady Byfield and George Stanhope were well-known. What if they really were lovers? He'd judged it so himself at first, and he'd seen stranger relationships between men and women, particularly when one of them was married to another. What if he went blundering in to save a lady who didn't want saving?

Then he remembered how she'd wept with such genuine emotion when she'd spoken of her husband, and how roughly George Stanhope had treated her beside her carriage. No, that hadn't been lovers' play. Jeremiah's frown deepened when he thought of what the man would do to her when he had her under his own roof.

"How the devil can he expect to get away with that?" he demanded, as much to himself as to the girl. "This is supposed to be a civilized country, isn't it? A man can't haul off and make some woman his prize just because he wants her!"

The girl looked at him pityingly, the ruffles on her cap fluttering in the breeze. "I didn't think you was an Englishman, sir, on account of how you talk. Do you be Irish, then?"

"Nay, lass, American, and where I come from a lady's safe from rascals like your Mr. Stanhope."

"American! La, no wonder you don't understand our ways!" She spoke firmly, almost lecturing him, as if he were some half-wit savage—the opinion most English held of Americans.

"In England we all know our place," she explained. "Them that's our betters can do things different than me or you. Because Mr. Stanhope's bound to be an earl, he can do what he pleases with his new sweetheart, an' none will judge him the worse for it. There be no law against what they do with themselves, leastways for gentry like him. Can you fancy a constable knockin' on his door wit' a warrant for hidin' a lady's gown? That constable'd be lookin' for work for certain if'n he tried *that!*"

She giggled again, her red-knuckled fingers over her mouth, and Jeremiah forced himself to smile in return. As foolish as the little creature was, what she said was all too true, and it echoed Desire's warnings, too. No matter how convinced he was that Lady Byfield was being held against her will, he'd never be able to find an English judge to agree with him against George Stanhope. If he wanted to free her, he'd have to do it himself.

"Don't judge me bold for askin', sir," the girl was saying, swaying her hips suggestively beneath her apron as she looked up at him from under her stubby lashes, "but do all American men be so tall an' comely?"

"Nay, lass, not at all," he answered, his face impassive. "In Rhode Island I'm rated a poor fifth-rate runtling, not worth the trouble to feed or keep. Why else do you think I've been sent here?"

The girl gasped, speechless at the possibilities. Jeremiah chucked her beneath the chin and patted her cheek. "Good day to you now, darling. The lady I'm seeking is dark haired, not fair, but I still thank you for your help.''

He lifted his hat and turned away, but she moved quickly, blocking his path with her basket.

"Sir, oh sir!" she said, smiling as coquettishly as she could. "My name's Betsy White, sir, an' tonight's my turn t' step out t' visit my sister. She lives in Tower Street, does my sister, the last house near the pump, an' she don't mind if I have friends.''

"Miss Betsy, then.'' This time he was able to dodge the girl and her basket. "Your sister in Tower Street, this very night. You can be sure I won't forget it, lass.''

He wouldn't, either. He didn't want anyone in Stanhope's house who might recognize him tonight when he came back for Lady Byfield.

With another war imminent, many of the ships in the channel fleet had returned to Portsmouth for a final victualing and refitting before once again settling into the necessary tedium of blockading the French coast. Ships in port meant sailors in town, and the streets of the town were crowded with crews celebrating one last, boisterous shore leave.

Jeremiah was thankful for the sailors' excesses. Although the citizens of Portsmouth were generally tolerant of rollicking strangers, tonight decent folk would prefer their own company and keep to their houses. Even on this quiet street, no one would notice another man who kept to the shadows, albeit one who glanced repeatedly at the bright three-quarter moon for solace against the darkness around him.

He waited in the park across the street from Stanhope's house, watching until the last curtains were drawn and the lights put out for the night. To his surprise, Stanhope left in a carriage with several companions, all laughing and dressed for evening amusements. Though he knew he should be relieved that Stanhope had left Caro, Jeremiah was more disappointed. He'd anticipated thrashing Stanhope in his own house. Touching the pistols in his belt for reassurance, he crossed the street and rapped on the front door with his knuckles.

A sleepy-eyed footman finally opened the door a crack, his nightcap askew as he peered at Jeremiah. "Shove off before you wake your betters, Jack," he ordered, seeing the rough, anonymous sailor's clothing Jeremiah had chosen, "else I'll call the watch on you. We've no use for your sort in this neighborhood."

But as he began to shut the door, Jeremiah braced his shoulder against the heavy oak and thrust the barrel of one of the pistols through the opening and against the footman's ribs. The man made a garbled, gasping sound as he stared at the pistol, his hands fluttering off the doorjamb as he backed away. "Spare me, sir, oh sir, please don't kill me, not even the master's plate's worth my life!"

"Nay, I'd wager it don't even come close," growled Jeremiah as he forced his way into the house and shoved the door shut. A night-light hung overhead, the light from the floating wick tinted pale blue by the lantern's glass, the footman's round face beneath it ghastly pale. "Look at how you're all aquiver, you yellow-bellied little coward!"

"Please, sir, I beg your mercy! The master don't keep no hard money in the house, but I swear on my mother's honor that the pitchers there on that table are sterling, and—"

"Don't want 'em," said Jeremiah. "Where's the lady Stanhope brought here yesterday?"

The man's mouth turned down. "At the top of the last stairs, in Addy's old room. The door's locked, but the key's hanging on the peg opposite for Mrs. Warren."

"The devil take you if you play me false!"

"I swear it's true! But the master's orders—"

"Do you think I give a damn about that bastard's orders?" Jeremiah jerked his head toward the adjoining room. "In there with you, and be quick about it."

"Oh, no, sir, I won't let you kill me like that!" Clutching his nightcap, the man turned to run, and with a muttered oath, Jeremiah tapped him on the back of his head with the butt of his pistol. The footman slumped to the floor, his eyes still wide but now unseeing.

Swiftly Jeremiah dragged him into the drawing room and bound him to a straight-back chair with the line he'd brought in his pocket, tying a rag around the man's mouth as a gag before he turned the chair to the wall, far away from any windows or door. He was sure he could count on at least a quarter hour before the footman was missed, maybe more, plenty of time to find Caro.

But back in the hall he stared up the long, dark—*too* dark—stairway, the old fears returning, pressing down on him like a weight he couldn't lift. He'd counted on the footman bringing some sort of candlestick to the door, not realizing the man would rely on the night-light alone. His heart pounding and his palm damp around the pistol's butt, he tried to swallow back his growing dread. He could turn around and walk away alone in the bright moonlight, or he could climb up into the darkness to search for Caro. He could sail for Jamaica tomorrow, the way his sister hoped, and never look back.

A coward's comfort, or his friends and a woman who needed his help.

Another chance to fail, or another chance to prove himself.

No choice at all for a Sparhawk.

He swore beneath his breath as he headed up the stairs, trying to keep his footsteps quiet. Footsteps, hell. He'd wake the whole house with the pounding of his heart. One landing, then another, the light from the lantern below fainter with each turning. His fingers gripped the pistol more tightly. Three flights, the footman had said. He was almost there. He could just make out the single closed door ahead, a gray stripe of moonlight along the bottom.

Almost there, and still the demons hadn't claimed him.

"Lady Byfield?"

Lying awake, curled on the narrow bed, Caro held her breath and listened, her ears straining to hear again what she feared she'd only imagined.

"Are you in there? Lady Byfield, ma'am?"

She flew off the bed and ran to the locked door. "Captain Sparhawk! Whatever are you doing here?"

"What the hell do you think I'm doing?"

She heard the key scrape in the lock and then he was there, a pistol in his hand and a wild expression in his eyes. Each time she saw him she was startled again by his size, how much larger and stronger he was than herself, and unconsciously she drew back. He was, she supposed, her savior, but she hadn't counted on being saved quite this way, and she'd certainly no intention of throwing herself into his arms the way the heroines did in operas and plays.

"Has Stanhope hurt you, lass?" He was breathing hard, his face shiny with sweat, and she wondered what he'd had to do to reach her. She had no experience with men as purely physical as this one, but she'd guess that Captain Sparhawk could leave a whole trail of bodies behind him. "Has he used you ill?"

"Oh no, not like that!" She was glad that in the gray moonlight through the window he couldn't see how she blushed. He might not have meant 'like that' at all; it was only her thoughts that ran that way. "That is, I am well enough."

He rubbed his sleeve across his forehead, his gaze sweeping around the tiny room. "Damnation, didn't he even give you a candlestick?"

She shook her head. "George probably believed I'd try to burn his house down."

"Then let's shove off before that damned footman I had to cosh wakes. Come on, lass, hurry!"

"Have you lost your wits?" She stared at him indignantly. "I can't possibly go with you! Can you imagine what George would think?"

"I can't, and I don't care."

"Well, perhaps you just should. Do you think George has forgotten that you were the highwayman who robbed him the other night? He's already filed a complaint against you, and I shouldn't wonder if they're printing broadsides with your description even now. Of course this footman you so elegantly—what was the word?—*coshed* will say it was the same man who came here and kidnapped me, and you'll find yourself at the hangman's tree so fast you'll wonder how it happened."

Now it was his turn to stare at her. "That's the greatest pack of claptrap I've ever heard! *You* were the one who forced me into that nonsense about being a highwayman, and it was Stanhope, not me, who kidnapped *you* in the first place! No court in the world could make any of that stick!"

"Not in the world, no," she admitted, "but here in Hampshire George has enough friends that he probably could bring it to pass. I really wouldn't want you hung on my account."

"And neither, ma'am, would I." He held his hand out to her, more a command than an invitation. "So let's clear off while we can."

Still she hesitated. True, she'd sought the man's help for Frederick's sake, but she wasn't sure she wanted to be indebted to him for her own, as well. "I've made great progress with that Mrs. Warren, you know. I think she'd be willing to let me escape some morning if I paid her enough. George isn't the only one who can bribe servants."

Jeremiah swore. "Will you come, or do I have to carry you?"

"That won't be necessary." She lifted her chin and swept past him, the coverlet dragging behind her like a train.

"Damnation, I forgot you hadn't any clothes!"

She let the coverlet slip a bit, and grinned over her bare shoulder. "George has them somewhere, and I don't think he'd return them now if we asked."

"We'll deal with it later," he said. "Now hurry!"

She skipped along ahead of him, her bare feet silent on the stairs. With her hair loose and tousled around her shoulders, she looked like what she was, a woman roused from her bed, and in spite of everything else, Jeremiah couldn't forget it as he followed close behind.

Close enough that he could smell her fragrance, close enough that he could see the soft curves of her body through the coverlet—God help him, was she naked beneath it?—close enough to remind him all too well of how sweet she'd been to kiss. . . .

Blast, did she mean to be so teasing, or was it just another of her unending games? She'd made it clear enough that she loved her husband, and Jeremiah would respect that, not wishing to poach on another man's well-staked territory. He never had before. But still Caro seemed determined to play the coquette with him, even now, when he should have been concentrating on getting her safely from this house. Any other woman would have been terrified, clinging to him from sheer gratitude, but she was treating the whole business like a lark. Telling him he'd be dancing on a rope's end for kidnapping her! His sister was right: the sooner he disentangled himself from Lady Byfield's affairs, the better.

And then at the bottom of the steps to the street, she turned up and smiled at him, a smile so breathtakingly artless in the moonlight that he nearly forgot all his intentions and kissed her. "You did it, Captain Sparhawk, didn't you? Rescued me from the dragon's lair like some poor fair damsel?"

"Not quite. The dragon could still wake and eat you up." He grabbed her by her elbow and hustled her across the street to the little park. She seemed shorter somehow, and then he remembered her bare feet. "Oh, hell, you can't walk, can you?"

"Of course I can walk. I'm a countess, not a ninny. I've told you before I rather like doing without shoes." She looked around the trees, her curiosity as frank as a child's. "How far is your carriage?"

"There isn't any damned carriage." His frustration growing, he uncocked the pistol and shoved it back into his belt. "Hired carriages are easy to trace. I'd thought we'd walk down near the waterfront and hire a chaise there to take you to your friends."

"Then I suppose we should begin walking, shouldn't we?" She hiked the coverlet higher over her shoulders and began striding resolutely off in the wrong direction. He caught her by the arm and turned her around, and she laughed merrily at her own mistake.

"Hush now, lass," he said uneasily. "Won't do to call attention to ourselves."

She clapped her hand over her mouth, then lowered her voice to a conspiratorial whisper. "Forgive me, Captain. I forgot that strolling along Queen's Court in my shift at midnight isn't enough to get me— even me—noticed."

"We'll find you some clothes soon enough." Damnation, why had she had to tell him *that*? She was as good as naked beside him, and he felt his own body responding with alarming interest. "Now tell me the names of your friends here in town I could take you to."

Her head bowed, she didn't answer at first. "There aren't any."

"All right then, in the countryside," he said, exasperated by her pickiness. "I forget you fashionable gentry don't believe in living in towns."

"No, that's not it." Her voice was so soft that he had to strain to hear it. "I meant that I don't have any friends. Before Frederick married me, none of his friends' wives would receive me, and afterward Frederick decided we wouldn't receive them. So you see we've always kept to ourselves at Blackstone House, and that's always been enough. Until now, anyway."

"Then there must be a someone else. An aunt or uncle, or some business acquaintance of your husband's?"

"Only George on Frederick's side." She smiled bitterly. Once she would have turned to Mr. Perkins, but now she didn't trust George not to have poisoned the lawyer against her, too, just as he had her own servants. She'd always suspected how little they'd respected her, no matter how much she'd tried to be fair and kind, and now she had the unhappy proof.

Her eyes were troubled, her manner uncharacteristically hesitant, as she glanced up toward Jeremiah. "Your sister Desire lives near Portsmouth. Could I possibly stay with her?"

Jeremiah sighed, unsure of how to answer without wounding her more, but that sigh was answer enough for Caro.

"No, of course not," she said quickly with forced cheerfulness, now trying to spare him. "Whatever am I saying, inviting myself into her house like that?"

"It's not what you're thinking, Caro," he said. "My sister's not much for any guests these days, not with her husband just gone off with the fleet and her third child due within the month."

Caro's face softened. "Oh, a baby!" she murmured. "How fortunate your sister must be to have a family like that! I've always wanted—no, I shouldn't go wishing for more, not after all the good things life's given me. Of course your sister couldn't take in a stray like me at such a time. Please wish her well when you see her again."

But this time her attempts to be the grand, gracious Lady Byfield failed miserably. Her words might be brave, but the forlorn slump of her shoulders told a different story that didn't escape Jeremiah.

Gently he slipped his arm over her shoulders. "I'm not about to cast you off alone, Caro. First we'll find you something more suitable to wear and a decent place to stay, then we'll consider the rest one step at a time."

"The poor damsel is most grateful," she said with more wistfulness than she'd intended. "And I do intend to pay you back."

"Oh, hush," he scoffed gruffly. "I'll hear none of that. My coin spends every bit as well as yours, and since I've brought you this far, you'll be my guest."

She smiled, thinking how different Captain Sparhawk's offer of hospitality was from George's. He didn't resemble any other gentleman she'd ever known, but she liked him. She liked him very much. "I didn't mean to pay you with guineas, though your offer is most generous. You've done me a great favor, and so, if you'll let me, I'll do one for you. Your friend Mr. Kerr—"

"Later, Caro," said Jeremiah sharply, drawing her closer beneath his arm. "We've company."

They had come to a neighborhood that Caro didn't recognize, one with narrow streets and ancient, dilapidated buildings whose upper stories jutted crazily over their heads. The paving stones beneath her bare feet had been replaced by hard-packed dirt, and the stench wafting from the street made her long for shoes of any sort. Two sailors were weaving toward them, navy men with long pigtails down their backs and round, flat-rimmed hats with embroidered ribbon bands, and unsteady as they were on their feet, there was no mistaking the eager hunger in their eyes as they stared at Caro.

*A lifetime ago, but she'd never forgotten that look in a man's eyes. Greed and lust, a predator's cold need, marking her, using her, ruining her beyond redemption. All she had, all she was, to be sold to the man with the deepest pockets.*

"Tumbled the chit right out o' her hammock, sheets an' all, did you, mate?" asked the first seaman, fumbling in the bag around his neck for another coin as he leered at Caro. "Saints, but she's finer than any o' the drabs we seen in the fancy houses on Water Street. How much'll you take for a turn wit' her?"

"Not a farthing," said Jeremiah with a quiet authority that startled Caro.

"Ah, mate, we's only askin' to share yer good fortune!"

"The lady's with me," said Jeremiah, his voice rumbling deeper. "And she's not for sale."

The man raised his hands and backed away, intimidated by the threat in Jeremiah's voice. "Meanin' no offense, gov'ner. She's yours, an' there it ends. No offense."

But his companion had had his courage bolstered by more rum, and he lurched toward Caro to snatch the coverlet away. "Come on, lovey, let's have some sport."

The knife was in Jeremiah's hand in an instant, the long blade flashing in the moonlight. The second sailor yowled and stumbled back, clutching his arm where blood was already darkening the slashed sleeve of his jacket.

"I told you," said Jeremiah as he guided Caro past them, "the lady's with me."

"You would have killed him, wouldn't you?" whispered Caro. The ease and violence with which he'd defended her stunned her. Frederick would never have dreamed of doing such a thing, even if he'd been able. "Just like that, you would have killed him."

Jeremiah made a disgusted sound deep in his chest as he wiped the knife's blade clean. "If I'd had to, aye. But that bit of English foolishness wasn't worth the killing."

She tried to smile. "But this bit of English foolishness was worth defending that way?"

He glanced at her sharply, surprised by the quaver in her voice. She looked small and waifish, her mouth pinched and her eyes still wide from what she'd just witnessed. Belatedly he realized that while dockyard arguments and drawn knives were nothing new to him, she'd be accustomed to more tender circumstances. He longed to take her in his arms and reassure her, to hold her until the fear left her eyes, but the memory of that well-loved husband stood uneasily between them, and instead all he did was slip the knife back in the sheath at his waist and clear his throat.

"There's nothing foolish about you, lass," he said gruffly, "except, maybe, the way you've rigged yourself out. But we'll remedy that directly."

He pounded on the door of a shop with men and women's second-hand clothing hanging from a rod in the window until a sleepy old woman answered the door.

"Can't ye read the sign, ye great bluff baboon?" she said. "We're closed."

"Not now, are you?" Jeremiah raised a guinea in his fingers to glitter in the moonlight, and at once the woman opened the door. "The lady needs a gown, and whatever else she pleases."

"Ain't ye the Lord Generous," grumbled the woman, eyeing Caro critically. "What's become o' yer own clothes, girl?"

"She lost 'em throwing dice with a crimp," answered Jeremiah dryly. "Look quick about it, ma'am, we haven't all night."

# Chapter Six

Within an hour Caro was dressed decently, if not fashionably, in a linsey-woolsey gown with a checkered scarf tied around her throat and over her breasts and a chip bonnet with a limp pink rose on her head, and perched on a bench across a table from Jeremiah in a bustling tavern near the water. Before her sat a slice of onion pie topped with yellow cheese and a tankard of cider, and nothing in her life had ever tasted so good. Although she guessed the hour must be closer to dawn than midnight, the tavern was full of sailors, shipwrights, carters, colliers and their women, and Caro leaned closer to Jeremiah to hear him over the din of their laughter and shouted conversations and the fiddle player near the hearth.

"I said, Caro, that Stanhope will think you've vanished from the face of the earth." He thumped his own tankard of ale down on the oak table for emphasis. "As far as he's concerned, you have. Look at you! No one would ever believe you're a countess now!"

She grinned, and took another bite of the pie. To see Jeremiah Sparhawk across from her now, his face relaxed and his green eyes warm as he teased her, made it easy for her to forget the pistols and the long, bloodied knife at his waist. He really wasn't much better than the highwayman they'd pretended he was. Maybe no Americans were. His gift for self-preservation would make him perfect for the task she meant to set before him, and with his chivalrous inclinations on her behalf he'd be bound to agree. Now if only she could convince herself that her own feelings toward him were equally mercenary!

For the first time, she wished she knew more of men and the world. Before she'd met Captain Sparhawk, she'd been able to divide them neatly in two: there were the precious few like Frederick and Jack Herendon, who treated her with kindness and respect, and then there were all the others, who looked at her with a blatant mixture of contempt and lust. But no man she'd ever met treated her like this oversize American, teasing and bantering with her one moment and then willing to fight to the death for her honor the next, and to her confusion, she liked it. She liked *him*, more than she should, certainly more than was proper for her as Frederick's wife.

Jeremiah covered her hand with his and the warmth of his touch raced through her. "You're quiet, lass," he asked with real concern. "Weariness, or is there something else that ails you?"

"Weariness." How could she ever admit that he was what ailed her? "Nothing more, nothing less."

Self-consciously she withdrew her hand, but as she sipped her cider, her eyes met his over the tankard's battered rim. There was gray streaked through his black hair at the temples, and from the deep lines that fanned from his eyes when he smiled, she knew he'd seen much of life, not all of it good. But she also knew better than to ask. She had more than her own share of secrets to keep hidden.

"Then I'd best find us lodgings for what's left of the night." He kept his hand on the table after she'd pulled hers back, unspoken admission of her rebuke, and he studied it now as if surprised to find it there. "Though truth to tell, I like where I am just fine."

In the crowded, noisy, smoky room his smile was for her alone, an invitation she had no right to accept. She must end this now, while she still could.

"I told you I would pay you back your kindness with the information you wished about your friend, and I will. But first I must tell you of Frederick."

"You don't have to," said Jeremiah quickly, perhaps too quickly. But he didn't want to hear again of the paragon that was Caro's husband, or how much she loved him. No, he didn't want to hear that again at all. "You've told me more than enough already, and I wouldn't want you to speak of anything that might cause you pain."

*Selfish, conniving bastard!* He couldn't believe he'd actually said that, especially after the lovely, grateful smile she gave him that he didn't deserve.

"No, Captain, I've scarcely told you anything." With a sigh she pushed the pewter plate to one side and clasped her hands on the table before her. She looked very young in the old-fashioned bonnet, her face framed by the curving brim, and he'd meant it when he'd said no one would believe her a countess now. "Frederick's mother, the dowager countess, still lives, though she is very old and not well. I've never been presented to her. Before I was Frederick's wife there wasn't any question of it, but when she learned we planned to wed, she left England for Naples so she wouldn't have to acknowledge me. It was—is—very painful for Frederick, though of course I understand entirely."

Yet the way Caro looked down at her hands, rubbing one thumb against the other, told Jeremiah that she didn't understand at all, and that the elder Lady Byfield's scorn wounded her every bit as much as it did Frederick. Pompous old bitch, thought Jeremiah angrily. His sister had told him how she herself had been snubbed in certain aristocratic circles simply for being an untitled American who'd had the audacity to marry the younger son of an English lord, and he imagined what those same overbred vultures would make of poor Caro.

"Two years ago this summer Frederick's mother finally agreed to see him again," she continued sadly, "and with great joy and eagerness he booked his passage to Naples. She specifically excluded me from her invitation, but Frederick held great hopes for their reconciliation. I wept for days and days after he sailed. We had never been apart, you know, not since my fourteenth birthday."

Jeremiah nearly choked on his ale. He'd known she'd been young, but fourteen, for all love!

"I had one letter from him," she said, unaware of his reaction, "brought by another ship that had met his, and then nothing more because—why is everyone running away?''

All around them men were shouting and abandoning their drink and their women to crowd out the back door, some not waiting their turn and climbing through the windows instead.

A laconic barmaid reached over to take Caro's empty plate and swipe a rag across the tabletop. ''It's the press-gangs again, lamb,'' she explained. ''They've been at it so hot all this week that the few men left run like frightened coneys at the very hint o' a lieutenant an' his bullyboys.''

Slowly the woman straightened, hands on her hips and her full breasts jutting out above her bodice as she languidly surveyed Jeremiah. ''Best tell your pretty sailor man here to turn tail with the others 'less he wants to spend the next seven years servin' against the French.''

Caro gasped and shoved her bench back from the table. ''Oh, Captain, she's right! There must be three score navy vessels in the harbor now—I saw them from the window at George's house—and they'll all be looking for men! Come, hurry, you don't want them to take you!''

''Hush now, lass, they'll not take me.'' He caught her wrist and gently forced her back down to her seat. ''I'm an American, mind?''

The barmaid sniffed. ''Don't be so sure, Yankee. There was two New Yorkers here the other night had their protections torn up right afore their eyes. The lieutenant called them bloody liars an' read them into the king's service anyways.''

Alarmed all over again, Caro tugged at Jeremiah's hand. "Hurry, then, there's little to be gained taking chances like this!"

"There's no chance to it, Caro," scoffed Jeremiah, touched and pleased by her concern. "I'm an American, and I'm a captain and owner of my own vessels. Six of 'em, last I counted. They can't touch me."

Pointedly the barmaid studied how he was dressed and sniffed again, not believing his claim for a moment. "Please yerself, *Cap'n,*" she said with a dismissive shrug, "for here they be now."

Abruptly the fiddler stopped playing in the middle of his tune, and every one of the people who remained—women, toothless old men and those missing limbs, sailors already serving with a ship and watermen protected by the crown—turned to stare in hostile silence at the six men standing in the doorway. At their head was a young navy lieutenant in a blue coat and two marines in red, and behind them stood three more seamen, clearly chosen for their size and fearsomeness.

The lieutenant scowled as he scanned the room. Empty seats with half-full tankards and tumblers before them were testimony enough that they'd arrived too late to find any useful men.

"An empty net tonight, eh, Lieutenant?" taunted one old man, his cackle echoed by the others. "The fish all slipped through yer net again?"

Angrily the officer searched the room for the man who'd mocked him. His gaze stopped when he spotted Caro and Jeremiah at their table near the far wall, and with a tight-lipped, predatory smile on his face he headed toward their table. One of the bad men, decided Caro uneasily, one of the ones who only wanted to hurt.

"You there, skulking behind the petticoats!" he said sharply. "What ship, eh?"

Her anxiety mounting, Caro watched as Jeremiah slowly rose to his feet, using his height to his advantage as he towered over the others. It seemed to her he was twice the size of the little lieutenant, and despite his rough, common clothing, there was more authority in him alone than in all three of the uniformed Englishmen combined.

The lieutenant knew it, too, and didn't like it. "I asked you your ship, you insolent dog."

"I'm not a dog, but a captain," answered Jeremiah with a mildness that didn't fool Caro. She thought of the pistols in his belt beneath his coat and the knife at his waist and who only knew what else, and prayed he wouldn't be half-witted enough to use any of them now.

"An *American* captain," continued Jeremiah, "a shipmaster and an owner of nearly twenty years' standing. I stood my own quarterdeck before you were breeched, you English puppy, and I'll thank you to remember it before I report you to your betters for ill breeding."

The others in the room hooted and laughed derisively. "Silence, all of you," bellowed the lieutenant as his men raised their cudgels around him, "or I'll have you all taken in for disrespect to an officer of the crown!"

The cudgels, not his threats, brought an uneasy silence, and the officer turned back to Jeremiah. "You claim to be an American captain. What ship? What port? Where, sir, are your papers?"

"I am Captain Jeremiah Sparhawk of Providence, in the State of Rhode Island in New England." There was no mistaking the pride in his voice as he handed the lieutenant a document with a heavy red seal stamped into one corner. "Most recently of my own brig the *Chanticleer.*"

"The *Chanticleer?* I know of no ship by that name in port."

"She was lost," said Jeremiah softly, "last November."

The lieutenant grunted as he took the document. "That's convenient, isn't it?"

Caro held her breath as the officer scanned the paper, his lips moving slightly as he read to himself. If what Jeremiah said was true, then the man must be satisfied and leave them alone.

But instead he tossed the paper scornfully onto the floor at his feet. "A Yankee forgery, and an amateurish one at that. Were I in Boston, I'll wager I could buy another like it for half a crown. But I don't even believe you *are* American. Sparhawk, that would be a Scottish name, wouldn't it?"

Caro could see Jeremiah tense, how he consciously flexed his hands at his sides to keep them from making fists.

"In Cromwell's time, it was English," he said, his voice unnaturally calm, "but it's American now, and has been since we tossed your kind off our shores twenty years ago."

"He lies, sir," spoke up one of the marines, his role obviously rehearsed. "The rascal's from Greenock, sir. I knew his people there."

The lieutenant smiled with triumph. "Then he shall do his duty in the maintop of the *Narcissus*, or be flogged for the lying, sneaking Scotsman he is. Seize him, before he makes off!"

But outnumbered though he was, the fury in Jeremiah's green eyes kept the Englishmen at bay. "If you do not choose to believe me, then perhaps you'll believe the word of Vice Admiral Lord John Herendon—your captain's superior, aye? Herendon will vouch for me, for he is married to my sister."

"A rogue like you married into Lord Jack's family?" The lieutenant sneered, and now it was his men's turn to laugh. "Next you'll be telling me that this little strumpet is lady-in-waiting to the queen!"

The tension that had been building in Jeremiah suddenly exploded. He pulled Caro to his side and tipped the heavy oak table over with a clatter of pewter and breaking crockery, scattering the Englishmen on the far side of the makeshift barricade. With a grunt he lifted the bench and swung it like a club, knocking the first marine senseless to the floor. The second one had his rifle lifted clear from his hands, and while he stared openmouthed after it, Jeremiah struck his chest so hard that the man folded in two and fell gasping for breath on top of the other marine.

But then came the unmistakable *snap* of flintlocks being cocked. Jeremiah froze, staring at the lieuten-

ant's pistol aimed at his heart and two seamen's rifles
pointed at him, as well. Behind Jeremiah, Caro stared
at the guns with her knuckles pressed to her mouth,
sick with dread over what would, inevitably, come
next. The hatred between the American and the Englishmen was palpable, and the only sound in the
room came from the groaning marines on the floor.

"That will earn you an extra twenty lashes, you
filthy liar," said the lieutenant. "Now drop it."

With an oath Jeremiah tossed the bench over the
table and at once the English sailors were on him,
shoving Caro aside as they roughly jerked Jeremiah's
arms behind his back to tie his wrists with tarred cords.
They found and claimed his pistols and long knife,
and a second blade hidden in the sleeve of his coat,
and struck him with a cudgel when he tried again to
protest. Blood trickled from his mouth and stained his
shirtfront, and when they prodded him toward the
door he stumbled, and they laughed again with a cruelty that tore at Caro's heart.

She couldn't let them do this to him. He deserved
better from them, but even more from her. Three
times this night alone Jeremiah Sparhawk had come
unbidden to her defense, and though she didn't have
his experience or his strength, there had to be a way to
save him now.

For Frederick's sake, she told herself as she rushed
after them. She was doing all of this for Frederick, not
for Captain Sparhawk, and never for a moment for
herself.

"Jeremiah, love!" she cried as she flung her arms around his neck. "They cannot take you like this, my darling husband!"

Confusion, then irritation, showed in Jeremiah's eyes. "Hush, Caro, this is none of your affair. They won't make any of this stick. I'll be out and free tomorrow, and I don't want you in the middle of it."

"No, love, no!" she wailed, fervently kissing his cheek before she turned to the lieutenant, wringing her hands with despair that was only partially feigned. "Please, oh, please, kind, dear, just sir! We are newly wed, only this very night! Could you be so cruel as to rob a bride of her heart's one true love on this day of all others?"

Behind her Jeremiah groaned. "For God's sake, Caro—"

"No!" She clutched at the lieutenant's sleeve, pleased that her histrionics had made him look so uncomfortable. The other men in the gang were hesitating, too, looking to him for reassurance, and around them the tavern's patrons were muttering and grumbling among themselves. She had him, she thought triumphantly; he'd have to let Jeremiah go now.

But instead of agreeing, the officer shoved her away. "Where would his majesty look for his navy if every wife wished to bind her husband with her apron strings?" he said curtly as he motioned for the others to continue. "It's your misfortune, not mine. My duty is to fill the company of the *Narcissus,* and I mean to do it no matter how many dubious brides weep at my feet."

"No, wait!" She rushed back to Jeremiah, her arms flung across his chest to protect him. She wasn't as certain as he that they'd set him free tomorrow. She'd heard too many stories from Frederick about the abuses of the navy's press-gangs in Portsmouth, and it was all too easy for her to imagine Jeremiah shipped out on a British frigate, beyond her reach for years and years. They'd already mocked his nationality, his rank and his protection papers, and laughed at her new bride's ploy, but there was one last, desperate gamble she still could try.

"You speak of your duty, and what his majesty expects," she said breathlessly, "but not even the king himself would expect my husband to serve as a mariner after what he has suffered at the hands of the Turks!"

With Jeremiah's hands pinioned behind his back, his coat was open over his shirtfront. Her hands trembling from her own audacity, Caro yanked his shirt clear of the waistband of his breeches and lifted the linen high over his bare chest. Gasps of horror filled the room as the light from the fire danced over the long, livid scar that sliced across Jeremiah's body. It was worse than Caro remembered, far worse, but it was also testimony that no one would ever question.

"God's shame on you if you take that poor lad!" called a woman near the back, and her cry was echoed over and over by the others. Caro let the shirt slip from her fingers, but left her hand resting lightly on Jeremiah's chest. She could only guess what her dramatic gesture had cost him, and she prayed he'd understand.

The lieutenant stiffened with displeasure and defeat. He waved curtly to the others, who jerked the ties from Jeremiah's wrists and tossed his guns and knives onto the table beside him. They pulled the two marines to their unsteady feet and, without another word among them, retreated out the door and into the street, followed by jeers and catcalls and a thrown heel of bread.

The tavern owner rushed over to Jeremiah. "God keep you, Cap'n, and whatever you wish tonight is my gift to you." He winked broadly and cocked his thumb toward Caro. " 'Tis not every night a man outwits the press and gains a clever bride like this one, eh? Whatever you wish, Cap'n, but name your fancy and it's yours."

"Thank you, no." His expression grim, Jeremiah stepped clear of Caro, leaving her to stand with her hand awkwardly in midair. She swallowed hard and tucked her hand beneath her other arm. He hadn't understood what she'd done; he couldn't make it any more apparent, not to her or anyone else in the room.

He shoved his shirttail back into his breeches and hooked the pistols back on his belt. "Though I appreciate your hospitality, sir, I must needs have a word with my *wife* in private."

He grabbed Caro by the elbow and ushered her roughly out the door. She tried to pull free but he held her fast, half-dragging her across the courtyard and past a curious stable boy at the pump. To her surprise the sky was beginning to pale with dawn. Was it really only last evening that he'd come for her at George's?

"You shouldn't be angry with me," she began, breathless at the pace he'd set. Her hat slipped from her head and though she grabbed for it he jerked her relentlessly onward, leaving the crumpled rose face-down in the dust. "If you'd only stop and consider—"

"Nay, ma'am, I shall not. Not here, not now. You've entertained the world enough tonight."

He pulled her into the open door of the tavern's small stable and back among the stalls. Beneath the single lantern the space was warm with the heat of the close-packed horses' bodies, the air thick with their smell.

"At least these beasts won't repeat what they hear or see, which is more than can be said of your last audience." With a last little shake Jeremiah released Caro's arm and she backed away, glaring at him as she rubbed her arm where he'd held it. "What the hell was all that about, anyway? Have you lost what few wits you possess?"

"I did what I judged best under the circumstances." Around them the horses shifted and nickered uneasily, made restive by the unchecked emotions in the human voices. "And don't you dare call me witless!"

"I'll call you whatever I damned well please! Why did you decide I needed a *wife?*"

He took another step toward her, trapping her in the corner with his body. She could feel his anger like a force between them, a white-hot violence barely contained, and any other time she would have been terrified of him. But her own furious resentment blinded her, and she lifted her chin defensively.

"I thought being married would make the lieutenant pity us, and he'd let you go. I saw it once in a play, though of course the hero was a Scottish laird, and—"

"A *play*?" He stared at her, appalled that she would even admit such a thing. "All that 'darling husband' claptrap was from some damned play?"

"It worked, didn't it?" she said stubbornly.

"Listen to me! They would have kept me at the press house for an hour or two at most, then let me go!"

"You trusted them too much! This is England, not America!"

"Oh, aye, my fine Lady Byfield, as if I'd forgotten! I don't need you to tell me that. I don't need you for anything!"

"Don't you go making any of this my fault!" She felt tears smarting behind her eyes and she didn't know why. "You're not being fair. You were the one who forced your way into George's house to rescue me. All I did was try to return the favor, and now you're free."

"I'll never be free, you damned selfish bitch!" Tormented by a pain she couldn't understand, he slammed his fist into the post beside her. "You claim fair play. You turned my private life into a penny curiosity. What of you, eh? What if I took you back in there before the others and told them all your shame, your sins? Would that be fair?"

"You wouldn't dare." She shook her head wildly. "You can't!"

He tore the kerchief from her bodice, and with a frightened gasp she pressed her hands over her neckline, striving to cover herself with her spread fingers. Instead he caught her wrists and pinned them high over her head, mercilessly forcing her back against the rough planks of the stall. She was painfully aware of how she stood trapped between the rough stable wall and the equally unyielding barrier that was Jeremiah Sparhawk.

Yet her body sensed the difference between the two, her softness matching and melting against the lean, muscled planes of his, warm with the heat of his anger. It had been this way the one other time he'd held her in his arms, and she shivered with an anticipation she desperately wanted to suppress. Long, long ago her mother had told her of such feelings between men and women, and their inevitable result. No wonder Captain Sparhawk could taunt her about her sin and shame when her body betrayed her like this!

When he bent his head over hers, she knew he meant to kiss her, just as she knew too late how wrong she'd been to trust him. By trusting him she had made herself vulnerable. She squeezed her eyes shut, the last defense she had.

"I thought you were different," she whispered rapidly, her voice barely containing her tears of fear and disappointment. "When I saw that scar and guessed what you had suffered, I thought you were the only man who could help me, the one who had fought Hamil Al-Almeer and survived. I believed you were strong and brave, but I was wrong, wasn't I? I was wrong! You're a coward, just like you fear. A *coward!*"

She felt him go still, his ragged breathing matching hers, the only sound between them. Though by infinitesimal degrees his grip on her wrists relaxed, she kept her eyes closed, both unsure of what he'd do next and unwilling to break the strange spell between them.

Gently his fingers caressed the narrow bones of her wrists, his thumbs sliding along the inside of her upstretched arms as he traced the pale blue veins that ran to her heart until, at last, he eased her arms down to her sides. Gently, so gently, he cradled her jaw in his hands, his breath warm on her forehead, and she felt the roughness of his beard on her skin as his lips feathered across the loose wisps of hair near her parting.

"A coward, you say," he said so softly she nearly didn't hear him. "Dear God, I never wanted to hurt you."

Then his hands, his touch, were gone. Bereft, she opened her eyes and saw he'd retreated across the stable, his back against the slatted boards of a stall as he crouched down in the straw, his arms folded tightly over his bent knees and his chin resting on his arms. The light from the lantern hanging overhead was harsh, sparing him nothing. His jaw was bruised from press-gang's beating, already swollen and mottled, and in his eyes was the same empty, haunted look Caro remembered from that first night.

The nightmare, she thought miserably. Something that she'd said or done had brought it back.

"I didn't mean that about you being a coward," she said softly. "I'm sorry."

"Don't be. You believed it when you spoke, and God knows it's the truth." He sighed and rubbed his fingers into his eyes. "So let me guess. Hamil has your precious Frederick prisoner, and you wish me to go fetch him home. That's it, isn't it?"

"Only to Naples, to his mother," said Caro eagerly. "She is the one who has heard through the Neapolitan court—they maintain diplomatic relations with the Pasha of Tripoli for their trade, you see—that Frederick still lives, and that Hamil would consider a ransom for him and your friend Mr. Kerr, too. I thought that because you'd fought Hamil before you'd like the chance to meet him again. Not as a friend, of course, but as men do, you know—oh, dear, that's not coming out at all how I intended!"

"You mean would I like another crack at killing him the way he nearly did me? A bit of bloodthirsty revenge amongst the savages, with a nice little errand delivering dear Frederick's ransom on the side? Is that what 'men do'?"

Caro winced. "That makes it sound vastly foolish, doesn't it?"

"Men *are* vastly foolish, sweetheart, though I've never had reason to judge women much better." He plucked a piece of straw from the floor and twirled it absently between his fingers. "So to make all this work, you must rely on the promise of a heathen pirate, the good will of an old woman who despises you, and the vengeful wrath of a coward you scarcely know?"

"I told you I don't truly believe you're a coward!"

"Ah, but Caro, I do." He tossed the straw away and slowly stood. "You've chosen the wrong man to be your hero."

She looked down, unable to meet his eyes. "It wasn't a choice. There were no others. You were all I had."

"Damnation." He didn't want to do it, and he'd be ten times a fool to agree. He didn't trust the old countess in Naples or George Stanhope here in England, the Pasha of Tripoli or Hamil Al-Ameer; any of them could play Caro false in a minute. And God in Heaven, what he himself could do to her hopes without even trying, a pitiful battered Yankee who was afraid of the dark!

Yet there was Davy, and maybe others. To turn his back on them would be to admit far worse of himself than cowardice alone.

And then there was Caro herself, waiting for his decision there by the post like some poor felon in the dock. An exhausted, bedraggled countess in second-hand clothes who'd tried to do her best to save him just as he'd saved her. A beguiling, unpredictable creature who mixed world-weary airs with unstudied innocence. A luscious, desirable woman who melted in his arms and tempted him with lips redder, plumper, sweeter than summer berries on the vine.

A woman who expected him to risk his life for the husband she loved.

Damnation, indeed.

## Chapter Seven

"You've gone too far this time, Jeremiah," declared Desire furiously, "too far by half!"

"Oh, hush, Des, 'tis not so bad," scoffed Jeremiah, standing beneath the rack of polished pans and kettles in the grand kitchen of his sister's house. He sipped coffee from the cup the scullery maid had brought him with a curtsy and a giggle, and enjoyed the fuss as the staff pretended to go about their preparations for tea, their collective ears straining to hear what their mistress and her brother said. "Considering some of the scrapes you've gotten yourself into over the years, I'd say that drinking coffee stands pretty far down the list of offenses."

"That's not what I mean, as you know perfectly well!" She glared at him as she rapped her knuckles impatiently on the tabletop. "You've no business coming skulking back here, not now, not after what you've done!"

He smiled innocently. "Here? In the kitchen?"

"I'm in no mood for you now, Jeremiah Sparhawk! I've seven captain's wives in my drawing room for tea, all in a fluster over this *highwayman* loose on the Portsmouth roads. One of them even brought me the handbill that's been posted since the villain was last seen so close to my home.'' She glared at him, her green eyes a match for his own, and lowered her voice against the eavesdropping. "A sight closer to my home than any of them realize. For all love, Jere, they have you down to the buckles on your shoes!''

Jeremiah laughed, remembering how George Stanhope had trembled and squeaked while he was being robbed. Amazing he'd recalled enough to tell the magistrate.

"This is serious, you great oaf!'' whispered Desire urgently. "They've put a price on your head!''

Jeremiah's laughter vanished. "They've put a bounty on me because I took a worn-out purse with a handful of guineas and tossed it in the poor box?''

"You can forget being Robin Hood, at least as far as George Stanhope's concerned, and he has friends enough to make it stick. No English gentleman wants to be at the mercy of some roving brigand, and they'll hang you for certain if they catch you.''

He set the cup down on the table, his pleasure in its contents abruptly gone. "But they don't know this thief's name, do they? They won't come looking for me here without it.''

"I can't protect you in this, Jere,'' she said wearily as she rubbed her back with both hands. "With a new war coming, the whole countryside's suspicious of foreigners, even Americans like us. The only thing worse would be if we were French.''

"Amen to that," he said gruffly. This whole conversation made him uncomfortable. All their lives, he'd been the older brother watching over her. Now Desire seemed somehow to be chiding him for irresponsible behavior, and with every right, too.

"French or American, you're the man that's described on that handbill. Anyone who knows you would recognize you at once. You're not exactly the kind of man who can lose himself in a crowd."

She glanced around the kitchen and sighed. "For all I know there's someone on my own staff who'll put those hundred pounds before their loyalty and turn you in. They might be doing it even now."

"I'm sorry, Des, as sorry as can be." He'd been wrong to underestimate Stanhope; the man was more clever—or just plain mean—than Jeremiah had given him credit for. The last thing he wanted was to put his sister and her children at risk, and by simply being here in the house he was doing just that. "Who'd have thought it would come to this?"

"I tried to warn you, Jere, but you've always been too stubborn to listen to anyone, even when your own neck's at risk." Her initial anger gone, she brushed back a lock of hair that had fallen across his forehead. "And now there's this other rumor that Captain Richardson's wife is busy whispering upstairs, that the wicked highwayman has stolen some poor lady from her bed! How their hearts are racing over that one!"

Jeremiah drew in his breath, wishing he'd something else to offer than the truth. "It's not a rumor, sister mine. Not exactly."

Her mouth dropped open in disbelief. "Oh, Jere, you didn't! Not after you'd promised me you'd stay clear of that woman's business!"

"Oh, my lady, please don't blame him!" cried Caro, rushing forward, unable any longer to keep on the far side of the cupboard where Jeremiah had told her to wait. "It's all my fault, every bit of it!"

"Lady Byfield," said Desire faintly. "I must admit I didn't expect to see you here."

Jeremiah groaned, wishing Caro had been able to contain herself until he'd had time to prepare his sister. Desire didn't need shocks like this, not this near to her time, and from the way she was staring at Caro, her cheeks flushed and her eyes a little too wide, she'd definitely been surprised. He slipped his arm around Desire's waist, startled by how readily she leaned into him for support. "Come along, Des, let's find someplace where you can put your feet up."

"I'm not an invalid, Jere," she said with half-hearted rebellion. "But a bit of privacy would not be amiss. I don't think Mrs. Curlew would object to us using her parlor, there, to the right. Lady Byfield, you come. too. You're already so thick in the middle of my brother's affairs that I'd scarcely want to leave you out now."

Caro bowed her head contritely, her humility increased by the woebegone bonnet. Jeremiah tried to catch her eye over Desire's head and couldn't, not with her head ducked so low. He remembered how she'd been scorned by other "ladies," and he feared she was assuming the same with his sister. He'd put an end to that as soon as he could; Caro was every bit as good as her so-called betters, and he was too much a New England democrat to believe otherwise.

Yet in the housekeeper's small, cluttered parlor, Caro refused to take the chair that Jeremiah offered, preferring instead to stand by the wall near the canary's cage as she watched Desire try to make herself comfortable in an old-fashioned wing chair. Though obviously in the last month of pregnancy, far beyond the time most ladies retreated from the world, she was still dressed with quiet elegance in a dark red kerseymere pelisse over a white muslin gown, and the resemblance between her and Jeremiah was striking. Nor was there any mistaking the bond between brother and sister as Jeremiah tucked another pillow into the chair behind his sister's back, a bond that Caro noted with both wistfulness and growing dread.

She had met Lady John Herendon once before, at a ball in honor of some naval victory or another, and had been struck not only by her beauty, but by the knowledge and confidence with which the American woman could speak as easily of politics and ships with the gentlemen as the other women spoke among themselves of their modistes. There was no other woman in the county—perhaps even in all the country—quite like her.

But Lady John had warned her brother against Caro, had referred to her as "that woman" in a manner that was all too familiar to Caro. Not that Caro could fault her. How could she, if Lady John loved her brother as much as it seemed?

"You mustn't blame Captain Sparhawk, Lady John," she said, speaking up before her courage faltered. "All of this, from the very first, has been my doing."

"Here now, Caro, no more of this Lady This-and-That," said Jeremiah sternly. "No more 'Captain,' either. If you felt free enough to call me your darling Jeremiah last night before a score of witnesses, why then, you can do it again when it's just us—though you'd best leave off with the 'darling' for your poor true husband's sake. And my sister's Desire, nothing more or less."

Twisting her bonnet strings uncertainly, Caro looked to the other woman for reassurance.

" 'Tis well enough with me," said Desire with a little shrug. "Though you're the countess, wife to a peer, and by rights we should be deferring to you instead."

Caro shook her head vigorously. "I'll do whatever you wish, Lad—Desire." She blushed self-consciously at the intimacy of the given name. Titles still intimidated her, it had taken her two years of marriage before she'd been bold enough to call her husband Frederick instead of Lord Byfield. "But as for all the rest—"

"I'll tell her, Caro." And tell her Jeremiah did, in a far different version than Caro would have dared tell, herself. There was no mention of the kiss in his chamber in this very house, not a word of the undignified scrambling through the Yellow Room at Blackstone, and nothing at all of the two sailors who'd attacked them in the street or the awful scene in the stable. Instead he spoke of how badly George had treated her and how important it was that she find Frederick and his crew mates. Caro listened, bewildered. Was he only protecting himself, or did he care enough to shield her too?

"I had no choice but to bring her back here with me, Des," he argued. "If she goes back home, Stanhope will only cart her off again."

"Just the way you did," said Desire, her voice brittle as she glanced at Caro. "I'm sure you realize that that ship bound for Jamaica cleared this morning with the tide."

"Desire," said Jeremiah, the warning in his voice clear, "don't."

But though he hoped to spare Caro's feelings, she wasn't listening any longer. Instead she was staring intently at Desire's belly, a look of wonder on her face.

"Your baby just moved, didn't it?" she asked softly. "I saw it stir through the muslin of your gown."

Desire nodded, her brows raised with surprise at such a question from a woman she barely knew. "He's always running races this time of day. Preparing himself for tea, I suppose."

"You know it's a boy?" Desire leaned a little closer, eager for information on a subject on which she was abysmally ignorant. Frederick was an educated man who had taught her many things, but there were definite gaps in his learning.

Desire smiled for the first time since she'd met Caro. "Only as much as any mother does. But this child moves so much like my son did that I cannot help but believe it's a boy, too." She reached out for Caro's hand and placed it on her belly. "There! That was a good kick, wasn't it?"

Caro gasped. "I did not know a baby could be so—so lively!"

Desire laughed. "'Tis nothing compared to what they do once they're born. My son Johnny was born on board a frigate, and you've never seen a child wriggle and squeal with delight as he did every time they beat to quarters. But then, you know how boys love drums, even tiny baby boys."

"Well, no, I don't really." With obvious reluctance Caro lifted her hand, though she kept her fingers spread as if still feeling the baby beneath them. "I have no brothers."

"No children of your own?"

"None." Deliberately Caro closed her hand, drawing her fingers up tight. "My husband and I have never been blessed."

"You may still be," said Desire. "You're still a young woman, and with men age never seems to make a difference. Lord Byfield may yet see the day when he'll embrace an heir other than George Stanhope."

But Caro shook her head, sorrow clouding her face. "I've spent more than half my life with Lord Byfield, and if there's no heir by now—no, it won't happen."

"I'm sorry, Caro." Tears of sympathy welled up in Desire's eyes. "I didn't mean to make you sad."

But Caro shook her head again, this time with a fierce determination that the other woman never expected. "You mustn't pity me, or judge my life empty. I may not have children, but I do have Frederick's love, and he has mine. For me that is more than enough."

"You love your husband that much?"

Caro's chin inched higher. "That much, and more."

"So it is with me and my Jack," said Desire softly, her hands cradling her unborn child. "I'll pray for your husband's deliverance, and rejoice in your happiness when he returns to you."

Yet Desire's expression was anything but happy as she turned back to her brother, standing these past minutes as a silent witness to the women's conversation, his face shuttered and his thoughts his own. Gently she touched his sleeve. "That's your answer, too, isn't it, Jere?"

He cocked his head and frowned. "Meaning?"

Desire took a deep breath. "Meaning that you intend to sail for Naples on this lady's behalf, and nothing George Stanhope or Hamil Al-Ameer or I can say or do will make you change your mind. Not that I'll be foolish enough—or selfish enough—to try again."

In that moment he realized she knew everything: what had happened on the *Chanticleer,* his failure to save his ship and crew, the fears that haunted him still. She knew, and she understood why he couldn't turn his back on the one chance he would have to find peace with himself. What was it she'd said about Jack? That she loved him enough to let him leave? Not that he'd ever doubted the bond between them, but now he realized how strong a woman his little sister had become.

"You're wrong, sister mine," he teased with more tenderness than he knew. "I've no intention in the least of acting on this lady's behalf."

Caro's heart plummeted. Though he'd said nothing to her of his plans on the long ride from Portsmouth, she had assumed that he'd agree, or else he would have left her behind. Instead he meant to abandon her here, now, crushing her last fragile hopes forever. For what must be the final time she looked at him, the tall, handsome man she'd believed would be her champion.

But to her confusion, he met her gaze and grinned. "I've never done anything in anyone else's name, Desire," he said, "and I'm not about to begin now. If the lady wishes me to sail to Naples, why then, she'd damned well better be coming with me."

Thomas Perkins sat back in his leather-covered chair and pursed his lips with displeasure. He had put off seeing this particular gentleman as long as he could, hoping that perhaps he would leave the offices on his own, but here it was nearly dusk and still the man had insisted. Clearing his throat, Perkins drew off his spectacles and lay them in the exact center of the packet of papers on the desk before he answered the gentleman who sat opposite him.

"I don't believe I can accommodate you, sir," said the lawyer in the careful, clipped speech that had served him so well in the courts. "I don't understand how such gutter-born gossip can have any relevance at all to the well-being of my client."

"What's gutter-born is your client, Perkins," said George Stanhope sharply. "Her current behavior is absolutely no better than anyone can expect."

"Her ladyship's behavior both past and present has never been anything less than exemplary, Mr. Stanhope. I pay no heed to rumor, sir, and instead make my judgments on my own knowledge. And I *know*, sir, that Lady Byfield is incapable of the activities of which you charge her, just as I know she has gone visiting friends, as her butler told me last Thursday, when these rumors first surfaced."

George struck his fist on the edge of the desk. "Then she's tricked you, too, just as she tricked my uncle! She winks once and shows her dimples, and you old men turn into blathering fools. You know she's taken young lovers for years. She's even made overtures to me—told me what she'd do with me if we was ever alone, bold as brass. Like mother, like daughter, they say. She's probably given my uncle more horns than a ten-point buck."

"You go too far, sir." Perkins realigned his spectacles a fraction more to the left. "I have told you before, Mr. Stanhope, that I've no wish to discuss her ladyship with you. Now if you will excuse me—"

"No I will not, Perkins! Dash it all, how can you defend the creature? She has run off with a common thief, the very man who robbed us both on the road! They'll hang him when they catch him, and God help her if she's with him when he's taken."

"But I thought you'd said earlier that her ladyship had been kidnapped by this ruffian, that you were waiting on tenterhooks for his ransom note?" Though Perkins's expression didn't change, he did allow a breath of irony to creep into his voice. "You've been quite thorough in that, haven't you, Mr. Stanhope?

The warrant, the handbills, the whispered story that's nearly as common as the one about the French war.''

Flustered, George eased a finger around the edge of his fashionably high neckcloth. ''You must have misunderstood, Perkins,'' he said weakly. ''Misheard it all, eh?''

But Perkins continued as if George hadn't spoken. ''So thorough, in fact, sir, that I almost suspect the entire escapade to be of your own invention.''

George dropped back into his chair, rubbing the thumbnail he'd earlier bitten to the quick against the inside of his palm. It took all his self-control to keep the telltale fingernails—or what was left of them—hidden from the lawyer. Why the devil hadn't he thought to wear gloves? If Perkins were to guess how brashly he was bluffing, the lawyer would be on his neck like a weasel.

He couldn't let that happen. He needed to have his uncle declared dead, and to do that he needed Perkins's help, not his antagonism. If he didn't become the Earl of Byfield soon, his whole extravagant empire of credit and promises would collapse beneath him. He'd never dreamed he'd slip so far into debt, but then two years ago, when he'd first heard his uncle's ship was missing, he'd never dreamed he'd have to wait so long for what was his by every right, either.

God, how he hated Caro Moncrief! It was her stubbornness alone that was stifling him, making him wait the full seven years until the law would declare his uncle dead, instead of going through the motions herself. He didn't have five more years. He didn't even have five more months.

But he did have one last card to play against her, one final trump that she'd never expect. That is, if she were even still alive. When his footman, his head bandaged, had haltingly confessed that an armed man had kidnapped the lady in the attic room, it had been all George could do not to shout with joy. If a ransom note had appeared, he was determined to ignore it, but when the hours stretched into days with no word, he'd allowed himself to imagine, quite delightfully, how that huge, violent brute had seized Lady Byfield for his own amusement. To have her gone so effortlessly was a true wonder, a sign that surely George's luck was changing for the better.

Perkins cleared his throat again. "Good day, Mr. Stanhope. The porter will show you out if you've forgotten the way."

"Not yet, Perkins." George reached into his coat for the letter, his trump card. "You're determined to be deuced ill-mannered to me, but you won't be so quick to be rude once you've seen this."

He snapped the heavy writing paper open and sailed it across the desk. A nice flourish, he told himself. "It's from my grandmother, the dowager countess. Her hand's a bit rickety, but if you take your time you can make it out well enough."

The lawyer lifted the letter gingerly, almost as if he expected it to bite him, and turned it over to finger the dark green seal stamped on the back.

"Oh, it's genuine enough, Perkins," said George, enjoying the other man's discomfiture. The letter had come as a surprise to him, as well, the first he'd ever received from his grandmother. He could barely remember her face and doubted she could do any better by him, but there was no point in sharing that with the lawyer. "She wrote to me because she doesn't trust you, and you can guess why she didn't write to Caro. Fourteen years she's chosen to live on the continent instead of being forced to meet the little harlot who bewitched her Frederick. Consider that well, Perkins. Fourteen years that poor old lady has been in bleak exile."

Perkins hooked his spectacles over his ears and quickly scanned the letter. He remembered the dowager countess all too well, and he doubted that even fourteen years would soften her to the point she'd be considered a poor old lady. As for the bleak exile— he'd arranged her allowance at Lord Byfield's request, and there were entire towns Perkins could name that got by quite nicely on less.

"I can understand why she would wish to return home," said the lawyer as he read, "but that's her own decision, not one for the courts. I certainly can't see why she would think her vendetta against her daughter-in-law would give her legal precedent for rushing the proceedings regarding her son. That right remains with the present Lady Byfield."

"But certainly a lady of her stature in the country—"

"Would be treated much the same as anyone else," concluded Perkins. The old countess' letter was sprinkled with her usual obscure threats and insults, and it pleased him to know they'd hold little weight with anyone now if she returned to England. "Oh, I suppose she could try to buy a judge or two, but the dowager countess would find that the present earl and countess are generally well liked throughout the county, and public sentiment wouldn't be in her favor."

"But to deprive a lady her age of the satisfaction of seeing her family's noble lineage continued, to watch an ancient title wither and languish while she waits in vain for the offspring of the rightful heir to bring her joy in her final days—"

"I can read your grandmother's words better than you can recite them, Mr. Stanhope," said the lawyer, privately doubting whether George Stanhope knew the meanings of half the words he was trying to quote as his own. "I suppose she is looking to you for these great-grandchildren? I didn't realize you yourself had such prospects in the matrimonial line."

George smiled smugly and plucked at his cuffs. "The youngest daughter of the Marquis of Coverdell has indicated she would smile upon my suit, once, of course, my estate and title are confirmed."

"Of course," said Perkins dryly. He refolded the letter and held it out to George. "In five years, I've no doubt they will be. In the meantime, please express my regards to your grandmother when you write to her next. Good day, Mr. Stanhope."

"Wait. Damn you, Perkins, *wait!*" Panicking, George refused to take the letter as he tried to think of another way. He'd been so sure that his grandmother's letter would be enough that he hadn't considered what would happen if it wasn't. "What happens if Caro don't come back? What happens if she decides she prefers this highwayman fellow, and doesn't return home ever again?''

"You're asking me what would happen if her ladyship disappears entirely and completely, and thereby abandons her responsibilities?''

George nodded eagerly. "Then I'd be the one to start having them both declared dead, wouldn't I? Then it would be my decision, and I wouldn't have to wait on the whim of some selfish little tart playing at being a lady!''

The lawyer's eyes were icy behind his spectacles as he leaned across the desk and stuffed the letter into George's hand. "What would happen, Mr. Stanhope, is that I would immediately suspect that her ladyship had met with foul play. And you, sir, would be my first choice as the villain.''

The sun was nearly at its peak when the hired carriage came to a halt near the last of the merchant wharfs. With two vessels scheduled to sail with the next tide, the wharf was crowded with activity: final bits of cargo and supplies being hauled or trundled aboard, sailors making teary farewells to wives and sweethearts, merchants with ventures giving their last orders and advice to the captains and their mates.

The tavern at the foot of the wharf was busy, too, with the majority of both crews embracing the final opportunity to become blissfully inebriated before the long voyages ahead. Some had brought their tankards to sit on the benches outside, singing and swearing happily in the late morning sun as they made life briefly miserable for any women who walked too close. With war in the air, life beyond this day was uncertain. If their ships were stopped by a short-manned frigate in the channel, any one of these merchant seamen could find themselves navymen by nightfall—reason enough for drinking and calling to the lasses one last time.

The sailors watched the carriage's arrival with curiosity, craning to see better when the driver swung the door open for the passengers. The lady's ankle when she lifted her skirt to step down was neat and trim, more than worthy of admiring comment, but the lady herself was swathed in deep new mourning, her veil so dark that even on this sunny morning no hint of her features showed. At once the sailors looked away, the more pious ones crossing themselves. On sailing day, no man needed so sharp a reminder of death and grief.

The lady leaned heavily on the driver's hand, her head bowed beneath her hat and veils, and when the carriage's other passenger, a tall, grim-faced gentleman also dressed in black, climbed out and took her arm, she swayed against him, eager for support. As they slowly made their way down the wharf, sailors, merchants and longshoremen alike stepped from their path, raising their hats in respect.

"I don't like this, Jeremiah," whispered Caro beneath her veils. "To hide in mourning when I pray to find Frederick alive must be wrong."

"Steady now, lass, don't turn skittish on me," murmured Jeremiah as he patted her hand solicitously. "That's nothing but superstition, pure and simple."

"But he never wants me to wear black! White, that's what he wants, always white. He says that even if I outlive him, I'm not to wear mourning, and I don't—"

"Caro, stop it now, unless you want to make damned sure you'll never see Frederick again!"

She didn't need reminding. Desire had shown her the handbill about the highwayman, and Caro had had plenty of time to repent that one silly trick to fool George. But worse than Jeremiah's warning was the way he said it, as curt an order as he'd give the lowliest sailor in his crew. It hurt, that order. Though she'd spent no time alone with him this past week as they'd hidden at Desire's house, still Caro thought they'd gone beyond that. She'd thought they were friends, and a friend would have understood her unhappiness at wearing black. Wondering what she could do to set things right, she was miserably silent as they walked the length of the wharf to the sloop *Raleigh* tied to the very end.

"This little boat will take us clear to Naples?" she whispered anxiously.

"She's not large, I'll grant you that, but she looks sound enough," answered Jeremiah gruffly. He wished now he hadn't snapped at her, but damnation, if she'd kept up that business about Frederick, her voice getting louder and more panicky with every word, someone would have been bound to hear her. "The proof will lie in how the sloop takes the wind."

"I suppose you're right." She stopped and looked up to the very top of the mainmast, holding her hat in place with one black-gloved hand. "It's just that Naples is so very far away, and I'd imagined something more substantial. The ship that took Frederick was twice this size.''

He nearly remarked where that larger ship had gotten Frederick, but wisely didn't. Instead, he merely patted her hand once again. He'd no right to make light of her misgivings when his own doubts could have sunk every ship in the harbor. He wondered if she was thinking the same thing, that a passenger's cabin on board a sloop of this size was going to be scarcely big enough for them to turn around, and powerfully close quarters for two people who were only pretending to be married.

''Mr. Sparhawk?'' The ruddy-faced man at the gangway squinted earnestly into the sun and wiped his palm on the front of his waistcoat before he held his hand out to Jeremiah. ''I'm William Bertle, master of the *Raleigh*, and I welcome you and your lady here on board, indeed I do.''

Jeremiah took his hand, reassured by the other man's calluses. He didn't trust a captain who didn't work beside his men, the way he always did. No, the way he *had*, when he still had a crew and ship.

Bertle bobbed from the waist toward Caro, a perfunctory bow at best. ''My sympathies, ma'am. I'm sure your brother was a noble, fine gentleman, surely too good to die at the hands of those French rascals.''

Caro only nodded in return. Jeremiah and Desire had concocted an entire family tragedy for her, but she wanted none of it. After what had happened with the highwayman ruse, she was determined to stick as closely to the truth now as she could, or at least not volunteer more than she had to that was false.

But it was enough of a response for Bertle, who had already turned back to Jeremiah. "I don't generally take passengers, you know, especially females," he said briskly. "They're in the main too much trouble, making the men all restless, but I figured since you two was man and wife, Mr. Sparhawk, you'd keep her out of mischief. I wouldn't have granted you passage otherwise." He spat over the side and glanced shrewdly at Jeremiah. "You *will* keep her out of mischief?"

"Captain Bertle, my poor wife is so devastated by her loss that she scarcely has the heart to breathe, let along cause mischief among your men. And if she did, rest assured that she would answer to me."

"Very good, sir, very good." Bertle nodded with satisfaction as he ushered them aboard. "A tight rein in a light hand, a crop when they need it. Good policy for horses and wives alike, eh?"

"What an odious man," said Caro as they stood by the quarterdeck rail, watching as the last lines were tossed away. "Nor are you much better."

"At least he won't bother you, because he knows he'll have to answer to me, and he's bound to spread the warning to his men." He hadn't liked Bertle's manner any more than she had, and it put an unintentional edge to his voice. "Being a jealous husband has certain advantages for us both."

She didn't try to hide her resentment and bristled in response. "And here I thought you didn't want a wife at all."

"I didn't, sweetheart." He wished she hadn't reminded him of the brawl with the press-gang; not his finest hour on any count. "I wanted the passage, and you came with it."

"And I can assure you that I'm quite satisfied with the husband I already have." As soon as she'd spoken she knew it was a hopeless rejoinder, prim and obvious, but she never had been very good at this kind of banter. "Bother this veil! I can't see a wretched thing."

She wrestled to control the yards of veiling that were catching the same wind that was beginning to fill the *Raleigh's* sails. Gradually the sloop began to swing around, away from the wharf and land and toward the channel and the open sea. With an excited gasp, Caro grabbed Jeremiah's arm as the deck slanted beneath her feet like a live creature.

"Oh, Jeremiah, we're sailing!" she cried with delight, her displeasure with him forgotten, and with one hand she swept her veil up. Her smile was as jubilant as a child's with a new toy, and he was struck again by how lovely she was, her face glowing against the black.

"We've done it, Jeremiah!" she crowed. "We've left Portsmouth and we've left George, and now all we have to do is bring Frederick back home!"

Done? Lord, they'd barely begun. But faced with such happiness, Jeremiah found he couldn't bring himself to tell her the truth. Why should he? She'd learn it for herself soon enough.

# Chapter Eight

The setting sun washed red across the sloop's sails as Caro sat perched on the coil of rope on the quarterdeck, her feet propped up on the empty hamper that had held their supper. Tomorrow she and Jeremiah would be at the mercy of the *Raleigh*'s cook, but tonight they had dined on the best that Desire's kitchen could offer, and that, decided Caro contentedly, had been very good indeed.

It had taken all afternoon for the little sloop to weave in and out among the navy ships that crowded the harbor, slipping gracefully between seventy-four-gun men-o'-war that towered high above them, before at last she had reached the open water of the channel. There had been so much that was new to watch that Caro had loved every minute of it.

But to her great surprise, Jeremiah hadn't. Oh, he'd stayed by her side and patiently answered all of her questions, but the distance she'd earlier sensed between them seemed to be growing into a gap she felt helpless to broach. He'd eaten little of dinner, though he'd drunk freely enough of the wine, and he'd resisted all of her attempts to coax him into speaking of himself.

She glanced at him now as he stood at the rail, his dark hair tossing in the wind off the water. She'd always considered him a handsome man in a wild, rough way that made him larger in spirit, as well as size, but since they'd reached the open water he'd seemed to become even less like the English gentlemen she knew and more of a man. He was so obviously in his world here, crossing the deck with the same physical ease as she would her drawing room, and he moved instinctively with the feel of the sloop on the waves beneath them.

Yet clearly Jeremiah wasn't happy. She could see the sorrow in his face when he stared out across the water, withdrawing deep into some secret inner suffering brought on by the familiar sights and smells of the sea. Maybe it was being a passenger instead of a captain. He'd told her once he'd held his first command when he'd been only eighteen, on a ship that his family owned. How hard it must be for him now to stand by and watch with nothing more useful to do than shepherding her! Perhaps, then, what he needed wasn't company, but the chance to be alone with his own thoughts. She had to remember that a man like Jeremiah Sparhawk wouldn't feel the pain of loneliness the way she did.

She stood, steadying herself on the railing. "I'm going downstairs," she said, slinging the basket over her other arm. "I'll leave the lantern lit for you."

He swung around to face her, his expression blacker than it had been all day. "It's 'below,' not 'downstairs'. And why the hell do you think I'll need the lantern lit?''

"To see where you're going, of course." No matter how sad he was, he didn't need to use that tone with her. "Though if you'd prefer to trip over your own belongings in the dark, why then, I'll be sure to chink every glimmer of light before I go to bed."

"It's not a bed, it's a bunk," he growled. "This isn't your precious Blackstone House, you know."

"And you, sir, aren't my husband to lecture me." In the wind the veil spun up before her face and irritably she yanked it aside. "Good night."

"Wait!" He grabbed her arm as she tried to pass him, pulling her close so he could speak for her ears only. "I *am* your husband, at least in the eyes of Captain Bertle and his men, if not God. Don't make a mistake like that again."

She glared at him. "What's the point in pretending now that we've left Portsmouth? Why don't we just go back to being who we are, with our real names?"

"Because if Bertle thinks we lied to him and we're doing sinful things together under his deck, he'll put us both off the first chance he gets, and I don't have a great wish to be marooned in some blasted little Portegee fishing village." He pulled her closer, so close his hair blew across her face. "Now I'm going to bend down and kiss your cheek for whoever's watching, and I'll thank you not to slap me."

She closed her eyes as his lips brushed across her cheek, a kiss so cold it might have come from Captain Bertle. Maybe Jeremiah was strong enough to say one thing to her and then pretend otherwise before others, but she wasn't, not about this. She felt close to tears, all pleasure in the day gone.

"Why are you doing this to me?" she asked, almost pleading. "I've done nothing to you, have I? I keep reminding myself that you've been kind to me before—look at how you agreed to come to Naples!—and that you will most likely be kind to me again, but now, now you're making it very hard for me to even like you."

"Then don't," he said sharply. "It will be easier on us both that way."

She shook her head, not understanding. "How can that help anything?"

"Dear God, Caro, think!" He raked his fingers through his hair, clearly searching for the right words. "You're trying to remember how I've been kind to you, and I'm trying not to forget that you're another man's wife!"

"But it's not like that between you and me! I love Frederick too much to—"

She broke off, appalled by the longing she saw in his eyes, a longing that she realized echoed the one she felt within herself.

"Too much to do what, Caro?" asked Jeremiah harshly. "Too much to do what with me?"

Her face hot, she shook her head again, this time understanding too much. "What you want I will not give you. Even if I—I wished to, I could not, for it is not mine to give."

He released her arm so swiftly that she had to grab on to the rail to steady herself. "By God, I've never forced any woman—especially a married woman—against her will, and I won't—"

"You don't understand!" she cried with anguish. "I mean my soul, my loyalty, who I am. That is what Frederick has given me with his love, and that is what I owe him in return."

"You owe your husband your soul?" he demanded, incredulous. "You may have more in common with Captain Bertle than I realized."

She couldn't argue with him. She knew that no matter what she said he wouldn't understand. "Why did you insist I come with you?"

"Why?" The single word hung between them, so much behind it that he couldn't find the words to tell her.

*Why?* Because he would need her connections to arrange Davy's release? Because she would suffer at George Stanhope's hands without him to defend her, because she was too lonely, because the yearning she didn't understand herself seemed to mirror his own? Because she needed him, because she gave him hope and faith in the future and himself?

All of these. None of these. Did he dare tell her the truth?

She stood very still, waiting.

"Because," he said hoarsely, "because, God help me, I want to be there with you if Frederick is—"

"No, Jeremiah, don't say it!" she cried. "I beg you, please, I—I hope you never have your blasted wish!" She turned swiftly and left him before he saw her tears, her black skirts swirling in the wind, black against the bloodred sky of the finished day.

* * *

Jeremiah stared out over the taffrail, watching the creamy wake the *Raleigh* left behind as she cut through the dark water. Over and over again this afternoon he'd caught himself gazing up at the sloop's sails, gauging the wind and how he should trim the canvas or steer a bit closer, as if he were captain still. Better to look back to where they'd been, to something he couldn't hope to change. A course once sailed could never be retraced, any more than the past itself could be relived or changed. So why, then, was he torturing himself with what he'd said to poor Caro?

Behind him he heard the bell that marked the end of one watch and the beginning of another. How long had he been standing here, anyway? Long enough for the sun to vanish and the moon to arc across the clear night sky, and long enough for his arms to become stiff as he leaned against the rail and for the cool air from the water to make the long scar beneath his ribs ache.

He had intended to remain on deck only long enough to give Caro time to undress and hide herself decently away in her bunk. And be asleep. If she were asleep, then he wouldn't have to talk to her, or apologize, or do whatever other damned thing he should to set things right. How they'd manage the question of privacy had been something they should have discussed earlier, but he had kept putting it off, until now, after what they'd said this evening, any such discussions would be impossible.

Three weeks he'd be alone with her each night, three weeks they'd torture each other, whether they meant to or not.

He sighed, a sigh that stretched into a yawn. High time he went below and tried to sleep, or he'd be in an even worse humor in the morning.

"You're still about then, Mr. Sparhawk?" asked Bertle as he came to stand beside Jeremiah. He cupped his hands to light his pipe, the spark flaring briefly across his full-cheeked face. "Mighty late for a stroll."

"But a fair night for one." Jeremiah didn't welcome the other man's company, but how could he decently object to Bertle walking his own quarterdeck?

"True enough, true enough." Bertle sucked on his pipe, studying the sky intently. "You're a seafaring man, ain't you, Mr. Sparhawk?"

"I was once, aye," said Jeremiah cautiously. "Not now."

"Not now, maybe, but it never leaves your blood, or your legs. You can put on those fancy shore-going clothes and pretend you're the same as any other lubber, but you won't fool another sailor, no, you won't."

Jeremiah didn't answer, offering no encouragement.

"You're a Yankee, ain't you, Mr. Sparhawk?"

"And you ask a lot of questions, Captain Bertle."

Bertle shrugged. "Nothing uncivil about questions, Mr. Sparhawk. How can you learn about a man if you don't ask him what he don't give up himself?"

"You can ask away, Captain Bertle, but you might not hear what you want."

Bertle peered at him shrewdly above his pipe. "So you're still touchy after your skirmish with the missus, eh? I guessed things was still not what they ought if you was still here."

Jeremiah's brows dropped lower over his eyes, warning enough. "My wife's no concern of yours, or any other man on board this sloop."

"You keep it that way, Mr. Sparhawk. When she put aside that veil, why, she had half my men crazy in love with her right then and there." Bertle sniffed and spat over the side. "She's a handsome woman, your wife. Got breeding, don't she? More'n you'd expect in some godforsaken Yankee jack's wife."

"You know, Bertle," said Jeremiah so calmly that only a fool would mistake the current of violence that ran beneath it. "I could pitch you over the side and no one would ever be the wiser. A man gets to feeling sleepy during the dogwatch, the ship heels a bit, and he tumbles overboard in the dark. Happens all the time at sea. But you being a sailor and all, you'd know that, wouldn't you?"

"Are you making threats against me?"

"Are you still asking questions?"

"The devil take you!" Angrily Bertle jerked the pipe from his mouth, using its stem to punctuate his words. "You can't threaten an English captain, sir, and brag about it. One more time, sir, and I'll have you put in irons below! Is that what you want?"

"Don't try it," said Jeremiah, "unless you mean to swim to Gibraltar. Good night, Captain Bertle."

*   *   *

Caro had left the cabin door unlatched, and Jeremiah frowned and shook his head as he bolted it from the inside. He must warn her against that, especially if Bertle and the others were eyeing her like the whitebelly sharks they were. He felt sure that the only reason one of them hadn't tried her door already was that none had guessed she'd be so careless.

She had left the lantern lit as she'd promised, a single stubby candle swaying gently in its gimbal with the sloop's motion. To his surprise she'd taken the top bunk, and at once he imagined what he'd see, lying below, whenever she climbed up or down, her skirts hiked far up her long legs. He almost groaned aloud. He'd just have to make sure he faced the bulkhead when he heard her stir. God help him, he was going to need the patience—and the purity—of a saint to survive this voyage.

Asleep, she lay curled on her side beneath a coverlet, one hand lying with the palm open beside her face. Her hair was loose and tangled about her shoulders and her lips were parted, and relaxed like this she looked both young and vulnerable.

How, he marveled, had she held onto that appealing innocence after living the life she did? He knew from how long she'd been married to Frederick that she must be close to thirty, but by the shifting candlelight she could have been ten years younger. With him it was the opposite. Experience and hard living had weathered him beyond his years, and some mornings he feared that the face he saw in the shaving mirror belonged to some old man he didn't know.

She sighed and shifted in her sleep, and he caught a tantalizing hint of her scent, jasmine and musk. At Desire's suggestion they traveled with their own linen, and Caro's pillow slip was trimmed with elaborate cutwork lace that matched her pale, gossamer-fine hair. As incongruous as that pillow slip was against the rough pine bulkheads of the tiny cabin, Jeremiah was glad she'd brought it. Frederick was right: she didn't belong in black.

Still watching her sleep, he shrugged his coat from his shoulders and unwrapped his neckcloth. Regardless of how she looked now, she really wasn't as helpless as he'd first thought, and she probably didn't need half the protection he was determined to give her. To confront him the way she had today took more courage than most men had. Certainly more than Bertle. Likely more than he himself. And that time when she'd spoken up before the lieutenant with the pressgang: he'd been too caught up in his own misery then to thank her the way he should have, but she'd fought like a terrier on his behalf. So much, he thought wryly, for the dainty, delicate Lady Byfield.

Shaking his head at how besotted he'd become, he climbed into the lower bunk, lying on top of the coverlet in his shirt and trousers. He didn't know what she was wearing to bed, but he wasn't going to tempt fate or himself by shedding any more clothes than he had to, at least not this first night.

Would Caro be tempted, too? The longing in her eyes had been unmistakable, and the way her lips had parted had begged for his kiss. Innocent though her face might be, she was a worldly, experienced woman.

She'd know both how to please a man and how to be pleased in return, and he almost groaned aloud with frustration.

With his head pillowed in his hands, he closed his eyes and tried to forget the woman lying so close above him. Instead of the soft, measured rhythm of her breathing, he forced himself to listen to the sounds of a well-ordered ship: the thrumming of the wind through the standing rigging, the rush of the waves against the hull, the creaks and groans of the timbers and the calls of the men on the watch overhead.

The sounds were so familiar that he almost didn't hear them, and gradually he let his body relax with the rocking of the ship's motion. It had been so long since he'd been at sea, endless months landlocked in his sister's house, and yet now he felt as if he'd never left.

*He lay on his back, still comfortably full from dinner. Instead of the salt pork that had seen them clear across the Atlantic, there had been fresh meat, for this morning the cook had slaughtered the hog Jeremiah had bought for the crew when they'd touched briefly at Gibraltar. Because the meat wouldn't keep in the hot Mediterranean sun, they had all eaten their fill, relishing the plenty after weeks of dwindling rations. Along with the pork had been bread, real bread, and not the dry, flat crackers that passed for it at sea, fresh green peas, sweet oranges, and a custard pudding made from cream and eggs.*

*Davy had joined him in his cabin, and together they'd drunk to the fastest passage they'd ever had between Providence and Marseilles. If this wind held steady, thought Jeremiah as he drifted off to sleep, they'd reach the French port by tomorrow evening, in time for him to call on that saucy little innkeeper's daughter he'd met last year. Bernadette, or was the name Antoinette?*

*With a jolt he woke to the crack of splintering wood, then the crash of his cabin door as it gave way and slammed open against the bulkhead.*

*"What the hell—"*

*But the man was already on him, hurtling across the dark cabin like a huge cat to land on Jeremiah's chest. He was nearly as large as Jeremiah himself, and he fought with the strength of one who relished killing. In the inky blackness of the moonless night, Jeremiah struggled for his life against an attacker he couldn't see, only feel, pressing down on his heart and lungs like the darkness itself: muscles that were lean and hard, a stiff, curling beard, folds of rough linen that tangled around them like a woman's gown.*

*And then Jeremiah felt the blade of the knife, cold and curving, pressed so close against his throat that each breath was a risk. On the deck overhead he heard running footsteps, a strangled cry of terror, and the guttural voices in a language that wasn't his own.*

*"Ye bloody infidel," said the man with the knife, breathing hard, his face so close to Jeremiah's that he could feel the hot hatred on his skin. "Ye shall die like the other lowly swine ye slaughtered today."*

*"Infidel be damned," rasped Jeremiah. "You're a bloody Scots pirate!"*

*"I am Hamil Al-Ameer, and praise Allah that ye have the chance to die in his name." The knife pressed still closer into Jeremiah's throat, and he knew then*

*that the man was right, he would die. But he didn't*
*want to, not like this, not now, and he struggled vainly*
*against Hamil and the darkness and the pain that*
*seared like fire.*

"Hush now, they can't hurt you any longer," murmured the woman's voice. "You're here with me, and you're safe."

Shaking and disoriented, he turned toward the sound of her voice. Kneeling beside him was a woman dressed all in white, bathed in soft light like an angel. Was he already dead then, beyond life and death?

"Jeremiah, look at me." Her voice was gentle but firm. "Look at me, darling. See? It's Caro. Whatever happened is done, and you're here with me."

"Caro?" He searched her face desperately, his breathing still ragged and his voice trembling as he fought for his own sanity. "Caro, you don't know what I did, what happened."

She saw the terror grow again in his eyes as the nightmare returned and swiftly she put her hand to his cheek, determined not to lose him. "What was your mother's name, Jeremiah?"

He turned his head away, confused. "Mama?"

"You all lived together on the farm on the island, didn't you, Jeremiah?" she said softly, coaxing him to trade the terror for happier memories. She wasn't sure it would work, but she wasn't going to sit by and let him drop back into the black torment again without trying. "Your Mama and your father and your little sister Desire?"

*"No."* He covered his eyes with his hands and the deep, shuddering sigh that racked his body was almost a sob.

She leaned closer, her voice more urgent. "I know you remember the farm, Jeremiah. The grand house on the hill near the water? You told me before it was the grandest house in the colony when you lived there."

"But not with Mama." He took his hands from his eyes, stretching his arms out over his head, and for a long time stared, without seeing, at the rough planks of the bunk above him. "Father took us to live with Granmam and Granfer at Crescent Hill after she died."

"Oh, Jeremiah, I'm sorry!" She'd meant to turn his mind down more pleasant paths, not to this.

"At least she didn't live to see what the British did to Newport during the war. She died soon after Obadiah was born, from the fever, I think."

"I didn't know you had a brother."

"I don't, at least not anymore." His voice was flat, wrung clear of emotion, but at least the blind panic had left his eyes and his breathing had slowed. "The English killed Obie, just as they killed my father. They're all dead now. Desire and I are the only ones left. And, of course, the children she has with Jack, though because of him they'll be raised English, not American. In England there's more to being the son of a lord than a Sparhawk."

His regret touched her. "You never thought to marry and have children yourself?"

"Never found a woman mad enough to take me." He sighed and tapped his fingers against the bulkhead. "My mother's name was Elizabeth Pattison Sparhawk. She had red-gold hair and clapped her hands when she laughed."

"She laughed often?" asked Caro wistfully.

"All the time when Father was home. She loved him, said Granmam, as much as any woman could. He wept at Mama's burying, the only time I ever saw him do it."

He rolled over onto his side, propping his head on his elbow to look at her. He was, she knew, trying very hard to look as if nothing had happened, as if his face weren't still pale and lined with suffering, and though she'd never humiliate him by saying so, her heart went out to him for wanting so badly to hide his weakness from her.

"But here I am babbling about myself as if it's the word from the mountain," he said. "What's more boring than another family's history?"

"Oh, but it's not boring at all!" Suddenly conscious of being in her nightgown, Caro sat back on her heels and tugged the fabric modestly over her knees. "I have no family of my own, you know. Orphans don't."

He raised one brow in question. "Someone raised you on that Hampshire farm."

"Not my mother," she said, and quickly looked away. "She died when I was quite young, just as yours did. I can scarcely remember her at all."

Jeremiah knew she was lying, and too late he remembered what his sister had told him of Caro's mother. If the old gossip was true, then it wasn't that Caro had forgotten her mother. Instead, he guessed, she remembered too much.

He reached out and gently took her hand in his, lifting her fingers to his lips. "What a pair we are, eh, Caro?" he said wearily. "Both of us plagued by a past that cannot be undone."

"What a pair, aye," she whispered with an infinite sadness beyond tears. She slipped her hand free of his and rose, glancing over her shoulder at the lantern. Though she did not move herself, the shadows from the lantern swinging back and forth made crazy patterns across her fine-boned face. "Will it trouble you if I keep the lantern lit? All the sounds of a strange place make me uneasy in the dark."

"No, sweetheart, it won't trouble me at all," he said softly. "Whatever you please."

The swinging light caught and framed her smile, a glimpse of bittersweet empathy for him alone. For him, from her. And he knew then, as somehow he'd always known, that she was the only woman he would ever love.

Alone in his cabin, Bertle grumbled angrily to himself as he refilled the battered pewter tankard with rum and lime water. He should never have agreed to have the woman on board, no matter how much gold the husband had flashed in his eye. Since Eve in the garden, women had brought nothing but sorrow and grief and discontent to mankind, and this pretty little chit with the silver-blond hair and bullyboy husband were no different than the rest. Damned impudent bas-

tard, challenging him like that on his own quarterdeck like some Yankee fighting cock in spurs!

Muttering another oath, Bertle reached into the
tankard, fished out a lime slice between his thumb and
forefinger, and lowered it carefully into his mouth.
Sucking noisily, he pulled the heavy leather mail pouch
from his sea chest and dumped the contents onto his
desk.

The letters slipped and scattered like a little drift of
snow, and with both hands Bertle sorted through
them. The smallest ones, addressed in dainty hands
and reeking of scent, would be from ladies to their
sweethearts, mostly sailors serving in the English ships
stationed at Naples, and Bertle put them aside. Later
in the voyage, when he needed amusement, he might
turn to them; some of those dainty ladies wrote the
most lubricious love letters imaginable.

But tonight the letters Bertle sought would be from
men of business or in the government, the letters with
information that could do him the most service. Some
of his most profitable ventures had come from just
such information, that little extra advantage over his
competitors, and Bertle smiled with satisfaction at the
large pile of business letters before him now. With the
situation with France so uncertain, every worried
merchant in Portsmouth had taken what could be the
last opportunity to write to his factor or agent in Italy.

With a surgeon's delicacy Bertle slid a thin-bladed
knife beneath the seal of the first letter and worked it
free without cracking the stiff blob of stamped green
wax. The sender's name had meant nothing to him,
but the recipient's—that ancient harridan of a count-

ess, Lady Byfield—had attracted Bertle's attention immediately. The countess was said to have the ear of the Queen of Naples herself, which in that court was far better than the king's. News sent to her might be interesting indeed.

But Bertle's hopes fell as he scanned the letter. Only some impoverished grandson living beyond his means and begging for funds, whining over a horse gone lame at Newmarket and a dispute with an aunt who'd refused him money, as well. Nothing useful, nothing interesting. But just as Bertle was ready to toss the letter aside, a sentence caught his eye. The tightfisted aunt had run off with her lover, abandoning her husband and his fortune to the hopeful avarice of the letter's writer and, he prayed, to the rejoicing of the countess. The missing aunt's name was Caro, the present Lady Byfield, her lover a huge, violent outlaw, and where they had so completely vanished to was anyone's guess.

Anyone's guess, and Bertle's surety. He plucked another wedge of lime from the tankard, savoring both the rum-laced juice and his own revenge. As tempting as it would be to confront that Yankee braggart, it would be better still to wait until *Raleigh* reached Naples.

He would call on the countess himself, pay his respects, tell her how honored he'd been to carry Lord and Lady Byfield themselves in his sloop. He'd tell her how he'd naturally respected their wish for anonymity and accepted the false surname they'd used, but the lady's breeding was unmistakable. As for the so-called husband—well, he'd let the man's real identity be discovered soon enough, and decide at the time which would pay the best, a reward for his honesty or blackmail for silence. Either way there would be gold, gold guineas and plenty of them.

A reward, and revenge. Bertle laughed aloud, spewing bits of lime rind as he imagined the fate of the brash, bullying Yankee in the hands of the Dowager Countess of Byfield.

TO

# Chapter Nine

"You have the look of a fightin' man, Mr. Sparhawk," said Hart, the earnest young man who was the *Raleigh*'s mate. Jeremiah had come on deck while he waited for Caro to wake and dress, and while the mate's cheerful company was not exactly his choice for so early in the morning, at least Hart had none of Bertle's belligerence.

With obvious pride, the young man patted the stubby little cannonade he was polishing, and swiped his rag over the barrel again as he grinned at Jeremiah. "We're only a merchantman, but the cap'n insists we be able to hold our own in a fight. You can see for yourself, sir, how far he's gone to outfit us proper."

Though Jeremiah considered himself a merchant shipmaster by trade, he'd seen a good deal more fighting one way or another than many captains in the American navy. The boy had guessed right enough there. But Hart's estimation of the four pitiful cannonades with which Bertle had armed his sloop was inflated by pride, or perhaps loyalty. To Jeremiah's eye the guns were probably older than Hart himself, and all the polishing in the world wouldn't make the antiquated barrels aim true or far enough to frighten any enemy. Arming a merchant vessel like this one was asking for trouble, for any attacker would consider the cannonades excuse enough to fire first.

"How I'd like a good crack at a Frenchman myself, wouldn't I though!" continued Hart. "Why, put anything French within my range and I'd give them a taste of British courage!"

"Be careful what you wish for, lad," said Jeremiah dryly. Once, very long ago, he'd been every bit as eager to chase after the enemy. His first encounter with one of that enemy's frigates and the carnage a single broadside could bring had instantly toppled his youthful bravado. "The press-gangs would make a prize of you in an instant."

"Oh, they can't take me," said Hart blithely. "My father paid old man Bertle twenty guineas to rank me mate so I'd be clear of the press. Masters and mates, by law the press can't touch them."

"Don't be so certain." Judging by what else Jeremiah had seen of Bertle's character, he wouldn't trust the man not to sell poor Hart, mate or not, and collect the navy's bounty himself. He glanced at the horizon, gauging the time by the level of the rising sun, and wondered uneasily why Caro hadn't joined him by now. She'd been stirring when he'd left, and that had been at least an hour ago.

"Not that it matters," Hart was saying, his disappointment clear. "I'll lay you odds we won't see even a hair of a Frenchman between here and Naples, let alone get to fire at one. Have you ever killed one yourself, Mr. Sparhawk? One of the French bastards, I mean?''

Jeremiah almost winced at the young man's innocent callousness. ''They're men, Hart, not grouse in season, and they tend to bleed and die the same as the rest of us.''

''Then you *are* a fighting man, sir!'' he exclaimed excitedly. ''We was talking in the mess and we were sure you were, no matter what the cap'n said. He said you was mean and dangerous, and we should steer clear of you, but I thought you looked like a man who'd know things worth knowing. A sight more than old Bertle would, anyway.''

Jeremiah looked past the young man to the water. He knew things, all right, such wonderful things that made him shake and weep helplessly as he had last night, things he'd give much to forget if he could. There had been a time in his life when he'd been proud to be known as a man who never walked from a fight because he was confident he'd always win, but now he wasn't as certain. These days it seemed he wasn't certain about much of anything.

He thought again of last night, wondering how Caro would treat him this morning. Like the young man before him, she had wanted so badly to believe him a hero who could solve her problems through the magic of his courage alone. Well, she couldn't believe that any longer. He glanced again at the empty companionway. Where the devil was she, anyway?

"So how many Frenchmen have you killed, Mr. Sparhawk?" persisted Hart, his eyes shining with bloodthirsty ardor.

"Enough to know I'd rather not kill any more of them."

Hart's chubby face fell. "Even to defend English soil?"

"The only thing I've done for English soil is send English men under it." He knew he'd be quoted in the mess, and he didn't give a damn if he was. "If you ever bothered to listen to your captain, you'd know I'm American, lad, not English, and I'll thank you not to forget the war—*our* war—that made the difference."

He turned on his heel before Hart could answer and headed below. God, he sounded as if he were a hundred years old! If Caro had been with him, he wouldn't have made such a pompous fool of himself. Caro would understand. Caro would—damnation, why had he left her alone for so long?

He skipped the bottom three steps of the ladder and raced to their cabin. He tried to open the door and found it latched from within, and though last night he'd wanted her to lock the door, he now found it nothing but frustrating.

"Caro, open the door," he ordered, thumping his fist on the pine for good measure. "It's Jeremiah, Caro!"

Yet all he heard in return was a faint, muffled voice from within, and his frustration turned to fear for her. He remembered the way Bertle had leered as he'd spoken her name, how he'd said half the crew was already in love with her. Dear God, if anything had happened to her because he'd been careless . . .

"Caro, sweetheart, are you all right?" he asked urgently. "Can you come to the door?"

For an answer he heard only another incoherent sound, this one close to a sob. It was enough for Jeremiah. Without waiting to hear more, he threw his shoulder against the door, determined to break it down if he had to and free her.

But as he braced himself to strike the door again, Caro herself threw it open from within. Though in the sunlight that slanted down from the open hatch, her cheeks were flushed and her hair was tumbled wildly about her face, the only part of her that seemed amiss was her temper.

"What in God's holy name do you think you're doing, Jeremiah Sparhawk?" she demanded furiously. "First you disappear for hours on end when surely you must know I need you, and then, when you finally decide to grace me with your presence once again, you try to break the door down like some sort of rampaging barbarian!"

"You needed me?" repeated Jeremiah, mystified, fixing on the only part of her tirade that might make sense. "Needed me how?"

"Oh, stop hanging about there in the hall and come inside!" She opened the door wider and stepped back so he could pass, one hand on the door and the other awkwardly behind her back. "Though I suppose I've said that all wrong, too, haven't I? Well, come along then, correct me!"

"It's a companionway, not a hall," he said as he reached out and shut the door. Though it was day above, in the windowless cabin she'd been forced to light the candle in the lantern again to see enough to dress, and on her coverlet he saw her brush and a mirror, and the little ivory combs she used to pin up her hair. "But that's the least of what doesn't make sense, Caro. What the blazes did you expect of me?"

"It's what you expect of *me!*" she cried indignantly. She shoved her hair back from her face. "You toss your coat over your shoulders and fumble a knot into your neckcloth and there you are, decent enough to breakfast with the king himself, while I'm trapped here, struggling like some poor cat in a sack, desperate for a little decent consideration of my plight!"

"Enough, Caro, enough!" He'd never seen her fuss and fume like this, and he didn't care if he never saw it again. "How can I defend myself when you won't even tell me what I haven't done?"

*"This!"* She turned abruptly to face the bulkhead. In the candlelight he saw how her hand bunched together the black bombazine of her gown, holding it tight at the waist. Above and below her hand the gown was open, to her hips, the lacings hanging loose from the eyelets on one side, and to his stunned surprise, that was all: no shift, no petticoats, no stays or corset, only creamy, flawless skin that seemed almost luminescent in the candlelight.

"Now you understand, don't you, Jeremiah?" she asked over her shoulder, oblivious to his speechless response. "There is absolutely no way I could do up those lacings myself. I know, because I've tried and tried until I nearly wept with my own clumsiness.''

He reminded himself he was a man of the world, a man of experience, but though he knew he should look away he couldn't, his gaze riveted in admiring fascination to the angled glimpses of her skin. How the devil was he going to act as her lady's maid, politely ignoring this sort of display? He'd always tried to be a gentleman where ladies were concerned, but this was more than any gentleman should have to withstand. And here he'd been worrying about seeing her in her nightgown!

"Caro, sweetheart," he began, his mouth dry. "Caro, I'm not sure I can do this."

"Certainly you can," she said promptly. "Sailors are supposed to be very good with knots and lines and ropes and things. How different can this be?"

"Oh, it's different, Caro. Trust me." He cleared his throat, running his hand back through his hair to keep it from touching her. "Now I'm no expert on such kickshaws and furbelows, sweetheart, but shouldn't there be more—more petticoats or some such?"

"Of course there should be, but please, please don't tell your sister!" She turned gracefully halfway around, beseeching him over her shoulder. "I wore the petticoats yesterday because she'd ordered both these mourning gowns for me for this voyage, and I did want to please her, but they're hot and heavy and stiff and I hate how they tangled between my legs when I walked."

Lord help him, she wasn't making this any easier at all. Tangled between her legs, for all love!

"Several years ago, when the fashions were so very bare, one wasn't supposed to wear a stitch beneath one's gowns, and I—well, I didn't. I still don't, if I don't have to." She smiled, the quick conspirator's grin he'd come to recognize meant trouble for him. "You're a man, Jeremiah, so you'll never know how dreadful it is to have whalebone stays and hoops jabbing into your ribs whenever you laugh."

"I can imagine." Oh, he imagined, all right, imagined everything there was to imagine.

"Then you'll understand that I'd rather Desire didn't know. I don't want her to think me ungrateful." She turned away from him again, releasing the fabric she'd bunched in her hand. "Now help me, please, Jeremiah, so we can go up on deck together. I'm sick to death of this wretched little cabin and I can't wait to see the sun again."

If she could be so cavalier, than so could he. He took a deep breath and forced himself to study how the back of the gown was constructed. There was one wider tie that seemed to pull the high waist together, and then a narrower cording that must weave the two halves of the back together. No challenge at all, really.

"You must remember I'm only pretending to be a married man," he said gruffly. "I suppose you've grown so accustomed to your husband doing this for you that you think nothing of it."

"Frederick? Helping me dress?" She laughed, not scornfully but with genuine amusement, yet enough to rankle Jeremiah.

"I suppose you have a whole flock of maidservants to help you instead in that big house of yours," he said as he untangled a knot she'd worked into one of the laces. "Things are different for a countess, aren't they? Where I'm from, husbands and wives help each other, and not just because of a lack of servants, either."

"That's not the reason," she said quickly. "It's that Frederick does not choose to be so familiar, not that we've so many servants."

" 'Familiar'? Is that what you English call it?" Jeremiah laughed but without much enthusiasm. "I thought that was the whole reason for bothering to marry in the first place."

"Don't make judgments about my marriage, Jeremiah." With her face turned away he couldn't see her expression, yet he could feel her body tense, her amusement replaced by edginess. "I don't doubt that what we have differs from your notions of a husband and wife, but in our way we're happier than most married people I've seen. Frederick understands me."

"Will he understand you asking some other man to do up your clothes like this? Will he understand you pretending to be my wife, sharing this cabin with me?"

"He would understand the circumstances," she said firmly, though she'd hesitated a moment too long for her conscience to be as clear as she wanted Jeremiah to believe. "In any event, it's not as if the gown laced in the front. What can my back alone signify?"

"Oh, Caro," he whispered roughly, "you shouldn't tempt me to prove you wrong."

With just his fingertips he traced the long, sweeping curve of her spine, grazing so lightly along her skin that he felt her shiver. Smiling to himself, he ran his hand upward, spreading his fingers so he felt not only the shallow valley, but the soft rise of her back on either side, and this time she gasped. But she didn't move away, and she didn't tell him to stop.

And he didn't.

Caro never would have asked him if she'd thought it would lead to this. But how could she have known? No one had ever touched her like this before. She felt both his hands now as he kneaded the tension from her shoulders, his thumbs working deep into her muscles, and she closed her eyes as her heart quickened and a delicious languor swept over her.

Her conscience told her the freedom she was giving Jeremiah was wrong, no matter how wonderful it felt. She had tried so hard to be a good woman, a lady, and no lady would ever let a man touch her like this. Look what had happened to her own mother, and what had nearly happened to her, as well.

But as she felt Jeremiah ease the silk of her gown further off her shoulders, she couldn't stop him, not when she felt his hands slide once again down the length of her back, his fingers splayed to cover as much of her as he could. This wonderful, wild sensation that only he seemed able to bring to her simply felt too good. His hands were warm and sure wherever they touched her, learning where her waist narrowed and her hips flared, reaching forward to find the softest flesh on the underside of her breasts. She gasped with surprised pleasure and instinctively arched against him, seeking the strong support of his chest as her own knees turned wobbly as a new lamb's.

"Oh, Jeremiah, what you're doing to me," she whispered with what little breath she still controlled. "Oh my, Jeremiah!"

He chuckled softly, knowing and masculine, as he slid one arm around her waist to steady her. "Exactly what am I doing?"

"You—you know." Grateful for his support, she turned her cheek against his shoulder, the wool of his coat rough against her skin. With her eyes still closed, she was almost painfully aware of his touch, the stiff hair on his forearm grazing against her side, the rustling silk bombazine of her gown gliding over them both.

"I didn't know you wanted me to play lady's maid," he teased, his lips so close that his breath was warm on her ear, making her shiver yet again. "Don't be so sure I know what you want now."

"But you do," she said breathlessly. "You know better than I do myself."

"Do I now, sweet Caro?" His other hand moved higher, her breast filling his palm as his work-calloused thumb teased her nipple into a taut peak. She caught her breath as the first hot flames of desire raced through her blood, her whole body tightening, coiling in a way she didn't begin to understand. Seeking some kind of release she moved restlessly against him, not realizing the agony she was bringing to him until she heard him groan, his grasp on her tightening as he tried to hold her still.

"Steady, lass," he said, his breathing now as ragged as her own. "There's naught to be gained for either of us that way, is there?"

"Oh, Jeremiah, I'm sorry!" Unaware until he'd spoken that she'd done anything wrong, she twisted about in his arms, clutching her gown modestly over her breasts as she faced him. "I told you I didn't know what I was doing, but you refuse to believe me."

"You're right, I don't." He swept her pale, tangled hair back from her forehead and tipped her face up toward his. "I'll need convincing."

He had, she thought with giddy conviction, the most beautiful eyes she'd ever seen on a man, as green and as ever changing as the sea he loved.

"I'm not very good at arguments," she said softly. "I doubt I could convince you of your own name."

"Don't use words, sweetheart, and you'll do just fine." Gently he raised her chin and captured her mouth for his own. She remembered what joy it had been to kiss him before, and eagerly she parted her lips for him.

But the heady sweetness she'd remembered from before wasn't there this time. Too much had happened since then to change the subtle stakes between them, and that easy, careless attraction between two strangers had been irrevocably lost. In its place was something deeper, darker, that Caro sensed from the instant his lips began moving over hers, something she welcomed even as she realized it could lead only to her ruin.

Now when his mouth moved so surely over hers, she felt his heat like a fire licking at her soul. Seamlessly their mouths joined, his tongue savoring her velvety sweetness, plunging deeper and then withdrawing in a seductive dance that left her desperate for more. In return she kissed him the only way she knew how, with a shy eagerness, the way he'd taught her the first time, and he rewarded her with a low growl of masculine satisfaction.

The gown between them slipped forgotten from her fingers as she reached her hands beneath his coat to curl around his neck, drawing him closer as she arched into him. Her breasts tightened against the rough linen of his shirt and the hard muscle of his chest beneath it, and little cries of pleasure escaped her lips to be swallowed by his.

His large hands slid deep into the black silk to caress her body, lifting her against him so she could feel how well they fit together. With an intimacy that at once shocked and excited her, her legs fell open on either side of his, and through the thin barrier of silk she could feel his rigid length as he pressed against her most secret parts, her softness melting around him, teasing them both with the promise of what completion would bring.

His mouth broke free of hers, his beard rough against her skin as he trailed kisses along her jaw. "We're so good together, sweetheart," he murmured, and even in her inexperience she knew he was right. "I'll give you paradise like you've never known."

Frustrated by the frail barriers still between them, he began pulling her skirts high over her legs, relentlessly guiding her toward the bunk as she clung to him.

In her ear she heard how he whispered her name over and over, his voice thick with desire, making the single word a prayer of passion and tenderness she'd never dreamed she'd hear.

"Love me, Caro," he whispered hoarsely as he licked at the salty hollow of her throat. "Love me, and let me love you."

*Love me.* He loved her, he wanted her: what else could a woman hope for from a man? Yet for Caro the awful reality of his words sliced through the haze of passion, and her eyes filled with tears of longing for what she could not—*must not*—have.

"No," she said softly, covering herself as she pushed away from him. "I can't, Jeremiah."

"Yes, sweetheart, you can," he breathed, still so sure of himself as he gently drew her back, kissing her again with an intensity that left her dizzy with longing. "You will."

She closed her eyes and pulled away again, trying to shut him out as she struggled to find the strength within herself to turn away. There could be no place in her life for the kind of love he was offering. Love like that was an indulgence that women could not afford. Love like Jeremiah wanted from her brought suffering, pain and sorrow. She had only to look as far as her own mother.

"I can't, Jeremiah. Please. *Please!*" She withdrew again, and again he reached for her, but now with a blind possessiveness she hadn't expected, crushing her hard against his chest. For the first time she found him using his size and strength against her, and too late she realized the force of the passion she'd raised in him.

Once he had told her he'd never taken a woman against her will, but if he tossed her onto the bunk now to finish what they'd begun, she knew she would have no one to blame but herself. Panicking, she tried to shove him away. "No, Jeremiah, I can't!"

"Can't, or won't?" The blood pounding through his body drowned out every thought except the overwhelming need for her. He had never known a woman who had responded to him so passionately and with so few inhibitions, the sinuous movements of her pale body half hidden, half revealed by the black silk more incendiary than if she'd been completely naked. Her eyes were dark with passion, her throat and breasts flushed; it was inconceivable that she'd wish to end this any more than he did himself, and the physical pain of interruption flared into anger. "I'm waiting, Caro. Can't, or won't?"

"Both," she whispered miserably, her own body aching with unfulfillment. "You must understand—"

"Damn your understanding!" He could take her now, here, while the fire she'd roused in him still throbbed in his body. Despite her words, he knew she wanted him. It would be so easy to bury himself deep within her, to lose himself in the hot promise of her love.

But instead he shoved her away while he still could, so roughly that she stumbled backward. Desperate for some sort of release, he lashed out furiously at the paneling over her head with his fist. "You parade about half-naked and rub yourself against me like a cat in heat, and then you want me to *understand* when you change your mind?"

She winced at his crudeness, tugging her gown back over her bare breasts. "I didn't mean it that way," she said softly. "There are so many reasons."

"Afraid you'll lose your title, Countess?" he snarled, as angry with himself for what he'd nearly done to her as he was with her for denying them both. "Afraid that if your precious Frederick learned how eagerly you'd spread your legs for some poor American sailor like me, he'd toss you out on the street like the little whore you are?"

Hot tears of shame ran down her cheeks. "It's not like that at all!" she cried. "It's just I—I cannot love you the way you deserve."

"You expect me to believe that?" Disgusted, he turned to leave.

"It's the truth!" she sobbed. "Damn you, Jeremiah, did I question you last night?"

He froze, his hand on the latch, his face rigid.

"I need you, Jeremiah," she said haltingly through her tears. "I need you and care for you, and I believe you care for me, too. But for me, for now, that's all it can be. I can't love you the way you want. I can't love anyone like that. It's not you, and it's not Frederick. It's my fault. All mine."

She sank down to her knees on the deck, burying both her face and her tears in her hands. He would hate her now. How could he not? She deserved it for what she'd done to him. But, oh, how hard his hatred would be to bear!

*She could still hear her mother's voice, raspy with consumption, as she and her friends had taught the little country virgin the cold, mercenary lessons in pleasing men so men in turn would value her. They'd told her things she'd thought impossible between men and women, then showed her themselves with their willing lovers if she'd dare doubt in their hearing. They had ridiculed her innocence and mocked her romantic ideas of love and happiness as readily as they had criticized her beauty. Such spiteful, jealous women, those friends of Merry Miriam Harris, their high-pitched laughter and their bright satin gowns making them seem like exotic, expensive tropical birds in the gray seaside mist of Portsmouth.*

*Though she had tried so hard to do what her mother and her friends wanted, every cruel word had found its mark in her thirteen-year-old soul, and each night she had cried herself to sleep on the pile of quilts, rank with stale perfume and old sweat, that was her make-shift bed in the corner of her mother's dressing room. Yet each night, too, she swore she wouldn't be like them, and when Frederick had rescued her she thought she'd succeeded. She was cherished, she was loved, she was treated as well as a favorite daughter by a gentle man old enough to be her father who never in fifteen years had asked her to perform the specialities she'd been forced to learn.*

*But now Caro knew she was no better than her mother and her friends. Only her price had been different. And God in heaven, how dearly it had cost her!*

For a long time Jeremiah stood watching her, crumpled there on the deck at his feet in the black sea of her tangled skirts. She was too lost in her sorrow to notice him, and as she wept softly to herself, he felt the blind anger that had so possessed him lessen and slip away. Overhead he heard Bertle shout an order, followed by the crewmen's footsteps as they hurried to obey. Strange how he'd forgotten he was even at sea. Stranger still how his whole world seemed to have narrowed to this one tiny cabin and the weeping woman within it.

Her hair had fallen forward to veil her face, leaving the nape of her neck and her back in the open gown touchingly exposed. He had never thought of her as vulnerable, yet as she was now he could think of nothing else, and he had done it.

This was his fault, not hers. The scars he carried were there on his body, plain as day, but the ones that marked her ran deeper, and were no less painful for being hidden. He, of all people, should have listened when she'd begged for his understanding. He didn't care now what had happened to make her believe she was so unworthy of the love she was born to give. What mattered most was that once again, one more time, he had failed another who had trusted him.

With a weary sigh he crouched down beside her, taking her hands in his to gently raise her to her feet. She kept her face lowered, unwilling to let him see how she wept. Wordlessly he turned her like a doll toward the bunks and began to lace her gown the way she'd first asked. The black cord crossed and recrossed her skin until, with a deft twist of his wrist, he pulled the two sides tightly together. He tied a neat little bow at the neckline and tucked the ends inside the gown.

And then, before she realized it, he was gone.

# *Chapter Ten*

"That rocky island to the nor'west is Sardinia," said Jeremiah as he handed his spyglass to Caro, standing beside him on the *Raleigh*'s quarterdeck. "With any luck at all, we'll make Naples by nightfall. For all that he's an unpleasant rascal, Bertle's done right well for us as a navigator."

"We'll be there tomorrow?" asked Caro wistfully as she took the glass, careful not to let her fingers brush his. "So soon?"

Jeremiah nodded, his hand tapping lightly on the rail as he gazed out across the bright blue Mediterranean. Even with a brisk breeze off the water, the morning was warm, and he'd left his coat in the cabin below and stood now in his waistcoat and rolled-up shirtsleeves, the wind billowing through the linen above his tanned forearms.

"Oh, aye, Bertle's made a first-rate passage for us. Couldn't be better." He glanced down at her from the shadow of his hat brim, his eyes very green in the light reflecting from the water. "I thought you'd be pleased, considering. The sooner we make Naples, the sooner you could have your husband back.''

''I am pleased, thank you,'' she answered evenly. ''It is only that the journey's been so easy that I wonder that we are there this soon.''

These past weeks with him she had become accomplished at such demonstrations of polite good breeding. By now she could let her eyes meet his without her face growing hot, and smile serenely when he offered his arm to her on the deck. It was all passing genteel, most correct.

She was sure he never guessed how she lay in the bunk above him each night and fought the fevered memory how his lips had felt on hers, the wildfire his touch had sent racing through her blood, and how shamelessly she had writhed in his arms as her body had begged for more. The vividness of the memory shocked her, returning whenever she was near him. She prayed he never noticed how many times she'd watched him covertly beneath her veiled hat and felt her pulse race as he climbed the rigging with an acrobat's grace, working alongside the *Raleigh*'s crew to relieve the tedium of the voyage.

Most of all, she wanted him to believe she was as happy and as carefree as he seemed to be himself. Why shouldn't Jeremiah be? Because he wasn't married, he'd done nothing wrong, while she had betrayed the trust of one of the kindest men ever created. It could hardly be Frederick's fault that though she loved him, she'd never been *in* love with him, a distinction she'd never known existed until now. And now it was too late, too late for all of them. But then she could hide her misery well. She'd had, after all, years of pretending she was something she wasn't.

Jeremiah watched as she delicately arched her wrist and lifted the glass to her eye, her hands so dainty in the black kid gloves against the polished brass. Damn these overnice, ladylike airs of hers! He missed her impishness and her impulsive laughter and the way she'd tug on his sleeve like an impatient little girl. With her veil knotted back from her hat's sugar-scoop brim, her face had the exact fashionable blandness expected of a countess. Only the freckles across her nose, like the gold pollen scattered across a lily, remained as he remembered.

Maybe it was the possibility of being reunited with Lord Byfield that had made her turn so proper on him, or maybe this really was the genuine Caroline Moncrief, and the woman he'd fallen in love with had been the artful imposter. Maybe his Caro, his passionate, impulsive, irrepressible Caro, wasn't his at all, and didn't exist beyond a handful of misadventures in Portsmouth calculated to bring him here to Naples with her, and those first two wretched nights aboard the *Raleigh*.

Whoever she was, she'd kept her distance since then. No more kisses, no more confessions, and somehow she'd rigged a way to get in and out of her clothes without his help. She didn't need him for anything. And that, he told himself fiercely, was all for the best and fine with him.

Too bad he didn't believe it, too.

"Is Sardinia a country in its own right?" she asked, focusing the glass.

"A kingdom, I think, if General Bonaparte hasn't swallowed it up wholesale." More of her polite small talk, he thought contemptuously. She wasn't even looking in the direction of the island. "I've never put in there, so I can't tell you much of the place."

"Do you know the colors of their flag?"

"Red with yellow bars, I think. They've so few deep-water ships that I can't have seen it more than a half-dozen times."

Caro's veil floated back up before her face, and impatiently she shoved it away without lowering the glass from her eye. "This flag might be red and yellow, but I don't believe it is. No, now that it's clear of the horizon, I can see it's blue and white with the red."

"What the devil?" Jeremiah grabbed the glass from her. Even at this distance, the tricolor of France was unmistakable, as were the three tiny dots of white topsail that crowned the masts of a frigate. And if Caro had spotted them from the deck, then the frigate's lookouts high in those same sails would definitely have seen the *Raleigh* by now, and Jeremiah swore under his breath. To come so close to their destination and then be captured—it was too much like what had happened to the *Chanticleer*. No more war, he prayed, please God, no more fighting.

"It's a French ship, isn't it?" asked Caro, standing up on her toes to try to see better. "If England's at war with them by now, as everyone said we would be, then they'll try to catch us, won't they?"

"Damned right they will." Jeremiah squinted up at the *Raleigh*'s own lookout, staring dreamily at the purple-blue hills of Sardinia, and he bit back the automatic reproach. This wasn't his ship, no matter how much danger the man's carelessness had put them in.

Bertle wasn't on deck, but Hart was, and in three steps Jeremiah was at the other man's side, thrusting his own glass into the mate's hands. "You wanted to see Frenchmen, Hart. Well, there the bastards are, large as life and on your tail."

With his eye to the glass, Hart twitched like a setter who'd just eyed a pheasant. "We'll have some sport now, won't we, sir?" he said as he chuckled with anticipation. "What luck! What bloody good luck!"

Jeremiah stared at him in disbelief. "If this is your idea of good luck, than I'd hate to see bad. Where's the captain?"

"In his cabin, with orders not to be disturbed. He always retires after breakfast, you know."

"I didn't know and I don't care," said Jeremiah curtly. "Send one of the men for him directly."

"What, and waste this chance to seize the glory ourselves?" cried Hart, his plump chin quivering with anticipation. "The cannonades, Mr. Sparhawk, the cannonades! I'll send Johnson below for the powder and balls, and then we'll—"

"Shove the damn things over the side for all the good they'll do you." Jeremiah looked back at the French ship, her sails now clearly visible without the glass. At last the sloop's lookout had spotted the frigate, and at his excited cry the rest of the sloop's crew had swarmed up the rigging to look for themselves. "A frigate that size carries at least thirty-six guns, each one capable of firing twice as far as your little brass popguns. You wouldn't even have a chance to aim before they'd blown you clear from the water."

He would have tempered his words if he'd seen Caro beside him, but instead of being shocked or frightened, she only nodded, her eyes bright with excitement. "Then we'd be fools to pick a fight, Jeremiah. Wouldn't it be better if we outran them?"

He glanced up at the sails, gauging the wind, and shook his head. "With their size and all the extra canvas they can set, they'd have us by sunset. Besides, if we run, we'll just be giving them the excuse to fire on us anyway."

"Look here, you're only a passenger," protested Hart. "You're not even English. You've no right to be giving orders to anyone aboard this sloop."

"And neither are you, you smug little jackass," snapped Bertle as he stumped up the companionway, still buttoning his breeches. "What's all this yammering about a Frenchman?"

"There, south-southwest," said Jeremiah, his patience fast disappearing. "I'd guess from the way they're chasing us that Bonaparte's declared war, and we're set to be that frigate's first prize. Start thinking fast, Bertle. My wife and I have no wish to risk our lives because of your indecision."

Hart elbowed his way forward. "I told them we'd fight it out, sir," he said eagerly. "I told them—"

Bertle cuffed the mate sharply, enough to send the younger man staggering to one side. "You could have told them you knew as much as a keg of salt horse and it would've amounted to the same thing. Use the brains God gave you, boy, and learn to keep your mouth shut when you can't.''

"What other papers do you carry?" demanded Jeremiah. "Dutch, maybe, or Swedish? Anything to fool them with when we're boarded?"

Bertle glared at Jeremiah as he pulled out a red bandanna and noisily blew his nose. "That's a low Yankee trick, bad as sailing under false colors, and I won't countenance it."

With his hands folded across his chest, Jeremiah looked down at the other captain. "You'd rather lose your ship and cargo?"

Bertle's mouth worked as he tried to come up with another, more respectable possibility.

"If we're going to try to fool them," said Caro, and all three men turned to look at her, "shouldn't we take down our flag? They might not have seen it yet, you know. The way the wind was blowing I couldn't make out theirs for the longest time, and they'd be looking into the sun to see us, too."

"Strike the king's flag, ma'am?" exclaimed Hart with horror. "To a Frenchman, ma'am?"

Bertle grunted. "Do what the lady says, Hart, and don't make a great show of it. Fray the line so it looks like we lost our colors in a blow. And mind, we're not so much striking to the bloody French as protecting what's ours."

Caro grinned, and for the first time in weeks Jeremiah saw a flicker of her former impishness. "Then give it to me for safekeeping, Captain Bertle. No *galant gentilehomme* would dare search a lady's belongings."

Clearly uncomfortable with her French, Bertle only grumbled some sort of halfhearted reply.

"You're registered out of Portsmouth, aren't you?" asked Jeremiah, and Bertle nodded. "Then we'll change your papers just enough to make 'em pass for American. There's a Portsmouth in Rhode Island, too, far up at the northern end of Aquidneck. We'll make that the *Raleigh*'s home port, and pray the French won't know the difference between an American and an English crew."

"They'll never guess if you pretend you're the captain, Jeremiah!" cried Caro gleefully. "All the rest of us can keep quiet while you speak for us. No one, not even a Frenchman, would ever mistake *you* for English!"

Jeremiah smiled at her, delighted that she'd suggested it before he'd had to volunteer. Given the circumstances, he was willing to overlook how the compliment was more than a bit backhanded.

But it was no compliment at all to Bertle. "Are you daft, woman? You expect me to turn over my pretty little *Raleigh* to some Yankee by-blow so he can play at being a captain?"

Caro drew herself up straight, her blue eyes snapping with indignation. "He is no by-blow, Captain Bertle, and he *is* my husband, and I'll thank you not to insult either of us any further," she said tartly. "As for his capability to sail your silly little boat, why, he's been a captain himself for years and years, and he sails ships so fine as to make this one look like no more than a peapod!"

Jeremiah lay his hand on her shoulder. "Steady, my dear, don't go overboard."

"It's all true, Jeremiah, and I won't have him say otherwise." She rested her hand on top of his with what she hoped would seem like wifely loyalty. "In America, Captain Bertle, my husband owns a half-dozen trading vessels in his own name, and holds shares in goodness knows how many others. If he is a passenger in your precious *Raleigh*, and not the master of a sloop—a finer, better sloop—of his own, why then, it's because he so chooses, not because he is incapable!"

Bertle's mouth worked furiously. "I've only your word that says so, ma'am. Even if the whole braggart tale's true, it still don't change the fact of him being a Yankee."

"No, it doesn't," agreed Jeremiah. "Nor does it change how that French frigate's bearing down on us."

"Damnation, Sparhawk!" sputtered Bertle. "What in blazes do you expect of me?"

"It's your decision, Bertle," continued Jeremiah relentlessly. He knew what destruction a warning shot from a frigate could bring, even if the others didn't. "We Americans aren't at war with anyone just now. My wife and I wouldn't be touched. You and your crew could lose your ship and your freedom, but we'd be merely inconvenienced. Your choice, Captain."

"May the devil himself take your choices, Sparhawk!" Bertle slammed his fist down on the railing. "I'm sorry I ever let the pair of you thieving rogues on board!"

But later that afternoon, when the frigate's long-boat bobbed alongside the *Raleigh,* it was Jeremiah who stood waiting as the captain to receive the French lieutenant. On Jeremiah's arm was Caro, and behind him, barely silenced by necessity, stood Bertle and Hart. As the Frenchmen began to climb from their boat up the side, Jeremiah took one final glance at Bertle and the rest of the sour-faced crew and sent a last, urgent prayer to heaven that the lot of them would behave. He wouldn't lay a penny that they could.

"You'll do splendidly," whispered Caro as she slipped her hand from his arm and instead twined her fingers into his, something she hadn't done since the first night. "However could you not?"

From the restless way her fingers moved, Jeremiah wasn't sure who was being reassured, but he liked knowing she believed in him, almost as much as he liked holding her small, gloved hand once again.

As he pressed her hand in return, he could just make out her smile beneath the shadow of her veil. He had insisted she drop it down again over her face, and he was glad he had. Not only did he jealously wish to keep Caro's beauty hidden from the notoriously flirtatious Frenchmen, but also because she was almost radiating excited delight. No one, not even a Frenchman prone to giving ladies the benefit of the doubt, would believe she was grieving for anyone.

*"Bonjour, Monsieur le Capitaine,"* said the lieutenant with a neat bow from the waist that seemed at odds with the party of four heavily armed marines and three seamen who accompanied him on board. The

lieutenant's red and white uniform glittered with brass and braid, and when he lifted his hat Jeremiah saw that the Frenchman still wore his hair clubbed back with a ribbon in the old style of the monarchists. "I am Lieutenant Jean Delafosse of the frigate *Beau Courage,* and because you do not fly a flag, *monsieur,* I fear I must ask you to show me your papers."

"Lieutenant." Jeremiah lifted his hat a fraction, but didn't bow. At least the man spoke English. His own French was serviceable but rusty, and he'd rather put the other man at the disadvantage. "Jeremiah Sparhawk, master of the American sloop *Raleigh,* bound for Naples. And we don't fly a flag because we lost it clean away in a little blow off Finisterre."

"Indeed, *monsieur?* One of my men swore he saw a British flag when he first sighted you, but perhaps he only wished it so." Delafosse's gaze swept the sloop's deck, a quick appraisal to match his ill-concealed skepticism. He glanced at one of the French seaman, and without a word the man trotted back to check the line that would have held the flag. "The men are always eager for prizes, and your sloop would bring a pretty sum."

"She would if she were English, Lieutenant," said Jeremiah evenly, offering Delafosse the leather portfolio that contained the *Raleigh*'s slightly altered papers. "But as I told you before, the sloop's American, same as I am myself."

The French sailor returned and whispered his findings to the lieutenant, who nodded and said nothing. Once again Jeremiah found himself praying, this time that the line on the jack staff had been convincingly frayed.

But Delafosse instead looked toward Caro with obvious interest, one hand over his heart as he bowed again. "My sympathies, *mademoiselle,* for your loss, whatever its nature."

"She's my wife, Lieutenant, not a *mademoiselle,*" said Jeremiah, the edgy possessiveness in his voice warning enough to make the Frenchman's black brows rise.

"A bloody Frenchman killed her brother," said Hart, loud enough for every man on deck to hear him. "A stinking, bloody *Frenchman.*"

The tension on the deck increased a hundredfold, and immediately Jeremiah swung around to face the mate. "One more outburst like that, Hart," he said, his hands clenched in fists behind his bark and his voice crackling with authority, "and you'll answer directly to me."

But Caro lay her hand on his sleeve. "Don't, love, please," she begged softly, her whole posture seeming to bend beneath the weight of her sorrow. "Mr. Hart meant no ill, I'm sure."

She turned toward Delafosse. "My brother was killed last year fighting in Spain, Lieutenant, but I—we—did not learn of his death until several weeks ago." Her voice was so tremulous that the Frenchman was forced to lean forward to hear her. "My husband is taking me to Naples and Rome to help me overcome my grief."

The Frenchman's face softened with pity, and Jeremiah realized that with those few sentences Caro had done more to save the *Raleigh* than all the other English on board put together. She was good at such deceptions, almost too good, and uneasily Jeremiah wondered yet again which side of her was the real one.

"Ah, *mademoiselle,* I did not know," murmured Delafosse. "The misfortunes of war are never kind, eh? But I marvel that an American like your brother was willing to serve the English cause."

*"Madame,"* insisted Jeremiah tersely. "Marrying me made her American, too, but my wife's English-born, same as her brother was."

"Of course, of course. So simple, eh?" With a little nod, Delafosse at last took the packet of papers from Jeremiah. Though he scanned the bills of lading and customs quickly, he lingered on the altered *Raleigh*'s certificate of ownership, tipping the sheet up to the sunlight.

"Everything in order, Lieutenant?" asked Jeremiah, anxiety making him testy. The longer the Frenchman fidgeted with the certificate, the more likely he was going to question it. "This wind's in our favor, and we've hauled too long enough."

"Patience, *monsieur,* patience. I must be able to satisfy my captain, as well as myself, that your affairs are as they should be." The wind thumping through the furled sails overhead was the only sound on the deck as Delafosse studied the paper more closely and Jeremiah held his breath. He'd used Bertle's own ink to change the sloop's origin, and to his eye the addition was indistinguishable. "It is most curious to me, *monsieur,* how when establishing colonies in your land the English so often chose to give names of their old towns to the new ones. There is no Paris or Marseilles in New France, yet here we have a Portsmouth in America, doubtless named for the Portsmouth in England." Delafosse ran his fingertip lightly over the town's name. "Your Portsmouth is in Rhode Island, is it not? Near to your capital city of Providence?"

Jeremiah answered warily. It was unusual for any European to know Rhode Island was a state, let alone the name of its capital, and he worried that perhaps, somehow, with this particular Frenchman, he'd been too clever. "Aye, it's in Rhode Island, but closer to Newport than to Providence."

"Ah, my confusion!" The Frenchman's dark eyes watched Jeremiah closely, ready for weakness. "But it is Portsmouth, is it not, that is home to that most excellent library of one of your citizens, a Monsieur Abraham Redwood?"

"That is Newport, too, Lieutenant." In return, Jeremiah studied Delafosse shrewdly. "As you know well enough yourself."

"Am I so obvious, then?" The Frenchman smiled wryly and refolded the papers for Jeremiah. "I was stationed in Newport with General Rochambeau during your country's war for independence. Though I was no more than a boy at the time, of course, I remember Rhode Island and its people with great affection and regard."

Jeremiah tucked the leather packet beneath his arm. "But still you'd question my word and test me?"

Delafosse shrugged. "A lying *Anglais* would not know of Mr. Redwood's library. I wanted to be sure. Your sloop would have made an excellent prize." Once again he glanced over the *Raleigh,* this time with obvious regret, and motioned for his men to return to the boat. *"Bonsoir, monsieur, madame, et bon voyage!"*

They were barely over the side before Caro's arms were around Jeremiah's neck. Giddy with relief, she giggled and hugged him tightly.

"I told you you'd fool them!" she exclaimed gleefully as she tossed the veil back from her face. Balancing on tiptoe, she darted up and kissed him quickly, retreating before he could kiss her back. "You were perfect, Jeremiah. No, you were better than perfect, and so vastly clever, too, to know all about those places in Rhode Island!"

"It's my home, Caro," he said, steadying her with his hands around her waist. "I should know about it. But your own performance wasn't so bad, either."

"Oh, pooh, I didn't do anything compared to you," she scoffed. She didn't dare kiss him again, but she couldn't resist laying her hand gently on his rough cheek for a moment. "But at least this time I won't have gotten the magistrate to put a price on your head."

He scowled dramatically. He wasn't ordinarily playful by nature—far from it—but Caro like this was hard to resist. "I should be thankful, then, for small graces."

"I'd call them quite large." She thumped his chest with her fist. "Who wants to be locked up in some dreary French prison?"

He grinned, letting himself enjoy the rare sensation of unexpected happiness. It had been like this before when they'd done something bold together, the camaraderie of a shared adventure bringing them close. He had been trying so hard these past weeks not to look at her in any way that might be misconstrued that now, in this moment when it didn't seem to matter, he drank in her beauty as if he'd never have enough.

Little gold tendrils escaped from the brim of the severe black bonnet, matching the pale gold of her lashes. Despite her bonnet and veil, the sun off the water had scattered more freckles across her nose and cheeks that, to his satisfaction, she didn't bother trying to hide with paint or powder. But most of all she looked happy, blissfully, joyfully happy in a way that he was sure must mirror his own feelings, even if each of them knew it could not last.

With the crew hurrying to get the sloop under way and Bertle once again the captain, they stood alone in the center of the quarterdeck, a two-person island of idleness in the rush of preparation. For the first time on the voyage, Jeremiah didn't mind being a passenger. How could he, with Caro once again in his arms and her laughter rippling merrily across the water?

"You seem to have routed them Frenchmen well enough, Sparhawk," said Bertle sourly behind them, and swiftly Caro separated herself from Jeremiah. "I suppose now I must thank you."

"Only if you wish it, Captain," said Jeremiah, determined not to let this one disagreeable man spoil his mood. "I saved my wife and myself, as well, so I wasn't being entirely selfless."

Bertle spat over the side. "It's how you did it rankles me. All that bowing and scraping and pretty talk to that Frenchman! I never thought I'd live to see a bloody French bastard treated so nice on my deck."

"You kept your deck, didn't you?" demanded Jeremiah.

Bertle grunted, unconvinced. "Seems to have improved your wife's spirits, though, didn't it? Seems like by being all lovey-dovey with the Frenchman, she's forgotten clear about her poor dead brother, and mighty fast, too, for an Englishwoman."

Caro gasped, her hand fluttering to her mouth, and retreated behind Jeremiah's broad back. He'd seen the agitation in her face, and whether it came from fear or surprise, he wasn't going to let the other captain's rudeness pass any longer.

"You've upset my wife," he demanded, his expression black. "What are you trying to say, anyway?"

"Not a word, Sparhawk," said Bertle, his grizzled chin still raised belligerently and his eyes filled with hatred. "Not against you or your little French-speaking *wife*. Not a blessed word."

He stalked to the rail before Jeremiah could speak again. Shaken, Caro watched him go, her hand pressed to Jeremiah's back for comfort. She'd heard the emphasis Bertle had put on the word "wife." Somehow, he knew the truth, most likely through her own carelessness. Rapidly she thought back on how she'd teased and laughed with Jeremiah here on the deck. No one would have believed they were husband and wife, not acting like that. Only lovers would be so oblivious to others around them. If even a dried-up old stick of a man like Captain Bertle could see it, then he'd know what to call her, too, a married woman who'd behave like that with a man she pretended was her husband—a slattern, a trollop, a bold-faced little whore. . . .

"I'm going below to the cabin," she told Jeremiah, and turned toward the companionway.

But Bertle had heard her, too, and he jerked around to face her. "Didn't mean to scare you off, Mrs. Sparhawk," he called, almost whining, as much an apology as he'd probably ever give. "Didn't mean for you to take offense."

She didn't believe him. She'd seen his kind of contempt all too often. "I'm weary, Captain Bertle, and should like to rest."

His glance darted nervously from her to Jeremiah, and he rubbed his hand across his mouth. "It would be a shame, Mrs. Sparhawk, for you to spend such a pretty afternoon tucked away below."

She hesitated, looking up to Jeremiah for reassurance. His mouth was tight, the expression in his eyes so daunting that she knew if Bertle made one comment against her Jeremiah would tear him apart. She didn't want that to happen, any more than she wanted to admit that the English captain *had* driven her away, and so, with some reluctance, she stayed.

Bertle had drawn his pipe from his pocket and he stood puffing away as he struggled to light it, his hands cupped to shield the spark from the wind and spray. "You ever been to Naples, Mrs. Sparhawk?" he said at last, the stem of the pipe clenched tight in the corner of his mouth. "Kind of a fairy-tale place, what with that crazy mountain shooting fire all the time. A volcano, they call it. Not that you'd ever find me living in a spot like that."

She glanced at Jeremiah again, praying that she might be able to repair some of the damage she'd caused. "I've heard—that is, my husband has told me—that the city is a most pleasant place for English-speaking visitors. That is why he has brought me here."

"It's a most fine place for mischief, if you ask me." Bertle drew on the pipe hard and stared purposefully down at the bowl, and as if by his command the sparks flared brighter, even in the sunlight. "Look at the sorry goings-on there! Do you think as fine a gentleman as our Lord Nelson would have gone astray like he did on English soil?"

He narrowed his eyes at her over the pipe, and she felt herself grow pale. She knew what was coming next, saw it like her own fate before her, and still she was unable to make herself leave before she heard it. God help her, somehow this wretched man knew *everything!*

"It was all that wicked, trollopy Lady Hamilton's fault, that and the volcano. She just had to dance for him like she was back in the brothel, and poor Lord Nelson came arunning with his breeches already unbuttoned. Two marriages that woman's broken, and for what?" Bertle nodded sagely and shifted his gaze to Jeremiah. "A trollopy woman and a volcano— nothing good will ever come of either one or t'other."

And with a strangled little cry, Caro turned and ran.

# Chapter Eleven

"Caro!" Jeremiah called her name again as he rushed after her, but she didn't stop, bunching her skirts in one hand so she could run down the steps of the companionway. A lifetime at sea gave him an agility she'd never have, and bracing himself on the rails, he dropped down the narrow companionway without touching a single step, to her side on the deck below. "Caro, wait!"

Still she plunged on, heedless, with her head down, ignoring him, until he grabbed her arm. Briefly she fought him, still trying to pull free. Then, abruptly, she turned to face him, yanking the bonnet with the trailing veil from her head.

"Why did you follow me?" she demanded, her eyes wild. "Aren't you afraid that I'll tempt and torture you, too, just like Lady Hamilton did?"

He pushed her gently back against the bulkhead, trapping her there with his body so she couldn't run again. Sunlight filtered through the grating of the hatch overhead, a checkerboard across her face like another, coarser veil. "If you've tempted me, it has nothing to do with volcanoes, or the indiscretions of some lords and ladies."

She stared at him and slowly shook her head, her smile incredulous. "You don't know what he meant, do you? Because you're American, you really don't know?"

"I know that weaselly little bastard managed to insult us both."

"It was more than that, Jeremiah. Much more." With a sigh, she slid wearily down the bulkhead to sit on the deck, her knees drawn up and her bonnet in her hand.

He crouched down before her. "How much more can there be, sweetheart?"

"Oh, there's more." To avoid meeting his eyes, she concentrated on the bonnet in her hands, touching the curving brim now stained white with salt spray and faded by the sun, and drawing the sheer veiling out between her fingers. "It's not the first time I've heard of Lady Hamilton's . . . *career,* though Captain Bertle is the first who's dared to say so to my face. Most others have preferred to whisper it behind their fans, taking care, of course, that their words were loud enough for me to hear."

She stopped, her head bent over her knees. He waited patiently, leaving it to her to tell him as he silently damned all the cruel, worthless gossips who'd made her life miserable.

Carefully, she smoothed the veiling over her knees, her voice detached. "Lady Hamilton and I are much alike, you see. She too was born quite common, and improved herself in the eyes of the world by marrying an older nobleman, Sir William Hamilton, who was kind to her."

"Whatever else you are, Caro," said Jeremiah softly, taking her hand in his, stilling her chilly, restless fingers. "You're most uncommon."

"You say that only because you're American." Her smile was fleeting, bittersweet. "The Hamiltons' marriage was scandal enough, no matter that Lady Hamilton devoted herself to Sir William and his position as the English ambassador. But then Admiral Lord Nelson sailed to Naples to save the king and queen from General Bonaparte, and he and Lady Hamilton fell in love."

She wove her fingers into Jeremiah's, searching for strength in his large, work-scarred hand. "They weren't—aren't—terribly discreet, for he keeps her now in a house outside of London. They can never marry, of course, for both of them are married to others, and some say Lord Nelson's career with the navy is quite ruined because of her. Sir William is sick near to death with a broken heart, and she—she will never be received again by anyone."

Jeremiah swore, his fingers tightening around hers. "I should have throttled Bertle for saying such things to you," he said angrily. "I had no notion that was what he meant, else I never would have let it pass."

Her eyes widened with alarm. "No, Jeremiah, you mustn't! No matter what Captain Bertle has said, he is still the master, and if you strike him the others will be on you in a moment. Let it go, I beg you. We'll be in Naples tomorrow, and I would not have you suffer on my account."

"After what he's called you—"

"No, Jeremiah, it means nothing," she said quickly, though the pain in her face said otherwise. "What worries me more is that somehow Captain Bertle has guessed who I am, or he wouldn't say the things he has."

"But you're blameless, Caro!" The unfairness of it infuriated him. "You've done nothing to be faulted for!"

"Haven't I?" She loved her husband, but she'd fallen in love with another man, and too late she'd learned the difference. Wasn't that sin enough?

She reached out one finger to trace the firm curve of his upper lip, and her eyes filled with tears of sorrow and longing. What would her life have been if she'd met him years ago, if somehow fate had sent her Jeremiah Sparhawk in place of Frederick Moncrief?

"My poor Caro," he whispered against her fingertips, kissing them lightly. "My poor, darling Caro."

Even as she told herself she shouldn't, she let herself lean forward into the waiting sanctuary of Jeremiah's arms. When he drew her across his legs, she sighed and nestled closer, pillowing her head in the hollow below his shoulder as he held her. Beneath her ear his heartbeat was steady and strong, and she closed her eyes to let the sound fill her.

"Whatever Captain Bertle says, I'm not really so much like Lady Hamilton," she said softly. "Why, I wonder? Is she that much bolder, more wicked, more wanton, more foolhardy than I could ever be? Or simply that she's happier, because she dared to follow her heart, no matter what the cost?"

Tears stung her eyelids, and she buried her face against his waistcoat. "I don't know, Jeremiah," she said, her voice fracturing as her heart broke. "I don't know, and now I never will."

The wind fell off that night, and despite their expectations, the *Raleigh* did not enter the wide, curving arms of the Bay of Naples until dawn of the following day.

"It is lovely, isn't it?" said Caro to Jeremiah as they stood on the deck. Washed in the rosy light of the rising sun, the castles and villas and pastel houses with their terra-cotta roofs and hanging gardens looked more like a painting from some artist's imagination. "Not quite real, somehow, at least not by English standards."

"Judge the world by English standards and you're bound to be disappointed," he scoffed, but without much bite to his criticism. "It will all be real enough when you're there in the middle of it. From here it's a pretty spot, but behind those gardens are more starving beggars than you'd ever dream could survive."

He had walked the deck the night through instead of sleeping, and instead, too, of being tormented by knowing she lay above him, always beyond his reach. He was sure she hadn't slept, either, no matter how still she lay when he'd finally returned to the cabin. Accomplished as she was at acting, she wasn't good enough to cover feelings that deep.

He pointed across to starboard. "There—that's Bertle's famous volcano."

"Don't you feel threatened?" she asked lightly. Misted by clouds of steam near its peak, Vesuvius this morning looked no more threatening than she felt herself. "Tottering on the edge of disaster with me by your side and a volcano before you?"

He cleared his throat. "The only disaster will be when you're no longer at my side."

"You shouldn't say such things," she said quickly. She looked up to find his green eyes watching her so intently that she blushed, and he smiled wryly.

"Am I that bad at speaking gallantry?"

"If you're that bad at speaking like a fashionable gentleman," she said, her voice too brittle for the banter she was attempting, "then I am even worse at listening. I don't, you see. I make that most grievous mistake for a lady of actually answering when I'm addressed. Frederick quite despairs of me."

He was touched by the way she was trying so hard to be brave, and how wretchedly she was failing. What had passed between them on this voyage would end here in Naples, and he drew her protectively into the crook of his arm, keeping her to himself just a little longer. Instead of a bonnet, she wore a dark cashmere shawl draped over her head and shoulders, for the chill of night was still in the air, and he liked the feel of the cashmere, soft, like her.

"Don't change, Caro," he said softly. "Whatever happens, I wouldn't want you to be any different than what you are now."

Quickly she looked back at the city, determined not to slide again into the treacherous quicksand of emotions and loyalties. She would be lighthearted, the way she once had been with him; she would be independent and levelheaded. She had never been a weepy woman, and she saw no useful reason to become one now.

"There are so many English in Naples," she said, striving for self-control by changing the subject, "that I don't doubt that we'll find some sort of decent inn for lodgings. Once we're situated, I shall dress and call on her ladyship this afternoon. Not even she can refuse to see me after I've come so far."

"You won't be staying with her?" asked Jeremiah with surprise. "Whatever your differences, she's your kin."

"Only by a marriage she doesn't recognize." She had dressed swiftly, without her gloves, and without thinking, she looked down at her wedding ring, an oval ruby in a ring of pearls. "You remember that was Frederick's reason for coming to her in the first place. He would still be safe at home in England if it weren't for me. I've no notion at all of what my reception will be at his mother's villa."

"Then I'll come with you," said Jeremiah promptly. "I won't let you face that old bitch alone."

Though touched by his offer, she shook her head, her expression wistful. "I can't take you, Jeremiah. You don't belong there."

"Why not? I've reason enough. I want to know what's happened to Davy just as you're looking for Frederick."

"Not this first time," she said as she drew the shawl up higher around her face. More pointedly than she realized, she eased herself free of Jeremiah's arm, already making the break from him. "For Frederick's sake and my own, too, I've no choice but to meet his mother alone."

She'd give the brazen little chit credit for courage, decided Dorinda, Dowager Countess of Byfield. But nothing more than that, not if she could help it, and certainly not another penny of her son's fortune.

Dorinda let her stand, Frederick's whore of a wife, the better to consider what her real place was, while Dorinda herself sat at the far end of the room in the gilded Venetian armchair with the ice blue damask cushions. If the creature was reminded of a throne, so much the better.

"I said come forward, girl, so that I might see you," said Dorinda, her voice echoing in the gallery's arched ceiling. One wall was windows, all now thrown open to catch the breezes from the bay, while the opposite wall was mirrored from the floor upward so no visitor need turn their back on the magnificent view. "If you've come this far from Blackstone, another few paces won't hurt."

At last the younger woman came toward her, her kid slippers making no sound on the polished marble parquet. Grudgingly Dorinda admitted to herself that Frederick had at least chosen a girl who looked like a countess, her silver-blond head held high and her walk a fashionable glide, her white Indian cotton dress drifting around her legs. Her face was lovely, fine boned but distinctive enough to be an original, with a inborn charm that no amount of paint or trickery could create.

No wonder Frederick had been so besotted, and no wonder, too, this wife of his had been so quick to replace him in her bed. His *wife,* considered Dorinda bitterly, and then let her thoughts travel to her grandson's letter, hidden in the lacquer box on the mantel, and of the greedy man who'd brought it this same afternoon. Who would have guessed so much would fall into Dorinda's favor when, months ago, she'd written the first letter to that idiot, George? If even a fraction of what they said of this Caroline was true, then at last Dorinda could avenge the wrong that had been done the Moncriefs.

And to her. Most especially to her.

"Come closer, girl, so I can see you properly," she ordered, beckoning sharply with her gnarled forefinger, the large square-cut diamond on it glittering in the sunlight. "I'm not a young woman any longer."

Not a young woman, thought Caro, but certainly still a vain one, with cheeks and lips painted bright rose and her deep-set eyes lined with black kohl. The dowager countess was a tiny woman, and though shrunk and bent with age, she was dressed in a costly variation of the latest *Directoire* fashion, her high-waisted satin gown cut low over her shriveled breasts and on her head an elaborate wig of black corkscrewed curls with a diamond-tipped arrow thrust through the crown. There were more diamonds swaying from her earlobes, around her throat, clasped to her wrists, far more than was considered stylish now but a king's ransom nonetheless, and Caro remembered how many times Frederick had worried that his mother might be wanting and ordered Perkins to increase the dowager countess' allowance.

Critically Dorinda's gaze swept over Caro. "You're not at all what I expected, girl."

"Neither are you, your ladyship." Caro smiled beatifically. She'd been warned by Frederick that his mother could be sharp-tongued, and she was determined not to let the older woman better her. Though they'd never met, in a way they'd already been warring for fifteen years, and though Dorinda might have the diamonds, Caro had Frederick. "And please, call me Caro."

Pointedly Dorinda ignored the request. "Sit, girl."

She motioned to the small taboret beside her own chair, and without protest Caro sat. Another chair would have been more comfortable and more appropriate than the backless stool, but Caro was willing to concede that much. Although there was nothing of Frederick in the old woman's face, little mannerisms—the quirk of her brow, the way she arched her wrist—were disconcertingly his.

With a sweep that was still graceful, Dorinda opened her fan. "I did not expect you to come to me yourself."

"And I wondered if you would receive me when I did," answered Caro. "But when you wrote to me that you had proof that my husband still lives, how could I not come?"

"It is a great distance for a lady to travel."

Attuned to such subtleties, Caro didn't miss the scornful emphasis on that *lady*. "I would travel any distance for Frederick's return."

"But I trust you did not make the journey alone." Dorinda's fan paused as she baited her trap. "No doubt you had a companion to ease your trial."

"I did, yes. An American gentleman who seeks word of other captives was so kind as to agree to accompany me."

The fan remained still, poised. "An American gentleman accompanied you? I would have expected Mr. Perkins, or perhaps dear George."

"They did not offer," said Caro, her cheeks warming in spite of her resolution. It wasn't exactly a lie. They hadn't offered, true, but then she hadn't told them of her plans. And oh, how different that long voyage would have been with either George or Mr. Perkins in place of Jeremiah! "Mr. Sparhawk graciously did, and I accepted."

Dorinda paused, letting the chit consider her own words. According to George, this Sparhawk was no better than a common footpad; in Captain Bertle's opinion, the man was some sort of seafaring adventurer, prone to intemperate violence and treasonous friendships with Frenchmen. Both, without question, believed him to be Caroline's lover.

"This Mr. Sparhawk must be an old and trusted friend to undertake such a journey with you," she said, watching with satisfaction as the little strumpet's blush betrayed the truth. "Perhaps a friend of Frederick's?"

*Damn her cheeks for blushing so!* Consciously Caro willed her hands to keep from twisting in her lap and wished she had the same control over the blood that rushed to her face.

"I have known Mr. Sparhawk only a brief time, but he has always acted with such honor and good grace that I felt my trust would not be misplaced," she said carefully. "Although he is American, his sister is married to Admiral Lord John Herendon."

"Ah, Britain's own pretty Lord Jack," purred Dorinda, remembering when Herendon, then a frigate captain, had been stationed with the other English ships in the bay. She had met him at the palace and found him much to her liking, tall and gold-haired like a Grecian god, and so much more like a hero than that poor bedraggled little Lord Nelson. Forty years ago, thought Dorinda nostalgically, no, even thirty, and she would have made a conquest of Lord Jack.

But for this man Sparhawk to be connected to the Herendons put a whole different coloring on Caroline's infidelity. Jack Herendon would have married a beauty, and her brother would doubtless be comely, too, and young. Trust both George and Bertle not to tell her what would matter most to a woman!

"Are they of a piece then, this Mr. Sparhawk and Lord Jack?" she asked archly. "Certainly any lady would wish for a man of Lord Jack's courage on a voyage in these uncertain times."

"No, they are not very similar at all," said Caro, imagining the two men side by side. "Jeremiah is taller than Jack, broader, with dark hair and green eyes. His life has not been easy, which sometimes makes him melancholy, but when he smiles, he makes one forget everything else, and he is very loyal, willing to fight to defend whatever he believes in."

*Jeremiah.* The way the chit said the name alone was enough to condemn her. Worse, she was so smitten that she didn't even realize her own error, babbling on happily about the man's qualities. Tall, handsome, a touch of melancholia for romance, a man of action and heartbreaking smiles. Oh, yes, thought Dorinda cynically, he was everything a woman could want in a lover, and everything, too, that Frederick—quiet, awkward, gentlemanly Frederick—never would, or could, be. As a woman, Dorinda might envy the creature's good fortune, but as a mother, she could only hate her more for scorning her son.

"Then it sounds as if you have chosen well, Caroline," she said, her smile creasing her paint. "Mr. Sparhawk will need all his strength on the next part of the journey."

"You have word of Frederick, then?" said Caro excitedly, forgetting all her promises to herself to be cool and distant with Frederick's mother. "He is indeed still alive?"

Lying little hypocrite, thought Dorinda angrily. Frederick had been captured for her love, and now the chit repaid his devotion with deceit.

"We can only pray that he is," she said, her voice smooth as cream. "They say the conditions for the prisoners are harsh, and as an English gentleman, Frederick is unaccustomed to deprivation."

Tears filled Caro's eyes at the thought of a man as kind and mild as Frederick suffering so. "Has anyone seen or spoken to him?"

Dorinda shook her head, the stiff black curls bobbing around her cheeks. "No, or any of the American prisoners, either. But my friends among the diplomats at the court assure me that Frederick lives, and is awaiting your assistance."

In fact there had been no such assurances, quite the contrary. The minister who had given her the list of hostages had cautioned that it was most likely a forgery, and that by now, after two years, Lord Byfield was most certainly beyond rescue, even through the efforts of a devoted mother. Dorinda knew he was right, for she had tried before on Frederick's behalf. It had been on that day, her grief for her son still fresh and raw, that Dorinda had written to Caro, summoning her, and to George, to reestablish her link with the future earl. George was a fool, but with him as earl she could return to die with dignity and respect at Blackstone House.

Languidly the fan moved through the warm spring air. Soon, thought Dorinda with grim satisfaction, soon the little bitch with the upturned eyes and handsome American lover would find the fate she'd earned so richly for herself.

"I would, of course, do anything I could for my son," she continued with a sigh, "but I am far too old to enter into such negotiations as will be necessary, or would I trust them to anyone who would not care for Frederick as I do."

"Let me do it, please, I beg you!" said Caro, eagerly leaning forward on her stool with her hands clasped. "I can make all the arrangements and arrange for the ransom. After all, that's why I've come, isn't it?"

Once again Dorinda sighed dramatically. This was almost too easy, without any sport in it. The chit was so gullible, so willing to believe, that it was no wonder that her son, another foolish idealist, would have fallen in love with her.

"Would that it were so easy, dear Caroline! But I fear that it cannot be done from Naples. No, no! The Tunisians are a sly, heathen lot who demand such business be conducted face-to-face. If you wish to help your husband, you must be willing to take your brave American and go to Tripoli, and bring Frederick back to me."

"Then I shall," said Caro without hesitation. Impatiently she rose to her feet, determined to begin planning at once. "Mr. Sparhawk is well acquainted with ships and sailing. I'm sure he can find us passage to Tripoli."

"Let that be my contribution," urged Dorinda, her eyes glinting within the dark rings of kohl. "I know the ways of this city, who to ask and who to bribe. Not even our Mr. Sparhawk will be able to find a vessel bound for Tripoli any faster than I."

Bound for Tripoli, thought Dorinda with a delicious sense of justice, destined for the slave market and a nightmarish, anonymous half life from which Frederick's little whore would never return alive. The lover would be killed; Dorinda would specify that, for the man had done no worse than choose unwisely. It was Frederick's Caro she wished punished. If the silly chit was lucky, she'd be bought for a rich man's harem, bound to serve only one infidel. If she were less so, then she would be the most costly houri in a brothel, drugged and forced to serve whichever man bought her favors.

Even that would be too kind for all she'd done: defiled the Moncrief family with her presence, banished Dorinda from England, sent Frederick to a painful death, degraded his memory with her lover. But it would do, thought Dorinda with satisfaction as Caro smiled with unfeigned joy.

It would do.

"Vesuvius, my lady?" asked the driver, his eager, florid face filling the window of the hired carriage. "The Castel Nuovo? Santa Chiara? The Royal Palace? Or would my lady see the antique statues taken from Pompeii? Very popular they are with the English gentlepeople, my lady."

"Whatever you please," said Caro wearily, burrowing back further into the worn squabs. In her present mood she wanted only silence, not a visitor's itinerary. "It doesn't matter at all to me. Simply drive until nightfall, or until I tell you otherwise."

Though the driver's face fell, he tugged on his forelock and climbed up on the box, ready to do as she requested. As much as he would have liked to show his city to the beautiful Englishwoman, his disappointment was tempered well enough by the fare she'd pay. Until nightfall, she said: *caro mio,* she'd owe him a fortune!

Inside the carriage, Caro closed her eyes and tried to let herself be lulled by the repetitious clip-clop of the horse's hooves and the rasping of the iron-bound wheels against the paving stones. She might as well have been back in Portsmouth for all the famous scenery meant to her. Certainly she would have been happier if she were.

For now she'd been assured that Frederick lived. In a few weeks, maybe even less, she would be reunited with him, and after returning here to Naples to visit his mother as she'd promised, they would sail back home to England. At the same time Jeremiah Sparhawk would redeem his friend, bid her and her husband farewell and leave for America. Most likely she would never see him again, and that was how it should be for a contented, married woman.

But deep inside, she knew she didn't want it to end like that. It was not that she wished ill for Frederick. Her joy for his survival was very real, and the thought of holding him again in her arms was wonderful indeed. But things were different since Frederick had gone away. *She* was different.

God help her, what was she to do?

The carriage passed a garden, and the heady fragrance of full-blown roses filled the carriage. She breathed it deeply, remembering.

*Another June, long ago, and she had held roses in her trembling hands when she stood beside Frederick in the chilly chapel at Blackstone. There had been no guests and only two witnesses—Mr. Perkins and the housekeeper—and the anxious young curate who owed his living to the Moncriefs had stumbled over the words of the service. Afterward she had signed her name after Frederick's in the register, prouder of the elegant penmanship she'd only recently mastered than of the new name and title she had written.*

There had been more roses in the earl's bedchamber, on the mantel in tall porcelain vases, on the desk, on the little tables beside the bed, and when Caro had drawn back the coverlet she'd discovered hundreds of rose petals scattered over the sheets, deep, velvety red against the white linen. With her long hair combed about her shoulders she had waited for Frederick in the center of his bed, the heavy curtains looped back against the posts, and felt the rose petals tickle against her bare toes as she'd listened to the thumping of her own heart.

Tonight he would truly make her his. Tonight she would do all the things her mother had taught her and please him, her new husband. She was now his by right and by law, and because she loved him she would do it, even as she prayed she would not shame herself and be sick.

At last Frederick had come, in a yellow dressing gown and nightcap, and she had hastily looked away, already embarrassed by the intimacy his dress implied. She had felt the bed shift when he sat on the edge, and her hand had been cold when he'd taken it in his.

"You know before this I have never done anything to hurt you, Caro," he had said gently. "I won't begin now."

Troubled, she had raised her eyes. "But as your wife—"

"I know all about what the world says of old men who take young wives," he said, smiling indulgently. "It's not much different than what is said of old men with young mistresses. What matters more to me in-

*stead is the love we share, pure and unsullied by ani-mal passions. You are in many ways more like a daughter to me than a wife, and like a father I've found great joy in the woman you've become."*

She had shaken her head, confused, and he had lightly pressed his finger to his lips to hold her silence.

*"Innocence like yours is a rare jewel, Caro, beyond any price. You are too young now to know the value of what you have given me today, but I am not, and I rejoice in the gift, however fleeting. Someday, per-haps, you will learn otherwise, and though I shall grieve, I will understand."*

*"But I love you, Frederick!"* she had cried from the depths of her heart. *"I will never love anyone else as much as I love you!"*

*"I love you, too, Caro."* He had kissed her on the forehead, his lips dry as parchment and his dark eyes full of tenderness and sorrow. *"And because I love you, I will understand."*

And now, at last, so did she.

"Pirates?" repeated the one-legged Englishman as he squinted up at Jeremiah. "Oh, aye, guv'nor, we've all manner of rogues here in this little harbor. Pirates, smugglers, corsairs, heathens and rascals of most ev'ry order."

Only half listening, Jeremiah looked over the man's head, across the Neapolitan waterfront to the ram-bling medieval castle that was the royal palace of King Ferdinand IV and his Court of the Two Sicilies, and to the lavish villas on either side that belonged to other aristocrats. Caro would be in one of them now, and he longed to know how she was faring with the dowager countess. Damnation, he should have insisted on going with her! She'd only been away from him for an hour at most, and already he missed her more than he'd ever thought possible. He picked up a stone and skipped it across the water, trying to concentrate instead on what the beggar was saying.

" 'Twas better when the fleet was here, of course," said the man, hopping after Jeremiah on his crutches. "Lord Nelson, well now, he wouldn't tolerate that sort of offal in his waters."

"Left behind here, were you?" asked Jeremiah, eyeing the stump of the man's leg and his tattered clothing. The English navy was notorious for ignoring its veterans and abandoning those who were too ill or wounded to serve.

"Aye, lost me leg in the service, but here I've a new wife and a new life and it never snows in Naples, so I don't be complainin'." The man winked broadly, contented enough even though he'd been whining for coins and tobacco when he'd accosted Jeremiah. "But as for the pirates, King Ferdy, well now, he'd jes' as soon wink as look the other way."

The man lowered his voice, confidential. "Are you lookin' for a berth yourself, guv'nor? Hopin' to make a quick fortune on the other side? If you is, I've got mates who—"

"All I'm interested in is information." Jeremiah flipped a guinea to the man, who caught it deftly in his palm. "I have a friend who's a prisoner in Tripoli, and

I mean to get him out. Taken by a thieving Scotsman who's renamed himself Hamil Al-Ameer.''

"Andrew Gordon, y'mean.'' The beggar tapped his nose. "He's a clever one, is Gordon, signin' over to the heathens that way. He chants their mumbo jumbo, takes a new name, and just like that, he's one of them, preying on Christians like he weren't born one his own self.''

"I know," said Jeremiah curtly. "Does he ever drop anchor here?''

The beggar shrugged, his shoulders propped high on his crutches. "Don't doubt but that he has, but I can't say when or for how long. You'll have t' go t' him in Tripoli if you want t' ransom your man. Lives fine as a lord there, they say. But even then don't expect much from Hamil. He hates Englishmen, an' he's just as like to take your ransom money and slit your throat as smile at you.''

All too easily Jeremiah remembered the feel of Hamil's blade pressing into his throat. Would Caro's husband have felt it, too, as it eased him into death? "Then it's a good thing I'm American, not English.''

"You're a Yankee, guv'nor?'' The man's eyes lit merrily. "You been deep water sailing, and not heard the news?''

"I'm arrived this day from Portsmouth, aye,'' said Jeremiah uneasily. "What news?''

"Why, news o' the wars, of course! The big one's France and England settin' to it again, with the Peace all blown to bits like tinder to a powder keg.''

"That one was brewing when we cleared the channel,'' said Jeremiah. "I knew the Peace had broken, for we were chased and boarded by a French frigate not two days from here.''

''But do you know what the Pasha o' Tripoli up an' done?'' said the beggar eagerly, grinning with anticipation to tell his story. ''Let that Yankee frigate *Philadelphia* run aground on his doorstep an' then calls it his, jus' like that, an' now your country an' his are at war, too.''

''At war?'' repeated Jeremiah, stunned, his thoughts immediately flying to Davy. ''America and Tripoli are at war?''

The beggar nodded dramatically, relishing the moment. ''True enough, guv'nor. What reason would I have for lyin', eh? You can jus' forget your ransom an' redeemin' your friend an' chattin' all cozylike with Hamil Al-Ameer. There's no Yankees goin' into Tripoli, an' even fewer comin' out, an' that's God's own truth.''

# Chapter Twelve

**W**hen he returned to the inn, Jeremiah ordered supper for two, then went to his room to change and shave. Because of Caro's uncertain relationship with her mother-in-law here in Naples, she had swiftly agreed to end their disguise as husband and wife, and take separate rooms. Perhaps too swiftly, thought Jeremiah gloomily as he scraped the razor across his jaw. Although he knew he had no real hold on her, he could feel her putting distance between them, preparing herself to rejoin her husband.

He'd known from the beginning that it would be this way. All too well he remembered sending her on her way that first night, how determined he'd been not to involve himself with a married woman, despite how lovely or lonely she might appear. Too bad for them both that he hadn't kept to his resolve.

Wiping a cloth across his face, he stood at the open window. Like nearly every building in Naples, the inn had a clear view of the bay, and in the setting sun Capri and the other, smaller islands were tipped rosy red against the deepening blue water. Cutting in and out among the islands were the striped sails of the last fishing boats straggling home, while fishermen who'd returned earlier and their wives spread their nets on the beach to dry.

Closer to the inn, a woman sang to herself, her language unknown to Jeremiah but the sadness in her song a match to his own mood. A vine with white, trumpet-shaped flowers framed the window, the tendrils weaving in and out of the red shutters and the heady fragrance of the blossoms more intense with the end of the day.

Caro, with her open, eager enthusiasm and delight in anything new or beautiful, would have loved the scene spread before him. Through her eyes he had once again come to appreciate life in a way he'd forgotten, and he hated how she wasn't here now to enjoy this.

He turned his back to the window and reached for his shirt, sliding it over his head. Tonight he would tell her nothing of what he'd learned at the waterfront, not only from the English beggar but from the port's officials, as well. Tomorrow would be soon enough for her to learn how the odds against their mission had increased. For Davy's sake and her husband's, he still meant to go to Tripoli, but now he could no longer offer any assurances that he'd return himself. With a sigh he pulled on his coat and went downstairs to wait for her.

The inn was owned by an Englishman married to a Neapolitan woman, and the establishment was a curious blend of the two cultures. While the rows of hanging pewter mugs and the keg of rum behind the grated bar in the common room could have been found in any shire, there were also little portraits of sad-eyed saints tucked into odd corners near the hearth, and the rich, spicy smells that wafted from the kitchen had no equivalent in an English cook's sturdy repertoire.

Jeremiah found an empty chair near the window, choosing the comfort of familiar rum and water over the house's customary red wine. Impatiently, he ran his fingers back through his hair, glancing down the street in the direction Caro's hired coach had gone. She was late. She'd sworn she would return by five, and by his pocket watch it was half-past.

"Has Lady Byfield sent word for me?" he asked the innkeeper's daughter as she refilled his tankard from a sweating crockery pitcher. "That she's been detained, or some such?"

"The English lady what came with you, sir?" asked the girl, and Jeremiah nodded. "No, nary a word, sir. But if she does, I'll be certain to bring it to you at once."

"Thank you." He swirled the rum in his tankard, no longer interested in drinking. Alone he watched the shadows lengthen and merge into dusk and then darkness, punctuated here and there by the wavering flame of a linkboy.

Perhaps, he thought morosely, she would choose to end it like this. She would patch things up with the old countess, become her guest in the villa, send a servant to bring a scribbled note of regret for him and collect her things. At least he would leave knowing she'd be safe here in Naples.

"Here, sir, for you." The girl bobbed her curtsy as she held the folded note out to him, and he snatched it from her hand. "The lady came in by the back stairs, sir, not wanting to cause a fuss on account of the hour."

The seal was hers, the Byfield crest, and in an instant he had cracked it and scanned the short note within.

> My Dearest Capn.: Forgive me I would be most poor pitiful company tonight the Morn will serve us Both better anon.
>
>                              Yrs. C.

"How long ago did she return?" he asked, tracing his fingers over the raised crest.

"Not long, sir, a quarter of the hour. Would you like me to take a reply back up to her?"

"No," he said with a sigh. "No reply."

Poor, pitiful company, indeed, he thought. Well, if he chose not to share his afternoon with her, then she was equally entitled to keep hers to herself, too. But still he wished she'd come.

"Will the lady be joining you, sir?" asked the serving girl timidly. "Should I fetch out your supper now?"

"No, lass, on both counts. I find I'm no longer hungry, and neither is the lady." He emptied the tankard and slowly headed back upstairs, taking a candlestick from the barkeep to light his way.

Searching for his key in his coat pocket, he noticed the strip of light shining from beneath his door and frowned. He knew he hadn't kept a light burning when he'd left; besides, by now, any candle would have guttered itself out. Instinctively he drew the knife he always carried, and hung back to one side as he shoved the door open with his foot.

"Jeremiah?" called Caro warily.

"Caro?" Feeling foolish, he quickly tucked the knife away as he came into the room and set his candlestick on the mantel. "What in blazes are you doing here?"

"I was lonely," she said. She was sitting on the bench near the window with her feet tucked up and her arms hugging her knees, her pale hair bright by the light of the single candle. Behind her the sky was full of stars, and the sliver of new moon was doubled in the bay. If he'd found the view beautiful earlier, now, with her in it, he found it downright magical.

She rested her chin on her knees, watching him. "Aren't you going to ask again how I got into your room?"

He shook his head. "This is Naples, not my sister's house. From the king on down, no one's expected to behave with any sort of propriety. Most likely you have to bribe the servants here to be able to keep to your own room."

She laughed. "Then I should have kept my money."

"I like the surprise, anyway," he said, shrugging off first his coat and next his waistcoat, tossing both onto his sea chest, followed by his neck cloth and his shoes and stockings. The room was warm, and like most sailors he felt more comfortable barefoot and with less clothing. After the weeks together in the tiny cabin, such casual familiarity before Caro seemed automatic. And yet because they now were in a bedchamber in an inn, an inn in Naples, he was aware of a new tension between them, a charged undercurrent swirling around them both. "And I was feeling a bit lonely, too."

She smiled, thinking how he never would have made such an admission on that first night. She liked watching him move about the room, even his simplest gestures lithe and spare. He was so handsome, she thought with a little catch in her breathing, and she loved him so much, that what she was doing couldn't possibly be wrong.

"I'm sorry about supper," she said softly. "But I wanted to see you alone."

She rose from the bench, and he stared. He couldn't help it. She wore a dressing gown of deep blue silk, nearly the same color as the night sky behind her, that draped and slipped around her in rich, shimmering folds. Where the dressing gown fell open in front, he could see that she wore a night shift of palest blue, the linen so fine as to be almost transparent across the darker tips of her breasts and the shadowy triangle at the top of her thighs.

"You never wore that aboard the *Raleigh*," he said, his voice low. He had never seen her in any color before save white or black. Hell, he'd never seen any woman dressed like this, tempting as sin itself, and he felt the temperature in the room rise another ten degrees.

"That's because I bought it this afternoon." The way he was watching her, his green eyes half-closed, made her shiver with anticipation. Before Jeremiah, she had found that raw, hungry look in men's eyes disturbing, even frightening, but with him she felt only excitement. "The shops in Naples, it seems, respect the local sense of propriety."

"Or lack of it. You couldn't find anything like that in Providence."

"Nor in Portsmouth, either." She smiled shyly, daring to ask the question she knew was rhetorical. "You like it, then?"

"Oh, aye, I like it. I like it very much." What the devil had that old woman said to her this afternoon? This time, there was absolutely no mistaking Caro's intentions, and he found himself torn between wanting her with an intense desire that was almost painful, and the knowledge that to take her would be wrong, dreadfully, disastrously wrong for them both.

She lifted her arms to smooth her hair back from her forehead, her breasts thrusting upward through the sheer fabric, and he felt his whole body tighten in response. If he didn't speak up soon, he wouldn't be able to.

He forced himself to raise his gaze to her face. "Caro, sweet, listen to me. Tomorrow I'm leaving for Tripoli to try to find Davy and Frederick."

"I know." Her eyes were luminous, deep blue like the silk in the candlelight. "That is why—"

"No, lass, hear me out. The pasha there has declared war on America, and though that won't stop me, it will make things damned difficult."

In spite of his resolve, he reached out to her, tenderly cradling her jaw in the palm of his hand. "The odds aren't smiling on us, Caro. The Barbary corsairs don't follow the usual rules of war for prisoners, and the one that has Davy and your husband is the worst of the lot. He could have killed them both already, sweet.''

She shook her head vigorously, her unbound hair swinging across his wrist. ''Lady Byfield says they're alive. She's had word through the envoys that all the prisoners on the list still live!''

''Pray she's right, Caro.'' He traced little circles on her cheek with his thumb, marveling as he always did at the softness of her skin. ''Then pray for me, too.''

''Why are you telling me this?''

''Because when I'm gone, sweetheart, I want you to remember the moonlight and the stars and the fishing boats with striped sails,'' he said tenderly. ''I don't want you to regret a blessed thing.''

Her smile was unexpectedly bittersweet. ''My whole life is too full of regret already. If I left you now, I would never forgive myself for what I had missed.''

''Be sure, Caro,'' he warned, knowing that this time there would be no turning back for either of them. ''Be very sure.''

She nodded, almost afraid to meet his gaze. Briefly her courage faltered. What if he said no? What if he dismissed her, or worse yet, laughed in her face? But she wanted more memories of Naples than moonlight and fishing boats. She needed this night with him to keep her warm through the lifetime of emptiness that remained before her at Blackstone House.

''You and I are always pretending we're what we're not, aren't we, Jeremiah?'' she said, hesitancy and daring mingled in her voice. "But tonight I would pretend one more time with you. I will be your Caro, yours alone. I will be innocent again, the girl I once was, untouched by any man except for you."

His eyes narrowed as he listened, lingering over her lush, rounded body in the blue silk, a woman's body, not that of an untried girl. Yet the game intrigued him, outlandish as it was; to pretend she was still a virgin was to make her husband and her marriage magically vanish. If this was what it would take to ease her guilt, than so be it. He wanted her too much to care any longer. Besides, the idea of being her first lover, even as a game, was enough to make his body quicken with growing interest.

"And what role am I to play in this, eh, sweetheart?" he asked, his voice low and intensely male. "A highwayman again, come to rob you of your virtue?"

"Oh, no, Jeremiah," she whispered breathlessly, realizing he was agreeing. "You must be yourself."

"Easy enough." He slid his hand back along her jaw to bury his fingers in the silvery silk of her hair. She let her head fall back, luxuriating in the pressure of his hand on the back of her neck, and unconsciously her lips parted, red, full, waiting for his.

He kissed her gently at first, his lips barely brushing against hers, sensitizing them enough to make her sigh with delight. Her hands slid down his shoulders, her fingers digging deep into the muscles as impatiently she pulled him closer.

"Don't be in such a rush, sweetheart," he whispered. "By my reckoning, we've all night before us."

Her hands stilled, her eyes so large with uncertainty that he chuckled. She was as good at this ruse as she'd been at all the other bits of playacting he'd seen from her. Maybe better. He could almost believe she'd never done any of this before.

Lightly he touched his finger to her lower lip, moist from his. "I'm not telling you to stop, Caro. I'm only reminding you that the journey can be every bit as fine as the destination."

She smiled tremulously and he lowered his mouth to hers again, dipping deeper to savor her sweetness. His tongue met hers, coaxing and caressing as he urged her to join him. She shifted closer to him, seeking more, and he gathered her into his arms, reminded again of how soft and willing she was to hold as his lips moved from hers to the little hollow beneath her ear.

Her laugh of sheer pleasure was almost girlish. "Come back," she ordered softly. "You taste too good to let go."

"It's only the rum," he murmured, taking his time to reach her lips again. "Middling rum at that, just like you'd taste on any other sailor."

"No one's like you," she whispered vehemently. "My own Jeremiah."

He had never belonged to anyone, and he was surprised by how deeply her words touched him. Was it only part of the game, he wondered, protecting himself against the pain of feeling too much, or did she really wish to be his alone, if only for this night?

When he kissed her now, he forgot about teasing and coaxing. Now he wanted to make her his in the one way he knew how, to possess her and mark her in a primal male way, and his mouth moved relentlessly across hers. He knew from the way she opened to him, drawing him deeper still, responding with the heat he remembered so well, that she felt the same need, moving against him with an urgent abandon that only inflamed him more. They had both waited so long for this.

Ruthlessly he pushed the dressing gown off her shoulders and down her arms, and he felt her shiver as the silk slid across her skin like another caress. The shift beneath was even more insubstantial than he'd first thought, held together only by tiny ribbons at the shoulders above her bare arms. The sheer linen was no more than a mist across her body, tantalizing him with how much it simultaneously revealed yet covered, and he felt his body, already aroused, grow hotter still.

Yet, though her face was flushed with excitement, her lips swollen from his kisses, there was an uncertainty in her eyes close to alarm. The game, he reminded himself, of course, it was part of the game, and he tried to tamp down the rising fire in his blood.

"Forgive me if I frightened you, sweetheart," he said gently, touching only her cheek to reassure her. "God knows I'd never want to hurt you."

"I know that," she said softly, her trust so touchingly genuine that it wrenched at his heart, "and you won't."

She turned her face into his hand to brush her lips across his palm, her eyes remaining turned toward his, their expression suddenly impish. "But it isn't fair that you are still so . . . covered."

Wryly he looked down at his shirt and breeches. "I'm afraid I haven't anything in my sea chest to match that shift."

"I'd rather see you," she whispered, her voice husky with shy suggestion.

He grinned wickedly and cocked one skeptical black eyebrow as he yanked his shirttails free of his breeches. "I don't think a modest young maid would want to see a naked man quite this soon."

"This one would." She took his wrist to unbutton the cuff of his shirt, the color of her cheeks stained darker despite her assurance. She stepped away as he drew the shirt over his head, tossing it carelessly across the back of a chair, and shook his thick, black hair back from his forehead. She swallowed as he unbuttoned the fall of his breeches, painfully aware of how he watched her face for her reaction.

And by the light of the two candles, he was well worth watching. A lifetime ago, in her mother's apartments, she had been shown men without their clothing, and she thought she knew what to expect. But Jeremiah was different from those men. Very, very different.

As he stood before her, comfortable with himself and enjoying her scrutiny, his shoulders seemed broader, his waist and hips even more narrow. There was not an ounce of extra fat on him, his body honed to lean muscle and sinew by a hard life. That life had left other marks on him, too, not only in the long, jagged scar across his torso but in a half-dozen older ones, as well. They covered his body, arms, and legs, reminding her again of how lucky he'd been to survive this long—long enough to find her. Finally she let her gaze drop lower, following the tapering path of dark, curling hair from his waist.

"Still not frightened?" God knows she should have been if she truly were the virgin she was pretending to be. Sweet heaven, he'd never wanted a woman as much as he wanted her now, and the proof was unmistakable, hard and throbbing before him.

She shook her head, her face on fire. It was, she knew, far too late to turn back, nor did she want to, but she'd never really considered exactly how large a man he was. Yet at the sight of him, she felt the heat he'd already brought to her blood grow hotter still, her palms damp and her heart quickening with anticipation, her breasts oddly tight and yearning for his touch.

Her reaction, he thought, was almost perfect, and another time he might have been able to laugh about it. Almost perfect, but not quite. No virgin's eyes would have shone so brightly as she faced her own ruin, the flush of desire spread across her throat and breasts. Sweet heaven, he'd never known a woman who responded this freely to him!

"Satisfied?" he asked, the single word rasping with the strain of holding back. "But now, Caro, I'd say you have the advantage of me."

She tipped her head to one side quizzically, not understanding. He reached across the small distance between them to untie the little bow on her left shoulder. Her eyes widened but she didn't flinch as the soft fabric slipped from her shoulder, stopping just above the swelling curve of her breast.

"Better," he murmured, "but there's better still."

His fingers trembling, he slowly tugged on the end of the second bow, watching the satin ribbon slide across her skin as the bow gave way. With a little shush the sheer linen dropped to her ankles like a pale cloud.

"Oh Caro," he breathed. "You're so beautiful I'm almost afraid to touch you."

"Don't be." She looked down so he wouldn't see the tears glittering in her eyes as she slipped her arms around his waist. "I'm here, love, and I'm yours."

With a deep groan he took what she offered, drawing her close. As his mouth found hers, his fingers sank deep into the soft curve of her hips, fitting his body against hers. She tasted his kiss like liquid fire, searing her blood, as the pressure of his body against hers overwhelmed her senses. When he lifted her against him, she moaned into his mouth, her nipples tightening as they brushed against the rough hair of his chest and the hard, hot power of his arousal against her belly.

He swept one arm beneath her knees and she gasped with surprise, clinging to his shoulders as he carried her the few feet to lay her on the bed. After the hard bunk of the *Raleigh*'s cabin, the feather bed felt light as dandelion down beneath her and the linen sheets were faintly redolent of rosemary. Alone, Caro looked questioningly up at Jeremiah as he shoved back the bed's curtains, the rings scraping along the iron rod.

"You're too fair to hide away in the dark, sweetheart," he explained, thinking how a real virgin would have pulled the sheets up tight beneath her chin instead of curling so invitingly naked against the bolsters the way Caro was now. "Whether by candlelight or moonlight, I want to see you. If it's not, of course, too much for your poor maidenly innocence?"

She chuckled, throaty and more alluring to him than she realized with her silvery hair tumbled across the pillow. Watching him with the same hunger that filled his eyes, she slid across the mattress to make room for him.

"Nay, Caro, not so fast." Lying down on the bed beside her he curled one arm around her waist and pulled her back, rolling her deftly beneath him. "No scuttling away from me now."

"Whyever would I want to?" she asked breathlessly. Although he supported most of his weight on his elbows, she liked the feel of his body on hers and the way the mattress gave gently beneath them. Exploring, she rested her hands on his lower back to feel the bunch of muscles there, the little indentations below his waist. She reached up to kiss him, teasing light as a feather.

"No reason on earth that I can consider." Past teasing, he caught her lower lip in his teeth, working it gently as his hand found her breast, and felt the tremor clear through her body. Beneath his fingers her nipple rose firm and taut, delighting him with her response. With a broken sigh, she arched her back into his caress, her hips instinctively rising beneath his to rub against him in a way that tore at his self-control.

"Easy now, sweetheart," he growled, intensifying the caress as her fingers clutched convulsively into his shoulders. His heart was pounding in his ears, his blood fevered, and the tension that had swirled around them all evening focused now on the beautiful woman beneath him. "My sweet, hot Caro."

"You make me feel so—so perfect, Jeremiah," she whispered raggedly, and closed her eyes with the heat that his touch brought her. She had never dreamed there could be so much pleasure in the world, so much sweet, agonizing pleasure.

"Almost there, love, almost there." He raised himself up just long enough to ease her legs apart, his hands gliding across the soft skin of her inner thighs until she trembled. When he touched her, wet and hot and ready, she whimpered, her legs curling around his hand as she desperately sought the release her body craved. "Almost home."

He opened her legs wider to take him and she stared up at him wildly, her eyes dark with passion and her breath no more than ragged gasps. "You won't—you won't hurt me, will you?"

He was so close he could feel her heat welcoming him, guiding him. He was long past playing games, long past pretending, past anything but the intense reality of her need waiting for him. Groaning, he buried himself in her with a single stroke, into her heat, deep into her velvety sweetness, and, unbelievably, through the very real barrier of her maidenhead.

## Chapter Thirteen

"*Caro.*" With the need pulsing in his veins and every nerve on edge, he couldn't say more than her name alone. How could he, when she was so hot and tight around him? Her eyes were squeezed shut and she'd stiffened beneath him, her breathing so shallow it was almost panting. Damnation, he'd hurt her, and he'd never wanted to do that. If only she'd told him the truth!

"Don't stop," she whispered with ragged, incoherent urgency, lifting and twisting her hips to meet him. "Oh, please, Jeremiah, don't stop!"

It was all the encouragement he needed, and she gasped as he began moving in her again, slowly at first and then faster, more demanding, in a rhythm she soon learned and answered. The first tug of pain she'd felt had vanished, and she curled her legs over his broad back, slick with sweat, drawing him in as deeply as she could. Hot tension coiled tighter and tighter in her belly, aching for a release that only he could give, and she cried out and clung to him desperately as they rocked closer to the edge.

"Oh, love, I'm sorry," he gasped, his face taut as he drove into her. "I'm sorry, but it's just too good. *You're* too good, Caro!"

She wanted to tell him it was all right and that she loved him, but he shifted higher, touching her deeper, and all her thoughts shattered and vanished before the wave of sensual pleasure. She had never dreamed her body was capable of this, and fleetingly she remembered all the ribald winks and leers from her mother and her friends so long ago. But this was different, because this was her Jeremiah, and she felt herself hurtling over the edge, crying his name, the exquisite ecstasy of her release beyond imagining.

Afterward she held him as they lay tangled together, gently stroking the long length of his back as his breathing calmed and his body relaxed. She knew she'd done the right thing, knew with all her heart. At this moment, their bodies still joined so intimately, she felt closer to him than she'd ever been to another person. But though she longed to ask him if he'd experienced the same joy from their lovemaking that she had herself, his face was turned away from hers, toward the pillow, and she fought back lonely tears of disappointment. Could she really have misjudged him—and herself—so badly?

Finally, with a sigh, he rolled to one side, propping his head up on the pillow to look at her, his hair falling damply across his forehead. There was, she thought unhappily, certainly no joy to be found in that grim, handsome face now.

"Caro," he said with more gentleness than she expected. "Why, love? Why?"

She swallowed hard, reaching for the sheet to cover herself. The way the shadows fell across the bed curtains hid his eyes, and she wished desperately she could see them now and know what he was thinking. Once again that single word of his could be the beginning of so many questions with so many different answers, but she gave him the only one that mattered.

"Because I love you," she said, her words quavering, "and because I dared to believe that you love me, too."

"But, damnation, Caro, what about your blessed husband?" There was confusion in his voice, and more than a share of anger. "You've been married to the man for fourteen years. I can't believe in all that time he never made love to you once, especially considering—well, considering the circumstances."

"No, go ahead and say it," she said bitterly. "Considering that Frederick paid five hundred pounds for my maidenhead, he should at least have had the privilege of taking it."

"Aye, something like that." He reached out then to brush his finger across her cheek, and only then did he realize she was crying. "Why, sweetheart?"

Another why, and this time the answer wouldn't be as simple. She turned her face away from him, instead staring up at the canopy overhead, and let the hot tears slide down her cheeks to wet the pillow.

"I was nothing when Frederick bought me," she said softly. "Only the fourteen-year-old bastard of a second-rate whore. There must be hundreds like me born every year, but at least I was lucky enough not to be tossed out to die on the dustheap, and instead was

sent to live in the country. It was, I think, the one kind
thing Mama did for me, and I thank her still. At least
I grew up healthy and strong. But my only 'educa-
tion' was what she forced into me during the last fortnight I was in her care, and oh, I was such an ignorant
little girl!''

She smiled bleakly through her tears, remembering
how much of an innocent she had been. ''If Frederick
hadn't bought me, I would have followed in my
mother's path, and I would have died years ago, from
the pox or consumption or some midwife's quackery.
Frederick saved my life, and for that I shall always
love him.''

''But not as a wife?'' asked Jeremiah gently, and she
shook her head against the pillow without looking at
him, her fingers twisting the sheet.

''That isn't what he wanted. Frederick was—no,
*is*—above the desires of the flesh. That's what he
called it—the 'baser side of man's animal nature'—
and he promised he'd never sully our love that way.
After what I'd learned from Mama, I wanted no part
of it, either, so we suited each other famously. I would
have if he'd wanted me to, yet he never did.''

''Then why the devil did he marry you?''

''He said it was to protect me. No one would dare
slander the Countess of Byfield to her face, and if I
outlived him, Frederick knew I'd be safe with his
name. Oh, I know what is said of me in Portsmouth,
but I was more his daughter than his mistress, let alone
his wife. It was enough for me, and I was happy.
Happy, that is, until Frederick disappeared. And then
I met you.''

"Come here," he said gruffly, and with a shuddering sigh she went to him, curling her body against him as his arm circled protectively around her. He should have guessed it all. The more he thought about what she'd told him, the more he realized she'd given him enough hints that a blessed idiot could have figured it out, just as he was ten times a fool for not realizing how much he was in love with her before this.

"I can't help but believe that what we've done will only make things worse, sweetheart," he said, "but you won't see me wishing it undone, either."

She searched his face. "You don't?"

"How can I?" He sighed again, stroking her cheek. "I love you, Caro, and that's the first time I've ever said that to any woman."

Her smile was magical. "You do? Truly?"

He brushed away the tangle of her hair and kissed her gently, sweetly. He could imagine few situations more futile than falling in love as he had with another man's wife, yet with Caro in his arms he still felt blissfully happy. "I do, truly, and more's the pity for us both."

"I loved you from the first time I saw you, sleeping at your sister's house," she confessed. "I tried then to guess the kind of man you must be to be so handsome, and I wasn't disappointed."

He grimaced, thinking how when she'd first seen him he'd been shaking and pale from a nightmare. "An ill-tempered, paid-out, rascally rogue?"

"No, of course not, and I won't hear you say it!" She punched his shoulder with her small fist, and he groaned dramatically. "I knew you'd be kind and gentle and clever and brave, and you are all those things. A kind, gentle, clever, brave, rascally rogue.''

"Impudent little baggage." As she laughed and wriggled out of reach, he tugged away the sheet that was twisted between them, wanting to feel again her skin against his. He pushed her back against the pillow, trapping her beneath his body, and kissed her until her laughter changed to little sighs of contentment and their kisses grew warmer, more impassioned. Reluctantly he broke away, seeing the dark smears of her blood on the sheet.

"Don't tempt me, Caro," he warned. "I've no intention of hurting you again tonight."

"You won't." She ignored him, running her lip across the rough beard on his jaw. "You only hurt at the beginning. You are, you know, a large man."

"And you're a lovely woman," he said softly. "The lovely woman I happen to love."

"I love you, too, Jeremiah." She found his lips and kissed him again, her happiness boundless. "Then I did the right thing after all."

He sighed and held her closer. "Not necessarily. I will never regret making love to you, Caro, but before this night you could have had your marriage to Frederick annulled."

She stared at him, shocked. "I would never have done that to Frederick. To shame him in front of the world like that—no, I could never have done it."

That stung Jeremiah's pride. "Then how shamed will he be if you present him with my child?" he said bluntly. "Or did the shopkeeper who sold you that dressing gown advise you on ways to avoid breeding, too?''

Embarrassed to be discussing such a thing with him, she shook her head. ''It wouldn't be likely, not the first time.''

''No? As you said yourself, there's hundreds of bastards born every year from just that kind of ill-founded trust. Exactly how forgiving is your precious Frederick?''

She rested her cheek against the curling hair of his chest, listening to the steady rhythm of his heartbeat. In all the time she'd spent this afternoon, agonizing over her feelings, she had, perhaps because of her own illegitimacy, never once considered conceiving a child.

''He would, I think, accept my child as his own,'' she said slowly. ''He cares so little for convention, and though he'd never admit it, he'd take great pleasure in displacing George as his heir.''

''Not your child, Caro. Ours.''

''Of course it would be ours. You know I've always wanted a baby,'' she admitted shyly. ''Your sister must have been brought to bed by now. I wonder if she had a little girl, or another boy like Johnny that looks like you?''

Jeremiah closed his eyes, fighting back the longing her words brought. A son of his own like his nephew Johnny, a boy to raise and teach and take to sea, a child conceived with the one and only woman he'd ever loved. Except that by law and the whim of Caro's husband, the child—*his* child—could become heir to an earldom, raised not as a Sparhawk but as a Moncrief, an English child, not American, and one who'd never know his real father.

"Whether boy or girl, Desire's child will carry its father's name," he said firmly, leery of Caro's dreamy expression. "I'd want the same for any child of ours."

"If there is a child," she said, "I will take care of the consequences myself."

"Nay, Caro, *we* will. When I return from Tripoli—"

"When *we* return from Tripoli," she said serenely. "I haven't sailed clear from England to be left behind now. Of course I'm coming to Tripoli with you."

His black brows lowered. "I can't allow it, Caro, not with the new war."

"*Your* country's war, not mine," she countered, serenity replaced by stubbornness. "*My* country has faithfully paid its tribute to the pasha for years."

"Yours, mine, ours," he said impatiently. "The devil can take the whole lot for all it will matter to you!"

She pushed herself upright, sitting against the bolster. "Listen to me, Jeremiah. Lady Byfield has arranged it all as her way of thanking us. There was a note waiting for me here at the inn tonight that she's already booked us places on a Neapolitan ship leaving with tomorrow's tide for Tripoli and Tunis, and ordered her bankers to pay the ransom for Frederick and your friend Mr. Kerr."

She paused and laid her hand on his arm. "She had the latest lists from Tripoli, Jeremiah," she said gently. "Mr. Kerr is the only one of your crew who survived."

Silently he shook his head. Though he'd known it was unreasonable, he'd kept on hoping that if Davy was still alive, maybe others were, too. Andrew Parker, Peter Collins, John Cramer, Jemmy Allyn, and all the rest, gone.

"I'm sorry, love," said Caro. "Lady Byfield said—"

"Damn Lady Byfield!" he said furiously, angry at the fate that had claimed his men. "She can damned well keep her thank-yous, and you will stay here with them."

"But I want to be there when you free Frederick!"

"What, are you afraid I might not bring him back after all?" he said angrily. "It would be easy enough, wouldn't it? Poor old Frederick didn't make it, sweetheart, so now you're all mine."

She froze. "You would not do that, Jeremiah," she said slowly, as much, he thought, to convince herself as him.

"Wouldn't I?" It *would* be easy, the only way he could know for sure he was hers forever, and for one tempting, dishonorable moment he let himself consider it. She could say all she wanted that Frederick was more father than husband to her; he still couldn't very well go to the man and ask for her hand. "How sure are you?"

But this time she didn't hesitate. "I'm sure. I love you, but I also trust you."

"Then God help you, Caro, for putting your trust in me," he said roughly. "No matter what you or the old lady say, the situation is far too dangerous, and I won't put your life at risk. Besides, I want to be able to do whatever I must without worrying about you.''

'' 'Whatever you must'?'' Suddenly his real reason dawned on her, and her eyes flashed with anger and fear for him. ''You'll save your friends and Frederick as you promised, but that's not all, is it? You're going to Tripoli to find the man who stole your ship. I put the foolish idea into your head, and now you're actually going to do it.''

He met her gaze evenly. ''I can let Hamil haunt my dreams for the rest of my life, or I can face him, and prove to myself that I'm not a coward. I'm a Sparhawk, Caro, and I don't see it as a choice.''

She shook her head wildly, trying to deny he could really want this. ''But how can you? If he captures you again, you know he won't let you go. He'll kill you. It's as simple as that, Jeremiah! *He will kill you.* You haven't a ship, or men, or cannons, while he's a *pirate!*''

''I don't mean to fight him at sea. You're right. I wouldn't have a chance. But the man's house is in Tripoli, and if I can reach him there—''

''No, I don't want to hear it.'' Agitated, she pushed herself from the bed and plucked her dressing gown from the floor, whipping it around her body. ''I love you, but I won't stay to listen to you plan your own death. It's time I returned to my own room anyway.''

He lunged for her across the bed but she kept beyond his reach. ''Damn it, Caro, come back here!''

''Damn *you,* Jeremiah, I won't!'' She retrieved the sheer blue shift and wadded it up into a ball in her hand, too hurt and angry to wish to be reminded of everything the shift had led to. With the silk shushing around her bare legs she went striding for the door.

"Caro, please. *Please.*"

Against her better judgment, she paused. She hadn't expected to hear that note in his voice, and slowly she turned back. He was sitting in the middle of the bed bathed in moonlight, his tanned body dark against the white sheets and his black hair loose around his face, and he was so achingly beautiful that she could have wept just from the sight of him.

He held one hand out to her, an offering, not a summons. "Please, love," he said softly. "This night could be all we ever have. Do you really want it to end like this?"

Still she hesitated, torn between sharing his love for tonight and the certain, bleak emptiness of a future without him.

He might have smiled; in the moonlight she wasn't sure. "You said your room was lonely. It won't have gotten any less so since you left it earlier."

"I don't want to be alone, Jeremiah," she said plaintively. "I've never wanted that."

"I never thought you did, love."

She sighed and took one step toward the bed, then another. "No more talk of pirates or pashas if I stay."

"Not a word." He took her hand and pulled her up onto the bed with him, letting her dressing gown slide back to the floor in a silk puddle. "Instead let me tell you one more time how much I love you."

Safe once again in his arms, her cheek resting in the hollow of his shoulder, she knew there was no other place under heaven she'd rather be.

His lips brushed the top of her hair, his eyes as clouded as their future together. Somehow he would find a way for them to be together. Somehow he would make their love last beyond this room, this night, and the magic of the moonlight in Naples.

With a sigh she burrowed closer, her hands sliding around his waist. "Now that I've finally found you, Jeremiah Sparhawk," she whispered, "I don't ever want to part with you again."

"Nor do I, love," he said softly, "nor do I."


"What are you doing here, my dear Caroline?" asked Dorinda, barely containing her irritation. She waved aside the dressmaker with the length of deep red Circassian draped across her arm and motioned for Caro to come closer. "I would have thought you'd be besieged with the details of your journey and not have time to make calls. Did you not receive my note about Captain Tomaso?"

"Yes, of course. Everything you've done has been wonderful, and I'll never thank you enough." Caro sank into the little gilt chair beside the older woman's, too distraught to notice the interest of the dressmaker and her assistants. "It's Jeremiah who's the problem."

"A bit of discretion, my dear," chided Dorinda. "It is unwise to advertise one's personal woes."

She glanced pointedly at both the lowered eyes and open ears of the dressmaker, mentally cursing her daughter-in-law's foolish outburst. By nightfall Madame Duval would have repeated every word she overheard to as many of her customers as she possibly could. But then, considered Dorinda, that in itself might not be such a bad thing. All of Naples knew of poor Frederick's capture. When his chit of a wife failed to return after attempting a rescue, a small show of grief on Dorinda's part would gain her much sympathy, and might help keep any unpleasant suspicions at a distance.

"You will excuse us, *madame*," she said. "As you can see, my daughter-in-law is concerned over a family matter that we must discuss in private."

Although the Frenchwoman bowed respectfully to Dorinda, her eyes were glinting with a businesswoman's eagerness as she studied Caro.

"I am honored, *Madame la Comtesse*," purred Madame Duval as she sank into a deep curtsy. "Perhaps your ladyship would be so kind as to permit me to call on you? I have in my shop at present a rose silk senchaw, *très belle, très riche*, that would suit your ladyship's—"

"She's not staying," said Dorinda curtly. "She leaves Naples this afternoon to seek my son, her husband."

Dramatically the Frenchwoman clasped her hands over her breasts. "Ah, *Madame la Comtesse*, I wish you *bonne chance*, I wish you and your husband—"

"Good day, *madame*," said Dorinda. As far as she was concerned, the dressmaker had learned more than enough to fuel her gossip, and she was in no humor to sit back and listen while Madame Duval lavished compliments on her upstart daughter-in-law. Capitano Tomaso's ship left on the late afternoon tide, and Dorinda fully intended that Caroline be on board.

Reluctantly Madame Duval and her assistants gathered their samples and bowed their way from the room. Dorinda sat back in her chair, one finger arched against her cheek and her eyes hooded as she considered Caro. No matter what the spat was between them, the chit had clearly just tumbled from her lover's bed, and Dorinda's anger rose another notch. She recognized the signs well enough: the chit's lips still swollen, almost bruised, her eyes shadowed from lack of sleep, her cheeks far rosier than they'd been yesterday. If the little harlot came any closer, Dorinda didn't doubt that she'd smell the man's scent on her still. What had her poor Frederick done to deserve such treatment?

But Dorinda knew the value of hiding her outrage, of biding her time. "Now then, my dear," she began sympathetically. "What exactly is the problem with Captain Sparhawk?"

Caro took a deep breath, steadying her voice before the countess. She didn't know how she'd survived Jeremiah's farewell this morning, and, feeling battered and vulnerable, she had come to her former enemy as a last resort. "Jeremiah refuses to let me go with him to Tripoli."

Dorinda sniffed contemptuously. So the man wished to be rid of her. Dorinda could not blame him, and in a way she respected him more for it. The Italians had a marvelous word, *cicisbeo,* that they used to describe the acknowledged, ornamental lover of a married woman, a title no honorable man would ever aspire to. What a pity she would never have the pleasure of knowing this Jeremiah herself.

"The way I view it," she said, "Signor Sparhawk has no choice but to take you with him."

"Jeremiah says it's too dangerous, that he won't put me at risk." *Because he loves me too much.* Caro stopped perilously short of saying the words out loud. Already she missed him. "He doesn't even want me at the dock to see him off."

"For God's sake, girl, use your wits!" ordered Dorinda, her anger too great to sustain the feigned sympathy any longer. "I'll wager you didn't get to be countess by wringing your hands and wailing. And don't forget that you *are* a countess, and no insolent Yankee sailor has any right to tell you what you may or may not do."

Caro's head drooped. "I've never done anything for myself," she said softly. "Frederick didn't wish me to. He considered it unseemly and ill fitting a lady of my station."

"Fah on what foolishness Frederick wishes! You're not helpless. You came here after him, didn't you?"

Caro shook her head, unconvinced.

"Listen to me, girl. I don't care how you do it—with your face, you should have no difficulty at all—but you owe it to my son to be on that ship. And you *will* do it, Caroline." The old woman jabbed at the air with her diamond-weighted finger. "Or you will answer to me."

As the hired skiff drew closer to the felucca that would carry him to Tripoli, Jeremiah's misgivings grew. The two stubby masts and patched lateen sails were bad enough, but the dozen oars that bristled from each side of the little ship inspired even less confidence. Oars like that needed men to row them, men that in this part of the world were most likely Christian slaves, and as both a free man and a Christian himself, Jeremiah despised all that galleys represented. As a sailor he wouldn't have trusted the shabby felucca on the river at home, let alone on the Mediterranean with its sudden storms and uncertain currents, and he wondered again if he'd been wrong to accept passage arranged by the old countess. Not that he had much choice; Naples was at war with Tripoli, too—at least theoretically—and all the other vessels daring to trade illegally between the two countries were bound to be as disreputable as this one.

For reassurance he thought of the pistols and knives hidden beneath his coat, anonymous, serviceable weapons. He had brought little else with him, leaving his sea chest behind at the inn until he returned. Once in Tripoli, he planned to purchase the loose robes that were worn there, and he hoped that with his black hair and weatherworn skin he could at least be inconspicuous.

He looked back over his shoulder at the fairy-tale city he was leaving and picked out the orange-tiled roof of the inn. He did not intend to be gone long, a fortnight at most if he could help it, and despite his warning to Caro, he had every intention of coming back. After a lifetime of sailing away, now for the first time he had a real reason to return.

Saying goodbye to Caro this morning in the bed they'd shared had been one of the hardest things he'd ever done. She hadn't wept or clung to him, or tried again to convince him not to go; but the wistful, silent love in her eyes was more expressive than a week's worth of recrimination from any other woman.

What he'd found with her last night went beyond happiness, beyond joy, to something he couldn't find words to explain. It was almost as if in her he'd discovered a part of himself that he hadn't realized was missing, a half that would make his life whole. He understood at last the wordless language that passed between his sister and her husband, and how impossibly dear love, real love, could be, even to a man like him. And passion. Who would have believed how much fire there was in his silver-haired Caro? He wiped his hand across his mouth as he caught himself grinning like a fool at the memory.

His Caro, his sweet, lovely, fiery Caro.

His Caro, who was wed to the man he'd sworn to risk his life to rescue.

Abruptly he turned his back on the city and concentrated instead on the felucca as the skiff bumped alongside. He grabbed the makeshift rope ladder and clambered aboard. For a moment he simply stood there, stunned by the noise and chaos around him.

Because of the felucca's narrow hull, space in its hold was at a premium, and the deck teemed with both passengers and animal cargo. Everyone seemed to be arguing and shouting at once, none of it in any language Jeremiah could make out, not spoken this quickly. Sailors and passengers alike wore either long, loose robes and turbans or fitted European clothing, or, in several cases, a combination of both, with one elderly man in a striped robe with a dirty sash and a pair of shiny leather shoes with outsize polished buckles peeking from beneath the hem. The slaves chained to their benches wore nothing so dignified, only filthy trousers or bits of draped loincloths, their broad-shouldered, unwashed bodies glistening in the hot sun, and Jeremiah prayed that beneath their unkempt hair and beards none were Americans. Beyond them, a handful of women clustered together in the scant shade of one of the forward sails, and Jeremiah looked hastily away, well aware of the peril of admiring women, no matter how shrouded, in this part of the world. Lord, what would Caro in her white silk and diamonds have made of this!

Beside the women on the deck were baskets of squabbling chickens, and tied unceremoniously to one of the felucca's lines were several goats, their stench unmistakable as the wind shifted toward Jeremiah. It was more a blasted ark than a decent merchant ship, he decided grimly, and however brief the voyage was—Tripoli was scarcely more than two hundred miles from Naples—it wouldn't be short enough.

"Ah, *signore* Capitano Sparhawk!" said a short, round-bellied man whose entire face seemed curved into his smile. "I am seldom so honored, eh? Another captain aboard *mia cara Colomba!*"

"Captain Tomaso," said Jeremiah, his voice determinedly noncommittal. The other captain wore a ring on his pinkie with an opal the size of a pigeon's egg and his hair was tied back with an elaborate silk bow, a macaronis' affectation, but his fingernails were ringed black and the cuffs of his shirt were grimy and frayed, and that told more than enough of the man to

Jeremiah. At least he spoke English, though after Nelson's occupation, most Neapolitans in water trade seemed to have some grasp of the language. "A fine day for sailing."

*"Bellissima!"* Tomaso beamed, his smile growing even wider as he patted his belly with both hands. "But wait until you see *mia dolce Colomba* fly across the water. Then you will see perfection!"

He bellowed a handful of orders to his men, and the felucca's sails were dropped to catch the wind. Jeremiah lifted his hat long enough to wipe his sleeve across his brow. It was hot in the sun, and his head ached dully from lack of sleep. Best to go find whatever wretched place passed for his cabin and get some rest.

Damnation, but he missed Caro!

"There, *Capitano,* I told you how she flies, eh?" bragged Tomaso. "Like an angel she is!"

More like a sow, thought Jeremiah irritably. To him the *Colomba* felt sluggish and low in the water, the long oars on either side making her unresponsive to the wind. "I'm going below, Tomaso."

"Alone, eh? You didn't bring your *graziosa amante,* eh? They told me you would." He kissed his fingertips and winked broadly. "A *bellissima donna!*"

"She's not coming." And a good thing, too, decided Jeremiah. Though Tomaso and Bertle were as different as shipmasters could be, there was still something intangible there in both men that made Jeremiah uneasy and on his guard. "This is no journey for a lady."

"She's not coming?" Tomaso's face puckered with sly regret and he clucked his tongue. "My poor fellow, to be scorned! Women, eh, so fickle, so cruel!"

"Not this lady," said Jeremiah curtly. He slung the canvas bag with his few belongings over his shoulder. "I'm going below."

"Ah, you English!" called Tomaso, not in the least offended. "Always eager for the next place to sling your hammocks!"

Jeremiah didn't bother to correct him. Not only did he want no further conversation with the man, but it might also serve him better for now to be believed an Englishman. An Englishman, for all love; Lord, how merrily Caro would laugh at that!

A gaunt little ship's boy showed him to what passed for a cabin, a dirty closet half below the waterline. Grateful again that he'd spared Caro this, he wearily hung his hammock and soon drifted off to sleep, lulled by the shuffling of the goats on the deck overhead. He slept deeply, only dreaming once, of Caro skipping along beside him in Portsmouth, the old coverlet sliding off her bare shoulders as she reached out to take his hand.

It was dark when Jeremiah woke and, disoriented, he tensed with terror, his hand at once on his knife, until he recalled where he was. The felucca and Tomaso and Naples and Tripoli and Davy and Caro, always Caro. He forced his sleep-thick brain to sort it through, striving to calm himself. At least there'd been no nightmares, no Hamil to haunt him, and he sighed, slipping the knife back into its sheath.

Above him there was a babble of indignant voices he couldn't hear well enough to understand, among them Tomaso's apparently trying to intercede. He rolled from the hammock, his mouth dry and his shirt plastered to his chest, and decided to go topside, hoping that the wind off the water might clear his head.

By the smoking light of an oil lantern hooked to the mast, he could just make out Tomaso's broad silhouette, gesturing alternately to three of the male passengers. Between them was a smaller figure, one of the women, and Jeremiah watched with idle curiosity, wondering what grievous insult one of the men had brought onto the other through the woman.

But perhaps it was the woman herself who'd caused the trouble. To Jeremiah's amusement, she tossed her head and waved one hand back defiantly at Tomaso. This one was no ordinary, obedient Turkish woman, and Jeremiah almost wished Tomaso would let her speak. He could use the entertainment.

Abruptly Tomaso turned, shaking his head, and then spotted Jeremiah. With a cry of joy he rushed forward, his arms outstretched.

"Capitano Sparhawk, I was just this moment going to send for you! Only you can answer this. Only you can return peace to my little *Colomba!*"

He spoke briskly in Italian to one of the seamen, who grabbed the woman by the arm and dragged her toward Jeremiah and the circle of the lantern's full light.

"I told you before, Capitano Sparhawk, that women give men no peace," declared Tomaso, "and here now is the proof. That *signore* there says this creature stole from him as he slept, but she swears he lies. She swears it, *Capitano,* but what is most amazing is that she says too that you will swear on her behalf. Can you believe it, eh? Come here, *mia bella cagna!*''

Roughly he shoved the woman closer to Jeremiah, and the black shawl she had wrapped over her head and shoulders slipped to one side. Silver gold hair spilled forward like the moon from behind a cloud, and even before she grinned wickedly, Jeremiah knew it was Caro.

## Chapter Fourteen

Caro had expected Jeremiah to be surprised, even a bit irritated, to find her on board the felucca with him. She had, after all, disobeyed his orders, and by now she knew him well enough to understand that orders weren't something he gave lightly. But she hadn't expected him to be as angry as he was now, staring as coldly at her as if she'd dropped from the sky.

"You might say you're glad to see me, Jeremiah," she said, her smile fading. She had so anticipated this moment, and now that it was here, it wasn't at all what she'd counted on. "I'm vastly glad to see you again, you know."

"Ha!" exclaimed Tomaso, shaking Caro by the arm. "You would dare to pretend you know this gentleman?"

"She does," said Jeremiah grimly, "just as I know her. This, Captain Tomaso, is Caroline Moncrief, Countess of Byfield, though she doesn't look like much of anything right now."

"I do not believe it, *Capitano*," said Tomaso flatly. "This creature a *contessa*?"

Delighted that her disguise was such a success, Caro's smile returned. She had done what the dowager countess had advised and taken responsibility for herself, and she was proud of how well she'd done. Remembering how in Portsmouth the secondhand gown and bonnet had hidden her in plain sight, she had literally bought the clothes from the back of a maidservant at the inn.

Not that anyone *should* guess she was an English countess, not dressed in a rough full-sleeved shift beneath a laced black bodice, two coarse petticoats, thread stockings and worn shoes that tied with dirty pink ribbons. She had tried to pin her hair severely back the way the maidservant had worn hers, but since Caro's fashionably cropped tendrils had refused to sleek back, she had been careful to cover her hair and shadow her face with the oversize black shawl that, too, had come from the maidservant.

"Captain Sparhawk's right," she said to Tomaso. "I am Lady Byfield. Didn't you receive word that I would be a passenger?"

Hearing the unmistakable upper-class accent in her speech, Tomaso hastily released her arm. "Forgive me, *ma donna,* I did not know! But how would I, eh? You dress yourself like *una domestica,* you pay for yourself on the wharf like all the others, you sleep on the deck with them. How would I know otherwise when this *ribaldo* accuses you of cutting his purse, eh?"

"You wouldn't, and that was the point." Free of the heavy shawl, she tossed her hair back in the cool night breeze, unaware of the interest that her pale, loose hair

caused among the sailors and other male passengers.
"It was a disguise."

Unsatisfied, Tomaso shook his head and raised his
shoulders. "But I do not understand. Why such a
disguise, eh? You are a great English lady. Is it some
jest, *una facezia,* that I cannot see?"

"That's two of us, Tomaso." Jeremiah took her
arm, his grip every bit as rough as the Italian's had
been. "Come along, love. I'm eager for answers."

She went meekly as he led her down the short companionway to the tiny cabin, and when he released her
to bolt the door and light the little lamp hooked to the
bulkhead, she stood with her hands folded, waiting
patiently. She had nothing to fear, nothing to hide.
Her reasons for joining him were the best.

Yet from the look in Jeremiah's eyes when he
turned around to face her, she knew at once he wasn't
going to agree.

"Don't start, Jeremiah, not until you've heard—"

"I'll start whenever I damned well please, Caro, and
nothing you say will change that." Pointedly he lowered his eyes to her clothing. The tightly laced bodice
accentuated the curve of her waist and hips in a way
that her more fashionable French chemises never
could. "What the hell are you doing here, rigged out
like that?"

"Like this?" She lifted the side of her skirt and
glanced down at it almost as if she'd forgotten herself
what she wore. "That's quite simple. I wanted to come
on board without any extra fuss, so I dressed myself
like this to look like the others. I remembered what
you said that night in Portsmouth."

"For God's sake, Caro, can't you see the difference?"

"The difference?" she repeated uncertainly, and looked again at her petticoats. "I suppose these are worse than what you bought me that night, smelling as they do of the kitchen. Frederick would be absolutely appalled to see me like this. That's why I brought a gown of my own to wear when we free him, white mull—oh, Jeremiah, I left my bundle on the deck!"

"Whatever was in it is gone now," he said. "You might be too fine a lady to steal from your fellows, but believe me, they won't feel such scruples about you."

Hoping to retrieve her belongings, she tried to squeeze past him. "But if I went and asked—"

"You really don't understand, do you, Caro?" He blocked her path, his body filling half the cabin and his fury the rest. "What's different isn't the rags on your back. It's that you were alone, among strangers who'd sooner do you harm than blink. Can you guess what kind of mercy you'd have found from that crew on deck if I hadn't come to vouch for you?"

Jeremiah could, all too vividly, and the horror of what might have happened to her, either on board the *Colomba* or wandering about the Neapolitan waterfront, fueled his anger at how much she'd foolishly risked.

"Damnation, Caro, this isn't some little masquerade for your amusement! Why the hell didn't you stay in Naples where I'd know you'd be safe?"

"Oh, yes, and Naples is such a fine, safe place!" Her own temper flaring, Caro shoved at the hard wall of his chest. "Have you ever considered what would happen to an English lady if Bonaparte's army returned? Why do you think Frederick's mother is so eager to make peace with me so she can go home to England? She told me that I—''

"Why are you suddenly so thick with a woman who despises you? How can you trust a blessed word she says?''

"At least she believes that I can do things for myself!''

"Don't argue with me, Caro," ordered Jeremiah, his voice as stern as if he stood on his own quarterdeck.

"And don't give orders to me!" Furiously Caro lashed out at him, her hand nearly reaching his cheek before he grabbed her wrist.

"Stop it, Caro," he said, more softly this time, but with the same commanding tone. "Do you want that whole pack of jackals topside to believe you've lost your wits?''

"I don't care a fig what they believe!" With a cry of wounded frustration, she struggled to pull free and try to strike him again, but he held her as tightly as if they'd been bound together. He was so much larger, so much stronger, and in that moment she hated him for it. "And you don't care, either, not about what they think or whether I'm safely left behind in Naples! All that matters to you is that I *obey*, like some well-trained little dog, so that you can feel free to go off alone and get yourself killed with a clear conscience. That's it, isn't it? *Isn't it?*''

"How can you say that after all we've done together?'' he demanded, his eyes glittering like green fire. She'd never guess how deeply her words cut into him, as surely as any knife. Didn't she realize how much he'd changed for her? The man he had been a year ago would not be here now, risking his life to save an English lord because his wife had asked him. For Davy, yes. He'd do anything for a friend like him.

But not for a woman. And never for love.

"I can say it because it's true!" she cried, her words shaking with emotion. "Whatever you do, you do for yourself, because you're the blessed American Captain Jeremiah Sparhawk!"

"Damnation, Caro, I'm doing this now because I love you!" His mouth crushed down on hers, stopping her words as he kissed her long and hard and deep. He felt the instant when her struggles subtly changed, when she stopped struggling to free herself and instead clung to him, when her anger, too, was channeled into the same desire he felt racing through his body. He let her hand go and she curled it around the back of his neck, her fingers tangling in his hair as she drew him closer.

He pushed her back the last few inches against the bulkhead, lifting her higher until her hips were level with his. He held her there with the pressure of his body, suspended, her toes grazing the floor as she steadied herself with her hands on his shoulders. The lacing of her bodice snapped through the eyelets as he hooked his fingers in the bow, tugging the neckline lower over her breasts.

She gasped as his open lips found her nipple, drawing it deeply into his mouth and suckling hard. Even through her petticoats she could feel the heat of his arousal, and instinctively she rocked her hips against his, her back arching against the rough timber of the bulkhead and thrusting her breast more deeply into his mouth. As much as he gave her, she desperately craved more, more that only he could offer.

His hand plunged beneath her petticoats, following the sleek length of her thigh above her garters to her bare hip, and she whimpered as she moved against him. Rapidly he unfastened the fall on his trousers, freeing himself as he swept away the last barrier of her skirts and shifted her long legs around his waist.

She was open and ready for him, her need shameless, and when he guided himself into her aching flesh, she raggedly cried out his name. With her legs crossed over his back she drew him in deeper, intoxicated with the way he filled her as he drove into her so powerfully that he lifted her against the wall.

She didn't care; she didn't care about anything except the feverish, spiraling ecstasy that was coiling in her body, making her limbs shake and her heart pound, her breath hot in his ear. Passion swept them both beyond sense, beyond reason, until at last their self-made world of pleasure exploded, and with a final sob of release she melted in his arms.

They stayed there joined together as their heartbeats slowed and their breathing grew more regular, her eyes closed and her cheek resting against his shoulder, his face buried in the damp silk of her hair, relishing the languid, animal fragrance of her satisfaction.

Finally, slowly, he lowered her to the deck, but even as her skirts dropped between them he still could not bring himself to let her go, touching her gently, caressing her, kissing her eyelids and the little dimples that framed her smile.

"You are so precious to me, love," he murmured. "Can you wonder that I'd want to keep you safe?"

She smoothed his dark hair back from his forehead. "But not if it means being apart from you. As soon as you'd said goodbye, Jeremiah, I thought I'd go mad from missing you."

"Ah, sweetheart," he said sorrowfully. "Did you think it was any easier for me?"

"Then you will understand." She reached up to brush her lips across his. "I followed you because, inside, I had no choice. I loved you too much for that goodbye."

He sighed wearily. "I'd still send you back if I could."

"But you can't."

"No." With one finger he traced the bow of her lips, thinking how she was at once both impossibly fragile and strong as steel. "You must promise me that you will do what I tell you."

She opened her mouth to protest, and he laid his finger across it. "Hush, and hear me out. You must do as I say because to stop and argue with me may cost both of us our lives. This isn't England, or even Naples."

"I could help you," she offered eagerly. "The way we fooled the captain of the French frigate."

"Don't even consider it, sweetheart," he said firmly, though touched by both her offer and the innocence behind it. "I admit that I'll be inventing this as I go along, but I won't expect you to exercise your charms on my behalf. In Tripoli, it plain won't work. You'll be a heathen, an infidel. Nor will anyone give a damn about you being a countess, except, perhaps, if they stop and consider how much of a ransom they could ask for you."

"I'm not sure there's enough money in Frederick's coffers to redeem us both," she said, striving to be playful and failing. With a troubled sigh, she searched Jeremiah's face as her own expression became uncharacteristically serious. "Tell me truthfully," she asked. "Do you still mean to find Hamil?"

"I must, love," he said softly, cradling her face in his hands. That much of the truth he could tell her. The rest, that which frightened him most, wasn't death itself at Hamil's hands, but that he would meet Hamil and be too much the coward to do what he must. "If I don't, I'll never be the man you deserve."

She nodded, knowing how futile arguing would be, and told herself that it was the smoke from the little lantern that was making her eyes sting.

"And what will you do when we find Frederick?"

Silently she thanked him for that *when,* not *if.* Already she did not deserve a man this fine, this noble. "I don't know," she said, her words barely audible. "I must see him first, and decide then."

"I will not let you go, Caro," he said with quiet determination. "No matter what, I will not give you up."

But before she could answer, he suddenly pulled away, every muscle tensed. "Something's wrong."

She shook her head, bewildered. "Wrong?"

"We've hauled aback. Stopped. Can't you feel the difference?" He was shoving his shirt into his trousers, his head cocked toward the louvered cabin door as he strained to listen. "I can't think of a single good reason for Tomaso to order it, but there must be a dozen bad ones."

Matching his haste, Caro laced her bodice and tugged her shift back into place. "Whyever would he stop now? We must be in the middle of the Mediterranean, quite in the middle of nowhere!"

"Doesn't sound good, does it?" He checked the powder in the pistols, hesitated a moment, thinking, then held one out to Caro. "Do you know how to use this?"

She stared dubiously at the offered gun and shook her head. "Frederick wouldn't countenance firearms at Blackstone. He wouldn't even allow hunting the deer from the park when they came and ate my roses."

"We're not talking about deer, love." He put the butt of the pistol in her hand and arranged her fingers over the catch and hammer. "First pull back this, then this, and don't be flustered by the smoke. Aim along the barrel as best you can, and don't be fancy. Just aim for the broadest part of a man—usually his belly—and you'll bring him down."

She nodded, determined to prove that she wouldn't be a liability, and concentrated hard on what he said.

But he sighed, watching how the gun wobbled in her grasp. "Tomorrow when we've more time, I'll show you properly. Mind, if you don't have time or the willingness to fire, just grab the barrel and use the brass part of the butt to rap your man on the head. Does well enough."

Her smile was lopsided with uncertainty, and his heart lurched at what she might have to face. "I'll do my best, Jeremiah."

"I know you will, love, though I pray you won't have to. Now hide that away in your pocket, beneath your skirts. Most likely this will all come to nothing."

Overhead he heard shouts and calls, though no alarms. He probably was overreacting, yet better that than the same complacency that had cost him the *Chanticleer.*

Caro smoothed her petticoats over the pistol, and her grin widened. "I'm glad I'm not in Naples," she said, and he realized she was breathless with excitement, not fear. "And I love you, Jeremiah, oh, so much!"

Quickly he swept her into his arms to kiss her one more time. No, not the last time. He wouldn't even consider that. Yet as they embraced, the pistol's weight beneath her petticoats thumped against his thigh and his conscience, too.

"I love you, too, Caro," he said gently. "Whatever else you think of me, remember that. Now we'd best go."

The horizon was red with the coming dawn, and the passengers who had slept on deck had already awakened and gathered in little groups for makeshift breakfasts. But every eye now was to the east, to the black silhouette of a large, sharp-nosed xebec riding easy on the waves not one hundred feet away. Staring into the rising sun, it was impossible for Jeremiah to make out much about the xebec, but he saw enough to fuel his uneasiness. Xebecs were the choice of pirates and corsairs, and he'd never known one used for honest trading.

There was no flag flying to announce the xebec's nationality, and none of the usual good-natured calling back and forth when two vessels fell in together at sea, despite the boat that was being rowed toward the *Colomba.* He strained his eyes for the black squares of

gun ports in her side, or a glimpse of a gun on her
deck. He'd bet a hundred pounds they were there, and
another hundred that the xebec's captain had purposefully set her into the sun to hide her.

With Caro's hand tight in his, he made his way
across the deck to where Tomaso stood talking with
his mate. Despite the early hour, the *Colomba*'s captain was newly shaven, the ribbon in his queue freshly
tied, ready for the company he obviously expected.

"What the devil's going on, Tomaso?" demanded
Jeremiah. "What's that ship?"

*"Buon giorno, Capitano, Contessa,"* said Tomaso, his smile more of a smirk. "I am surprised to
see you from your sleep so soon. Most especially you,
*ma donna.* Did you not rest well?"

There was no mistaking what he meant, and Jeremiah's first impulse was to knock Tomaso down where
he stood. But Caro's hand was on his arm, and it was
she who spoke first.

"Why, thank you, yes, Capitano Tomaso," she said
graciously, a countess even in rough homespun. "How
kind of you to ask."

Unsettled by her demeanor, Tomaso belatedly lifted
his hat to her, and another time Jeremiah would have
laughed out loud. Caro as Lady Byfield could be a
formidable creature indeed.

Languidly she waved her hand toward the xebec.
"Why have we stopped for this other ship?"

Tomaso's face reddened beneath his tan, and he
glanced uneasily at Jeremiah. "A bit of business between two merchants, *Contessa.* Nothing out of the
ordinary, eh?"

"You tell me, Tomaso," said Jeremiah curtly. He wished the man still smirked; this guilt and lying were sure signs of worse things to come. "Is it ordinary for you to trade at sea with a ship that doesn't dare show its flag?"

Tomaso shrugged elaborately. "I am not a wealthy man, *Capitano*. This war between you English and France, eh, it has ruined Napoli. I must trade wherever I can."

Sheer will alone kept Caro from ducking behind Jeremiah's back. Jeremiah had been right: there was something very wrong here, more than just Tomaso's insolence. Did Jeremiah too see how only the captain stood near them, how everyone else, passengers and seamen alike, had inched away and left them to stand alone on that crowded deck? The pistol weighed heavily in her pocket, and she wondered if she'd have to use it after all.

The xebec's boat bumped alongside the felucca, and with obvious relief Tomaso hurried to larboard to meet it.

Jeremiah squeezed Caro's hand for reassurance. "Stand firm, love," he murmured beneath his breath for her ears alone. "You couldn't be doing better."

She turned to smile her thanks to him, and froze. The six men from the xebec's boat were climbing on board the felucca, and even in her inexperience she knew these were no ordinary merchant sailors.

All six were tall and broad shouldered, fierce, dark-skinned men with white turbans on their shaved heads and black beards that curled to their bare chests. Instead of shirts they wore short, brightly colored vests over their bronzed arms and chests, and tucked into their sashes and belts were pistols and curving sabers. As each one slung his leg over the felucca's side, his gaze swept the deck with the practiced air of a warrior, and though none of them drew the weapons at his waist, those looks alone were enough to silence every idler and sailor on board the *Colomba*. In spite of her resolution to be brave, Caro shrank closer to Jeremiah's side.

"God in heaven," she prayed, her voice barely audible. "Whatever can they want?"

Protectively Jeremiah pulled her close to him, his arm circling her shoulders. "Steady now, love. We'll find out soon enough."

*But he already knew. From the instant he'd seen the first man, he'd known. How could he not? He'd played his nightmare over so many times in his mind that every sound, every smell, every last detail was engraved forever in his memory. But dear Lord, what had he done in his life until now to have fate deliver such a dreadful coincidence to him?*

The last man over the side was the leader; from his almost princely bearing alone he could be nothing else. To Caro's surprise he was European, perhaps even English, his long beard reddish gold and his eyes bright blue, and he surveyed the deck before him with a haughty stare down his long, arched nose.

His vest was richly embroidered with gold and silver thread that glittered in the dawn's light, and beneath it he wore a white silk shirt, also heavily embroidered. Tucked into his scarlet sash was a pair of beautiful silver-mounted pistols. A saber in an enameled hilt hung at his waist, and in the center of his turban was pinned a large cut amethyst. Unlike his barefoot men, he wore soft boots of red leather, and he stood with his arms folded and his legs widespread, well aware of the impression he was making.

As he glanced their way, one of the passengers let out a wail of uncontrolled terror and folded to the deck, shaking and sobbing, his outcry the only sound on the silent felucca. Around him, the others shuffled away, afraid to share in whatever horror the man felt, but the red-bearded man didn't deign to notice. Yet Caro felt Jeremiah's fingers tighten into her shoulder, and she heard him swear softly beneath his breath.

Tomaso rushed forward, bowing so low over his outstretched leg that his forehead touched his knee and his black bow flopped forward from his neck. "I am honored, *vostra magnificenza, vostra superiorità, vostra—*"

"None o' your ass's prattle, Tomaso," interrupted the red-bearded man irritably. "I haven't time t'waste. The message said ye had a gift for me to ensure the safety o' your miserable felucca."

Impatiently his gaze again swept across the deck, but this time it stopped at Caro, lingering over her with an interest that made her blood turn to ice.

"Jeremiah," she whispered, too terrified to look away. "Who is he?"

"Hamil Al-Ameer," he said hoarsely. "And God help us, we're the gift."

## Chapter Fifteen

Caro gasped. Hamil Al-Ameer was the man who had imprisoned her Frederick, the man who had captured Jeremiah's ship and crew and tossed him for dead into the sea.

The man Jeremiah had sworn to kill.

She twisted about in Jeremiah's arms to see his face, his expression rigid with a bitter, complete hatred she'd never before seen, then looked back at Hamil and his men standing in a line on either side of him. If Jeremiah tried to attack Hamil now, they would be on him instantly, and they would cut him to pieces before her eyes. They were ready for him, their hands resting easily on the hilts of their sabers, almost daring him to try.

Seven against one were odds no sane man would risk. But where Hamil was concerned, Caro wasn't sure Jeremiah was sane; he had suffered too much, been pushed too far. Fear tightened in her breast, her heart pounding wildly as she realized what she must do to save him from himself.

In the tension that bound the men together, no one noticed as she slowly slipped her hand into her pocket.

With trembling fingers she unhooked the catch on the gunlock and wrapped her sweating palm around the butt. She swallowed hard, and in her thoughts said a prayer for Jeremiah. She loved him enough to do this, this and more, if she must. Then, as quickly as she could, she jerked the pistol from her pocket and aimed it at the chest of the red-bearded man as she squeezed the trigger.

"Caro, *no!*" She heard Jeremiah's anguished shout as the gun seemed to explode in her hands. Through the acrid gunpowder smoke she saw the stunned faces of Hamil's men and Captain Tomaso's gaping mouth as she slammed down onto the hard planking of the deck, the pistol flying from her fingers.

What had happened? she thought crazily, gasping for breath. She had shot Hamil, yet she was the one who had fallen. She thought she'd done what Jeremiah had said, release the lock, draw the trigger, aim where the man was broadest. . . .

"Caro, love, look at me!" said Jeremiah frantically, his face above her, his eyes wild and his hair falling forward over her. She wanted to laugh from relief and joy, if she could only catch her breath. He was well, unhurt, and the force she'd felt pressing her into the deck was the weight of his body on hers. She'd done it! She'd saved him, her own Jeremiah.

Then abruptly his face was gone, his body torn from hers, and, still dazed, all she saw above her was the pale blue morning sky. She heard grunts and the scuffle of bare feet, the scrape of steel against steel, and by the time she had rolled over onto her hands and knees, the deck of the *Colomba* was silent again. Before her lay Jeremiah's motionless body, his dark coat slashed and torn to show the white linen of his shirt, his face turned away from her, the wind from the water lifting and tossing his black hair above the spreading circle of blood. Unable to comprehend, she could only stare as Hamil, alive and unharmed, prodded Jeremiah's chest with the toe of his red boot.

With a small whimper of denial she crawled across the deck to where Jeremiah lay. On her knees she bent over him, her pale hair tangling into his. He was so still, his face relaxed, his lips parted with some final word she'd never hear. She touched his cheek, cool and unnaturally pale beneath his sun-browned skin, and let her fingers fall into the blood, his blood, that stained the silvery deck beside him.

Wild with grief, she looked up at Hamil. "You've killed him," she cried bitterly. "I was the one who fired at you, yet you killed *him* instead!"

Hamil frowned. "This shrew is a countess, Tomaso?"

"*Sì, sì,* yes!" said Tomaso, desperately eager. "Would I insult you with a gift of anything less? Mark her hair, her skin like porcelain beneath the dirt!"

The Scotsman stroked his thumb through his beard, studying Caro.

"Surely you will grant me safe passage now, *signore!* Who else but I, Tomaso, has ever brought you an English lady for your amusement?"

"She has not the look of a lady."

"But the other one, the *grandiosa contessa Inglese*, assured me it was true!" exclaimed Tomaso, clutching his hands anxiously before him. "Would she have paid me so handsomely if it were not so, eh?"

Abruptly Caro raised her face, tears streaming down her cheeks. "The Dowager Lady Byfield did this? Betrayed me when I trusted her friendship, sought her help for her only son? Frederick's mother hated me enough for *this?*"

Tomaso shrugged. "You were an inconvenience, *cara mia,* a difficulty she wished gone. You betrayed her son, eh? Now she has betrayed you."

Caro bowed her head over Jeremiah, overwhelmed by sorrow and guilt. This was her fault, not just for firing the gun, but for everything, from the very beginning. If she had not gone to Jeremiah that first night, he would live still. She had brought the death of the only man she'd ever really loved. Her body still bore the warm evidence of their lovemaking not an hour before, and the enormity of her loss swept over her.

"On your feet, woman, so I might look at ye," ordered Hamil. "Stand, or I'll have ye dragged to your feet!"

Slowly Caro rose to face him, forcing herself to meet his gaze even as she swayed on her feet. No matter what Dorinda had done to her or what she had done to herself, she was still the Countess of Byfield, and for the honor of Frederick's name she must not cower.

Oh, dear Lord, poor Frederick, and her heart sank even lower. How she'd failed him, too!

Hamil's eyes narrowed. "Your name, woman. The truth, or with Allah as my witness I shall end your miserable English life now."

"Caroline Harris Moncrief," she said softly. "Countess of Byfield."

"You swear it by all that ye infidels hold sacred?"

She nodded, her eyes filling again. "But why did you have to kill Captain Sparhawk?"

Hamil sniffed contemptuously. "He's no more dead than I, m'lady, no thanks to ye. He'll wish he were when next he wakes, but no ways worse. If I wished him dead, I woulda seen it done right, but what use would a dead man be to me?"

Her eyes widening with disbelief and hope, she began to drop down beside Jeremiah, but Hamil's hand jerked her back to her feet.

"Come," he said harshly. "I am your master now, and ye must think no more of him."

Slowly, painfully, Jeremiah fought his way back to consciousness. He was on a ship. He knew that much from the slow rocking and the distant rushing sound of the waves, and the familiar sound was the one thing of comfort to him. His whole body ached and throbbed, but the searing, blinding pain was concentrated in his left temple, as if whatever had caused it still hammered against his head. He wanted to curl into himself against the pain and retreat again into unconsciousness, but his legs felt strangely heavy, too heavy to move.

From a distance beyond the water, he heard a woman call his name. Her voice was gentle, familiar, and instinctively he turned his head toward it for comfort, groaning at the pain the slight effort caused him.

"Jeremiah, love, you're going to be all right," murmured Caro as she placed another damp rag, torn from her petticoat, onto the angry, bruised lump on

Jeremiah's head. All she'd been given to tend him was a bucket of water and a tiny lamp to keep away the rats here in the hold of Hamil's xebec, and she knew she should be grateful she'd been granted that much. The gash on Jeremiah's head had been relatively minor, as Hamil had predicted, but the bruise worried her for the damage that might lie behind it. "You'll be fine, I swear it, you will. Oh, love, will you ever forgive me what I've done to you!"

"What the devil have you done now?" croaked Jeremiah.

With a startled gasp Caro bent closer. "You *are* alive!"

"Barely." He forced himself to open his eyes a fraction, her taut, worried face spinning before him in dizzy circles. "Damnation."

"Here, drink this." Gently she lifted his head enough for him to sip from the dipper of water. "But don't move any more unless you wish to. There's no reason to, anyway."

"I can't. What happened to my legs?"

"Nothing," she said angrily. "Hamil's men put you in irons, though where he thought an unconscious man would run I'll never guess."

*Hamil.* At once the whole bitter scene on deck came back to him. "I should never have given you that pistol. They could have killed you."

"I was afraid of what you would try to do," she confessed. "I thought I could shoot him first because no one suspected me. If you had even moved, they would have murdered *you.*"

"It seems they half did anyway."

"I know." She hung her head forlornly, the dipper clutched tightly in her hand. "There's more that's my fault, Jeremiah. It was Frederick's mother who betrayed us first, selling us to Tomaso like sheep at the market. Your only misfortune was to be with me. Oh, I know I should never have trusted her, but for Frederick's sake, I—I believed what I wanted to."

Jeremiah reached out to take her hand, fitting his fingers into hers. He understood why she'd done it, maybe better than she did herself. With a family as strong as the Sparhawks behind him, it pained him to imagine poor Caro so starved for a parent's affection and approval that she would turn to a mother as evil as Frederick's.

"It's done, and I'll live," he said, wondering whether it was love alone that had changed him, or if being struck on the head had had something to do with it, too. There'd been a time when he would have berated her for her misplaced trust and blamed her for how desperate their situation had become. But now all he saw was how much worse it could be; they were both alive, relatively unharmed, and they were still together. "I'll hear no more about it being your fault."

She would have wept if she'd had any tears left. "You're too good for me, Jeremiah," she whispered. "Far, far too good."

"Good for nothing and fit for less, is closer to the mark," he said gruffly. "But how are you, sweetheart? I knocked you harder than I intended, but I wanted you out of Hamil's way."

"I'm fine, now that you are, too." She lifted his hand to her lips, her smile shaky. "Most likely I would have come closer to hitting Mount Vesuvius than Hamil."

"True enough," he agreed, thinking how strangely wonderful it was that, even as Hamil's prisoners, they could still make jests. "We shall have to work on your aim."

With a loud scrape the hatch overhead was lifted off, and a beam of bright sunlight pierced the gloom of the hold. Swearing, Jeremiah lifted his arm to shield his eyes. Three of Hamil's crewmen dropped through the opening without bothering with the stairway, and motioned for Caro and Jeremiah to climb the steps to the deck above.

Caro scrambled to her feet, her hands squared defiantly on her hips. "Captain Sparhawk can't be moved," she said sternly to the tallest man. It didn't matter that the man spoke no English; her voice and manner were expressive in any language. "He has suffered a very grievous wound to his head, and I don't want him injured further."

The man lifted his bearded chin higher, clearly offended to be addressed so insolently by a mere woman. His hand went to the hilt of his saber, another kind of wordless message.

But Caro held her ground, unimpressed. "I'm not going anywhere without Captain Sparhawk, and so you may tell Mr. Al-Ameer if—"

"Caro, lass, hush," warned Jeremiah, unsteadily rising to his feet by leaning against the bulkhead. "This isn't worth your neck. You know it could be we've made Tripoli and they'd like us to go ashore."

"Oh." Slipping her shoulder beneath his arm to help him walk, she glanced at him sideways, the proud, haughty countess suddenly gone and only a scared, vulnerable woman in her place. "Somehow everything will be all right, won't it, Jeremiah?"

He sighed deeply, wishing he could be both truthful and encouraging. "Somehow, aye, it will, love. With you by my side, it always is."

He knew he didn't deserve that bright smile from her, but he claimed it anyway. God only knows when she'd have reason to smile again, and wherever he was bound, that lovely memory might be all he'd have to comfort him.

The midday sun off the water was blinding, slicing like razors into Jeremiah's head, and he stopped at the top of the companionway, struggling to adjust to the brightness before he must face Hamil. He had a brief impression of a coastline, the curving arms of a wide bay, the white fortress city of Tripoli.

One of the seaman jabbed him in the back to hurry, and with enormous effort he raised himself from Caro's support and forced himself to walk unassisted, the heavy iron chain dragging between his feet. Hamil stood aft near the wheel, watching them approach, and Jeremiah prayed not to falter or fall beneath his enemy's eyes.

"Sparhawk." Hamil looked him up and down, his lip curling at how torn and dirty Jeremiah's clothing had become. "I didna remember the name until this morn."

"Hamil or Gordon, I didn't forget yours." Jeremiah's disdain equaled Hamil's as he studied the Scotsman's opulent dress, the silk sleeves billowing in the wind and the gold thread and sequins on his waistcoat twinkling like tiny reflected suns. Gotten up like some ten-guinea French whore, thought Jeremiah contemptuously, all spangles and tinsel and empty show.

"I took your *Chanticleer,* Sparhawk," said Hamil slowly as he studied Jeremiah, the gentle burr of his accent softening the calculated cruelty of his words. "A bonny little brig. I sold her to the Bey of Tunis, who fancied a Yankee-built toy. Alas, the bey's men are better suited to camels than the sea, and she broke up on the rocks off Zembra not a fortnight after I sold her off."

Jeremiah felt as if he'd been struck again, and feeling Caro's fingers tighten around his in silent sympathy did nothing to ease his sense of powerlessness. To learn that his *Chanticleer,* lovingly built to his own designs not four years ago on the river at home, had been casually, carelessly destroyed at the whim of a heathen ruler was to lose another friend. Until then he hadn't realized how some part of him had planned to rescue the brig along with Davy. Grimly he wondered if the *Chanticleer*'s fate was some awful premonition, that he and Caro and Davy were all doomed to die like the brig on this same bleak, cheerless coast.

"I took your vessel last winter, Sparhawk," said Hamil. Swiftly he reached out, grabbed the neck of Jeremiah's shirt and tore the front in two. Instantly Jeremiah recoiled, his hands bunched in fists at his side as the two halves of his shirt fluttered back in the breeze. His chest was left bare, the jagged pale scar unmistakable beneath the whorls of dark hair, and Hamil's smile was wide.

"I took your *Chanticleer*," he continued, satisfied by what he'd seen, "and ye gave her up with nary a fight or a whimper."

"Damn your lies," answered Jeremiah sharply. "Isn't this scar proof enough? We fought your thieving deceit to our dying breath."

"Then why, Sparhawk," taunted Hamil, "do ye still live?"

"To see you go to the devil first, Hamil." Forgetting all caution, Jeremiah spat at the Scotsman's feet. "God help me, I'll see you in your grave."

"As Allah wills," said Hamil, glancing briefly at the spittle on his red boots, "ye cowardly son of a Yankee bitch."

Jeremiah lunged toward him, the shackles clanging across the deck, and immediately four of Hamil's men seized his arms. He lashed out against them blindly, furiously fighting as much against his own sense of helplessness as the four men who held him fast. But he was still weak and his own strength soon exhausted, and as they jerked him, panting, roughly to his feet, Jeremiah barely had breath enough to curse them all.

But Caro, where was Caro? Twisting wildly, he searched for her and found her, standing pale and rigid with self-control, with a turbaned sailor holding each of her arms. The longboat for shore was being lowered, and clearly she would be a passenger in it. With sickening clarity, Jeremiah realized how neatly he had let his temper play into Hamil's hands. What easier way could there have been for her to be separated from him?

"Where are you taking her?" he demanded. "By God, if you harm her—"

"Ye shall do what, my fine Yankee captain?" The Scotsman stepped closer, his blue eyes bright with malicious amusement beneath his bristling ginger brows. An ill-fed boy rushed to kneel at his feet and wipe his master's boots clean, and when he was done Hamil carelessly kicked him aside. "Ye canna help yourself. How can ye help the lady?"

Nothing Hamil said could have wounded Jeremiah more, for what he said was the truth. She was at the ladder now, her pale hair blowing around her face and her blue eyes wide with longing and despair as she looked to him for the help he couldn't give. They were going to take her and he might well never see her again, and there wasn't a blasted, bloody thing he could do to stop them. So much, he thought bitterly, for the power of love. He had failed them all, his ship and crew and now his own dear Caro.

"But ye are not the only cowardly American," continued Hamil scornfully as he pointed over the larboard rail. "Ye have much company."

There in the shallows of the harbor lay the frigate *Philadelphia,* once the pride of the tiny American navy, run aground and then surrendered in confusion by her captain to the pasha's men. Now in place of the stars and stripes that Jeremiah himself had proudly fought beneath flew the green flag with three white crescents of the frigate's captors, and even at this distance Jeremiah saw how sadly ill kept the once-great ship had become.

The three hundred Americans of the *Philadelphia*'s crew were already prisoners in that white city; Jeremiah would make it three hundred and one. He thought again of the wreck of his own hopes here in the same harbor, and craned his neck for one more glimpse of Caro.

But the space where she had stood was empty, and so, he knew, was the place where his heart had been.

"Where are you taking me?" asked Caro as the spray from the boat's oars blew into her face. She clung to her seat as they raced across the bay, her gaze never leaving the xebec where Jeremiah still remained. "To some other prison?"

Hamil frowned. "No prison, m'lady. Ye are a countess. Ye shall be a member of my household for so long as it pleases."

She didn't want to know who would be pleased, or how. "I can tell you now you'll get no ransom for me."

He shrugged. "It's not for the ransom that I took ye, m'lady."

She could no longer make out the people on the xebec's deck, and she wondered with despair if they'd taken Jeremiah back to the hold. Dear God, she prayed, let the lamp still be there, for she didn't know what would happen to him if he was forced alone into the darkness. She could not forget her final sight of him earlier, exhausted and defeated as he sagged between the sailors supporting him, the pain and defeat in his eyes already almost beyond bearing. "What will you do with Captain Sparhawk?"

"For his insolence, I should send him as a slave to the quarries. A man his size would be useful there, and the sun and the lash would go far to curing his temper." His smile chilled her more than his words. "In a year ye would not recognize him."

She could not imagine a man as proud as Jeremiah a slave, toiling in a quarry like a pack animal. "It would kill him."

"Aye, perhaps it will," said Hamil as casually as if they were discussing the likelihood of rain. "But ye best think no more of him, m'lady."

"But I love him," she cried with anguish, "and I cannot forget him simply because you order it!"

"Ye can, and ye must." His face was stern, his voice disconcertingly quiet despite the threat it carried. If she had been a man, realized Caro, he would have killed her, too, without another thought. "Ye are in Tripoli now, m'lady, and I am your master. Ye have no others. Ye will do well not to forget it."

The city was enclosed by a high, thick, white wall, flanked by two fortresses, bristling with cannon to protect the harbor from invasion. Caro, Hamil and a small party of his men entered by the northwest gate that led to the harbor, riding on horses that had been waiting at the waterfront for them. As they rode slowly through the crowded, narrow streets, people were quick to run from Hamil's path, some men bowing respectfully low and others merely staring with open awe at their country's most notorious corsair.

For Caro, there were only stares. At first she wondered why there were no women in the streets, until she realized that they were the shapeless, scurrying figures wrapped so completely in black that only one eye showed. Caro, sitting sidesaddle in her European clothes, her face uncovered and her pale hair loose to her shoulders, was a sight few Tripolitans could resist. She kept her eyes straight ahead, ignoring the leering men as best she could, but by the time they reached Hamil's house, she was too hot and exhausted from the strain to notice much except the tall marble pillars that they passed between.

With more gallantry than Caro either expected or wished, Hamil himself came to help her from her horse, his large, freckled hands familiarly taking her by the waist and lifting her from the ground. He was a large man, nearly as big as Jeremiah, and equally accustomed to the power his size granted. As soon as her feet touched the ground she swiftly eased herself away from his hands.

He noticed her skittishness, his eyes narrowing, but said nothing, merely beckoning for her to follow him through a short passageway. To her surprise they entered an elegant courtyard, two stories high with open piazzas that faced onto the courtyard. More columns of polished Egyptian marble supported the piazzas, and the floor of the courtyard was inlaid with elaborate porphyry.

In the center was a carved marble cistern and a bench beside it, shaded by the nodding fronds of a small date palm. On the bench were plump red cushions, a pitcher and a goblet, a small book left open, and discarded on the floor lay a pair of green openbacked lady's slippers, but no sign of the reader who'd left them. Yet Caro's hopes rose. If there was already a lady in Hamil's house—a lady frivolous enough to wear embroidered green slippers with red heels—then perhaps his interest in Caro would be only as a hostage.

Two servants, a thin man in a turban and an older woman, rushed to Hamil, bowing low enough to touch their foreheads to the floor before him. He waved his hand impatiently for them to rise and gave them orders in a language Caro didn't understand. The woman turned to her and bowed, though not so low as she had to her master, and nodded vigorously.

"Abidzu will take ye to your room," explained Hamil. "She will bathe ye, and see that ye are dressed more befitting your station. Ye may go wherever ye please in my house, but if ye try to leave without my permission, ye shall be punished."

"So I am in fact your prisoner?" asked Caro tartly, and immediately regretted it. What was she doing, baiting him like that?

But to her surprise, Hamil looked disconcerted, not angry, as he glanced away, running his thumb through the thicket of his beard. "In my home ye shall want for nothing, m'lady," he repeated. "Ye shall have every comfort."

"Except my freedom?"

He ignored her question. "Tonight, when ye have bathed and rested, ye will dine with me. Abidzu will bring ye to my rooms."

He turned swiftly, his boot heels echoing across the stone floor as he left with his men. Caro sighed, rubbing her fingers into her temples. She didn't want to dine with Hamil tonight, especially not in his rooms, but there was probably no way she could refuse without earning that promised punishment, whatever it might be. Could it be so much worse than being alone with the man in his bedchamber?

Wearily she followed Abidzu up the stairs to a room that overlooked the courtyard, a room that was clearly intended for favored guests, not prisoners. Rich car-

pets were laid across the marble floor, and the walls
were inlaid with painted porcelain tiles. For sleeping,
there was a kind of raised platform with a mattress,
coverlet, and cushions in the center of the room. Besides a large mirror on the wall and two low chests, the
room's only other furnishings were two old-fashioned
English armchairs that looked as out of place as Caro
herself felt. She went to the single arched window, its
shutters thrown back to catch the breezes from the
water.

She leaned outward, looking to the fortress at the
southern corner of the city's wall. As a warning,
Hamil had pointed it out to her as the prison for infidels. If Frederick still lived, if Jeremiah's friend David Kerr were still a captive, then they would both be
kept there. Whenever she thought of Frederick, he was
always in one of the comfortable, elegant rooms at
Blackstone House, and she could not imagine him
surviving two years in that bleak, windowless fortress. Perhaps all the warnings from others had been
right. Perhaps he was already long beyond her help,
and this entire disastrous voyage had been nothing
more than a pointless chase to rescue a dead man.

She looked to the harbor for the xebec, Jeremiah's
prison. She had done that to him, just as she'd been
the cause of Frederick's capture, and overwhelmed by
the odds against the men she loved, her eyes filled with
tears.

Yet tears would solve nothing, help no one, and she
forced herself to try to think instead. Three men, three
prisoners. She, too, was a prisoner, but one bound
only by threats, not shackles. If any of them were ever
to return to a Christian world, it was up to her to find

a way. Neither Frederick nor Jeremiah would like having their fates decided by a woman, but she had no choice. There was, quite simply, no one else.

Jeremiah had promised her everything would be all right, and Jeremiah would never lie to her. He loved her too much. Somehow they would be reunited. Of course everything would be all right.

Somehow...

Caro closed her eyes as Abidzu drew the comb through her wet hair to help dry it. She had been bathed in perfumed water by Abidzu, all the salt from the sea scrubbed away, and in place of the rough clothing of the Neapolitan serving girl, she now wore a loose robe of blue striped silk banded with gold braid.

Yet instead of relaxing her, Abidzu's attentions had only reminded Caro of what Hamil would expect from her in return. No matter what he'd said, she couldn't believe that all of his guests were treated so indulgently, and as Abidzu finished braiding her hair, her apprehension grew.

This could be her first step toward freedom, the first time she must depend on her own resources to defend herself. Though Hamil's men had taken the pistol Jeremiah had given her, there was sure to be a knife at dinner that she could hide away in her skirts for later, when she might need it. Her fingers tightened on the carved arms of the chair as she remembered the hungry way Hamil had looked at her on the xebec.

"Abidzu," said a woman's voice curtly in accented English. "Leave us at once."

Caro's eyes flew open, and she turned about in her chair as Abidzu hurried from the room, bowing low to the two beautiful young women who stood in the doorway. The taller one was nearly as fair as Caro herself, with dark eyes in startling contrast to her blond hair, and a full, ripe figure beneath a silk robe identical to the one Caro was wearing. The other had hair as black and shining as a raven's wing, drawn up under a silver fillet to show the hoops she wore in her ears. She stood with her hands clasped over her belly, rounded with the first months of pregnancy, and watched Caro with shy, heavy-lidded eyes.

Her gaze intent on Caro, the blond woman lifted her hand to smooth back her hair, and a score of silver bangles clattered down her forearm. "Are you the English noblewoman that came this day with Hamil Al-Ameer?"

"Of course she is, Bella," whispered the smaller woman, still loudly enough for Caro to hear. "Who else could she be? But look at her! What could Hamil be thinking of? She must be as old as my mother!"

Slowly Caro rose to her feet and walked around the chair to face them. She bit back a retort to the comment about her age. They were scarcely more than girls, and to them she probably did seem like an ancient old crone.

"I am the Countess of Byfield, yes," she said. "Who are you?"

The smaller woman sighed wistfully. "Hamil didn't tell you?"

"Hamil is a busy man, Leilah," said Bella impatiently. "He can't do everything."

"But Bella—"

"Hush!" Visibly straightening her shoulders like a soldier before a battle, Bella looked back to Caro. "We are the wives of Hamil Al-Ameer," she said, "and if you wish to become his concubine, you must now speak to us."

# Chapter Sixteen

"His *concubine?*" Caro shook her head in disbelief as she looked from one girl to the other, and very nearly laughed from the sheer preposterousness of the situation. "Is it the custom here for a wife—or wives—to interview a husband's mistress?"

Leilah flushed and stared down at the floor, but Bella's brown eyes met Caro's without flinching. "It is not an interview, Countess of Byfield. If Hamil chooses to keep you, that is his decision."

"Believe me," said Caro dryly, "it will be as much my decision as Hamil's. And please, call me, Caro. Your name is Bella?"

"Isabella, though Hamil prefers Bella. This is Leilah. And we must call you 'my lady,' for Hamil wishes it so." She pursed her lips, determined not to be distracted. "We want you to know that only we wives and our children will be entitled to a full share of our husband's goods when he dies. As a concubine, you and your children will only receive half a share."

"Though you would naturally prefer not to divide the estate by even that extra half." Caro sighed, thinking how whether in Portsmouth or Tripoli, she still seemed to be in the middle of such quarrels. "You needn't worry at all, you know. I have no wish—none whatsoever—to become Hamil's mistress."

"None?" Bella narrowed her eyes suspiciously. "Hamil is a man all women desire, my lady. He is strong and virile and very handsome."

"And he has blessed us both with sons!" blurted Leilah, then at once stared back at the floor.

Caro's glance fell to Leilah's thickening waist. "You have other children? But you are scarcely more than children yourselves!"

Bella smiled knowingly. "I was thirteen when Hamil took me from my brother's ship, and within the year he married me and gave me my first son, Allah be praised. Another son and a daughter have followed, and I am yet but eighteen. You cannot doubt how potent a man my husband is."

"I most certainly would not," said Caro hastily. She had been barely older than Bella when she'd wed Frederick, but she herself had been all the children Frederick wanted. By the time Bella reached her own age of twenty-nine, she could well be a grandmother. No wonder they thought she was so appallingly old! Yet in a way she envied them the same way as she'd envied Desire Herendon, and she thought wistfully of how much she'd give to bear Jeremiah's child.

She smiled gently at the two young faces before her. "You love Hamil, don't you?"

"Of course I do," answered Bella fervently, and at her side Leilah nodded in agreement. "*We* do. We love him, and he loves us, as it should be between husbands and wives."

How simple Bella made it all sound! "Then you will understand that I would not wish to come between you."

"No?" Bella remained skeptical. "Why wouldn't you?"

"Because I, too, have a husband that I love very much, and there is no more room in my heart for another," said Caro, painfully aware of how much more her words meant. Between Frederick and Jeremiah, her heart was overflowing. "My husband was captured by Hamil and is his prisoner. I came to Tripoli to find him, not to become Hamil's mistress."

Swiftly the two girls exchanged glances. "If your husband were returned to you," asked Leilah carefully, "would you leave and swear never to return?"

"I would swear it now," said Caro fervently.

Another look passed between Hamil's wives, and slowly Leilah nodded.

"Leilah's father is a special friend of the pasha's," explained Bella. "If you swear you will leave Tripoli with your husband, and if, until then, you hold true to what you profess and keep yourself from Hamil's bed, then we shall pledge to help you."

"I swear, by whatever you wish." It would be the easiest promise to keep that Caro had ever made, and impulsively she kissed each girl on the cheek. "You will never have anything to fear from me."

Both Bella and Leilah went still, stunned by such a sign of affection from the woman they'd feared as a rival, then suddenly began to giggle with relief like the young women they were.

"We thought you would be very grand, my lady," confessed Bella, her serious role as mediator done.

"Hamil is most proud of having captured you. A British noblewoman! He told us we must be respectful to you, and speak only English in your presence."

Caro laughed, amused to hear that anyone would consider her grand and daunting. Certainly no one ever had before. "Your English is better than that of many people born in England itself."

Bella's cheeks pinked with pride. "That is Hamil's doing. He wished his wives to speak his language, and he bought us a tutor, a slave, from your royal city of London, so we might learn only the best."

"Poor Mr. Peck!" Leilah sighed sadly. "He was a good teacher, but he wasn't very wise."

Bella sighed, too. "He was greedy, you see. He stole one of Leilah's gold necklaces and tried to sell it at the market. Of course he was caught, and Hamil punished him himself, using his own sword to cut off Mr. Peck's hands. Then he nailed them himself onto the walls near the east gate to warn other thieves against stealing from Hamil's wives."

She smiled contentedly, oblivious to the look of horror on Caro's face. "You see why we cannot believe you wouldn't want such a man as Hamil for yourself. What other man would show such love, such devotion, to his women?"

"Now I can see that Tomaso was right," said Hamil with satisfaction. "Ye are every bit the noblewoman he promised ye were."

At the other end of the dining table, Caro smiled faintly. It was one thing to swear to Bella and Leilah that she would keep away from their husband, but it was quite another to be alone with Hamil himself. His gaze had not left her since she had entered the room, and too well Caro knew that the hunger in his eyes had nothing to do with the mountain of food between them. Through an arched doorway, beneath a large framed looking glass, she saw another mattress on a raised platform much like the bed in her own room, only larger, broader, piled even higher with silken pillows and coverlets in luxurious invitation—an invitation Caro had every intention of refusing.

"An English countess, from one of the greatest families in Britain," continued Hamil with relish. "No one would e'er doubt your blood an' breeding to see ye tonight."

She wondered uneasily what he would say if he knew the truth of her background—not, of course, that she'd any intention of telling him. "A countess, yes," she said, "but hardly an English one, not dressed like this."

"These garments are not proper for your rank?" he asked with a strange mixture of outrage and concern. "Ye would wear richer in London?"

"Not richer, no," she said quickly, not wishing to anger him over something so inconsequential. "Few ladies at any court in Europe would dress so grandly, except, perhaps, General Bonaparte's wife Josephine."

"Proper, that is. The general is a great man." Hamil himself was dressed even more splendidly than usual tonight, wearing a fitted waistcoat so thick with gold embroidery that the silk beneath was completely hidden. To Caro's surprise, he had left off his turban, and unlike the other Tripolitan men, he had did not shave his head. Cherubic red gold curls surrounded his forehead, completely at odds with the cruel lines of his face. Caro thought again of the poor tutor and shuddered.

"And your chambers, m'lady? Are they pleasing?"

"My room is lovely, thank you, as is this meal." The table was set with European silver and porcelain dishes—doubtless plunder—but no utensils, for Hamil had adopted the local custom of eating with one hand, scooping the food into his mouth with his fingers. So much, thought Caro unhappily, for claiming a knife for her defense.

Hamil grunted. "Your friend Sparhawk would weep to have such quarters this night."

"Where is he?" she asked quickly. "Is he still on board your ship?"

"My ship?" He lewdly sucked the mutton grease from his thumb as he watched for her reaction. "The hold would seem like the very palace compared to where he lies now."

Caro's fingers gripped the arm of her chair. "You have taken him to the quarries?"

"I told ye, m'lady, ye are to waste no more time considering a cowardly brute like that one," he said carelessly, and tossed the mutton bone onto the floor behind him. "Ye are a lady. Ye deserve better."

As desperate as Caro was for news of Jeremiah she realized that Hamil had no intention of telling her more, at least not then. He was toying with her, testing her. If she was ever to learn anything from him, she would have to do the same to him.

But while Hamil could taunt her with Jeremiah, all she had to bargain with in return was herself, and to

succeed she must remain every inch the highborn
countess Hamil believed her to be. If she faltered even
for a moment, she would lose all her value to him. She
would become simply another female captive, little
better than a slave, and there'd be no hope for her,
even less for Jeremiah and Frederick.

Oh, yes, the stakes were very high, thought Caro
grimly, and it would be the most dangerous game
she'd ever played.

"So you believe I deserve better," she said slowly.
"Better meaning yourself?"

He smiled, supremely confident, and sat back in his
chair to study her. "Ye met my lassies this afternoon,
didn't ye? They've no complaints, the randy little
creatures."

Caro shrugged and crossed her knees, the striped
silk gliding seductively across her long legs in a way
that riveted his gaze. "They are charming girls, but
then they have seen nothing of the world for compar-
ison."

His smile faded. "And you have, m'lady?"

"I'm not a girl, Hamil Al-Ameer." She smoothed
the silk across her thighs with her open palm, praying
that her words sounded more convincing to him than
they did to her. "I thought you'd noticed that for
yourself."

Hamil didn't answer. He didn't need to. The look in
his eyes was beyond words, a wolfish predatory look
that made her feel like a bleating lamb waiting to be
devoured. No, worse than that; she felt as if she were
thirteen again.

*"No, Caroline, no!"* said her mother furiously,
*cuffing her across the ear while her mother's friend,*

*the out-of-work actor who was pretending to be Sir Harry, had waited for the chance to fondle Caro again. "You cannot flinch when the gentleman touches you! The gentleman has something you want—his gold—and in exchange you must give him whatever he desires, and that is yourself. Do you understand?"*

*"But Mama—"*

*Her mother's hand had struck her again, harder. "Do you* understand, *daughter?"*

*She had pressed her hand to her jaw, fighting back the shameful tears that would only earn her another blow. "Yes, Mama," she whispered miserably. "I understand."*

Abruptly Caro pushed her chair back from the table and swept across the room to stand before the window, her back to Hamil as she struggled to regain her self-control. She wasn't thirteen, and she didn't answer to her mother any longer.

Be calm, she ordered herself fiercely, breathing in the scent of orange blossoms from the garden below. You must not let Hamil see your agitation or know your fear. Be gracious, be genteel. Be Lady Caroline Moncrief, Countess of Byfield, because that is what you are.

"This is a long way from Edinburgh, isn't it?" she asked lightly. She would make him speak of himself, not her. What man wouldn't do that? "Why did you leave?"

He didn't answer at first, and when she looked over her shoulder she found him standing not a foot away from her, and she gasped. How had he crept up on her so silently like that?

"What was in Scotland to make me stay?" he asked with a bitterness that Caro hadn't expected. "What could I have been there? A fisherman like my father, toiling ev'ry day of my life for less than nothing, a little man livin' in fear of being taken up one more time by the English press and forced to serve against the French?"

"You would rather kill and imprison your own countrymen?"

"Aye." His expression was cold, without mercy, and it took all her will not to move away from him. Standing, she saw he wore his saber even now, and a dagger with a long, curving blade tucked into his sash. Was that the same knife that had so scarred her Jeremiah? How many others had died by the same blade, even, perhaps her own poor Frederick, God help him?

"I kill who would kill me first, m'lady," he said, "and take those prisoners my master the pasha wishes. For ten years I served your King George in his navy. I learned my trade but earned no reward for it."

"None? I thought that when a prize was taken, even the lowest boy received a share."

"A pitiful handful o' coins for the men, m'lady, while the officers need wagons to carry away their share of the gold." He grunted with disgust. "Oh, aye, your king is eager to have a poor Scotsman fight for him, but without influence or a fine English name there was to be no advancin' through the ranks for such as me. The pasha values a man for what he is. Here I have power, riches, my bonny little wives and my sons, and I am second only to the pasha himself."

"Doubtless the pasha is grateful to have you sailing on his behalf instead of against him." She turned away toward the window to hide her revulsion, thinking of how many lives Hamil had ruined.

"No question of that, m'lady," said Hamil proudly, "for I've filled his coffers as well as my own."

"You've earned fame as well as riches, you know." She leaned from the window to pluck a cluster of white blossoms from the tree below, trying not to think of how misplaced a man's pride could be. "Didn't you see how all on board the *Colomba* knew you by sight alone? Even in London they fear your name."

"Fear is respect, m'lady," he said, watching how the silk slid over her hips as she bent forward at the window. "The only true way to rule other men."

"And what of your soul?" she asked as she turned back toward him, twirling the flowers beneath her nose. "Is what you gained by converting to Islam worth damning yourself as a Christian for eternity?"

Hamil made a guttural sound of disgust deep in his throat. "When the bloody priests can offer me the same as the pasha, then I'll go back to the church."

She sleeked back her hair and tucked the white flower behind her ear. "Then here in Tripoli, Hamil Al-Ameer, it would seem you have all you could ever wish."

"Aye, m'lady," he whispered roughly. "Almost."

He reached to touch her, the curling hair on the back of his hand glinting red gold in the light of the setting sun. As in a dream she watched his hand come closer. A pirate's hand stained forever with death and sorrow, a hand that had brought such suffering to the ones she loved, ready to mark her with the same sins, closer and closer....

302      *Sparhawk's Lady*

*"You must give the gentleman whatever he desires, Caroline, and that is yourself. Do you understand that much, daughter? Will you ever understand?"*

With a hiss Caro jerked beyond Hamil's reach, her striped skirts swirling about her.

"You think that because you have stolen and killed enough to make you rich that you are a gentleman, too, don't you?" she cried, panicking. "That is why you want me, isn't it, an English countess to add to your collection of stolen jewels and plate!"

"What I want, m'lady, is a woman who knows better than to trouble me." He grabbed her arm and effortlessly twisted it behind her back until she yelped with pain.

"Let me go, Hamil!" she cried, trying desperately to free herself. She could feel his breath warm on her bare shoulder, and the stiff gold threads on his waistcoat prickling into her arm. "Oh, please, let me go, you're hurting me!"

"That's what I intended, m'lady," he said, taking pleasure in her pain. "Countess or whore, all women are the same beneath their skirts. Ye would do well to remember it."

He shoved her roughly away and she stumbled forward, catching herself on the edge of the table. She turned swiftly to face him, her breathing ragged with pain as she gingerly held her arm. "You've no right to do that to me, none at all!"

"I've every right in the world, m'lady," he said, his smile curling upward through his beard. "*My* world. Ye are my prisoner, and I can do whate'er I wish with ye. I can sell ye, or rape ye, or kill ye, m'lady, it's all the same with the pasha."

"Then why not do it all, and be done with me?" she asked bitterly.

He laughed with his head thrown back, and she hated the sound of it. "Ah, but that would be a waste of Allah's gifts, wouldn't it? I've scarce begun to know ye. I've never had a countess before, and mayhap ye *shall* be different from the others."

She backed away, holding the edge of the table. If only there had been a knife!

"Ye have the fire in your blood for me, m'lady. Ye can deny it, but I can see it clear in your eyes." He laughed again, his voice growing softer. "But not tonight, m'lady, not so soon. I'd rather take my time with ye. Ye shall dine here with me every night, and ye must strive to make yourself agreeable to me, before ye can know the pleasure of loving Hamil Al-Ameer."

"The devil I will!" The white blossoms behind her ear had been crushed in the struggle, and with trembling fingers she tore the white flowers free and let the little branch drop to the floor. She'd lost, at least for tonight, and she hated herself for failing, almost as much as she hated the man before her. "I'll never do anything to please you!"

"Oh, ye will, m'lady, ye will." His laughter vanished as he absently fingered the jeweled hilt of his saber. "Because if ye don't, it will go hard on ye, m'lady, very hard."

His gaze never leaving her, he deftly swept the dagger from its sheath, flipped it over and around the back of his hand in a single elegant motion.

"And if ye do not try your best, m'lady," he said, his eyes glittering with anticipation, "then Sparhawk shall be waiting to feel my displeasure."

* * *

"You kept your word, my lady," said Bella the next morning when they met beneath the palm tree by the cistern. "You did not lie with Hamil in the night."

Caro stiffened, wondering how the younger woman could know. Bella stretched languorously against the cushions on the marble bench and smiled, a smile far beyond her years.

"When he left you, he came to me," she purred, "and he did not leave until dawn. His ardor was such that I knew he could not have taken another woman before me. Countess or not, last night he wished only for his Bella."

She swung her legs over the edge of the bench and leaned close to Caro. "You have kept your promise, and now it is time for Leilah and me to keep ours, and seek your husband's freedom."

Caro took a deep breath, knowing how much she was going to gamble. "My husband, and two Americans with him."

"Three men?" Bella lowered her chin. "We had agreed on your husband and no more."

"Last night Hamil was eager to make love to me," said Caro evenly. "I turned him away and sent him to you, but he is intrigued enough that if I say the word he will return to my chamber."

"The Americans will be most difficult," said Bella with obvious reluctance. She pulled one of the cushions into her lap, holding it tightly in her arms. "Our countries are at war. The American prisoners from the warship in the harbor are obstinate and ill-tempered, a bane to the pasha and his men."

Caro's expression didn't change. "I don't know how long I can refuse Hamil. Clearly he's not a man accustomed to hearing no."

"That is true." With a troubled sigh, Bella rested her cheek on the pillow in her arms. "Then give me the three names. I shall do what I can."

Jeremiah stumbled again, and again felt the cudgel jab into his ribs to prod him along, his leader's derisive laugh loud in his ears. Before Hamil's boat was out of sight, his crew had stolen Jeremiah's shoes and every scrap of clothing except his trousers. Maybe they'd been ordered to do it; Jeremiah wouldn't put anything past Hamil now. But even those thieving jackals had been taken aback by the scar on Jeremiah's body, pointing with their dirty fingers and talking excitedly among themselves. Maybe they even remembered how he'd earned it.

He stumbled again, swearing to himself at his own infernal helplessness. It was hard enough walking barefoot through the hot, rocky streets of Tripoli, the heavy iron chain of the shackles dragging between his legs with each step and his wrists tied tightly behind his back, but worse still to do it blindfolded, led along like a pack animal with a rope around his shoulders, spat upon and mocked by any stranger who wished the pleasure.

Where, he wondered as he cursed his ignorance, where were they taking him? He took small comfort in the rag tied around his eyes, for it meant they considered him troublesome enough to hide their secrets from him. If he'd been bound only for the quarries that were the final destination for so many captives, they wouldn't have bothered.

The best he could hope for was that they'd put him in the prison with the other Americans from the *Philadelphia*. There at least he'd receive better treatment than if he were alone, and have the solace of being among men who spoke his language. Perhaps in the prison, too, he could learn of Davy's fate, and Jeremiah's wildest dream was to find Davy himself, alive and well. With Davy, he knew they'd be able to escape and then find Caro.

*Caro.* He remembered her smile, her laugh, the way she always trusted him to make things right, and oh, he'd done it up royally right this time, hadn't he? He'd seen the way Hamil had looked at her, and he couldn't bear the thought of what the bastard was doing to her now. Not his Caro, his lovely, precious Caro...

The man with the rope jerked Jeremiah to one side, and his foot struck something hard. Steps, he thought, feeling his way upward, then the air on his bare skin turned cooler as they moved out of the bright sun and into a building. The rocky ground beneath his feet was gone, replaced by a cool, polished floor of stone. Once more, briefly, he felt the sun, and with it the sweet, surprising fragrance of oranges and the distant murmur of women's voices. Jeremiah frowned, turning his head toward the sound. What manner of prison could this be?

The rope pulled him onward, down more passageways and steps, until Jeremiah heard the man call to another. There was the sound of a door opening, a heavy door from the creak of the hinges. The man said something more and cut away the tarred cords that had bound Jeremiah's wrists. Jeremiah gasped as the blood returned to his hands, but as he did, the man shoved him hard, pitching him off balance and sprawling to the stone floor. The man laughed one last time and the door slammed shut, followed by the scrape of the bolt being pulled across. Then footsteps echoing, fading in the hallway, then silence.

Painfully Jeremiah dragged himself to his knees. "Is anyone else here?" he asked, his words echoing back at him quickly enough for him to know the room was small. "Any other poor beggars here, or am I the only one?"

No answer, no reply, crushing his hopes for company. His fingers shook as he tried to unfasten the cloth around his eyes, unable to get a grip on the fabric. He didn't want to be alone. He hated not seeing, hated the darkness, the old fears that would surely come with it. Desperately he clawed at the blindfold, finally tearing it from his eyes.

And all he saw was more blackness. The cell had no windows, no cracks in its walls, not even a tiny strip of light where the door had closed behind him. Nothing but darkness so complete he could feel it pressing in around him, on him, heavy and endless, ready to steal his breath, his sanity, his very life....

Damnation, he wouldn't let it happen! He crouched against his heels, his fists clenched like knots at his side, and struggled against the panic. It was Hamil who'd done this to him, and he refused to let the bastard have this last victory. He couldn't. *He couldn't.*

Because Caro needed him.

He whispered her name, and suddenly her face was there before him, shining with happiness against the black, the way it had been that morning on board the *Raleigh*. Her upturned eyes were the same blue as the summer sky, her lips as rosy as if he'd just kissed them, and he could almost count every gold-dusted freckle across the bridge of her nose. She laughed, and he smiled, both at her and the wonder of the love he'd found. With her, the darkness would never be the same. Caro would always be his candle, a bright spark to drive away his demons.

Slowly, so slowly that he didn't know when it had begun, his hands began to relax and uncurl. His heartbeat slowed, and the ragged terror of his breathing eased. He sat back on the floor, finding the wall and leaning against it. He tipped his head against the cool stone, closed his eyes and opened them again. The darkness stayed the same, and, miraculously, so did he.

Because Caro needed him.

Because he needed her.

It was, thought Hamil, better than any entertainment he had yet devised. The more obvious kinds of torture, the kind he'd favored in his earlier years as a corsair, were over so quickly, no matter how strong his victims. Bloodletting alone bored him now. Now he knew that the most exquisite suffering wasn't caused by a sword or a lash, but rather the more devious, more lasting damage that words and images could bring to the spirit itself. And what he had arranged tonight—praise Allah—it would be a finer show than anything at the pasha's court.

The countess sat beside him, her legs folded beneath her on the cushions as he had ordered. He had chosen her costume, too, the robe of sheerest silk that revealed more beneath the gold embroidery than it hid, and ordered Abidzu to paint her eyelids dark with kohl. He had hung gold chains around her neck and put rings on each of her fingers until she looked like what she soon would be, the favored concubine of Hamil Al-Ameer.

He smiled to himself, thinking how she was the rarest jewel among his possessions. That he, Andrew Gordon, a lowly Scots brigand who could barely make his own mark to a paper, had risen so far as to have the wife of an English peer as his mistress! Truly Allah had smiled upon him in a way that the dour God in the kirk never would.

She was quiet tonight, his countess, pale beneath the kohl. But soon there would be color enough in her cheeks, and then he would be the one to quench the fire in her blood. She shifted on the pillows, tucking her legs more closely beneath her. Such long legs she had! He could scarcely wait until they were wrapped around his waist and her cries would fill his ears. Perhaps he would consider forcing the American to watch as he took her, plunging deep into her lush, quivering body, and then make her the spectator when the man was slowly killed, breath by breath.

He heard the guards in the passageway, and he leaned forward with anticipation. Everything was as it should be. He lay his hand on her thigh, and though she trembled, she didn't draw away. Aye, she was

learning her part well, well enough to withstand what
would come next.

And when the three men came through the arched
doorway, he felt the shock of recognition race like a
current clear through her body.

## Chapter Seventeen

She had never thought to see Jeremiah here. She had believed him far away, in the quarries or in the pasha's prison, and yet here he was, not twelve paces before her. Though Jeremiah kept his face impassive beneath Hamil's gaze, she knew from the sudden fierce happiness that lit his eyes when the guard pulled off his blindfold that he, too, had not expected this meeting. The man she loved was still alive, and only the steady pressure of Hamil's hand on her leg, a reminder she could not afford to ignore, kept her from running to his arms.

But as the first joyful shock of seeing him again passed, she noticed how his arms and body were covered with bruises and welts. A week's worth of black beard shadowed his jaw, and she nearly wept to see the angry red sores that the heavy shackles had cut into his ankles. And where, she wondered, were his clothes? Here she had been given embroidered silk, while he had been left with no more than the ragged tatters of his trousers.

"Do ye remember Captain Sparhawk, m'lady?" asked Hamil as he slid his hand higher along her thigh.

"He was taken with ye from the *Colomba,* but he is such a base, cowardly scoundrel that I wouldna doubt if ye had scorned his company."

She nodded, her cheeks flushed with shame at the way Hamil was touching her. Yet if she struck his hand away as he deserved, Hamil had promised to vent his displeasure on Jeremiah, and she couldn't bear the thought of causing him more pain. How many of the bruises that marked him already now had come from some indignity imagined by Hamil?

Helplessly Jeremiah watched as Hamil's caress grew more intimate. He saw how Caro closed her eyes, her lips pressed tightly together as if to stop herself from weeping, and his rage grew as he imagined all she must have endured. He wished nothing more than to leap at Hamil now and throttle the despicable life from his body for what he'd done to his Caro.

But before he could do anything, Hamil drew the curved dagger from his sash, and Jeremiah sucked in his breath. Though in the darkness he'd never seen the knife that Hamil had used against him on board the *Chanticleer,* he'd swear this was the same one. He had first felt the blade against his throat, and then, when he'd tried to fight back, his last seconds of consciousness had been spent in agony as the same knife ripped at his belly. *That* knife, in the same hand that held it here again.

The same knife that Hamil now slipped gracefully beneath Caro's chin, yanking her head back by her hair so that her throat was taut against the blade. She made no sound, but her eyes were wild with terror, and Jeremiah could see how the blue vein on the side of her throat throbbed in silent echo to the pounding of her heart.

"A lovely woman is the countess, eh, Sparhawk?" Hamil turned just far enough to brush his lips and beard across Caro's cheek in a mockery of a kiss. "So well-bred, too, that I've never had to worry a moment that she'll misbehave. But ye, Sparhawk, ye have brought naught but trouble with ye, and so I must make the poor lady pay your debt."

"Don't hurt her, Hamil!" said Jeremiah desperately. "Take me instead if one of us must die, but spare her!"

"Nay, Sparhawk, I dinna mean to kill the lady outright! She's far too useful to me for that." Hamil curled his fingers deeper into her pale hair. "I mean for her to serve as a safeguard for ye. If ye donna behave, then she will perish. If ye can control yourself before me, then I leave her unharmed. Can ye understand that, Sparhawk? Do ye care enough for the lady to agree?"

As frightened as she was, Caro wanted to shout at Jeremiah to stop, not to make any deal with Hamil. Didn't he of all people know not to trust this man? Whatever Hamil threatened, she was sure he would not really hurt her, at least not yet. She was, as he'd said himself, too valuable to him to harm, and with the enormous Mameluke guards who'd brought Jeremiah still standing on either side of him, there wasn't much use for this insurance that Hamil wanted. Couldn't Jeremiah see that, as well?

But all Jeremiah saw was how close to death she was in Hamil's hands.

"Of course I agree," he said quietly, praying that Hamil's knife would not slip. He'd agree to anything to save Caro. "You have my word."

"I accept it, Sparhawk, for what little worth the word of a coward may hold." Gently Hamil stroked the blade of the knife back and forth along Caro's throat.

Jeremiah stiffened at the word *coward* but said nothing, this time refusing to jump at Hamil's insults. Last time on board the xebec he had, and his temper had cost him dearly. But soon, he told himself, soon he'd have his revenge, and make Hamil feel the blade of that knife himself.

"I've heard it said," continued Hamil, "that all ye American captains can write as fine a hand as any clerk. Would ye consider that true?"

Of all the things Jeremiah expected to hear from Hamil, surely this had to be the last. "I can't vouch for every American shipmaster, but all I know keep their own logs and records."

"Including yourself?"

Why the devil did Hamil care if he were literate? "Aye, including myself."

Hamil nodded with satisfaction and barked an order. A pair of slaves rushed into the room, carrying a small, low table that they set on the floor before Jeremiah. One left and returned with a sheaf of paper, tied with ocher ribbon, a quill pen, a bottle of ink and a little box of sand for blotting. Carefully the slave arranged them all on the table, placing everything in a neat, ceremonial line before Jeremiah, and then, to Jeremiah's surprise, with another nod Hamil dismissed the two Mamelukes, as well.

"The countess tells me I am famous in London," said Hamil grandly. "If that is so, then there must be many who seek t'spread lies about me and my past, the way all great men are slandered. But I won't let the filthy liars have their way. Nay, I will give them all the truth about Hamil Al-Ameer, the most famous of the Barbary corsairs!"

He paused for a moment, clearly expecting Jeremiah to comment.

"The truth, Hamil?" repeated Jeremiah at last, too stunned by the man's self-created grandeur to say much else.

"Aye, the truth, with Allah as my witness! I mean to see my life published in London and Edinburgh, for all the Christian world to read and learn from!"

Jeremiah glanced down at the table with the pen and paper before him. "You want me to write this book?"

"Nay, just write the words I tell ye!" Hamil sniffed haughtily. "I want it to be the truth, and that must come from me alone."

Jeremiah sighed wearily. "Then why have me act as your clerk? Why not write it yourself, to be sure it's exactly how you wish it to be?"

Hamil's gaze turned cold and remote. "There was no time to waste on schooling when I was a bairn, nor since. Scratching with a pen is not fit work for a man."

God help us all, thought Jeremiah, the most notorious corsair on the Barbary Coast was ashamed that he couldn't write his own name, ashamed enough that he'd rather send his own guards away than have them guess the truth. "Surely there must be other men in Tripoli better fit for the task? I told you I keep my own log and books, but my hand's hardly genteel enough for a clerk.''

''Ye shall do it, Sparhawk,'' ordered Hamil. ''Being a shipmaster yourself—if a cowardly one—ye shall know the proper words for what I wish to have writ. And I know that ye will do it proper, for if ye don't, the countess here will suffer.''

Once again Jeremiah looked to Caro and the unspoken longing that filled her eyes. As he'd spoken, Hamil had relaxed his grip, but still the knife was there against her throat. Lord, what a choice! Awkwardly he knelt at the table, the chains clanking around his ankles, set a sheet of paper before him, dipped the pen into the ink and waited for Hamil to begin.

Twenty pages later, Jeremiah's hand ached and his back was stiff, and Hamil, it seemed, had only begun. Most of what he dictated was either self-serving or outraged or both, but mingled in his rambling, too, were details of the harbors along the coast, the activities of the other corsairs, and the pasha's own plans for defense, information that would be as priceless to the American navy as it would be to Jeremiah himself if he managed to escape.

No, *when* he escaped, with Caro and Davy at his side and Hamil cold and dead for what he'd done to them all. Hamil had long since lowered the knife from her throat, but still Caro sat like a statue on the pillows beside him, her face pale from the strain. If only he could have a moment alone with her to give her courage, to tell her how much he loved her.

Hamil yawned, drinking deeply from his goblet of *aquadeut,* the spirits distilled from dates that he liked so well; abstinence wasn't one of the aspects of Islam he chose to embrace.

"Enough, Sparhawk. We shall continue tomorrow night." He turned and prodded Caro. "Go, m'lady, and read to me what he's written."

Caro looked swiftly from Hamil to Jeremiah and back again, not really believing the corsair wished her to go to Jeremiah. "You wish me to read all of it aloud?"

Hamil yawned again. "Nay, not all. But find me the part about capturing the Romish brig filled with nuns."

Her legs stiff from sitting, Caro walked slowly toward Jeremiah. Fleetingly, she considered throwing herself into his arms and refusing to be parted from him again, but then she thought of how badly she'd bungled her one attempt at freedom before, on board the xebec, and sorrowfully knew she shouldn't try again.

"Here's the page he wants," said Jeremiah softly. "There in the middle."

His fingers brushed hers as he handed her the page, enough contact to make her heart beat faster. Beneath Hamil's watchful gaze, she didn't dare speak, and instead she prayed her expression alone would tell him what lay in her heart.

Mechanically she began to read, her eyes jumping ahead a line or two beyond the words she spoke out loud. Strange that this was the first time she'd ever seen Jeremiah's handwriting. Strange that—

She stopped abruptly, halted by the passage so clearly meant for her eyes alone:

I love you, Darling Caro, so much that to see You here makes me feel both Joy & Sorrow, but I promise, Sweetheart, that I will find a way to Freedom. I love you with all my Heart Now & Forever Caro my Lass

"Is there an error, m'lady?" demanded Hamil. "By Allah, if he has gotten it wrong—"

"There is no error," said Caro, not daring to look back at Jeremiah for fear the tears that filled her eyes would spill over. "None at all."

"Countess, waken, I beg you!"

Groggy still, Caro tried to focus on Leilah's round face as the girl shook her shoulder again. Behind her stood Bella, shading the lamp with her hand. Half-turned toward the doorway, she stood guard and listened for any sound that they had been followed.

"Come, my lady," whispered Leilah urgently. "Come, you must hurry!"

Caro pushed herself upright, shoving the hair from her face. "Why? Where are we going?"

"To the prison," said Leilah, anxiously twisting her hands in the trailing hems of her robe. "There is no man by your husband's name among Hamil's prisoners—your English names are so difficult!—but my father says there are several of your countrymen and he may be one of those. The only way we can be certain is if you come yourself, and we must go and return while Hamil sleeps. Oh, hurry my lady, please!"

Leilah's words jarred Caro awake. She heard only the possibility, and none of the warning that the news might be bad. *Frederick was waiting for her.* At once she rolled from the mattress and searched frantically through the clothes she'd been given. Frederick would expect her to wear white. He asked so little of her in return for everything he gave, that she always did this for him, but tonight she was forced to settle for a silk robe with cream and yellow stripes. It was pale, but it wasn't white, and as she slipped the robe over her head, she felt a superstitious uneasiness envelop her as completely as the striped silk. If only she'd found a robe that had been white!

Wrapped in blankets that hid all but their eyes, the three women left by a small side door that Caro had never noticed. Waiting outside were two men, one of them Leilah's brother Morad, and quickly they hurried toward the prison. It was the first time since she'd come to Tripoli that Caro had left Hamil's house, and she found herself soon lost among the narrow, twisting streets. From the height of the moon she guessed it must be past midnight; the streets were empty, and in the distance she heard the soft shush of the waves on the beach of the harbor.

"That is the bagnio where the Americans from the ship in the harbor are held," whispered Leilah as they passed by a small square warehouse with guards posted by the door. "The pasha's prisoners are kept within the castle itself, but Hamil has his own prison, there near the north wall."

"Why?" asked Caro, pulling her blanket higher over her face. Though shrouded to her ankles, the guards still stared at them with an interest that made her wary.

Leilah's whisper shrank even lower as they reached the smaller, windowless building that was Hamil's prison. "As great a friend as Hamil is of the pasha, still he does not trust him, especially with prisoners. By rights Hamil can claim the ransom on all prisoners he takes, and this way he can be sure he receives it."

Morad led them past another Mameluke guard and into a small courtyard, and motioned for them to wait on the bench in the shadows. "He says we must stay here," explained Leilah, "out of the lamp's light so we might see the prisoners, but they cannot see us."

Her mouth dry with anticipation, Caro sat beside the other woman on the little bench. It had been so long since she'd last seen Frederick that she couldn't decide what to tell him first.

One by one, a motley parade of prisoners was brought before them. Young and old, fat and thin. The only thing they had in common was that they all were English, and complaining bitterly about being roused in the middle of the night. That, and that not one of them was Frederick.

Sadly she watched as Leilah's brother prodded the final man shuffling back toward the gate. "Ask them if that is all," she said, unwilling still to abandon hope. "Ask him—oh, dear God, *Frederick!*"

He was last because he couldn't walk on his own, and relied on the slave who supported him with each step. In the yellow lamplight he was so shrunken and pale that he seemed almost translucent, like a figure made from wax instead of flesh and blood. He had lost so much more of his hair that all that remained was a wispy fringe around the crown, and all of that was white, not the iron gray she remembered so well.

She called his name again and ran to him, taking the place of the slave to lead him to the bench. She was shocked by how frail he'd become, the man who had carried her through so much now unable to support himself. He had always been older, but when had he become *old?*

She knelt at his feet, his hands in hers as she searched his face. "Frederick, it's Caro," she said softly, "and I've come to take you home."

He stared at her in bewilderment, so clearly unable to accept her presence that she lifted his hands to touch her face. "See, Frederick, it really is your Caro. I'm really, truly here."

"My pretty little girl," he whispered hoarsely. "Whatever are you doing in this desolate place?"

"I told you, I've come to take you home. It's been so long, Frederick! You will scarcely recognize the east rose garden, I've made so many improvements!"

He smiled fondly, wearily. "My sweet Caro, as dear as you are to come for me, you must realize I'll never see Blackstone House again."

"Of course you shall!" she cried. "The sea voyage will do you good, and then Cook and I will set about filling you full of so many good things to eat, you'll be plump and merry by Christmas!"

"Look at me, Caro. I'm an old scarecrow of a man, and the first strong gust will topple me for good." His fingers trembled as he stroked her cheeks. "I thank God that I lived long enough to see you one more time."

"Don't say that, Frederick, please!" She was crying now, her tears wetting his fingertips. *"Please."*

"No sadness now, my girl. Remember instead that you were the greatest blessing in my life." He coughed, a ghastly rattle that shook his entire frail body. "Does my mother live still?"

"Oh, yes, she does, and Frederick, she and I have become great friends." She had never lied to him before, but this one, this one she could not help. "Can you ever believe such a thing? I visited her at her villa in Naples before I came here."

He smiled again, his eyes too bright beneath his paper-thin lids. "You're not my girl any longer, are you, pretty Caro?"

"Of course I am, Frederick, and I always will be!"

"No, sweet child, that's not what I meant. You've changed since I left, bloomed like the summer roses in that east garden of yours." Gently he brushed a curl back from her forehead. "Will this man make you as happy as you've made me? If he doesn't, you know, he'll have to answer to me."

Her throat too tight with tears to speak, she could do no more than nod her head.

"You love him that much, then?" he asked quietly. "That is good. That is how it should be."

She pressed her face against his knee, her shoulders shaking with her sobs. "But I love *you,* Frederick!"

"My lady, we must go," said Leilah urgently, her hands on Caro's shoulders. "We have been gone too long already. We must leave now, or Hamil will miss us."

Caro looked at her husband through the haze of her tears. "I'll come back for you, Frederick. I promise. I won't leave you here."

"My lady, please, there is no time to waste!"

Caro rose unsteadily and bent to kiss her husband's cheek. She looked over her shoulder as she followed Leilah and her brother, but Frederick didn't notice, his head bowed and his features lost in shadow.

"Your husband is an old man, my lady," said Leilah as they hurried back to the house. "Pray to Allah that he will be strong enough to escape."

"I won't leave him behind, Leilah."

Leilah sighed, resigned. "Any other woman would be content to save one man, but you must have three. At least the other two can walk. David Kerr will be brought out with your husband, so perhaps he can help him."

Caro was almost afraid to ask of Jeremiah. For the past five nights she had seen him when he came to write Hamil's book, but the guards who brought him never said where he'd come from, and blindfolded, Jeremiah wouldn't know himself. "And the other one?

"Jeremiah Sparhawk? Why, my lady, I thought you already knew." Her pause stretched like an eternity to Caro. "Jeremiah Sparhawk is held in Hamil's house."

Tonight would be the night, or at least that was what Bella had told her near the cistern. Caro swallowed her excitement as she sat next to Hamil, only half hearing as he recited one more exaggerated adventure for Jeremiah to copy down. Tonight, God willing, they would all be free.

She wished there had been a chance for her to explain it all to Jeremiah. As often as he could, he had written messages for her in the middle of Hamil's manuscript, but she had never found a way to write or speak to him in return. To her the plan that she'd devised with Bella and Leilah seemed as foolproof as any could be. She only hoped that Jeremiah, when he learned of it, would agree.

She glanced at Hamil and the dagger in his hand, the way it had been every night. Though she told herself each time he pressed it to her throat that he would not hurt her, it still terrified her, and she hated him for using her fear that way. After tonight, she vowed, he'd never do it to her again.

Now she watched the dagger twist in his hand as he toyed with it, doing little balancing tricks that seemed to her to belong more in a traveling circus than a corsair's xebec. Deftly he flipped the dagger over the back of his hand. But this time to her surprise, he judged the motion wrong, and the knife clattered to the marble floor.

Hamil swore, his words slurring, and as he reached down to pick up the knife, he pitched forward himself, knocking over the empty goblet that had held the drugged *aquadeut*. He lay sprawled facedown on the green and white tile, his eyes closed and his beard fanned out like a bristled pillow beneath his head.

"Jeremiah!" In a breathless instant she had clambered off the pillows and raced into his arms, hugging him fiercely. "Jeremiah, listen to me, we're going to escape!"

"You did this?" he asked with disbelief, looking past her to Hamil's crumpled body.

"With help. Hurry, here's the key for the shackles."

"Good lass!" He bent down and quickly unlocked the irons around his ankles with the key that Bella had given her. But then, to Caro's horror, he seized Hamil's curving dagger from where it had fallen and raised it high over the unconscious man's back.

"No, Jeremiah, no!" she gasped, grabbing his wrist to stop him. "You can't do it, not like this!"

"And why the hell not?" he demanded, his eyes wild with the need for vengeance. "Caro, for all that this bastard has done to you, to me, to *us,* he deserves no better!"

With both hands she fought him for the knife. "You can't, because I promised his wives you wouldn't! They love him, monster though he is to us, and because of that they have arranged for us all to go free! Jeremiah, listen to me! *Listen to me!* If you kill him now we will never leave Tripoli alive!"

He could not believe Caro was doing this to him, stopping him from the one act that would truly free them both. He wrenched the dagger from her hands and she cried out his name again. As she did, he saw the two young women in the doorway, their arms wrapped tight around each other as they stared at him in terror, the same terror he'd seen before in Caro's face. Hamil's wives. Damnation, would he be the monster to them that Hamil had been to Caro? Where in God's name would it end?

"They love him, Jeremiah, the same as I love you!" cried Caro frantically. "You don't need to kill him this way. We can escape without you doing it, all of us, you and I and Frederick and David Kerr. They're waiting for us now, at the prison. Can you understand, love? To murder Hamil now, when he cannot defend himself—where is the honor in that?"

He looked at her, wavering. She was right, there'd be no honor in killing him now, and yet the way Hamil had attacked him deserved no honor. He stared down at the dagger in his hands, his fingers flexing around the hilt. How sweet it would be to end Hamil's life with the same knife he'd felt himself!

A small cry like an animal's came from the doorway and, startled, Jeremiah looked again to Hamil's wives. The dark-haired one had turned away so she would not have to watch, and now he could see the swelling of the child within her. Dear God, was he really the kind of man to leave an unborn child fatherless? He thought of his sister and her baby, and Caro and the child he hoped they'd created between them. If he killed Hamil now, like this, then Hamil would have the final victory, for Jeremiah would have become as evil as the corsair himself.

Damnation, he couldn't do it.

No, he *wouldn't* do it. Swearing again, he pulled the belt from Hamil's body, buckled it around his own waist, and thrust the dagger into the scabbard. He couldn't make out the strange look on Caro's face, and so he kissed her instead.

"Come along," he said gruffly. "Tell me where we go next."

## Chapter Eighteen

With his black beard beneath the borrowed turban and long tunic, Jeremiah made such a passable Tripolitanian that Caro laughed and clapped her hands.

"You look vastly fierce," she said as they hurried to the side door of the house to meet Morad. "I'd wager even Desire wouldn't know you."

"Nor you, love," he said, watching as she wrapped the thick black blanket around herself. "Lord, what a pair we seem to be for fancy dress and pretending to be who we're not! When I get home it's going to be nothing but plain Jeremiah Sparhawk in homespun."

At the door she turned and hugged Bella and Leilah one last time. "Thank you both for all you've done," she said and shyly laid her hand on Leilah's belly. "Good luck to you, too."

Leilah leaned close to whisper. "You take this one as your husband," she said, glancing back at Jeremiah, "and he will give you many fine sons of your own. But please, I beg you, take him forever away from Tripoli!"

Caro smiled wistfully. "In England one spouse is considered enough," she said. "As for the other, I'll do my best."

"Come, love, we must be off," said Jeremiah, and together they slipped through the door to the street. But Morad's face when he greeted them was worried, and though they lacked a common language for him to explain why, Caro herself saw that the city tonight was a far different place than it had been just a few days before. Men with drawn swords or muskets ran wildly through the streets, some toward the castle and some away from it, and the air was filled with the wails of women. A deep explosion from the castle's artillery rumbled through the night, the reverberation shaking the ground beneath their feet.

"What the devil is going on?" demanded Jeremiah.

Morad shook his head as he urged them to follow. *"Americanos,"* he said helplessly, the only explanation he could offer that they might understand. *"Americanos!"*

"I'll wager we'll find out soon enough," said Jeremiah grimly, taking Caro's arm. "But as an *Americano* myself, I can't say I like any of this, especially—"

But his fingers grasped at empty air beside him where she had been. Frantically he scanned the jostling crowd of men in the street, a restless tide of turbans and angry bearded faces. "Caro! Caro!"

He barely noticed when the man nearest him whipped around at the sound of an English-speaking voice and shouted furiously in Jeremiah's direction. Morad grabbed Jeremiah's sleeve, trying to draw him away to safety, but Jeremiah jerked free, his own saber now drawn as he plunged into the swirling mass of white tunics that had swallowed Caro so completely.

"Caro!" shouted Jeremiah, his fear for her growing every second. "Damnation, Caro, where are you? Caro!"

"Jeremiah!" Her voice was more a frantic shriek as she called to him from a doorway half a block away. She was braced against the door's arched frame, her arms drawn tight against her body to protect herself, and her black blanket had fallen from her head. As Jeremiah shoved his way to her, he saw how men in the street slowed to look at her, her blond hair and pale face like a beacon that marked her as a foreigner, a Christian, perhaps even an American....

*God in heaven, they would tear her apart for that!* Wild to reach her, Jeremiah surged forward, slashing with the saber at the men who blocked his path. When he reached her at last, she leapt out to him, clinging to his shoulders like a drowning woman. Even in the shadows he saw how her face and blanket were streaked with dirt, and to his horror he guessed she'd been knocked to the street when she'd been jostled away from his side. Lord, how had she ever managed to get herself clear without being trampled and kicked to death?

She opened her lips to speak but he lay his fingers across them and silently shook his head, understanding now the terrible risk they both were under if their identities became known. He pulled the blanket back across her face and wrapped his arm tightly around her waist. No matter what else happened, he would not let her slip away again.

Then Morad was there beside them, his eyes wide with trepidation as he motioned anxiously for them to follow. The heavy guns were firing regularly now, bright flashes like fireworks in the sky to match the thunderous explosions of their gunpowder.

There were no guards outside Hamil's prison when they reached it, the single door bolted shut. Morad pounded his fists on the door while Jeremiah and Caro pressed close to the wall, their arms still wrapped tightly around each other. Here in the shadow of the castle itself, soldiers and Mamelukes, too, swarmed through the streets, their drawn sabres glinting like silver. At last the door was opened just enough for Caro, Jeremiah and Morad to slip through, and then slammed shut after them.

The man who let them in was Seid, the father of Morad and Leilah, and above his gray-streaked beard his face in the lamplight glistened with sweat and fear. "Praise Allah that this night will end soon," he said anxiously. "Is Leilah well, unharmed?"

Wearily Caro pushed back her blanket and nodded. "Well enough when I left her," she said, unwilling to think of how close she herself had come to being killed in the street. Her heart was still racing with fear, her hands trembling, and she knew that if Jeremiah hadn't come to her she would now be dead. Instinctively she reached for his hand again, needing the comfort of his touch. "You know she'll be safe at Hamil's house."

"More than can be said for us." Impatiently Jeremiah leaned forward, wiping the sweat from his forehead on his sleeve. "What the devil is happening in this city tonight, anyway?"

Seid sagged forward in a dispirited little bow. "The *Americanos* have retaken their frigate *Philadelphia* in the harbor," he said, the bow turning into a shrug. "Beyond that I do not know what is truth or lies. I have heard they have brought more of their warships into the harbor and mean to take the city, while others say the *Americanos* who were prisoners have broken free and captured the castle itself. But I cannot say if any of this is true. I know nothing for certain."

Jeremiah's fingers tightened around Caro's, his heart pounding with a mixture of excitement and dread. Chaos like this was perfect for their escape, for any kind of alarm that Hamil put out would be swallowed up in the panic of a terrified city. And then there was the tantalizing possibility of being rescued by the same American ships that were said to be in the harbor itself—he'd never dare dream of anything this tidy!

But one look at Caro beside him, her grimy face a reminder of what she'd survived already this night, and all Jeremiah could think of was the risk. Over and over again she turned to him to keep her safe, and each time she'd ended up in far greater danger than either one of them anticipated. And tonight—tonight, he didn't even want to consider all that could go wrong.

"We'll take the two men we've come for, then, and be on our way," he said, slipping his arm around Caro's shoulders. Instantly she nestled closer against his chest, and he thought again of how impossibly dear she was to him. "David Kerr and Frederick Moncrief."

"The American sailor and the English lord." Uneasily Seid looked away. "You were expected, and they were soon to be separated from the other prisoners, but Allah has willed otherwise."

"What do you mean?" asked Caro, her voice trembling. "Where are they?"

"It was the pasha's Mamelukes," he said defensively. "They came with the first word that the American prisoners were trying to capture the city. I couldn't stop them—I had no right, not the pasha's men. They took all the Americans away to the castle and killed them."

Stunned, Jeremiah swore beneath his breath, unable to believe the trick that fate had played on him. How could he have come so close to rescuing Davy and then have lost him like this? After all the months apart, to have missed him by no more than an hour! A single, blessed *hour,* and Davy would have been at his side when they sailed from the harbor.

"Oh, Jeremiah, I am so sorry," murmured Caro, wrapping her arms around his shoulders. "I'm so very sorry, love."

He closed his eyes, numb with grief, and pressed his face against her hair. At least he had her, his Caro. At least he had not lost her.

Seid ducked his head and cleared his throat. "But I do have the Englishman for you," he said, striving to make the best of a very bad situation. "The Englishman was unharmed! Here, see, so you may judge for yourselves!"

Eager to be reunited with Frederick, Caro turned toward the doorway. But the man the jailer brought was too young and too tall, his shaggy brown hair and beard as much testimony to how long he had been a prisoner as was his disbelieving smile at being released.

"There is some mistake," she said slowly. "This isn't Lord Byfield."

"Davy, by all that's holy!" Jeremiah grabbed the other man in so fierce an embrace he nearly lifted him from his feet, then shoved him back to look at him. "They said you were dead, but here you are. By God, here you are!"

Caro stood alone and watched them, her hands clasped tightly around her body. "But where is Lord Byfield?" she asked plaintively. "Where is my husband? You said he was saved. I don't understand."

But she did. She knew Frederick too well not to guess this last gift he'd given her.

"It was the damnedest thing you've ever seen, Jere," David was saying. "The Mamelukes came in looking for blood, shouting out the names of all us poor Yankee bastards. I was to the back, and before they get to me that old English gentleman stands up near the door and says he's David Kerr, and off they hauled him in my place before I could say a word."

Caro pressed her hand to her mouth to hold back her sob, trying not to imagine the cruel, curved sabers of the Mamelukes. She had loved Frederick so much, and oh, what he had done for her!

"My poor, dear love," said Jeremiah gently, now the one to offer consolation. He held his arms open to her and she crumpled into them, burying her tears against his chest.

"I loved him so much, Jeremiah," she sobbed. "I *loved* him, and now he's gone!"

"I know you did, sweetheart, and he knew it, too," he said as he held her. In his more selfish moments he'd longed for Frederick's death so he could rightly claim her as his alone, but now that she was free to be his, her grief was too deep, too real for him to feel anything but the shared weight of her sorrow. The circumstances, too, with Frederick trading his life for Davy's, were almost beyond believing. Whatever his other faults, Lord Byfield must have been a rare man, indeed, and Jeremiah prayed his end had been swift and easy. "He must have loved you dearly."

"He did," she whispered hoarsely through her tears as her arms tightened around Jeremiah. Because Jeremiah understood about losing Frederick he was all the more dear to her. What had she done to deserve two such men in her life?

"Lady Byfield," said David gravely, holding his hand out to her. "Your husband spoke so often of you that we all envied him. He was a good man, ma'am. I know there's no way I'll ever make up to you what you lost, ma'am, but you can always count on me to do whatever I can."

Fresh tears welled up in Caro's eyes, leaving her unable to answer. Learning that Frederick's love for her and his kindness for others had not gone unappreciated even in prison was almost more than she could bear. She turned her face again into Jeremiah's chest, seeking comfort in his strength.

*Poor Frederick, poor, sweet, loving, generous Frederick!*

But even as Jeremiah held her, he was listening to the sounds of the guns and the mob in the street. "We must go, Caro," he said. "We can't risk staying here any longer."

Seid ducked his head again. "It is all arranged as my daughter wished. The camels are waiting for you at the east gate, and from there—"

"Camels!" scoffed Jeremiah. "I've no mind to go riding on camels!"

"But it is the safest route!" protested Seid. "Tonight of all nights! You can travel across the country to the next port and find your passage there. But to attempt to leave from this harbor tonight would be madness!"

"Then madmen we are," said Jeremiah firmly. "Davy here and I are deep-water sailors. There's no way under heaven we're going to go hanging onto some animal's hairy hump to traipse across the desert when there's plenty of ships and boats in this very harbor, and—"

But his words were lost as an enormous explosion rocked the town, drowning out the sounds of the cannons and the screams of the men and women in the street alike.

While Seid sank to his knees, shaking with fear, Jeremiah's expression grew sterner still as he strained his ears to hear more. "They've either blown up the castle or the pasha's whole damned navy, and I'm not about to wait to find out which."

Gently he tipped Caro's tear-streaked face upward. "We must go now, love."

"But Frederick—"

"Frederick's dead, sweet," he said firmly, "and you know as well as I that he died hoping that you'd return home safely."

She closed her eyes, fighting back the tears. Jeremiah was right, of course; Frederick wouldn't have sacrificed himself if he hadn't believed his weakened health would have held her back. From the first time she had met him, he had wanted nothing more than for her to be happy. As much as she longed to stay in Tripoli until Frederick's body could be found, she knew in her heart he would insist on her going.

Slowly she pushed herself away from Jeremiah's chest, sniffing back her tears and drawing her shoulders up as straight as she could. For Frederick's sake, and Jeremiah's, too, she would be brave. "I'm ready."

"That's my Caro!" Jeremiah's instant smile was so full of love that she nearly began to cry again. He kissed her quickly on the forehead and glanced over to David. "What of you, Davy? Are you well enough to reach the water?"

His friend's mouth quirked upward. "Ah, Jere, just try to stop me."

Quickly David dressed in the tunic and turban they'd brought for him, and slipped a knife and saber into his belt. With Morad as their guide, they hurried through the streets toward the waterfront as quickly as they could, the two tall Americans on either side of Caro.

The shouts and confusion of the crowds around them grew louder as they approached the gate to the quay, and Jeremiah's hand gripped the hilt of his saber more tightly as his instincts warned him to be ready for whatever might lie ahead. His eyes met David's over Caro's head, the look they exchanged confirming Jeremiah's uneasiness, and silently he prayed he wasn't leading Caro into the greatest disaster of her life. But as at last they passed through the gate to the quay, the sight before them was beyond imagining.

The explosion they'd heard had been the *Philadelphia* itself, run aground and in flames that even now shot hundreds of feet into the night sky. Bits of burning timber and rigging drifted across the water's surface like floating candles, and smaller explosions continued to rip through the burning hulk as flames found one more pocket of ammunition or turpentine. Plumes of acrid smoke from the burning tar and tinder-dry timbers billowed inland across the harbor. The roar of the heavy guns in the batteries along the wall continued, and the shriek of solid shot and grapeshot from the gunboats in the harbor added to the din. Caro looked to where he pointed, and could just make out another vessel, riding in the open sea safely beyond the range of the castle's guns.

Pausing only a moment, Jeremiah plunged on toward the beach, pulling Caro along with him. In Hamil's rambling reminiscences, the corsair had mentioned a little sloop he'd captured from a Venetian nobleman that he now used himself for pleasure cruises. The sloop was supposed to be tied at the end of the quay, and as they ran across the pounded earth, Jeremiah prayed that this time Hamil wasn't lying. The usually crowded quay was deserted tonight, with no one else willing to risk their necks in so open a place. No one except us madmen, thought Jeremiah, and in spite of the shells flying overhead, he grinned to himself at his own foolhardiness.

To his amazement, the sloop was exactly where Hamil had described it. With sabers drawn, he and David dropped over the side and swiftly searched the little vessel, but found no guard at all on board. Like everyone else along the wharf, they, too, must have abandoned their post and fled the explosions and cannon fire.

Jeremiah held his hands up for Caro as she joined them, clambering down the swinging ladder with her skirts tucked high. As quickly as the two men could, they cast off the sloop's lines and pushed her away from the wharf. Caro sat with Jeremiah at the tiller, while David manned the sails.

"Keep low," Jeremiah warned her. "We're too small fish for them to aim at us directly, but there's always the chance we'll be hit by something gone awry."

Crouching down beside him as ordered, Caro stared back at the city they were escaping. If Naples from the water had reminded her of a fairy-tale city, then Tripoli was one from a tale out of the Arabian Nights. The white stone of the castle walls and tall minarets of the mosques were lit bright as day by the fire, the night sky behind it dark blue and dotted with stars.

As swiftly as they could, the two Americans cut their course through the harbor filled with burning debris. Jeremiah steered as far as he could from the burning *Philadelphia* without risking the little sloop on the same rocks and currents that had grounded the frigate. Although by now the fire in the *Philadelphia*'s shattered hull was dying, the sound of the flames was still a dull roar punctuated with crackles and hissing as the fire relentlessly consumed the miles of dry timbers, cordage and canvas, the heat so intense that Caro was forced to shield her face with the blanket.

"The Americans must have tried to cut her out," shouted Jeremiah over the noise of the fire. "Look, out there beyond the bar!"

Caro looked to where he pointed and through the wobbling haze of heat from the fire she could just make out the lights and shape of another ship, riding in the open sea safely beyond the range of the castle's guns.

"I'll wager fifty gold pieces that she's American," continued Jeremiah. "If we can get to her, we'll be home free."

"Are you sure, Jeremiah?" American though it might be, the other ship still seemed impossibly far away, and Caro thought regretfully of the placid camels waiting in vain for them at the other gate.

"Of course I'm sure." He had pulled off the turban, and with the beard and his black hair flying in the wind, he looked far more like a pirate than Hamil himself. "'Tis no more than a hop and a skip across a pond to me."

"A burning pond, with someone lobbing rocks at you!"

He grinned. "No trial, Caro, no trial at all."

Suddenly a stray ball plummeted into the water not twenty feet before them, sending a column of water shooting high into the sky. Caro shrieked and grabbed at Jeremiah and he held her tight.

"It's all right, love," he said when she finally raised her head. "We're fine, fine as we can be. The worst's really past, you know. I'd wager we're likely out of the range of the batteries by now."

"Truly?" she asked, searching his face for reassurance. "We came so close to being killed!"

He smiled crookedly, his teeth white against his beard. "That seems to happen to us over and over again, doesn't it? But here we are one more time, spared for another day's mischief."

"That's a merry way of putting it." She pushed herself upright and stretched, her muscles cramped and aching from the hard planks of the deck. In all the years she'd lived with Frederick, she'd never once been in any danger, but since she'd been with Jeremiah, it seemed she was always ducking one near-disaster after another, exactly as he said. Not, she admitted to herself, that she really wanted it any differently. "I suppose that it's just one more way that you Sparhawks differ from the rest of us mortals."

"Aye, love, I suppose it is." Jeremiah's smile went a bit more lopsided as he pulled off the belt with the saber, his gaze never leaving her face. "Would it be any easier for you to understand if you became a Sparhawk, too?"

"What, have you become a conjurer now as well as—" She stopped abruptly as she realized what else his words could mean. His face told it all by the light of the burning ship, his emotions so patently exposed that her heart raced in instant response. She swallowed hard, but her heart still felt the same way, and she knew. Dear Lord, she *knew*.

"Oh, Jeremiah," she said at last, her voice unsteady. "This has nothing to do with conjuring, does it?"

"I'm afraid it doesn't, no." Carefully, as if he worried that somehow she'd shatter at his touch, he laid his hand over hers.

"I didn't think it did." She stared down at how his larger hand covered hers, wishing desperately for the right thing to say. How very much she loved this man! Losing Frederick had made her realize all over again how fragile life, and love, could be, and nothing now was going to make her wait to seize the happiness that Jeremiah was offering.

"Tell me, Captain Sparhawk," she said, feeling oddly shy and uncertain, "are you proposing marriage?"

"Yes, Lady Byfield, I am," said Jeremiah, feeling ten times a fool for having done it. The poor lass was barely a widow, and here he was, with bombs and grapeshot flying overhead, blurting out his proposal like the worst greenhorn swain. But he couldn't wait. She was the one thing, the only thing, that made his life worth living, and he could no longer imagine it without her by his side. "Will you marry me?"

For a long time she didn't answer, her face so serious he was certain she'd refuse. Then, suddenly, she grinned, the irrepressible grin that was Caro's alone.

"I will," she declared, "if you can get me to that American ship as easily as you've boasted."

"Done!" He swept her into his arms and kissed her, fast and sweet. Only when the sloop pitched so crazily that they almost tumbled over the side did he realize he'd let the tiller go. He grabbed for it as David shouted crossly, unaware of the circumstances, and Caro laughed as she picked herself up from the deck where she'd fallen. It was, she thought giddily, miles away from a proper drawing room proposal on bended knee, yet because she loved Jeremiah so much, she couldn't imagine one any finer.

"I love you, Jeremiah," she said as she leaned across the tiller to kiss him again. "No matter that you're a pitiful excuse for a sailor."

With one hand he pulled her face closer, kissing her hungrily before he let her go. "It's you that's addled my wits, woman," he said, pretending to be stern. "What poor sailor stands a chance against your wiles?"

She laughed again, feeling giddy with joy and relief. "I'd rather you didn't stand at all, Captain Sparhawk," she teased. "I've something quite different in mind."

"I do, too, but not before we hail that ship and have the captain make a decent woman of you. Don't tempt me any further, mind?" He scowled darkly, but she wasn't fooled. "Why don't you go below and see if there's anything in the galley to help us celebrate? Surely Hamil wouldn't have sailed without a bottle or two of that blessed date wine of his on board."

"I'll go look." She kissed him briefly, her lips savoring the taste of his. "Since the captain orders it, of course."

"Be sure you take the lantern near the companionway, love," he cautioned as she shrugged off the heavy blanket. "And don't be long."

She smiled over her shoulder as she made her way unsteadily aft to the hatch, the pale silk of her robe fluttering around her legs. The little sloop was much more lively in the water than any of the larger ships she'd traveled in, and she was careful to feel her way down the steps of the companionway. She unhooked the small lantern that Jeremiah had lit, and opened the door to the galley, bending slightly to peek inside.

But as she did, a man's hand closed over her mouth while another snaked around her waist, jerking her hard against his chest. She clawed desperately at the man's hand and dropped the lantern to the deck, where it guttered out at once and left her to struggle in inky darkness. She wrenched awkwardly to one side as she tried to break free, and mercifully the hand disappeared from her mouth. But then she felt the cool blade pressing flat into her throat, the sensation all too familiar.

"Ye shouldna run from me, m'lady," said Hamil softly, his lips close to her ear. "Did ye really think ye would get clear of me?"

Too frightened to answer, she closed her eyes in the darkness. She had thought this was done, finished, that she could marry Jeremiah and forget any of it had happened.

*But not this, God help her, not this!*

"There's some that say Hamil can see in the dark like a cat, like a panther," he taunted. "Dare ye test me yourself, m'lady?"

"How did you find us?" she whispered miserably.

"The lasses, o'course," he said. "I knew they'd betrayed me—who else could've done it, eh?—but even when I told them I'd sell them in the slave market, they told me that ye had gone to the desert, the foolish, lying creatures!"

Caro thought of Leilah and Bella, and the sorrow their help had cost them even as they'd told the truth. "You won't sell them, will you?"

"Nay, o'course not!" he scoffed. "They meant no harm. They are but women, with nary a thought for intrigue between 'em. Much like ye, m'lady. I know 'tis Sparhawk who's behind this, who brought ye here, and it's Sparhawk who shall pay.''

"You can't!" she cried wildly, and the blade pressed closer to silence her.

"Oh, I can, m'lady, and ye shall be the one to help me." With his free hand he deftly seized her wrists and forced them behind her back, pinioning them with rough cords that bit so harshly into her skin that she cried out despite the knife at her throat. Roughly he turned her around and shoved her against the bulkhead to tie the cords to the grating so she could not move. He was so good at this, she thought wretchedly, so efficient that it all happened almost before she realized it. How many other captives had he treated the same way?

"Now call to him, m'lady," he ordered. "Make him come to ye."

"I won't do it," she said, her trembling voice robbing her words of their defiance. "Why should I have him come here so you can kill him?"

"M'lady, I mean to kill him with your help or without it," said Hamil with surprising patience. "I could just as easy slit your pretty throat now an' be done with ye, an' go up that hatch after him."

"Maybe he'll kill you first! He has a sword—no, two swords!—and a knife, and he has a friend there, too, David Kerr, who's every bit as willing to fight as Jeremiah himself!"

Hamil chuckled softly. "Ah, m'lady, your loyalty touches me! So much like my own lasses ye are, that I've half a mind to take ye home again, if it weren't for the trouble ye have already caused. The great coward may have all the swords he wishes, and it matters not, for I've a pretty pair o' pistols here, ready with a ball for each o' them topsides.''

Caro's eyes had gradually grown accustomed enough to the darkness here between decks to realize that it wasn't as complete as she'd first thought. A faint, hazy twilight, reflected from the burning ship, filtered down through the hatch, and by it she could barely make out Hamil's face and the shape of the two pistols in his hands.

"So why not kill them outright?" she asked bitterly. "Cut my throat and then shoot them, and you'll be done with us all."

"Too easy, m'lady. And this way, ye know if your man is what ye believe he is, then he could have a chance, too. He could kill me, an' free ye, m'lady. But only if ye call him here."

Frantically she tried to sort out what he said. She wasn't foolish enough to trust him, but after listening night after night as he recited his battles and victories for Jeremiah, she knew that even Hamil had his own skewed code of honor. He really would rather fight Jeremiah than shoot him, for the glory would be greater when he won.

But he also believed that Jeremiah was a coward and not a serious challenge. Caro knew otherwise. Whatever else Jeremiah was, he wasn't a coward, and he knew how to fight, especially when his life, and hers, were at stake. She didn't doubt that Hamil was a fighter, too, but she'd put her faith in Jeremiah. What other choice did she really have?

"You will not shoot him if he comes down here?" she asked.

"With Allah as my witness."

"You'll fight fairly?"

He sighed. "M'lady, we shall fight as men. Sparhawk would not want it otherwise, would he?"

As much as she wished it otherwise, she knew Jeremiah wouldn't. Praying she was doing the right thing, she took a deep breath and shouted his name.

At the tiller, Jeremiah frowned when he heard her call. What the devil was she doing, anyway? She'd already been below far longer than she should have. Was this another one of her games? As much as he'd come to enjoy her surprises, this wasn't really the time or place, but then he'd thought she'd realize that.

She called again, and his frown deepened. Her voice sounded odd, strained somehow. Even if she hadn't called for help, something must have happened to her. He shouted to David to mind the tiller for him, and headed below.

"Caro?" He paused on the steps, wondering uneasily what had happened to the lantern and where she could be. "Caro, love, are you all right?"

"Come down here, if you please," she said, her voice almost pleading. "There's something I'd like to show you."

He came down the last steps, feeling his way in the dark. "Caro, what's wrong? Where's the candle?"

He heard her gasp and caught a shadowy glimpse of her face beside the bulkhead, her eyes wide with fear, and then the other man crashed down on him, knocking him from the steps to the deck.

*Hamil.* God help him, he knew the weight, the size, the very smell of the man as they struggled together. It was the nightmare all over again, this man and this terror and this darkness that smothered everything but the fear.

"Jeremiah!" cried Caro with anguish. "Your knife, love, oh, get your knife!"

This man and this terror and this darkness, but Caro was here, too, his Caro. This time, for her sake, he wouldn't lose. His Caro, his woman, and the devil could claim Hamil for daring to touch her. He, Jeremiah, would win, and he would live.

As hard as he could, he shoved Hamil back, buying himself the split second it took to yank his knife from the sheath at the back of his waist. Then Hamil was on him again, grabbing his wrist with the knife just as Jeremiah seized his, forcing him back as they rolled over and over across the canting deck. It would be this kind of fight, as rough as any he'd known, with only raw strength and luck to mark the winner.

The darkness that robbed him of sight heightened his other senses, and he could feel the other man's muscles tighten as Jeremiah fought against him, heard him grunt with the strain.

They struck against the bulkhead, unable to roll any further, and Jeremiah braced his arm against the wood for more leverage. He had to get his knife lower, to where he could strike, but as he did Hamil managed to twist his wrist a fraction lower in Jeremiah's grip, and Jeremiah felt the sharp slice of pain where Hamil's knife cut across his cheek. An inch more in the other direction, and he would have lost his eye.

Hamil's wrist twisted again, wrenching to break free, but this time Jeremiah was ready. Relentlessly he forced the other man back, driving his arm against the deck. He slammed Hamil's hand into the planking as hard as he could, hard enough to break half the bones in his hand. He heard the catch in Hamil's breathing, the only sign that he'd been hurt, and then the scraping noise of the knife sliding from his open fingers across the deck.

Still Hamil fought, writhing beneath him as he tried to protect his chest, but Jeremiah knew he'd won. His heart was pounding, sweat streaming from his body, but he had his knife and he'd won, and all that remained for him to do was to end the life of the miserable cur beneath him.

Tied to the bulkhead, Caro could see nothing of the two men fighting except a tangle of twisting shadows. The thumps and grunts terrified her, and desperately she strained her ears to distinguish one man from the other, to know how Jeremiah fared.

*Keep him safe, God, please keep him safe!*

Then suddenly Hamil twisted across the deck into the little square of twilight, clawing with his left hand at something just beyond the light. As he rolled back into the darkness, she caught the faint glimmer of polished metal, the flintlock on the pistol he had shown her earlier.

"Jeremiah, he has a—"

But her warning was lost in the dry explosion of the gunshot, echoing repeatedly in the narrow space of the companionway as the gunpowder smoke stung her eyes. Then silence, awful, ominous silence that threatened every hope for happiness she'd ever had.

"Jeremiah," she said, her voice keening high with raw grief. "Oh, my God, Jeremiah!"

"I'm here, love," he said, his breathing ragged beside her in the dark, his arms around her. He realized her hands were bound and cut the cord. "It's done."

She held him as closely as she could and it still wasn't enough. "You're alive," she sobbed. "You're alive, praise God, and Hamil is dead!"

"Yes, love," he said wearily. "Hamil's dead, and at last we're free."

# Epilogue

*Portsmouth*
*One year later*

Caro lay back on the striped pillows in the bow of the little boat, her ruffled silk parasol tipped to one side to shade her face from the afternoon sun as she trailed her fingers over the side in the cool water of the Herendons' pond.

"Tell me again about Providence," she said as she smiled lazily at Jeremiah. "I want to know everything."

"You must know it as well as I do by now," he said, returning her smile as he pulled slowly on the oars. Not that he minded telling her one more time about her new home; he'd promised to do whatever he could to make her happy, and this small request pleased him as much as it did her. "Besides, you'll be there yourself soon enough. Sailing next week as we are, with a fair wind we'll make Narragansett in six weeks at most."

"Then just tell me about your house," she said. "*Our* house."

"It's a fine house, built by the best housewrights in the state," he began, delighting in how the sun filtered through her parasol across the golden freckles on her nose. "My father would have nothing less for my mother. There's a parlor and a dining room and a first-rate kitchen below, and of course the office in the back, and above stairs there are four bedchambers and a little sewing closet."

She sighed contentedly. "It sounds vastly fine to me."

"It sounds vastly small, once we try to pack in all that you've carried off from Blackstone House. In return for gaining the title without a fuss, that lawyer of yours has seen to it that you'll scarce leave Georgie boy the roof over his head."

"George is welcome to it," she said promptly. "It leaks most confoundedly."

He laughed, as much with sheer pleasure in her company as from what she said. "Nay, I've a mind to build you a new one. Brick, I think, as many rooms as you wish, with white marble steps and black shutters like all the grandest houses on Prospect Street."

"Oh, Jeremiah," she said softly, her brows raised with surprise. "You don't have to do that. Truly. Your father's house sounds more than grand enough for me."

"Nay, my father did his best for his wife, and you deserve the same," he said gruffly. "I don't mean for you to give up your silk gowns. You might have been a countess here, but I'll see that you're the first lady of Providence."

She smiled wistfully. "You know I'd love you no less if I had nothing better to wear than my shift."

"Of course I know it," he said, grinning wickedly. "There was a certain night in Portsmouth that I recall you did just that."

"And you, Captain Sparhawk, are quite beyond redemption." She poked him with her toe. "And the devil take you if you ever try to change."

"I think we're going to find the devil a good deal sooner than you intended," he said as he maneuvered the boat around toward the dock. "At least that's my guess from the way that my sister's hopping up and down over there."

Caro's eyes widened as she turned to peer over her shoulder. "Oh, Jeremiah, we must be dreadfully late!"

"Most likely we are," agreed Jeremiah mildly. "What of it?"

By the time they finally reached the dock, Desire had been joined by not only her husband, but all three of their children, two small dogs, and a nursemaid, as well.

"For all love, Jere," she said, her exasperation clear, "it's high time you stopped paddling about! Dr. Abbott has been waiting in the library for the past hour for this christening, and if I offer him a drop more claret he won't be fit for anything."

Jack leaned over to help tie the boat, the sun glittering off the gold bullion on his uniform. It was only purest luck that his leave home had coincided with Caro and Jeremiah's last days in England, and they all considered it a fine omen for the future to be together like this.

Gallantly he held his hand out to help Caro from the boat. "Your sister's right, you know," he said to Jeremiah. "If you let old Abbott tumble any further into his cups, then your precious baby will be no more than just another brat begotten 'tween decks in a frigate."

Jeremiah grunted contemptuously as he climbed onto the dock. "At least it was on board a Yankee frigate with a Yankee captain and crew, which is more than can be said for your own brats."

"Hush, the both of you!" scolded Caro as she took her daughter from the nursemaid's arms. The baby gurgled happily to see her mother, waving her tiny plump arms above the trailing lace of her christening gown. "I won't hear you call my daughter a brat, nor will Desire wish it of her children, either."

"Here, let me have her," said Jeremiah as he reached out for his daughter. He had never imagined himself as a man who'd willingly hold a baby, but then he'd never imagined himself so smitten with such a tiny creature, either. She was exquisitely perfect, his daughter, with her mother's elfin eyes and the black Sparhawk hair, and when she smiled at him he felt his heart lurch in ways he'd never dreamed possible. "Come to your papa, Betsy, my girl."

"Elizabeth," said Caro firmly as she handed their child to him. "Elizabeth Fredericka. If you say 'Betsy' to Dr. Abbott, then Betsy she'll be for all eternity, and I shall never, ever forgive you."

"Ah, love, I promise not to shame either of my pretty lasses." He settled the baby into the crook of one arm and curled the other over Caro's shoulders, drawing her close enough to kiss her gently on the forehead.

"Mind Betsy doesn't shame *you,* Jere," warned Desire as she herded her two older children up the hill toward the house and scooped up little William under her arm. "You're wearing your only decent coat, and Nurse says she was fed not a quarter hour before."

Jeremiah only grinned. He was a father of eight weeks' standing now, and he felt sure there was little more his daughter could do that would shock him, at least so long as she remained a baby.

"We'll be along in a few minutes, Desire, I swear we will," promised Caro, unwilling to end just yet the magic sight of her daughter and her husband together, the two people she loved most in the world. "Please give Dr. Abbott our apologies and tell him we've been detained, but shall join him directly."

Fondly Jack slipped his arm around Desire's waist, steering her to follow the children running on ahead. "Come, dearest, let's leave these besotted Sparhawks alone and fish Abbott out of the claret before he drowns."

They walked on without Jeremiah and Caro, who lingered another few moments near the pond. Caro bent to kiss Betsy's forehead, trailing her finger across the baby's rosy cheek until she smiled.

"Oh, Jeremiah," whispered Caro, feeling so complete she almost wept with happiness, "however did we create anything so very beautiful?"

"How could we not, love, with you as her mother?" He saw Caro before him almost like a painting: her face with a charming half smile framed by the parasol over her shoulder, the diamonds in her ears, her pale pink muslin dress drifting around her legs, the rolling green lawns, the neat rosebushes in full bloom, the

Herendons' grand house of pale yellow stone behind her.

His wife, he thought with something close to awe; his Caro, his love, the one woman who had brought both peace and endless joy to his life. She had given him so much here in her world that he could only pray he'd be able to do the same when she came to his.

"Ah, Caro, my lass," he said gently. "How can I ever return what you've given me?"

Her eyes bright, she reached out to take his hand. "But you already have," she said softly. "You've given me your love, and that for me is everything."

\* \* \* \* \*

## What do A.E. Maxwell, Miranda Jarrett, Merline Lovelace and Cassandra Austin have in common?

They are all part of Harlequin Historical's efforts to bring you longer books by some of your favorite authors. Pick up one of these upcoming titles today and see what a difference an historical from Harlequin can make!

**REDWOOD EMPIRE—A.E. Maxwell** Don't miss the reissue of this exciting saga from award-winning authors Ann and Evan Maxwell, coming in May 1995.

**SPARHAWK'S LADY—Miranda Jarrett** From this popular author comes another sweeping Sparhawk adventure full of passion and emotion in June 1995.

**HIS LADY'S RANSOM—Merline Lovelace** A gripping Medieval tale from the talented author of the Destiny's Women series that is sure to delight, coming in July 1995.

**TRUSTING SARAH—Cassandra Austin** And in August 1995, the long-awaited new Western by the author whose *Wait for the Sunrise* touched readers' hearts.

Watch for them this spring and summer wherever Harlequin Historicals are sold.

HHBB95-2

## WOMEN OF THE WEST

Exciting stories of the old West and the women whose dreams
and passions shaped a new land!

Join Harlequin Historicals every month as we bring you
these unforgettable tales.

May 1995 #270—**JUSTIN'S BRIDE**
    Susan Macias w/a Susan Mallery

June 1995 #273—**SADDLE THE WIND**
    Pat Tracy

July 1995 #277—**ADDIE'S LAMENT**
    DeLoras Scott

August 1995 #279—**TRUSTING SARAH**
    Cassandra Austin

September 1995 #286—**CECILIA AND THE STRANGER**
    Liz Ireland

October 1995 #288—**SAINT OR SINNER**
    Cheryl St.John

November 1995 #294—**LYDIA**
    Elizabeth Lane

Don't miss any of our **Women of the West!**

ANNOUNCING THE

# PRIZE SURPRISE SWEEPSTAKES!

This month's prize:

# L-A-R-G-E—SCREEN PANASONIC TV!

This month, as a special surprise, we're giving away a fabulous FREE TV!

Imagine how delighted you and your family will be to own this brand-new 31" Panasonic** television! It comes with all the latest high-tech features, like a SuperFlat picture tube for a clear, crisp picture...unified remote control...closed-caption decoder...clock and sleep timer, and much more!

The facing page contains two Entry Coupons (as does every book you received this shipment). Complete and return *all* the entry coupons; **the more times you enter, the better your chances of winning the TV!**

Then keep your fingers crossed, because you'll find out by July 15, 1995 if you're the winner!

Remember: The more times you enter, the better your chances of winning!*

## PRIZE SURPRISE
### SWEEPSTAKES

## OFFICIAL ENTRY COUPON

This entry must be received by: JUNE 30, 1995
This month's winner will be notified by: JULY 15, 1995

**YES,** I want to win the Panasonic 31" TV! Please enter me in the drawing and let me know if I've won!

Name_____

Address _____ Apt. _____

City                State/Prov.              Zip/Postal Code

Account #_____

Return entry with invoice in reply envelope.

© 1995 HARLEQUIN ENTERPRISES LTD.                    CTV KAL

# OFFICIAL RULES

## PRIZE SURPRISE SWEEPSTAKES 3448

### NO PURCHASE OR OBLIGATION NECESSARY

Three Harlequin Reader Service 1995 shipments will contain respectively, coupons for entry into three different prize drawings, one for a Panasonic 31" wide-screen TV, another for a 5-piece Wedgwood china service for eight and the third for a Sharp ViewCam camcorder. To enter any drawing using an Entry Coupon, simply complete and mail according to directions.

There is no obligation to continue using the Reader Service to enter and be eligible for any prize drawing. You may also enter any drawing by hand printing the words "Prize Surprise," your name and address on a 3"x5" card and the name of the prize you wish that entry to be considered for (i.e., Panasonic wide-screen TV, Wedgwood china or Sharp ViewCam). Send your 3"x5" entries via first-class mail (limit: one per envelope) to: Prize Surprise Sweepstakes 3448, c/o the prize you wish that entry to be considered for, P.O. Box 1315, Buffalo, NY 14269-1315, USA or P.O. Box 610, Fort Erie, Ontario L2A 5X3, Canada.

To be eligible for the Panasonic wide-screen TV, entries must be received by 6/30/95; for the Wedgwood china, 8/30/95; and for the Sharp ViewCam, 10/30/95.

Winners will be determined in random drawings conducted under the supervision of D.L. Blair, Inc., an independent judging organization whose decisions are final, from among all eligible entries received for that drawing. Approximate prize values are as follows: Panasonic wide-screen TV ($1,800); Wedgwood china ($840) and Sharp ViewCam ($2,000). Sweepstakes open to residents of the U.S. (except Puerto Rico) and Canada, 18 years of age or older. Employees and immediate family members of Harlequin Enterprises, Ltd., D.L. Blair, Inc., their affiliates, subsidiaries and all other agencies, entities and persons connected with the use, marketing or conduct of this sweepstakes are not eligible. Odds of winning a prize are dependent upon the number of eligible entries received for that drawing. Prize drawing and winner notification for each drawing will occur no later than 15 days after deadline for entry eligibility for that drawing. Limit: one prize to an individual, family or organization. All applicable laws and regulations apply. Sweepstakes offer void wherever prohibited by law. Any litigation within the province of Quebec respecting the conduct and awarding of the prizes in this sweepstakes must be submitted to the Regies des loteries et Courses du Quebec. In order to win a prize, residents of Canada will be required to correctly answer a time-limited arithmetical skill-testing question. Value of prizes are in U.S. currency.

Winners will be obligated to sign and return an Affidavit of Eligibility within 30 days of notification. In the event of noncompliance within this time period, prize may not be awarded. If any prize or prize notification is returned as undeliverable, that prize will not be awarded. By acceptance of a prize, winner consents to use of his/her name, photograph or other likeness for purposes of advertising, trade and promotion on behalf of Harlequin Enterprises, Ltd., without further compensation, unless prohibited by law.

For the names of prizewinners (available after 12/31/95), send a self-addressed, stamped envelope to: Prize Surprise Sweepstakes 3448 Winners, P.O. Box 4200, Blair, NE 68009.

RPZ KAL